DEAD MONEY

TEARS OVER HAPPINESS

The Roll'z Roy$$ of $tory Telling

SHAWN L. BAILEY

This book is a work of fictional names, characters, places, and incidents that are the product of the Author's imagination or are used fictitiously, any resemblance to actual events, locations, or persons living or dead is simply coincidence.

DOLLAR4DOLLAR PUBLISHING

Avondale, Az

www.dollar4dollarpublishing.com

DEAD MONEY: TEARS OVER HAPPINESS

Copyright © 2025 by Shawn L. Bailey

First Edition

E-Book: 978-1-967441-30-3

Paperback: 978-1-967441-31-0

Dedications

First and foremost, I want to dedicate this book to my best friend, Lord and Savior Jesus Christ. None of this would be possible without your patience, guidance, teaching, remolding, and shaping me into whom you say I am. Calling me out of darkness and igniting a spiritual light in me to be a use to your sons and daughters. There is no greater calling or job to have than to be called upon by your Gracious Father. Being crafted by you, it was only you who could see in me what others need you to see and experience throughout your Word. It was a gift from you, handed to me to write and share stories to redirect the steps of others. I will only share the gift and spiritual light of change redirecting the mind and heart throughout my stories from your blessings. When everyone jumped ship, it was through my faith in you that when you called, I came trusting in you and your word. Without you, I'm nothing, but with you, I'm everything. Until your doors are opened here in this lifetime, just know that all I do, Lord, is for you.

With the highest regards, I want to thank Ms. Jean for stepping up and being a mother to me when I was kicked out in the streets at the age of 12, when my mother lost focus, God sent another Black Diamond into my life. It was you who predicted what I would grow up to be and what my future would be. I love you, Queen, for always keeping your doors open and making your home feel like home to me. Even in God's kingdom, I know you're saving a resting place for me. Rest in Peace.

I also want to dedicate this book to my brothers and sisters from another mother, Donald Austin, California Mike, Skip, Randy Colter, Q Ball, Robert Walker, Pupa, Ebony, Squirt, Elaine Devine, Ricky Colter and Family, Dunnie Colter, Al Bowman, Luther Ware, D-Money, Ice T, Dr. Alfred Craig, Beverly Craig, Uncle Ben from Texas, and DeMeka Bailey thank you for your support and assistance, love you and Rylen.

Reggie Nickelson RIP, Arthur Murphy RIP, Red Devil RIP, DMX RIP, and Kenny Red RIP, I want to thank each and every one of you for every moment that I spent with every one of you. They were valuable moments and very important to me being a part of y'all. All glory be to God for our encounters. I love and bless you all.

Acknowledgements

To everyone who counted me out, being the gentleman and scholar that I am, I want to give y'all a moment to strike a pose. Can y'all still see me? Can't stop, won't stop suckers! Yea, this is round 2 of many to go with y'all. I'm going to stay dethroning you, Haters. The ROLL'Z ROY$$ OF $TORY TELLING say, always applaud the Haters. They're the ones that are going to keep you relevant and make sure you get your blessings from them trying to block them Suckers:) They just won't never understand and learn that when God goes before you and says that it's done, there's nothing no one can do but watch your blessings pour through abundantly. My Gracious Father is going to keep you Haters perplexed because you'll never know when the blessing is going to come, start, or stop. Sometimes, we're looking for Haters to come from a far, but the majority of the time, the Haters are right up under you. Outwardly speaking blessings and inwardly praying and expecting you to fall.

I want to mainly acknowledge each and every one that supported me through my journey and had nothing but positive, uplifting words to encourage me to keep going. Special thanks to Ms. Gayla Williams for your kind words expressing my gift and the comfort my book brought to you, your family and your friends. It appears that everyone seems to keep telling me the same thing about my writing. So, I promise to take each one of y'all words to heart and continue to keep great books coming your way. It's an honor and a spiritual pleasure to take time out of my day and life to put a smile on my fellow brothers and sisters' faces. Just know that I don't consider none of you fans of my work but family, to share my blessing with. May God bless each and every one of you and y'all families. May y'all prosper as well in all that you do. No names needed; you already know who you are, and that are family readers.

To my son Elijah Bailey, you left me with such a heartfelt experience seeing how genuine you were to read and experience my gift from God. I take all you said to heart. I Love you and my precious grandkids Jayla and Elijah Jr.

To my best friend Danelle Gregory and business partner, God couldn't have brought you into my life at a greater time. You effortlessly work side by side with me, learning and being a blessing to others daily. It warms my heart to see who the people around you don't cherish the effortless love and joy that you offer them, but as you have learned, no one can block your blessings, and sometimes we have to separate in order to move forward, family and friends' weight can get heavier than we can carry. Thank you for your support daily, spiritual kind, encouraging words, and business knowledge that you share. What a phenomenal woman. I Love you, Queen. Keep shinning for God. You're on the right path.

To my beautiful daughters, I ask that y'all forgive me in my absence. I know how important my presence was needed, but I'm grateful that God gave me this opportunity to become a better father to each one of you. Just know that every one of you shares and has a special place in my heart, and I thank you for blessing me with such adorable, beautiful, and intelligent grandbabies. I Love each one of you with every breath that I breathe. I take full responsibility for anything that y'all have had to endure without me seeing you through and before the world. With that being said, I'm sorry if I've brought any hurt and pain to your heart. As a dad, all I can do is ask for forgiveness and become a better man moving forward. Changing the things I can change and asking God to change the things in me I can't. To me, y'all will always be my Black Diamonds, which is the purest of them all. I Love you, Queens.

To one of the most kindhearted and adorable daughters in my life that have always been very supportive in my life in any business adventure. You have always believed in me and have supported your dad. You were a big part of me being able to send out these great stories to my ROLL'Z ROY$$ reader family. I'm forever grateful for you, young lady. You are unique and a Queen in your own right. I love you and my beautiful babies. May God bless you and your family in all that you do, Tori Williams. You'll always hold a place in my heart, beautiful.

To my young Kings. I'm grateful that y'all are all at the age to better understand what I've endured and been through over the years. Now, y'all get to see what being a parent is like and dealing with baby mamas. I got the biggest smile on my face because I know what y'all are enduring with y'all baby mothers. As they say, you can't live with them or live without them. Just enjoy the blessings and the borrowed time that God gives you with them because no one knows when it all comes to an end. Remember, we're all on borrowed time. (Message) Each one of you gentlemen has made me proud of you. Y'all all are unique and talented and powerful in your own way, but if y'all ever come together, y'all will be a force to reckon with. Don't waste so much time on the playground with Satan. I offer the same words to y'all as I did my own brothers and sisters. Be a family of strength. Strength comes through exercise. Proverbs 24:10 say, if you faint in the day of adversity, your strength is small. Y'all came from me, so it's my job to make sure you get ahead and not be left behind. I Love you, Kings and very proud of y'all. Keep shaking the ground they walk in. That's that Bailey you love to Hate but got to love because we did it so well.

To all my readers, I always want to leave you with something to think about mentally and spiritually. There are going to be people who come into your life that you'll respect and love but just know when you're not being who they want you to be in their life then the evil comes from deep within them. These are some of the same people in your life who will stoop to their lowest to bring you down. Remember, everyone is seeking their own happiness, not yours, unless you're cooperating with their joy. Hate loves no one, but misery and misery will take you captive only if you allow it to. Psalms 1:1-6 says, Blessed is the man who does not walk in the counsel of the wicked or stand in the way of sinners or sit in the seat of mockers, but his delight is in the law of the Lord; and in his law he meditates day and night. He is like a tree planted by streams of water which yield its fruit in season and whose leaf does not wither. Whatever he does prospers not so the wicked. They are like chaffs that the wind blows away. Therefore, the wicked will not stand in the judgment nor sinners in the assembly of the righteous, but the way of the wicked will parish.

This is the joys of obeying God and refusing to listen to those who discredit or ridicule him. Our relationships, family, friends and associates can have a profound influence on us, often in very subtle ways. If we insist on friendships and relationships with those who mock what God considers important, we might sin by becoming indifferent to God's will. This attitude is the same as mocking. Do your friends and companions build up your faith, or do they hold you back and tear you down? True friends and partners with whom you share companions should help you draw closer to God's purpose and plan for your life, not hinder your relationship with Him.

God doesn't judge people on the basis of race, sex, or national origin. He judged them based on their faith in Him and their response to His revealed Will. Those who diligently try to obey God's Will are blessed. Their happy condition is like healthy fruit-bearing trees with strong roots. Kings and Queens, trusting in God is our only hope. Jeremiah 17:5-8 says, Thus saith the Lord; Cursed be the man who trust in man, and makes flesh his arms, and whose heart departs from the Lord. **V6**. For he shall be like the heath in the desert and shall not see when good comes; but shall inhabit the parched places in the wilderness, in a salt land and not inhabited. **V7.** Blessed is the man who trust in the Lord, and whose hope the Lord is. **V8**. For he shall be like a tree planted by the waters, and that spreads out her roots by the river, and shall not see when heat comes, but her leaf shall be green; and shall not be careful in the year of drought, neither shall cease from yielding fruit.

Mighty men and women, we are to apply this to our lives. To trust in the Lord gives one the "Fruit of the Spirit. Brothers and Sisters two kinds of people are contrasted here: those who trust in human beings and those who trust in the Lord. The people of Judah were trusting in false gods and military alliances instead of God, and thus they were barren and unfruitful. In contrast, those who trust in the Lord flourish like trees planted by water.

Psalms 1 say, Blessed is the man who does not walk in the counsel of the wicked or standing in the way of sinners or sit in the seat of mockers. In times of trouble, those who trust in human beings will be impoverished and spiritually weak, so they will have no strength to draw on. But those who trust in the Lord will have abundant strength, not only for their own needs, but even for the needs of others. Brothers and Sisters, are you satisfied with being unfruitful, or do you, like a well-watered tree, have strength for the time of crisis and even some to share as you bear fruit for the Lord?

Jeremiah 17:5-8 says, I and God promise to watch over them. God's wisdom guides their lives. In contrast, those who don't trust and obey God have meaningless lives that blow away like dust. My readers, there are only two paths of life that lie before us. God's way if obedient or the way of rebellion and destruction. Be sure to choose God's path because the path you choose determines how you will spend eternity. You can be a blessing or block your own blessings by hindering other's blessings. But hindering others just know God will step in. ROLL'Z ROY$$ OF $TORY TELLING, get in, let's ride.

To all book author's, I wish prosperity upon you and may y'all continue to elevate to that next level. Keep allowing God to direct your step, you are blessed. Psalms 1:1-3 says, Blessed is the man who walks not in the counsel of the ungodly, nor stands in the way of sinners. Nor sit in the seat of the scornful. But His delight in the Law of the Lord; and in His Law does He meditate day and night. And He shall be like a tree planted by the river of water that brings forth His fruit in His season; his leaf also shall not wither; and whatsoever He does shall prosper. Brothers and Sisters you are blessed.

About the Author

Shawn L. Bailey was born in Chicago, Illinois and was raised on the Southside at a time when he witnessed crimes, drug addictions, and deaths on a normal basis. His mother had him in 1967, and she was a single parent. He almost lost his life at the age of 6 years old. He was trapped in an apartment fire on 79th Troop, but God had a much bigger plan for him. Shawn became a legendary gentleman of leisure throughout his lifetime. God later called him to Minister his Word. He was ordained on October 3rd, 2019, where he was blessed with the gift that would leave his mark in the Urban Book industry for times to come. Some people say that he has a way to change someone's life; others have called him a prophet. But after reading his book, you'll know him as The Roll'z Roy$$ of $tory Telling.

Table of Contents

Chapter One
HONEY

Izzi sat in her driveway, flipping through the tracks on her CD player with the car idling. She was on her way to meet one of her close friends. It was Christmas time and Izzi had planned to fix her husband DuVall, a nice Christmas dinner that he'll never forget. Normally, at Christmas time, they would travel to Boston or New York to have Christmas dinner with either DuVall's family in New York or Izzi's mother and father in Boston. But this year, DuVall and Izzi decided to stay and spend Christmas together at their Scottsdale home in Arizona. Even though it was still cold in December in Phoenix, it would seem like summer weather there compared to Boston and New York this time of year. Izzi found just the perfect song on her CD that her bestie had customized for her. The song had gone perfectly with the mood that DuVall left her leaving home in. Mariah Carey 'All I want for Christmas' came booming through the 500 Mercedes Benz speakers. The Burgundy and Beige Mercedes was a birthday gift from DuVall for Izzi's birthday. One thing Izzi loved about her husband was DuVall loved spoiling her with expensive and lavish gifts.

Izzi put the biggest smile on her face when her cell phone started ringing. DuVall's face popped up on her cell phone screen and Izzi was wondering how DuVall missed her already as much as she was missing him. She pressed send on her Iphone10 Verizon cell phone, yeah Hun, "Wow baby, I just walked out the house. Are you missing me already?" Why, of course. You know that anytime you're out of my sight, you're being missed. Awe, honey, that's so sweet. I missed you too, honey, but I won't be gone shopping too long. I'm meeting Fuzzi, she is going shopping with me too. Baby, you know it won't take long for her to get on my last nerve. DuVall started laughing. Yeah, she is a handful; that's your boy-girl. Izzi started laughing. Baby, stop it! Don't even start on my friend, ok? "I won't." But hey, I just wanted to remind you to don't forget to stop by the cleaners to pick up my suit. Ohhhh! Yeah, baby, thank you for reminding me. I can't lie baby, I already forgot, thank you.

DuVall and Izzi both blew a kiss before ending their call. Just as Izzi ended her call with DuVall, her cell phone started ringing again. She thought it was DuVall calling back until Izzi heard, "Bitch! Where the hell are you at?" Izzi started laughing. Fuzzi, you do know my mother named me Izzi and not Bitch. Well, Izzi, where the hell are you at, Bitch? Izzi and Fuzzi both started laughing. Girl, I'm almost there. I'll be walking through the door even before you can read the next man that you see. I'll be there in a few minutes, Fuzzi, trust me. Well, honey, I doubt that because it ain't no man in this store. It ain't nothing but a bunch of pussy's up in here, and some of them need soap and water. Fuzziiiiii, no, you didn't just say that! Izzi put her hand over her mouth but still laughed. Bitch! What am I going to do with your ass? Child nothing, we got the same thing, and mine only want dicks. I'm coming, bye crazy ass. Click!

Izzi turned Mariah's song back up and started backing out of the driveway. Izzi was Caucasian and Hispanic. Her mother is White, and her dad is Spanish. When you see her pretty face and her 38-26-38 frame, she will put you in the mind of the R&B singer Mya. Izzi is just much taller than Mya; she is 5'9 with curly hair. But she normally keeps it straight, silky, and black. Izzi's skin tone makes her appear more Hispanic than Caucasian, but her blue eyes could clearly let you know that she has Caucasian traits in her bloodline.

Her husband DuVall used to be a star football player growing up in school and college. He even turned down an NFL contract to play for the Dallas Cowboys to open his own Law Firm in Phoenix and marry his childhood girlfriend. But after opening his law firm and hiring a much younger secretary 10 months later, DuVall and his first wife got a divorce. Lori started cheating on DuVall with a construction owner that DuVall's firm represented in a criminal case. DuVall won the man's case, while the construction owner won over DuVall's wife.

DuVall stands 6'2 and weighed 320 pounds at the time when he was held back by a 130-pound female who was his secretary. DuVall wanted to kill her and her lover. The day that he accidentally heard a voice recording of his wife and her lover, Lori told the construction owner that she would take that nigga for every dime that he had. Then she would come and spend DuVall's money on him. Lori came walking into DuVall's law firm that morning, asking for money to go shopping. DuVall removed twenty $100 bills from his wallet, then placed them in his hand and slapped Lori into an Encyclopedia book cabinet. Bammmm!

Before that day, DuVall had never hit his wife or any other woman, but after hearing the woman he has been sleeping beside every night and breaking his neck to keep happy call him a nigga to another Caucasian man, the only thing that went through his mind was the day he introduced Lori to his grandmother. DuVall's grandmother kept telling him to go and find an African American woman that looked like her or his mom. That girl only wants you because you are a great athlete, and that makes her look like she is somebody having the school hero on her arm. The day that Lori and DuVall got married, DuVall cried because neither his mother nor grandmother attended his wedding. The day that DuVall slapped Lori with that money, his grandmother's last words to him haunted

DuVall. "Boyyyy! No matter how many touchdowns that you score or no matter how many black penises you give that girl, to her and them white folks that's cheering you on, you're going to always be a nigga to them."

The same woman that saves Lori and DuVall's life from him killing her, two and half years later, DuVall got down on one knee and asked his secretary to be his wife. Six years later, here Izzi and Duvall were about to spend their first Christmas alone. They didn't have any kids together, being that both agreed not to have none yet. DuVall would put you in the mind of Tim Duncan, and he loved working out and keeping his body in shape. At the age of 42, DuVall was still throwing up 550lbs on the weight bar.

Izzi finally made it to the Super Walmart store to hook up with Fuzzi. She parked her Mercedes Benz as close to Fuzzi's Convertible Corvette as she could. Izzi exited her vehicle, really looking more like she was about to enter a nightclub the way that she was dressed. Her thigh-high pink, red bottom boots matched her short-waisted mink coat. Izzi was wearing a two-piece jean suit by Gucci and a pink silk blouse. She always looked sexy but kept it clean and respectful. All eyes were already cutting her way as she sashayed her way across the Walmart parking lot. Every part of Izzi's body spoke its own language as she made Gucci talk Izzi.

Just as Izzi entered the Walmart and almost made the old white man greeting the people almost have a heart attack, Izzi could hear a voice that she knew all too well. Well, damn Bitch, about mother fucking time you showed up. Come on here with your all-day taking ass. It smells like ass, coochie, cheap perfume, and cheerios up in here. Izzi slapped Fuzzi on the arm in a playful way and they gave each other a hug. Ohhhhhh, girl, I love them boots. You better not never take them off around me, cause a bitch definitely go steal them. That's okay, girl. You will be bringing them right back because yo ass can't get them big ass feet in my boots. Hell, why you playing, I'm loving that pencil dress that you got on Fuzzi, and that coat is bad. Fuzzi started spinning around in a circle like she was a model. Fuzzi was wearing a pencil dress but with lace in all the imaginable places that any man would envision himself being able to see. Yo, ass leaving that coat with me before I leave yo crazy self. Girl, what am I supposed to do, freeze and be sick for Christmas? Fuzzi's coat has every color you can think of, but it was a fur, low cut but puffed out on the neck and wrist. Fuzzi's shoes seem to match the coat with all the different colors and fur around the ankles. Christian Dior perfume could be smelled by Izzi when she hugged her. That smells good, Fuzzi. I know, don't it. I know I should have brought the bottle in here and started spraying it on some of these housewives. They busted up laughing and went and grabbed their shopping cart.

$ $ $ $ $

DuVall heard the doorbell ring; he had just stepped out of the shower and grabbed a towel off the rack. DuVall went straight to the living room curtain and pulled it to the side so that he could get a better look at who was at the door. There was a White Jaguar parked behind his H2 Hummer. A brief smile came across DuVall's face. He went and opened the door. A tall redhead stood at the door wearing a long white Donna Karen coat and white thigh-high boots. DuVall said, "Oh! So, you finally brung me my Christmas presents, I see." Of course, daddy, you know that I'd never allow Christmas to pass by without seeing about you. What did you bring me because I don't see any gifts in your hands? That's because it's right here, you need to unwrap it yourself. The redhead opened her Donna Karan coat, and all she had on was three gift-wrapped bows. One was taped to her Brazilian clean-shaven vagina, and the other two bows covered her nipples which were a couple of 40D breasts. I guess that look is saying that I should rewrap it up for another day. She was about to close her coat back up and walk away, but DuVall's manhood came alive and wanted the redhead gifts. DuVall took a deep breath and figured that he had at least a few hours before his wife returned. DuVall pulled the attractive woman closer to him, and they engaged in a passionate kiss. DuVall invited her inside and closed the door.

The female noticed the towel wrapped around DuVall's waist. Daddy, are you sure that you weren't expecting me? DuVall opened up the redhead coat and took one more look at her body. This was a day that DuVall found himself daydreaming about many times before, even at times when he was right there with Izzi next to him in bed. The redhead and Izzi just so happened to be childhood friends. Every time La'Bella came to their home to visit, DuVall had envisioned himself having a threesome with Izzi and La'Bella. But Izzi made it clear to DuVall a long time ago that she wouldn't share him with anyone. So, after DuVall made a few sexual advances at La'Bella, La'Bella learned that it would be to her advantage to accept his sexual offers. DuVall always seemed to be very busy dealing with a case, so every time he got the opportunity to fulfill his sexual desires, DuVall would wind up just giving La'Bella money or gifts and go home to his wife. La'Bella knew that if she would ever become DuVall's next wife, she had to let him experience everything that he had been missing out on. Another thing that La'Bella had at her advantage was Izzi had shared many of her and DuVall's sexual experiences with La'Bella, Emma, Ashley, Kahi'Lee, and their transexual friend, Fuzzi. So La'Bella already knows all the sexual things that DuVall experienced and hasn't experienced in the bedroom. But today, before La'Bella left Izzi's house, DuVall was definitely going to experience every sexual position that he'd never experienced. The reason why La'Bella knew it was okay to show up at Izzi's house naked was she called Izzi and learned that she was out shopping with Fuzzi. La'Bella knew just how long they would be out shopping because they were all close friends, and they had shopped together many times before.

$ $ $ $ $

Izzi and Fuzzi were going up and down each aisle, and Fuzzi was driving Izzi crazy. Many times, Izzi told Fuzzi that she would never go shopping with her, never again. They were on the aisle with all the feminine products, and Fuzzi had two boxes of Massengill Douches. She got loud and started telling all the females in the store, and I think y'all whores need to start cleaning those dead fishes between y'all legs before y'all try cleaning a damn turkey. Fuzzi took all the douches off the shelf and put them in her basket. Hell, bitch I won't be the grinch this year; I'll just stand up there with the old man and pass out douches for Christmas.

It was an old lady coming down the aisle and Fuzzi walked up to her and handed her one of the douches. Here, child, "I know you smell that. It's yourrrrrass that you're smelling." The woman gave Fuzzi a real mean, crazy look and walked off. She got down the aisle and threw the douches on the floor, and Fuzzi said, "I bought that for you, Bitch! You better pick that up and use it and Merry Christmas." Girl, you are so ignorant and embarrassing. I'm leaving your stupid ass in this store. Izzi started pushing her cart fast down the aisle, trying to get away from Fuzzi. Wait bitchhh! I'll buy you a box for Christmas too, bitch.

By the time Fuzzi caught up with Izzi again, she was picking up a few Patti Labelle's Sweet Potato Pies. Girl, I've been looking all over this store for you. Get away from me, Fuzzi, before I call the store security on your stupid ass. Go ahead bitch and call them. I already gave him my number and promised to suck his dick after he gets his income tax check. Yeah, he already got a full dose of this fu'dasshian ass. Izzi started laughing. I hate your ass, girl. You really make my ass ache, Fuzzi. Awe bitch, you know you love your little sister. Fuzzi kissed Izzi on the cheek. And bitch I put all those douches back. I'll be the Christmas Grinch again but only because of your stankin ass attitude. But I still do hope some of these bitches do pick up some of these douches, though. Girl, I really wasn't playing at all about that.

Fuzzi was born James Armstrong in the San Francisco Bay area. At a very young age, he knew that something was different about him. He was the baby of six children, four girls and two boys. James's face was so pretty that when he was younger, his two older sisters used to dress him up in girl clothes and then tell him, "Boy, you know you should have been born a girl!" James's father never came around and showed any kind of interest in James Armstrong Jr., plus his mother stayed in the streets and slept with all types of different men. It was actually one of his mother's boyfriends that turned James out to have a homosexual lifestyle. James's mother left him with a pimp named Do'Dirty at the age of 12, whom she sometimes turned tricks for when she needed money to keep up her bills. This time when she went out to turn tricks, she got arrested, and that pissed Do'Dirty off because he was left to care for a child that wasn't even his child.

This day when Do'Dirty was in the bedroom watching a football game, James was in one of his sisters' bedrooms and started to make himself up to look like a woman. James applied make-up to his face in the same way that he always saw that his sister did him. Then he found one of her miniskirts, and he stuffed her bra with tube socks, giving James a pair of 36D breast cups and he put a half top kitty shirt on and a pair of high heels. Then James got one of his mother's old wigs and brought it back to life. James used to watch all the little tricks that his mother and sisters used to do to their wigs. The one he got, James took it and put big Shirley Temple loc curls in it. He has on a pair of women's panties that he didn't know how to undisposed his private parts. But something he would later learn from another homosexual male prostitute. James stared at himself in the mirror. To his surprise, James looked more like a beautiful woman than his mother or sisters did. It was at that very moment in his young life that James Armstrong Jr knew that he was born in the wrong body. Everything that he saw in the mirror, he knew that he wanted to never separate from that young female who was looking back at him in the mirror.

Do'Dirty was on his way into the kitchen to grab himself another beer when he caught a glimpse of the young, pretty attractive female that was looking in the mirror. He thought that James had let some girl into the house without his permission. Well, hello, pretty lady, who are you, and where in the hell is James? James stood there and didn't say a word. He noticed that Do'Dirty was rubbing his penis while talking to him and that he was attracted to the female he was seeing. James was always curious as to what it would feel like to be with another boy, but here he was, standing in front of a grown man. James' heart almost jumped out of his chest when Do'Dirty walked over and placed his hands on his shoulders. What's the matter? You don't like talking, little momma? James put his head down, not allowing Do'Dirty to see his face. Before James could get out a word, Do'Dirty's hands started to explore James' whole body. Do'Dirty whispered in James's ear, "Oh, you one of them shy females. Are you shy and afraid of one of these?" Do'Dirty had removed his penis from his pants and had placed James's hand on his erect penis. Do'Dirty invited what he thought was a shy little girl to go down on him, and James accepted his offer. James dropped down to his knees, and that's when his first homosexual encounter occurred. Ummmmm! Ummmmm!

After Do'Dirty turned James out that night, James was walking down O'Farrell and Jones in San Francisco. After James turned 22, he met a rich trick who fell in love with him. James told the trick how bad that he wanted to become a woman. At first, the trick just paid for James to get breast implants, then two years later, James had a full, complete sex change. He no longer goes by James Armstrong Jr.; his birth certificate still has the same name. But the new script that he paid for from a good friend that changes your name turned James into what his new birth certificate and driver's license say Sabrina Renee Armstrong, but he still goes by his street name, Fuzzi that he got from Do'Dirty when he turned him out.

When James was growing up even his mother Tina used to call him Prince because he looked just like a young version of the rocker Prince. But a few years and few surgeries later, James was 5'9 light skinned and had a voice like Michel'le, turning himself into a spitting image of Amber Rose. Her new and improved measurements were 38DD with a 28 waist and 48-inch jungle gym backside. Ever since Dr. Kirkpatrick completed James' buttocks surgery, James learned that many men who claimed to be straight shooters really seem to have more Sugar in their Tea than James did. Every time that he tried to come clean with his sexuality before completing his sex change, every man that approached him on the street, it wasn't too many that wanted to turn him down even though he was gay.

$ $ $ $ $

Izzi and Fuzzi were in the checkout line when a really pretty Hispanic girl was checking them out. She seemed mesmerized by the two attractive women in her line. Well, hello, pretty lady, did y'all find everything okay today? Izzi and Fuzzi smiled at the cashier and thanked her for her compliment. Yeah, girl! "We sure did!" I feel like I been dodging men up in the nightclub up in this damn store. Being that it was so close to Christmas, Walmart was packed with shoppers. Yeah, I see they all are watching both of y'all now.

Fuzzi said, "I don't know what the Fuck for." They can't offer to buy us no drinks up here unless they are about to pay for these groceries. I don't do drooling, honey, unless a credit card is about to be swiped, like you about to do this one. Izzi said, "I heard that." You are so pretty, ma'am. Who does your make-up? Thank you, baby, "I've been doing my face since I was 12 years old." It's flawless; it looks like you had it professionally done. Well, I try to keep it this way until men start squirting all that gushy stuff on my face. Izzi slapped Fuzzi on the head. The cashier put her hand over her mouth and busted up laughing. Girl, what the hell you hit me for? Shit! Even she gotten some of that gushy stuff on her face, too. Child, please excuse my girlfriend, she is very special. Oh! "It's no problem, she okay. She seems like a lot of fun; I could talk to her all day." That would be $89.65, ma'am. Hold up, let me find this card because if I can't find it, then I'm going to have to jump up on this machine and swipe this ass across this register. They all started laughing, then Izzi said, "Child, and if she does that, the whole circuit breaker in the whole store going down, all that ass been through." The cashier laid on her station laughing. Izzi and Fuzzi finally finished paying for their groceries, and the cashier looked like she didn't want them to go.

The bag boy asked them if they needed help carrying their groceries. Fuzzi told him, "Hell, as tired as I am, you can carry me to the car, and I'll carry my own damn groceries." Can you handle carrying all this ass? The bag boy turned completely red in the face.

Izzi told him thank you, baby, don't pay this fool no mind; we can manage. Trust me, I'm about to take her ass back to the crazy house right now. Here, baby, Merry Christmas. Izzi gave the young man $5.00. Girl! Yo ass should have kept that $5.00 because Santa Claus about to hit our ass up as soon as we walk out of this store. Izzi and Fuzzi hugged each other, laughing, and they pushed their baskets out of the store into a waiting Santa Claus.

$ $ $ $ $

Merry Christmas, Mrs. Ratcliff. Oh! Hello Sam, how's your wife doing? She's doing just fine, calling me every hour to come home. Well, Sam, it's almost Christmas, can you blame her? Not really, but don't tell my wife I told you this, but Mrs. Ratcliff, it's the only time that I can smoke my pipe. My wife hates the smell of it, so I have to smoke here at work. Aw, that's too bad, Sam, I'm sure it's something y'all can work out. Yeah, I believe we did already with her demands. I'm not supposed to smoke anymore. They both laughed. Well, I guess you're here to pick up your husband's suits. Yeah, of course. So, how is he doing these days? It's been a little while since I saw him in the store. I'm sure he's at home in front of the television, enjoying his time off. Yeah, I'm sure with the type of work he does, I'm sure he enjoys time alone. Sam, he told me to wish you and your wife a Merry Christmas and a Happy New Year. Plus, he sent you a little something extra for your great service. Awe, that's nice, but it's not necessary, Mrs. Ratcliff.

Sure, it is Mr. Fatone; we insist that you accept our gift. He smiled at Izzi while he was passing her DuVall's suit. Oh! And I found two dresses that you bought a while back and forgot to pick up. Izzi saw the dresses, oh my goodness, I've been looking all over my closet for those dresses. Well, they been right here. Izzi paid him and gave him a $200 tip. They said their goodbyes, and even though Mr. Fatone was married, he still couldn't help but admire Izzi's bombshell physique as she walked away.

Izzi was on her cell phone talking to another close friend when she turned on her block, "Girl, who car this is in my driveway?" "Hell, girl, how in the hell am I supposed to know, Ashley said." You sound like I'm riding in the damn car with you. What type of car is it? A White Jaguar, girllll! Jaguar! Jaguar! Oh! Didn't La'Bella just buy a new Jaguar? I don't know, but she did call me earlier on my way to the store. I told her that I was going grocery shopping with Fuzzi, though. She never even mentioned to me that she bought a new car, maybe she brought it by to show me. Well, that's her y'all come pick me up? I'll treat y'all to some drinks. It's been a while since we all been together at the same time. Ok, then you call Emma and Kahi'Lee and have them meet us there. Ok, what about Fuzzi? Is she still with you, or did she go back home? Child, please don't even mention her name to me right now. Okay! Okayyyy! I can already hear it in your voice. Okay, call me back.

Izzi grabbed the black box that she had got for DuVall, she parked behind the Jaguar and got out. Izzi was whistling Mariah, "All I Want for Christmas" song again. All she took out of the car were DuVall suits and the black box. She figured that she and DuVall could remove the groceries from the car together. Just as soon as Izzi entered the house, it didn't take her woman instincts to know that something wasn't right. Izzi looked around her house after she noticed a woman's coat was lying at her front door. She quietly closed the door and hung DuVall suits on their coat rack. Izzi removed her boots because she knew her boots would make her presence known in the house. She walked into her house, surveying each room. It wasn't until she got close to their bedroom door that she could hear sexual moans from a woman's voice. Ohhhhhh! DuVall Yes! Yes! Yesssssss baby! Izzi almost felt like her heart was about to stop beating, but it wasn't until she peeped through their bedroom door and saw DuVall pounding away in La'Bella's legs.

Izzi grabbed her chest and slowly backed away from their room. How could her best friend and husband be having sex in her bed? Tears begin to roll down Izzi's face. Izzi headed to another bedroom and removed one of DuVall's guns from his gun collection case. Izzi loaded the gun just the way that he had taught her to, and she said a quick prayer to God. After praying, Izzi looked at the 9mm automatic weapon that she had just loaded, and she opened a jar in the room and grabbed a photo book. She left that room and headed towards the kitchen, and she removed DuVall's hunting knife.

DuVall was right at the point where he was about to cum, when he and La'Bella heard the loud thump at the foot of the bed. When DuVall turned around to see what it was, Izzi held the 9mm in her right hand, and she had his hunting knife in her left hand. It was the photobook that they heard on the bed that got their attention. DuVall nor La'Bella have never been caught in this position so neither one of them knew what to do or say. DuVall tried to get up off of La'Bella, but Izzi told him motherfucker if you don't finish fucking this bitch, I'll blow your brains out. You told her that you were cuming motherfucker, so you better cum. Because if you don't, it will be the last pussy that you get on this earth. Izzi pointed the gun, and DuVall followed her instructions. La'Bella was trying her best to push DuVall off of her and, at the same time, trying to tell Izzi that she was sorry. Izzi let one round off in the ceiling to let them know that she was serious about them finishing their sex rendezvous. Pow! Bitch, shut up and enjoy him on me this time.

Tears continued to roll down Izzi's face. DuVall sounded off as he was cuming in La'Bella. DuVall rolled over on his back. Are you happy now, Izzi? Is that what you wanted to see to divorce me Izzi? Izzi said, "Nope, buddy, not yet, but I'll let you know when I'm happy." She pointed the gun at DuVall and demanded that he open up the photo book. DuVall opened it up and finally saw what it was that Izzi wanted him to see. Duvall, do you remember that day? Yes, of course, honey. I remember that day. Pow! Izzi shot DuVall right in the leg. Motherfucker how dare you call me honey with that ashy bitch laying in my bed. Our Bed! Our Bedddd! Izzi's voice got louder. DuVall was backing up on the bed, holding his leg. Argggghhh Shit! La'Bella was slowly trying to get up out the bed. Izzi, please don't do this. You and your husband can work things out. Izzi pointed the gun at La'Bella, bitch get back next to your man because the only way you'll be leaving this house is in a body bag whore. La'Bella started crying and got back on the bed. Izzi kept making DuVall turn pages until he got to the page of their vows. Izzi tossed his hunting knife at him. If you want to live and see your 43rd birthday, you better take that knife and destroy that bitch like she did my marriage. DuVall and La'Bella's eyes got really big. You can't be serious, Izzi. As a mother fucking heart attack. Pow! Izzi shot him in the same leg again. DuVall grabbed his leg, Arggggh! Arggggh! But when he turned it loose, he leaped at La'Bella. Wham! Wham! Wham! Wham! Wham! DuVall kept stabbing La'Bella until her body went limp.

DuVall stared at Izzi with a malicious look on his face. He was a lawyer, so he knew that he could beat killing La'Bella because he had no choice. So, what now, Izzi? Now, you read our vows. DuVall grabbed their photobook with blood all over his hands. Izzi pointed the gun at him. Read it! Read it! Readddd it! Read it, you son of bitchhhhh! Izzi Marie Ratcliff, I just wanted you to know that there is not any woman in this world that have made my heart stop just by looking at them. You are a beautiful, special, attractive and phenomenal woman who completes me in every way in this world.

I can't think of another woman that I'd rather spend the rest of my life with Izzi than you. I promise to respect, love, honor and cherish you for the rest of our lives through sickness and health until death do us part. DuVall looked at his wife with tears in his eyes. Baby, can you please forgive me? I'm so sorry that I have done this to us. I'll do anything to fix this. Can you please forgive me, honey? Izzi shook her head yes, and then she said, "DuVall, I love you more than I love myself. Of course, I do, baby. I do forgive you, and you and I know that you're sorry, but I told you not to ever call me honey ever again. Pow! Pow! Pow! Pow! Pow! Pow! Pow!

Fuzzi's cell phone was ringing. "Hello! What do you want bitch?" Yo ass talking about me and look yo ass missing me already. Fuzzi, I killed them both. What! What! You done what, girl? The phone went dead. Click!

Chapter Two
WHEN DUTY CALLS

911, What's your emergency? Yes, I'm here at the Fry's Market on Indian School Road. Yes ma'am, what is your emergency? Yes, I was exiting my vehicle to go shopping and witnessed this woman slapping her daughter in her face. Ma'am, the little girl can't be no more than 10 or 11 years old. I overheard the little girl after slapping her that she wasn't stealing enough expensive stuff out of the store. Plus, she also has a young little boy stealing for her with the little girl. I heard them blaming each other for not grabbing what the mother wanted them to steal from the store. Ma'am, there's also an infant sitting in the sun crying, and she just ignores this baby. I'm about to go over there and slap her just like I saw her do this little girl. No, No, ma'am. I can just imagine how you're feeling, but don't go and get yourself in any trouble. You're doing the right thing by notifying us. We'll get a police officer dispatched to your location. It's being put through now; if I can just get you to keep an eye on them, I really appreciate it.

Where are the kids now, ma'am? The mother sent them back into the store to steal more stuff. Okay, where is the mother at right now? She's sitting her dope-fiend self in the car, tweaking and still ignoring her baby. Ma'am, can you see the type of vehicle she is driving and the color? Yeah, it's a blue Maximum, an old model like in the 90s. I know because I used to have that same vehicle, but when they first came out. Okay, ma'am, you're doing just great assisting us. I've already dispatched officers to that location. Ma'am, just in case we get disconnected somehow, can I ask you your name? No, I don't really want to be involved. No, I don't like what I saw, but I'm good at giving my name. Okay, ma'am, I do understand.

The 911 operator was just keeping her on the phone until the police arrived at the scene. Well, ma'am, you should be seeing a police officer pulling into the shopping store any minute now. Ma'am! Ma'am! Here come the kids running out of the store now. Her little girl was running real fast with a handful of merchandise. She was yelling and calling her mother's name and that made the woman start her car and back up from her parking spot. She could see her children running toward her one after the other right in stride. Now, she could hear the police sirens coming in her direction. Come on, baby, run, run. She was cheering them on to run faster to her. The little girl opens the front door and jumps into the front seat, dropping some of her merchandise. Run Jimmy, come on, brother, run. The mother had already started driving slowly, just as the little boy was opening the back door. Halfway jumping into the car, his mother saw the police turn down their aisle, and she hit the gas. Urrrrrrrrrr! But her son wasn't completely all the way inside the car. The body of the car hit his back. Wham! And sent him flying onto the hot pavement. The police vehicle came within inches, running the boy over. Urrrrrr! The police officer jumped out and ran to help the little boy, but his mother didn't even stop. She was burning rubber leaving the grocery store. The police radio dispatched the woman's license plate number and the direction she was headed in.

They stayed with the little boy and the woman that called the crime being committed in because she approached the officer when she saw the mother leave her child lying on the ground. She confessed to being the person who made the call. It didn't take long before the police had the woman's home surrounded by police officers. After the woman was taken into custody, her children were taken into the care of CPS, Child Protective Services. The case was given to Ashley, who was already in a murder investigation and was surrounded by police officers. Right after Ashley, Fuzzi, and Kahi'Lee showed up at their friend Izzi's house only to learn that she had shot her husband, DuVall and another close friend of theirs, La'Bella.

Izzi's neighbors were in their backyard when they heard multiple shots coming from Izzi's house, and they called the police and reported hearing gunshots. Before Ashley could learn all of what had happened, she was being called to remove two little boys and a little girl from a woman's home. Ashley Washington works for the social service; she is the person to decide whether to remove or return kids to their parents. But this was a time in her life when she didn't want to leave her best friend's side. Before Ashley left, she ordered Izzi not to answer any of the police officer's questions. Izzi was sitting in the back of a police car, and Ashley, Fuzzi, and Kahi'Lee were all standing there crying to see that she was arrested. They all heard the police officers say that it looked like a blood bath in Izzi's house. All they knew was that Izzi called Fuzzi and said that she killed them both. They kept trying to call La'Bella's cell phone, but they were not getting any answers. They were all wondering just what could have gone wrong between Izzi and DuVall. They both seem so happy and in love.

Ashley, being a social worker, caused her to have to leave because her job called her regarding her removing three children from their home. Ashley, before leaving, asked the police if she could have a word with Izzi. But being that it was an ongoing murder investigation, he couldn't allow Ashley the opportunity to talk to Izzi. The officer did, unfortunately, accept Ashley's phone number to give to Izzi. Ashley hollered to Izzi, "Girl, call me just as soon as you can, okay." I love you, don't worry, Izzi, you'll be okay. Ashley blew Izzi a kiss and she returned it to her. Izzi was feeling even more relaxed to see that her girlfriends had her back on this. Izzi was wishing that La'Bella was just the same type of friend, and she wouldn't be sitting inside that police car. But one thing Izzi did know about sitting in the back of the police car, she didn't have any regrets.

Ashley pulled up in front of a home on the lower west side of Phoenix. There were a few police cars at the home but nothing like they were in front of Izzi's house. Ashley exited her vehicle and showed her credentials to one of the police officers. They have been waiting for Ashley to show up and take custody of the kids. Ashley saw the mother sitting in the back of the police car just like she had just left Izzi. The officer begins to share the situation with Ashley as to the reason why she was called out to the home. Seeing the condition of the woman's house, Ashley was wondering why they hadn't been called to the house much sooner. The lights were off, and clothing was thrown every place, mixed with trash. The first thing that Ashley noticed was burnt candles and drug paraphernalia lying all over the living room table. Ashley opened the refrigerator, and she quickly closed it from the odor that almost made her throw up. Every room she looked in had clothes thrown everywhere and smelled like urine. When Ashley went to pick up the baby boy, his pamper looked like he had been sitting in urine and feces for days. It brought tears to Ashley's eyes to see the baby living that way.

Ashley loved doing her job because she really loved children. After talking to the little girl, Ashley learned that their dad got killed, and that's when the mother got hooked on drugs. The little girl was pretty much raising her two brothers and providing for her mother's meth habit. One of the police officers asked the mother if she wanted to say goodbye to her kids. The woman told the police that she'll make a deal with them. What's that, ma'am? I'll pass on the offer to say goodbye to my kids if you allow me to take just one more pull off my pipe before you take me. That's when he cuffed her and rushed her to his squad car.

She was a Caucasian female, and before the drug addiction, she would put you in the mind of GiGi Hadij, the model, but those looks are far behind her now. The little boy was five years old and was already calling Ashley Nigga's and saying that he wanted his mother. Being that Ashley was already used to these types of situations; she came prepared to deal with the problem to make the kids safe. Ashley's first priority was to get that pamper removed from baby Jordan. Ashley went to her car, got a diaper bag, and changed his pamper. One of the police officers had already sent out for McDonalds before Ashley got there. So, when the food came, that helped comfort the kids. Even though Ashley was just dealing with the whole situation of doing her job, no matter what was going on, Ashley's mind was still on Izzi and her problems. Right now, Izzi was feeling like her heart was being ripped in half.

$ $ $ $ $

Hello, ma'am, I'm here to see Mr. Pakulski. Oh! Yeah, I do believe that he is expecting you. Will you please wait one minute? I'll give him a call and let him know that you're here. Tyler looked around Mr. Pakulski's lobby and saw a magazine that caught his attention. So, he walked over to the table and picked it up. This was a magazine that Tyler knew that his face should be on the front cover of. He sat down to look through the magazine, and just as he opened the magazine, Tyler's cell phone started ringing. He already knew who it was because Kahi'Lee was on his screen saver. Hello baby, I was thinking about you too. Tyler got really quiet and listened to Kahi'Lee explain that Izzi had been arrested for murder. Tyler told Kahi'Lee that he was about to have a meeting with talent agent Mr. Pakulski, whom Kahi'Lee knew very well, being in both of their professions. Tyler and Kahi'Lee had hooked up together after doing a photoshoot together. They are both models but have two different agencies they are under. But no matter what agency you come from if you are expecting to land the big jobs and make it in this field, there wasn't no way that you could make it without Mr. Pakulski's assistance.

Tyler told Kahi'Lee that he would meet her back at their house just as soon as his meeting was over with Mr. Pakulski. Excuse me, Mr. Bronson, Mr. Pakulski will see you now, sir. He told his girlfriend that he has to go, and he'd see her later. Just be strong for her. I love you. Click! Tyler ended the call, but his mind was in a daze thinking about Izzi's troubles. Mr. Pakulski, Tyler, hello! It's good to see you have a seat. They shook hands. Oh, I see that you have been looking through the new elegant magazine. Tyler didn't even realize that he was still holding the magazine. Oh yeah, it's nice but it would be even nicer if my face was on this cover. Mr. Pakulski saw the sad look on Tyler's face and heard the depression in his voice. Yeah, everyone always seems to love to see a younger and newer face on the cover. I'm sure something good will come up for your likeness to the company. What the hell is that supposed to mean? What are you trying to say, Mr. Pakulski? Well, you know the game, Tyler, sometimes it costs a little more than just a person's look than what they have to offer. Mr. Pakulski stood up, walked over to a shelf, and removed two glasses and a clear crystal bottle full of liquor. You know Tyler, what sometimes means, right?

Mr. Pakulski gave Tyler a seductive look that made Tyler's skin crawl. So, what are you saying, Mr. Pakulski, we're back to this bullshit again? I already told you that I'm not into you or any of your friends' sexual fantasies. I have a beautiful woman that satisfies me and I'm good with just her. Oh, do you mean Mrs. Neidhart? "Yeah!" I see she seems to be doing quite great for herself. It seems that she must have figured things out in this business. Mr. Pakulski's words seem to cut through Tyler like a sharp knife. Tyler thought to himself, was this prick trying to say that my girl slept with one of her agents? Just hearing those words angered Tyler to the core. He jumped up, pointing his finger at his face and cursing Mr. Pakulski out. He got so loud that the secretary started knocking at Mr. Pakulski's door. Mr. Pakulski, open the door! Mr. Pakulski, is everything okay, sir? Yeah, Val, me and Mr. Bronson are fine. We just happened to disagree about a few things, that's all. Mr. Pakulski waved his secretary off, and she left the room and closed the door. But the whole time he was staring Tyler down until she walked out.

Mr. Pakulski told Tyler to calm down and take a seat. Hey, let's have a drink. I'm sure we can work this whole thing out. Mr. Pakulski went to pour them a drink, but not before he removed a valve from his coat pocket. He poured a little into one of the glasses, and then he fixed their drinks. Here, let's start over, Tyler, we seem to have gotten off on the wrong foot. Tyler took the glass, and he even apologized for getting loud and causing his secretary to come into his office. Man, please excuse me. I'm dealing with a little something right now; I was wrong. Tyler knew how easily Mr. Pakulski could make a phone call and end his career. No! No! No! Don't even worry about it. We're much too good of friends for that. Mr. Pakulski held up his glass to a new start. To a new start. They both toasted and downed their drink.

Mr. Pakulski went to retrieve a brown folder. Come on, Mr. Bronson, let me see what we can find that suits you. Tyler did realize that he was starting to get much older in this competition. He knew that the window was closing on his break in the modeling field. Mr. Pakulski invited him to come sit on his black sofa to discuss business. Forty minutes had gone by, and they were going back and forth, but Tyler's behavior began to change. Whatever Mr. Pakulski had put into Tyler's drink was starting to give him a high sexual arousal. Mr. Pakulski watched Tyler carefully and kept rubbing his leg, trying to help the drug take a more faster effect. Mr. Pakulski got up and went and locked his door. He grabbed the remote and turned up the music that was already playing softly in his office. Mr. Pakulski pressed another button on the remote before he placed it back on the table.

So, Tyler, are you ready to get your career off the ground now? Mr. Pakulski went back to join Tyler on the sofa. He placed his hand on his leg and looked Tyler right in the eye. Come on, Tyler, don't you know what I can do for you if you allow me to? Tyler looked at Mr. Pakulski for a moment, then he unzipped his pants and exposed his penis to Mr. Pakulski, and he happily got down on his knees and went to please himself and Tyler. Ummmmmm! Ummmmmm! Unfortunately, Mr. Pakulski and Tyler were interrupted by their sexual encounter. Valerie had buzzed in and told Mr. Pakulski that he had another very important appointment waiting. Even though Mr. Pakulski wasn't completely satisfied, he was content with what he had recorded on tape. They both stood up and cleaned up their act before Mr. Pakulski calmly escorted Tyler to the door and greeted his friend. Mr. Pakulski told Tyler that he would be contacting him real soon for his next job. They shook hands, and Tyler left. Mr. Wubben, what can I do for you today, sir?

Chapter Three
WHAT'S THE PLAY

itch, are you deaf or something? I told your pale-face ass once already that I mailed my bill in. Well, ma'am, I looked it up twice in our system, and it's not showing that the payment has cleared. I'm not the one who can authorize that your electricity can be turned back on. The only way I can send someone out to restore your power is that the bill is paid in full. Bitch! What are you the grinch that stole Christmas? Don't your stupid ass know that it's almost Christmas. How in the fuck am I supposed to feed my kids and give them a proper Christmas in the dark. Ma'am, I honestly feel for your kids, but I can't go against company policy. The best thing I can do for you is give my supervisor a call to speak with you on this matter. Would you like to talk to my supervisor? Yes, somebody with some damn sense because you don't seem to have any at all. The worker put her head down, put her close sign up, and went to get her supervisor. Hello Ma'am, I'm Susie Supervisor, what can I do to help you? Emma was trying her best to talk to the woman respectfully, but she wasn't happy with how Susy said she talked to her. The woman went right back to talking ignorant, acting ballistic, and drawing a crowd. Ma'am, if you can just lower your voice and give me your address, I'll see what I can do to solve your problem. Ma'am, thank you for your patience. I have someone in the account trying to straighten it out now.

For the first time being in this store, she calms down and puts a half smile on her face, thank you. Emma got back on the computer and kept searching for the files. Yes, Pamela, I'm still holding on. Emma listened and knew that everything was about to go all bad at this point. Emma took a deep breath again, okayyy, Mrs. Randall, we have checked our whole system, and there isn't any payment paid on this account showing that it has been paid, so at this point, there's really nothing that we can do to help you. Besides taking the payment right now in full, and if your other payment shows up at our company, we will gladly refund you, ma'am. Mrs. Randall stood there staring at Emma with rage in her eyes. Emma was about to say she was sorry, but Mrs. Randall spit in her face. Before she could even turn and walk away, Emma had started climbing over the counter, grabbed Mrs. Randall's hair, and started beating her. Wham! Wham! Wham! Wham! Get off of me, you stupid bitch! Wham! Wham! Wham! Emma was taking all of her frustration out on Mrs. Randall's face and body. Mrs. Randall will put you in the mind of Vanessa Williams; 5'9; 139 pounds with that hood rich, thick body with long deep wavy hair with blue streaks. Which right now was being pulled out by Emma. Emma, a Caucasian, but she grew up around nothing but black and doesn't take nobody's shit. Right now, Mrs. Randall was learning and experiencing at this very moment. Emma 5'8 real pretty face and look like a young Drew Barrymore but with an ass like that, she got some black in her with natural blonde hair and blue ocean water eyes.

Emma already knew how to deal with snobby women because her five friends taught her how to deal with any woman or man. One of her best friends Fuzzi just so happened to be born a man and now lives as a woman. Emma was the only one besides La'Bella that didn't have a man. Emma dates a lot but always made sure her male friends went home before the sun came up. By the time Emma's boss and coworkers pulled her off Mrs. Randall, it was blood and streaks of hair everywhere. Mrs. Randall had to be woken up because Emma had completely knocked her out. Mrs. Randall had to have forgotten that she was even at the electric company. The police and ambulance were called to the scene even though Emma was in the right to defend herself, she knew that she had just put her job in jeopardy. Also, besides that, she might even face criminal charges. Mrs. Randall wanted to press charges, but the officer told Mrs. Randall that Emma also could press charges against her. Because spitting on someone is an assault charge and a criminal offense in the State of Arizona. So, Emma and Mrs. Randall agreed not to file charges against each other. By the time all the attention died down, Mrs. Randall was released after being checked by the paramedics and Emma was sent home until further review.

Emma winds up calling Fuzzi, Ashley, and Kahi'Lee. They all agreed to go visit Izzi at the jail. But after they all showed up at the jail, they learned that Izzi wasn't even shown as being processed yet in their system. So, they all agreed to go have lunch together and try to figure out how to get Izzi a lawyer. They knew that DuVall kept all their finances mainly in his account. While they were having lunch, Ashley suggested that they go see a lawyer so that they have some type of idea as to what type of money they needed to come up with. But none of them have ever been in the type of trouble that Izzi was in right now. In fact, the only one out of the three, even been to jail before, was Fuzzi for prostitution. After their food came to the table, they chose to eat at Singh Hi which was a great Chinese food restaurant. They were sitting and eating next to a few lawyers at the time and didn't even know it. The restaurant was packed with all types of normal people. Business families and just plain normal people.

Everyone loved Singh Hi Chinese Food. Just luckily the four men that were dressed in business suits were all lawyers. Kahi'Lee just happened to hear one of the men say, "So, Adam how did the case work out for you in court today?" Kahi'Lee started kicking Emma under the table and pointed at the men next to them, but Emma's mind wasn't on men right now, it was only on getting Izzi free from jail. Girl, I'm not even thinking about no dick right now, Kahi'Lee, we must get Izzi out of there. No! No! That's not what I'm trying to get your attention for. I just heard that man say that their lawyer's girl. Maybe he can help and tell us who we need to talk to. Emma said, "Sir, excuse me, I don't mean to interrupt you guys' lunch, but we really can use some help right now." The lawyer turned around to have a conversation with Emma. While the other freeloaders were lusting off of Fuzzi, Kahi'Lee, and Ashley. After they all started talking, the girls learned that all four men were criminal defense lawyers. Two of the lawyers gave Emma their card, they both were good with murder cases. But when the girls learned that a case like Izzi's could cost up to $50,000 to over $100,000 to represent her, it would all depend on how many appearances the lawyer had to make and the hours and length of the case if it goes to trial. Both lawyers asked for Izzi's name and promised to look her up. They got a callback number to reach Emma and Fuzzi when they had some information on Izzi. They said they would see what they could do for her and promised to call real soon. After lunch, everyone went their separate ways.

$ $ $ $ $

Tyler sat in his jeep looking and feeling completely defeated. He had already thrown up three times after leaving Mr. Pakulski's office. He couldn't believe he allowed himself to stoop so low in his life just to keep his modeling career up. Tyler sat there wondering just how many other models have had to encounter that type of behavior from the talent agent that he lusted over. Tyler felt so humiliated that tears began to roll down his face. Right now, all Tyler wanted to do was go take his own life. Tyler didn't know what had just overcome him in that office. He promised himself that as long as he lived, he'd never have another drink in his life. Tyler was so deep in thought that he hadn't even noticed Kahi'Lee pulling up behind him in the driveway. Kahi'Lee tapped on his window. Baby! What's wrong with you? Why are you sitting here looking all crazy? Tyler never even responded, and Kahi'Lee noticed that he wasn't his normal happy self. Any other time that Tyler saw Kahi'Lee, he would be rushing and taking her in his arms. Kahi'Lee opened up his truck door, baby what's wrong, are you okay? No, I just feel a little sick. Kahi'Lee placed her hand over his forehead, but Tyler didn't have a fever. It doesn't feel warm, baby come on let's get you inside. Tyler was so broken he still almost couldn't move even with Kahi'Lee's help. After getting him into the house, Tyler just remained quiet and kept his distance from her. Kahi'Lee wanted to help, but she didn't know what was wrong with Tyler.

Right now, it wasn't the time for her to deal with this because her mind was on Izzi. Kahi'Lee was wondering how Izzi was holding up in jail around all those real criminals. Kahi'Lee rushed over to her answering machine and saw that she had missed many of Izzi's calls. Her heart almost stopped. What would Izzi think of her being that she wasn't there to accept her calls? Kahi'Lee grabbed the cordless off the wall and called Emma. She was so deep in thought that she hadn't realized she had completely stopped breathing until Emma answered her call. Hello! Emma, it's me. Has she called you yet? Girl, I missed her phone call when she called me. Yeah, Fuzzi and I talked to her girl, she sounds so terrible. They both started crying at the same time. Girl, what did they charge her with? What is her bail? Can we bail her out? They charged her with two counts of murder, and she doesn't even have bail. Emma started crying even more than she already was crying at first.

Kahi'Lee, Izzi said that her case is going to be a high-profile case because DuVall is a well-known lawyer. What's a high-profile case? I don't know, but Fuzzi does. Wait, I'll click her in now. Moments later, they were all on the line. Fuzzi, I got Kahi'Lee on the line now, too. Hello! Girl, I'm so glad y'all called. I just got off the phone with Mr. Shelton, the lawyer that we met earlier. I got some bad and good news. That other lawyer number that we have is a close friend of Duvall's so he said that there was no way he would or should take Izzi's case, but Mr. Shelton really didn't know DuVall, he only heard of him. Being that Duvall is a well-known lawyer it's not going to be any lawyer that's going to even take Izzi's case. Plus being who DuVall was, now her case is a high-profile case. What's a high-profile case, Fuzzi? Emma, that means that because DuVall was a lawyer the case would be highly publicized. Oh, okay, that makes a lot of sense. What did Izzi say happened? Kahi'Lee said that Fuzzi told Izzi not to say anything but to the lawyer. But in a roundabout way, Izzi kept saying that she didn't know that DuVall wanted her and La'Bella in their bed. Fuzzi spoke up, girl, all that I can think of is Izzi found that bitch in her bed and killed both of their asses. What? La'Bella would never do that. Emma, you don't know what one of these sneaky bitches would do behind your back. I sat there thinking that La'Bella wouldn't do that either. But while me and Izzi were shopping that dirty bitch was screwing her husband. But, honey child, she won't be sneaking and riding nobody else man's dick. Izzi fixed that, didn't she?

So Fuzzi, what's the good news because everything you said sounds terrible? Well, there is girl. Mr. Shelton agreed to take Izzi's case if I go out on a date with him. Kahi'Lee said, "What! Are you fucking serious?" Yeah, girl, but I was just looking him up on the internet, the man got very high ratings on here for murder, and they are saying that he's one of the best. He told me that if Izzi is found guilty she's looking at life in prison. Everybody got really quiet when Fuzzi said those words. Emma and Kahi'Lee started crying. Emma knew that none of them would have the type of money that Mr. Shelton would be asking for, so she finally said, "Fuzzi, what are you going to do to help us?" Fuzzi said, "Y'all, we can help Izzi, but we all have to be on the same page, though." I'm willing to do anything to help Izzi, that's my sister just like y'all are. "I'd do anything to bring any of my sister's home but what about y'all," Fuzzi said. But Kahi'Lee and Emma know Fuzzi, they both knew not to answer that question too fast. Emma told Fuzzi, "Come on with the bullshit, Fuzzi, what's on your mind?" Come on, Fuzzi, don't bullshit us, you know you're not the type of person to ever hold your tongue.

Well, I do have an idea as to how we can raise the money. Kahi'Lee quickly spoke up and said, "Fuzzi, I'm telling you now, I'm not about to kill nobody and wind-up cellmates with her." Fuzzi busted up laughing, don't trip cause I'm not willing to go to prison either, Kahi'Lee. Then what are you talking about? Well, it wouldn't be too wise to discuss this over the telephone. So, we'll have to meet up, and y'all can make that decision then whether you're in or out. But we have to do something fast, ladies. That's if we want Mr. Shelton to represent her. He said that she'll be arraigned on Monday. Kahi'Lee said, "damn, I don't know shit about the law." Fuzzi said, "Arraigned means to face the charges, girl." Oh! And then what happens? Then, she'll have a primary hearing to see if they can bond her over to face charges, which we already know that they have enough evidence to do. They got two dead bodies, weapons, and our sister. Do I need to explain anything else, Kahi'Lee? Damn, Fuzzi, as much as your ass knows, it sounds to me like you can go be a lawyer. For the first time, they all started laughing. Girl, I wish I could represent her. A bitch sure got the clothes for it. But even as much as I know about the law, by the time I get finished, child, they'll be putting me and Izzi's ass under the prison because I'll be then offered the judge and the prosecutor some pussy. Okay, so when and where are we meeting up? We can meet now. "Can y'all come by my house? Fuzzi said, Yeah, I can, Kahi'Lee said, but y'all give me a minute, I got to check on my man as he not feeling too good. Girl, once I get him settled, I'll be on my way. What about you, Emma? I'm grabbing my keys now, I got no man, kids, and maybe after today no job either. Why? What happened, Kahi'Lee asked her. Nothing, girl, I had to whip some bitch's ass at work today because of her dirty mouth. Ooooooh! Are you serious? Yep, I sure am. Just hurry up, and I'll tell you all about it when we get to Fuzzi's house. Okay, I'll see y'all in a few minutes. They all hung up. Click! Kahi'Lee went to see about Tyler, and Emma went to Fuzzi's.

$ $ $ $ $

Fuzzi had gone home and changed into a two-piece velour Gucci booty short set and tied-up laced heels. She went and poured herself a glass of Grey Goose and orange juice. Fuzzi knew that it wouldn't be easy telling Kahi'Lee and Emma what she was about to tell them. In fact, she expected them both to get up and walk out on her. Telling Ashley would definitely be out of the question. The type of job she had, Fuzzi, knew that if any of them had a chance at making it, it would be Emma. Kahi'Lee was much softer than all of them. But one thing that Fuzzi did know was each one of them was a man's dream to have any one of them on their arms. Just about anywhere, they all went together men and women would turn their heads. So, they all would be perfect for what Fuzzi has in mind. But after downing her first drink, Fuzzi was still asking herself would the girls go along with what she had planned. The telephone started ringing, and it took Fuzzi out of her train of thought. Fuzzi grabbed the receiver off the wall and the operator said, "Would you accept a prepaid phone call from; this is me, girl, answer the phone, to accept this call please press 5." Fuzzi accepted Izzi's call, and she tried everything to calm Izzi and let her know she'd be fine and that they found her a lawyer. But Fuzzi needed Izzi to help convince Kahi'Lee and Emma to help Fuzzi out. Izzi kept crying, it had finally set in on her that she wasn't about to get out of jail any time soon. Izzi had already called four times already, even before Emma had made it to Fuzzi's house. Izzi had no idea what it was that Fuzzi was asking her childhood friends to agree to. But Izzi promised that whatever it was, she would make it up to them when she got out. Emma loved Izzi so much that without even knowing what was going on, she told Izzi don't worry Fuzzi got a plan, and I'll help her. Trust me, we'll get you out of there, I promise you. Fuzzi looked at Emma when she said those words and knew there was no turning back from that. Izzi told her friends that she has to get off the phone, but she'll call back just as soon as she can. They all said that they loved each other and ended their call.

Okay! So, tell me, Fuzzi, what's the plan, girl? By the time Fuzzi finished explaining everything, Emma was shaking her head saying, "Bitch! Hell naw! Are you fucking crazy? You trying to get us all killed?" Fuzzi told Emma, "Well, I'm not the one who made a promise to Izzi that I'll get her out." Bitch, you did, but if you have a much better plan then I'm all in. By the time Kahi'Lee showed up, Fuzzi and Emma were in a heated argument. Hey! Hey! What's going on? Kahi'Lee didn't even knock, she just walked right into the house. But she walked in on a heated argument between her two girlfriends. Why are y'all at each other's throats now? Fuzzi walked over to Kahi'Lee and kissed her on the cheek. Ohhhh! That's cute girl. I like that outfit. She pinches Fuzzi on the cheeks of her butt because they were hanging out her shorts. Kahi'Lee don't be giving this bitch no compliment with that outfit on looking like she got on somebody's little girl's outfit. Emma turned her nose up to Fuzzi. Awe don't be hating on my body and Gucci outfit, Bitch. I don't hate on your no-name brand gear, step your game up. Step it up. She snapped her finger at Emma. Ok! Ok! Ok! Y'all stop it already, both of y'all look nice. Fuzzi said under her breath "mine name brand though." Has Izzi called yet? Yeah, you just missed her, but she'll be calling back. She had to go be counted like she a damn sheep or something. Poor baby, I miss her so much.

Ok then, so what's our plan to get her out of there? Fuzzi and Emma both looked at each other. Well, Kahi'Lee, that's kind of what we're arguing about. Why, if it's going to get her out of there what's wrong with it? Emma said, "You say that now but wait until she tells you what her little plan is." Kahi'Lee turned to Fuzzi to hear what her plan was. Kahi'Lee, the only type of people that have the type of money that we need right now are drug dealers and pimps. What girl, are you crazy? Now okay, that's the same thing I said, she trying to get us killed. Fuzzi started yelling, "No, I'm not, and stop saying that shit." Ain't nobody going to get killed, Nobodyyyy! Do y'all know how much money some of those dudes walk around with in their pockets? Let alone up in their cribs. Most of them are so stupid that they keep it under their mattress, in shoe boxes, or in an old car in the yard. All we got to do is get close to them and play their little bullshit games. And they will high side you right into their money. All their minds are on is making money and some pussy. Any pretty bitch quickly brings a distraction to their game. Because he go be sniffing up her ass and trying to impress the next man. That's one thing pimps and drug dealers have in common. Bitch, they all ain't nothing but a lottery ticket. You just keep getting them by playing the game and scratching it, bitch, until you hit the jackpot, you feel me? Now, Kahi'Lee and Emma both have a different look on their face. After Fuzzi gave her little speech, the wheels started to turn in their heads. Emma had a few dudes who came into her job to pay their bills. They all pulled out wads of cash trying to impress her in front of their girls. A few of the dudes even offered to spend some on her if she called their numbers. Emma took the numbers but never called them because she knew the type of lifestyle that they lived, and she didn't want any part of it. Emma spoke up, "Yeah Fuzzi, I do know a few guys that come at you with their money. I even still got a few of their numbers maybe we can call them." Kahi'Lee said, "Those type of men approaches me all the time, but they all just disgust me with all that bragging about what they got and what they can do for you."

Fuzzi saw now that she had their full attention, and she chimed right into their conversation. Why do y'all think that they do that? Emma and Kahi'Lee got quiet and started thinking, but Fuzzi saved them from even wrecking their brains. Y'all some sexy, beautiful, fine-ass bitches, and that's what they want. Bitch! Look at us, whose attention can't we get entering a room? Emma and Kahi'Lee started to see Fuzzi clearly now as to what she was trying to say. Besides, not only would we get Izzi a lawyer, but you bitches can buy yourself any motherfucking thing y'all want. Them two buckets out there will be brand-new cars. Everything y'all put on them stankin asses of y'all's will be brand new and name brand. Emma said, "Hold-up, bitch, my ass ain't stanky. That's that elephant booty of yours you bought, that's stanky." They all busted up laughing. But they were now starting to come to an agreement to do what Fuzzi was talking about. But, out of nowhere, Kahi'Lee said, "Wait! Wait! I can't do that; Tyler would kill me." If he knew that I been around or with another man, my ass would be killed like DuVall. Both of y'all trying to get me killed. I'm out of here, y'all crazy. Her words pissed Fuzzi off, but she knew that she had to play it cool. Girl, you can't be serious. I don't mean to blast your man but ain't he the same one who couldn't even buy you a Valentine's gift or flowers this year? How many presents are under y'all Christmas tree? Fuzziiiii! You didn't have to go there. Naw! Naw! It's okay, Emma, at least she is telling the truth. But my man is about to land something big, and we go be straight. At least, we love each other ain't none of us cheating on each other so my relationship is good and thank you for your opinion. Kahi'Lee grabbed her purse and keys and started walking out the door. But what saved Fuzzi's plan was the phone started ringing.

Kahi'Lee stopped at the door. See if that's Izzi before I leave. Fuzzi answered the phone, you have a prepaid phone call from, it's me, Izzi, Fuzzi smiled, yeah, it's her. Here you want to answer it. She extended the phone towards Kahi'Lee. Kahi'Lee accepted the call, and they all got on the loudspeaker to talk. It didn't take long before all of them were in tears. Izzi called back a few times, and by the end of their last call, they all had told Izzi that they were all going to work together and get her a lawyer. When they started talking about their plan, Fuzzi told the girls that you don't shit where you lay your head at. Our victims will all be from out of town. We have all got to go shopping, so I can buy y'all the right clothes. We need to get three cell phones, rent hotels, rent cars, and buy mace and good knives. "What do we need knives for?" Kahi'Lee asked. Before Fuzzi could say anything, Emma said, "To be safe, girl, just in case those people are dangerous." But if we do like we are supposed to, like Fuzzi said earlier, we'll just walk away with their money, right Fuzzi? Right! After Fuzzi had fixed them all a glass of Grey Goose, Emma was starting to feel more comfortable with the whole situation.

Fuzzi told them that first, before we do anything, I got to go put my hook in Mr. Shelton so that we can get him on her case while we put this money together for her. Come on, y'all can go help pick out something to wear tonight. You're going to meet up with him already? Kahi'Lee, we're pressed for time. She'll be arraigned, I'm sure, by tomorrow. So, when she goes before that Judge, she'll need Mr. Shelton there by her side, representing her. They were all in Fuzzi's room going through her clothes, and Emma picked up a red dress. Where are y'all going to eat? Hell, I don't know. Well, I'm sure this dress would definitely do the job. Your body and this dress would have his penis hard as a rock. They all slapped hands and laughed.

Chapter Four
SEALING THE DEAL

Fuzzie sat in her bedroom, looking through her vanity mirror. Even though he had completely had a sex change, he was still born a male. The female hormone shots that she often took being born the opposite gender sometimes facial hairs would appear on her face. Fuzzi was happy that she wasn't a natural hairy man, so the tweezers that she was using to pluck away her facial hair were doing the job. Fuzzi's skin was naturally smooth, and she was light-skinned, so Fuzzi hardly ever wore make-up or wigs. The hormone shots that she took over the years helped grow her hair, so she has long black silky hair past her shoulders halfway down her back. The one thing about herself that Fuzzi hated most was she wore a man-size 10 shoes. No matter what people do to change their appearance, some things just can't be changed. Fuzzi was a big fan of old-school music so Teddy Pendergrass, "Come Go With Me," played softly in the background. Fuzzi had even dated a millionaire who favored Teddy Pendergrass when she was younger working the streets.

Terrence was a fan of the LGBTQ community and picked Fuzzi up one night. Fuzzi thought that he was a gentleman and treated her like a woman. They even discussed Fuzzi becoming a woman from a young man. Terrence even encouraged Fuzzi to live out her dreams. The only problem was all he donated to her becoming a female was a fucking $100 for the oral sex that Fuzzi gave him. Later that evening, Fuzzi recognized the Rolls Royce that she was in earlier being crashed into a pole, and it turned out Terrence picked up another transgender female. Fuzzi had learned that he had paid for her operation. Fuzzi always joked with the other homosexuals, hell maybe I didn't suck his penis like she did because he didn't wreck his Rolls Royce when I was sucking his dick.

$ $ $ $ $

The doorbell rang, and Fuzzi checked herself once again in the mirror. She did agree with Emma about the red dress she picked out because it was showing off every curve, and the dress made her ass pop like Orville Redenbacher popcorn. Fuzzi sprayed her body one last time with that Prada Candy Kiss and headed to open the door. Wow, did I come to the right address? You make me feel like I don't deserve to be in your company. Fuzzi smiled at Mr. Shelton's compliment. Thank you for the compliment, but I do believe that that's a woman's choice whom company she chooses to keep, and tonight I choose you. Besides, you look quite handsome yourself. Mr. Shelton smiled, but he knew the plain-looking suit that he had on was just a normal suit that he would wear to go fight a case in court.

Shall we, he extended his arm to escort Fuzzi to his Black Maybach Mercedez Benz. He opened the door, and those seats melted Fuzzi's voluptuous butt cheeks like butter in a frying pan. Just as soon as Mr. Shelton started the car Fuzzi felt heat stimulating her backside. Wow, this is nice, you just shamed my little Corvette. Noooo baby! You actually got great taste in cars. He begins to tell Fuzzi everything about her vehicle. Before I bought my Maybach, I used to drive that same Corvette but after winning a lot of cases in court, unfortunately, I was able to purchase this car. Fuzzi turned to him, you're that good, huh! Well, let's just say, I take my job seriously. Hearing those words made Fuzzi remember why she was riding in the car with this white married man in the first place. So, she needed to take her job seriously, too.

Fuzzi quickly, upon opening the door, recognized his wedding band that she didn't care about because it wasn't like she was looking for a relationship. Her only job was to convince him to take her friend's case, and Fuzzi was about to do that just before Mr. Shelton left her company. They pulled into a nice-looking restaurant in Mesa, Arizona. The sign read Tiffany's. It wasn't a restaurant that Fuzzi was familiar with. Mesa wasn't a part of Arizona that she frequently went to. Upon entering the restaurant, Fuzzi could tell that it was a rich, romantic setting for couples. It has red eloquent tablecloths on all the tables with candles burning. Their waitress showed them to a corner table and began to offer to take their order. Mr. Shelton ordered a bottle of expensive smooth champagne. After a few glasses, the both of them seem to warm up to each other. They had moved closer to each other, and when Mr. Shelton wasn't commenting on her looks, he was telling Fuzzi how great she smelled. Several times, the waitress tried to take their order, but every time they declined.

The next time, when she came to take their order, Fuzzi wasn't sitting at the table. Ummmmmm! Excuse me, sir, where is your lady friend? I didn't see her leave. Mr. Shelton wanted so badly to answer her question, but every time he wanted to answer Fuzzi was taking his penis deeper and deeper down her throat. She had climbed under the table and decided to take control of Izzi's situation. Mr. Shelton laid his head back, and his eyes started rolling in the back of his head. The waitress thought that he was about to have a seizure. Sir! Sir! Are you okay? Do I need to call the paramedics? Fuzzi finally came from under the table. No, ma'am, he won't need a paramedic; maybe a warm towel will help then we're ready to order now. The waitress put her hand over her mouth and smiled at Fuzzi. Oh! Okay! Yes, ma'am. Let me see what I can do to help you. Fuzzi said, "I'm sure your assistance will acquire you a big tip." Mr. Shelton was so embarrassed, but he enjoyed every minute of it. It was Fuzzi's boldness that won him over. Mr. Shelton had never experienced a sexual encounter, never in life before like that.

During dinner, they discussed the price and what it would take to hire him to take Izzi's case. He told her that Izzi's case would cost $50,000. That it could also be more or even less. And if it was, he would return whatever money that he didn't work for. He told Fuzzi that it wasn't going to be easy representing Izzi being the type of man that DuVall was. If he could settle without taking it to trial, then things would work out for them all. But Mr. Shelton knew that he was about to take a lot of heat taking this case. After taking Fuzzi home, he thought that he would be invited in for sex. But Fuzzi told him that when he was ready to take $10,000 off her bill then she was ready to give him the rest of what she gave him as an appetizer before their meal. Fuzzi closed his car door and allowed him to take in her ass shaking as she entered the house. She knew his penis longed for an experience to learn what her vagina was like.

$ $ $ $ $

Izzi sat nervously in the courtroom chained to a few other female inmates. One of the girls who was African American and looked like a female version of Mike Tyson, kept on hitting on Izzi in a sexual manner. But, when Izzi didn't show any type of affection towards her back, the female started trying manipulating tactics to get under Izzi's skin. All the other females were afraid of Big Girl, whom she called herself. The ear piercings and all the tattoos made the female look more intimidating than she really is. She kept on telling Izzi, "Bitch I'm sucking on that strawberry sherbert before I leave this jail, watch!" Izzi never said anything, she just always stayed where the guards could see her. Before Izzi and the other females entered the courtroom, Officer Scott told them all that there only there to be arraigned for the charges that they were accused of. Nobody would do any talking but the Judge. You won't talk to any lawyer or anyone regarding your charges. You would just hear your charges and bail amount if there is one. Plus, your next court date and the Judge, you'll go before. If anybody talks or causes me any problems, I'll pull your asses out of court, and we'll try it again 30 days from now. Plain and simple, ladies, you respect me, and I'll respect you. You screw me, and y'all screwed yourself. It didn't take long before two females were being removed from the courtroom. After Izzi got her charges and was told that she didn't have bail, tears ran down her face non-stoppable. Big Girl smiled and laughed at her crying. After the arraignment, they were all taken back to the holding tank until they returned to their permanent housing.

Upon returning to jail, Big Girl wasted no time putting her plan together to get Izzi. She kept a close eye on Izzi because she had nothing to lose. Big Girl was a two-time loser and was on her way back to prison for distribution of Meth and Heroin out of a Motel 6. The guard announced five minutes to lock down, and all the females rushed around the pod to collect their final interactions with fellow inmates. Izzi was on the phone and talking to someone on the phone and hadn't noticed that Big Girl had slipped into her cell. Big Girl had switched with Izzi celli and went and covered herself up in the top bunk. Izzi walked into the room crying, still having been upset about not having bail. But she did learn that a lawyer would be in court to represent her. Girl, are you going to sleep already? But Big Girl didn't respond, so Izzi sat on her bed crying. Moments later, the guard does his final walk for the night. Big Girl made sure the guard saw movement when he did his walk passing the room. Thirty minutes passed, and nothing out of the ordinary happened, so Big Girl knew that her plan worked. Izzi was lying in bed, thinking and reliving her shooting DuVall when she felt her covers slowly being pulled back. When she turned around, Big Girl was looking at her face-to-face. Hello, strawberry sherbert, I told you; you were my favorite.

$ $ $ $ $

Fuzzi, Emma, and Kahi'Lee landed at Hartsfield International Airport in Atlanta. All the strip clubs around there have nothing but ballers floating around. Either they have a name or were trying to make one for themselves. But either way, it was known worldwide that they were making it rain in ATL strip clubs. Fuzzi already knew for sure that it definitely was a victim waiting to pay for their time. Fuzzi had taken Kahi'Lee and Emma to her hairstylist and made sure that their hairstyles were video-ready to accommodate the outfits that she personally picked out for them. ATL was about to get a triple dose of the dirty desert finest. Upon exiting the airplane, they went to retrieve their luggage from baggage claim. Then, they went to Avis's rental car and pushed off into two Convertible Corvettes. One white and the other black. Fuzzi knew about the young gang members, so she was sure not to rub anybody in the wrong way.

It was all business, nothing personal on Fuzzi's behalf. They checked into the Marriott. Fuzzi told them this is where we will lay our heads, because them white folks ain't going to let nothing happen to us here. There are cameras everywhere, and we're three attractive women that can pull anything or anybody, so we got to stay ready for our prospects. We'll check into another hotel to take our prospects to and handle our business. Bitches! We're in the motherfucking ATL. Are y'all ready to get sexy and go fishing for the fishermen with that green bait? "Well, I don't know about y'all, but my ass is hungry." Kahi'Lee said, "Girl, me too." Let's get dolled up, drop the tops on those Corvettes, and have some fun. They all hugged and headed to get dressed. Emma said, "Y'all can ride together because I'm not about to mess up my hair, girl. Y'all know a bitch looking real cute right about now." She smiled looking at herself in the mirror.

Emma was the first one to get dressed. She wore a short white jumpsuit with white open-toe pop heels. Her hair was up in a schoolteacher hairstyle, blonde and black. She topped it off with a Versace white and gold letter jacket, glossy lips, and light eyeliner white, gold and pussy pink. She sat sipping on her orange juice, waiting on Kahi'Lee and Fuzzi. Fuzzi had made it very clear to them that before they even left Arizona there would be no drinking at all on this trip. That was men's way of getting a woman comfortable to give in to their sexual desires. Plus, you will always have those slick ones that will try to slip you something to knock you out.

Fuzzi came walking out of the bedroom, wearing a pair of black lace see-through jeans and a shortcut gator high-back boot, wearing a pair of gator panties under the see-through jeans. She topped it off with a clear see-through black long sleeve shirt with a matching gator bra covering her breast. Her hair was flat ironed straight down with diamond hoop earrings.

Well, hello, pretty lady. Don't you look nice. Fuzzi commented on Emma's outfit. Thank Youuuuu! Yo ass looking like it's about to jump out of that lace, Girl! Stunning! Fuzzi spun around like a runway model, to only take in Kahi'Lee entering the room. A grand entrance is what Kahi'Lee was used to because she had done it for a living. She made every designer's clothes that she wore look like a million bucks. She for sure, goes out and buys before anyone else does. A Prada mini dress and 3-inch heels that she has on even made Fuzzi do a double take. It was a shiny gold color that demanded attention. Her hair was in loose long hanging curls. Her make-up looked like she was going to take glamor shots. Kahi'Lee showed Fuzzi how to really do a runway walk into the room. She came in twisting and turning like all cameras were clicking her way. Work it

Bitch! Work It! Work Itttt! All three of them busted up laughing. They grabbed their purses and keys and headed out the door. Fuzzi had put their destination in the GPS. They were looking for a good soul food restaurant. They knew all the important information that they needed to learn about ATL hotspots in all the right places to be.

It wasn't like they were looking for white collar, CEOs or corporate type of men right now. They wanted to be in the company of hood thugs, blood smoking, dice rolling, pistol carrying, loud rap music, fuck the police, or anybody else who wanted to stop their hustle with bags and bags full of money. That didn't take long because, sometimes, the things you're looking for find you. He pulled right up next to Fuzzi and Emma at the red light. His Cadillac EXT with candy paint and 26-inch rims stopped right next to them. Rick Ross featuring Meek Mill, "She on my dick" remix was rattling both the Corvettes. The driver smiled at Fuzzi with a mouth full of diamond teeth, the passenger, like the driver showed off diamond teeth, and they shined brighter than the sun. Which was accommodating the big flashy jewelry that hung around their necks, wrists, and ears. The driver was yelling something, but the music drained out every word he said.

Kahi'Lee watched the whole interaction unfold. It even gave her a better understanding of street players. There every movement was fuck the world. The light turned green, and Fuzzi knew just what to do. Let the dogs chase the cookie. She hit the gas, and the

Corvette did the rest. It even threw Kahi'Lee off guard. Why is she rushing off from the type of men that we're looking for? Kahi'Lee speeded up to catch Fuzzi and Emma. The two guys noticed a third sexy woman pass them in another Corvette, and the chase began. Fuzzi made sure there were several lights that she passed before she allowed the Cadillac truck to catch them. Hey! Hey! Shawty! Pull over let a boss holla at'cha. Fuzzi smiled, and both Corvettes pulled over. Kahi'Lee and Emma already knew to follow Fuzzi's lead. Flirtation and plenty of sex appeal always trigger the male hormones. Both men exited the Cadillac truck, trying to make sure that they put their bid in first and grab the most attractive woman out of the three. What's up, Shawty's? Where y'all headed moving so fast like some jungle cheetahs? Fuzzi said, "Oh, I'm sorry, handsome, I didn't know y'all was trying to holla at us." She lied but kept a poker face. We are not from around here. We are just trying to find this soul food joint. She pointed to the GPS, showing the men where they were headed. Naw shawty their food ain't all that good.

Let us treat you ladies to some real soul food. I'm sorry, please forgive us. I'm Tremendous, and that's my homeboy, Xerxes. Fuzzi introduced them to the two men. I'm Fuzzi, this Emma, and that's our girl Kahi'Lee. The two guys waved at Kahi'Lee. So, would y'all like to take us up on our offer? Yeah, we would love to try out the better restaurant, but we can buy our own food, sweetie. Tremendous pulled out a rubber band full of $100 bills. Naw, shawty, what y'all think, we some broke-- And before he could get off another word, Naw, sweetie, hold up, how bout we treat y'all for y'all showing us around y'all town. Now see, shawty, I like you, already. We know y'all ain't from around here. These shawty's around here, Tremendous and Xerxes slapped hands and, at the same time, said, "Greedyyy!" No, sweetie, we from Seatle, Washington, and we're all hard-working women. I can see y'all doing well for yourselves, but money is hard to come by these days. Tremendous told them to follow them then. And he and Xerxes went back to Tremendous truck. When the two ballers got out of earshot, Fuzzi told Emma and Kahi'Lee, "This is it ladies y'all know what to do." They all winked at each other and followed the Cadillac truck.

The restaurant wasn't all that big, but it was packed with hungry families, hustlers, and church-going people. The parking lot almost looked like a nightclub ending. Everybody was flossing their whips and showing off their little dime pieces. While they were parking, they could hear a Pastor approaching a group of men, and he told them that they needed to give their lives to God. One of the dudes told the pastor, "Man when you get some of that good cocaine that you use to have before you were serving God then we'll come fuck with you." All the young dudes started laughing and slapping their hands. The pastor and his wife just walked away. It didn't take long before their laughter came to an end. Fuzzi, Emma, and Kahi'Lee came walking up. The dudes started attacking them like flies. Even Tremendous and Xerxes couldn't believe the bodies that they had.

They knew that they were all beautiful females, but they didn't know that they made the two women they were risking their lives for were nothing in comparison to what was in their company. Damnnnn Ma! Tremendous and Xerxes almost said it at the same time. Emma was laughing at all the men's different comments. While Kahi'Lee was a bit nervous. She wasn't used to men attacking like they were doing. Fuzzi wasn't paying any of them any attention. She already had her mind set on Tremendous. He has to be the one with the money because he showed them over $10,000 like it was nothing. But she will quickly learn that her intuition was off just a little.

Tremendous and Xerxes jumped out of the truck, and all the attention Emma, Fuzzi, and Kahi'Lee were getting quickly turned to Tremendous and Xerxes. Hey! What's up, big hommie? All the dudes' manners and respect levels completely changed when Tremendous and Xerxes walked up. The respect for them didn't go unnoticed by the women. Say, fellows, can y'all give the ladies some room? Their pathway was quickly cleared. Hey! Big Hommie, let me holla at'cha. I got that cornbread, fluffy. Fuzzi figured that the dude was telling Tremendous that he was ready to buy some work. But Xerxes told the dude that he'll holla in a few minutes. When they walked into the BarBQ pit restaurant, it was like Tremendous and Xerxes were celebrities. All the people eating and the workers were giving them mad respect. All the tables were taken, but the owner, whom everybody called Big Swizzle, walked up and shook Tremendous hand but he hugged Xerxes. Hey baby boy, don't even trip, you know I got you. Come on, y'all follow me. Right this way, ladies. Big Swizzle took them to a special table that was already reserved for five people. Xerxes and Tremendous pulled out the chairs for Fuzzi, Emma, and Kahi'Lee. But Fuzzi could tell that he had his eyes on Kahi'Lee. He gave Kahi'Lee that look like I'll give you the world. It didn't take long for Xerxes's cell phone to start blowing up. He had to excuse himself a few times from the table. They even got to witness two men bring him a large sum of cash. One of the men told him that it was $30 thousand in the bag and the other said that he had $12,500.

While eating, Tremendous invited them over to their house for a few drinks. Do y'all smoke or drink? Emma was about to say no, but Fuzzi said, "Yeah, as long as nothing is expected in return." Xerxes laughed and said, "Y'all are all very attractive, but no disrespect, these types of hours my mind is focused on money not pussy." We can exchange numbers and get back later if y'all like. Kahi'Lee placed her hand on Xerxes's hand, I'm sure you already got a woman waiting on you at home, so we can just enjoy our lunch and attend to our normal lives. Thank y'all for showing us this place, the food is great. Xerxes's said, "Shawty, you know I'm just kidding. You are not about to walk out of my life that easily. I'm your future, and you just don't know it yet." Is that right? You better know it. When they left the BarBQ restaurant, Xerxes's rode in the car with Kahi'Lee to a private home that he and Tremendous have together. Xerxes was 5'9 with long braids in his hair, medium build with a lot of tattoos. He looked like the rapper Ice T, just much brighter. His homeboy Tremendous was 5"11, 270 pounds but mostly muscular, with low cut waves in his hair and dark-skinned, but he talks real country. You can tell that he was from Atlanta, Ga. Tremendous looked a lot like Headcrack on Dish Nation. It didn't take long before their little party started. Blunts and drinks were being turnt up.

To Fuzzi's surprise, the home was pretty nice, and it didn't appear to look like it was a man's hideout. They have big white plush, real nice, and expensive furniture throughout the house. Large platinum television screens on every wall. A large kitchen covered in marble full of food. But there wasn't a trace of any female living or being in their home. The only problem that Fuzzi saw that they had was Xerxes didn't seem to be the one to let his guards down, and he kept a .357 magnum no further than at arm's reach. And Tremendous carried a .40cal and a .25 that he kept strapped to his leg. Nobody would even think that he had it, but while he and Xerxes played Madden football on the big screen Fuzzi kicked Emma's leg to make her aware of the weapon. They were playing Madden for $1000 each quarter. Fuzzi even thought that if they didn't need their money, Tremendous and Xerxes would be great men to have in their lives. Kahi'Lee was sitting in between Xerxes legs while he played cheering him on. Fuzzi and Emma cheered for Tremendous. Xerxes kept telling Kahi'Lee to pick up Tremendous money after every quarter. He told her that they were going shopping with Tremendous cash. Without any of them realizing it, they were having so much fun when they noticed the day had turned into night, and everybody got hungry. Xerxes wanted to take them to another restaurant, but Fuzzi agreed to cook.

Kahi'Lee and Emma told them that Fuzzi was a great cook. Xerxes wanted Spanish food, so Fuzzi took to the kitchen and made that happen. Even Xerxes and Kahi'Lee left for a few hours. But when they returned, Xerxes couldn't believe his eyes. His kitchen table was filled with all types of Mexican food as if he walked into a gourmet Mexican restaurant. Damn! Are you serious? Fuzzi grabbed a spoon and started letting him taste everything. The last dish that he tasted she walked up to him and said, "How do everything taste?" I'm really, really impressed with your skills. Everything tastes wonderful. Fuzzi kissed Xerxes on the lips gently, don't speak too soon you haven't tasted me yet. Xerxes looked Fuzzi in the eyes, he couldn't believe she had done that, knowing that he was into Kahi'Lee. But it turned him on, and now he wanted to take Fuzzi, too. Me and my girls don't discriminate sweetie, it ain't no fun, right? Fuzzi grabbed him in between his legs and cupped his penis on her way, walking out of the kitchen to tell everybody it was time to eat.

After dinner, they all enjoyed a drink and a couple more blunts. Fuzzi and Kahi'Lee went into Xerxes's bedroom while Emma went with Tremendous. Fuzzi knew that Kahi'Lee nor Emma was about to give up no pussy. So, she knew that just like Queen Latifah she had to be the one to set it off. While Xerxes was eating Kahi'Lee's vagina, she started off giving him head to distract her next move. By the time that Xerxes realized what was going on, his own .357 magnum was being put to the back of his head. Motherfucker, if you move too fast or turn around, Kahi'Lee's pussy will be the last thing you see in this world. Xerxes said, "Fuck! Fuck! Fuck! I knew not to trust you, bitches." Shut up!

Do you know what all your mother has done to have you? We all bitches' sweetie when we have to be. Fuzzi ripped up towels from the bathroom and tied Xerxes up. While Kahi'Lee held his gun on him. She tied his hands, mouth, and feet up. Then, she told him, sweetie, you couldn't have handled me and her pussy, no way. Not this one, she grabbed his penis and put it in her hand. You're cute, but your penis ain't no bigger than the one I had that's why I got rid of mine. Emma had done everything she could to stall Tremendous from having sex with her but from him being so big and strong he tricked Emma like he was just going to eat her vagina. But he forced his weight onto her, and when Fuzzi and Kahi'Lee made it to her, Tremendous had her legs high over his shoulders and was pounding away at her pussy. Oooooooh! Oooooooh! Oooooooh! Oh! My God, please stop! Please stop! Take it out. Pow! Tremendous felt the warm pain go through the back of his leg. Motherfucker, didn't she say no. Tremendous rolled to the side of Emma, but he was hollering like a bitch. Argggggggh! Argggggh! Argggghhh! "Get up, girl, come on." Do you want me to kill this piece of shit? Emma was so mad and confused right now, she didn't know what to do or say. Kahi'Lee walks over to his pants and removes the wad of cash. She tossed it to Emma. Here, don't worry about it, girl, he just paid you well for that pussy. Fuzzi tied him up, and they took all their money. They left with $308,000 in cash. Fuzzi didn't know what it was when she saw it, but they left over 22 kilos of cocaine sitting in the closet. But Fuzzi, Emma, and Kahi'Lee weren't drug dealers, so they got what they came for, Izzi's lawyer money.

After they made it back to the hotel room, Emma went straight to the bathroom. They had stopped at a little convenience store, and Fuzzi bought her three Massengill douches, and Emma used them all. She sat in the tub, crying thinking about what had just happened. But, when she finally got out of there, Kahi'Lee and Fuzzi had $110,000 waiting on the bed for her. Emma picked up the money and counted it. All she went to ATL in her purse was $82.00 to her name. But she couldn't believe all that money was hers until Fuzzi told her that was her cut. Fuzzi told Emma that she doesn't think Tremendous relieved himself in her because he was beating her pussy like an African drum when they came into the room. Girl, that just goes to show you being the boss doesn't mean you the boss because his homeboy wasn't packing shit. Emma fell on the floor laughing hard. Bitch, you are one special person, girl. She shot that man. Hell, I ain't no crazier than your ass. You go tell him; he paid for Emma's pussy. Well, bitches, now y'all know what prostitution is like. But y'all made so much more money than they did in one day. Fuck y'all, my pussy is still sore, that felt like I was attacked by a horse. Fuzzi said, "Bitch I know, I saw it, I'm jealous. I wanted to stay there and rape his ass." They all busted up laughing. Even though they had accomplished their goal, nobody said anything, but what they didn't know was they all have been bitten by the dead president bug. Money! Money! Moneyyyyyy!

Chapter Five
I GIVE UP

Ooooooh! Ummmmmm! Yesssssss! Yessssss! Suck that kat, strawberry sherbert, suck it! Suck that, kitty kat. Izzi's body, mouth, and face were sore. She hadn't had any sleep as of yet. When she finally learned that her celli Caroline wasn't the one trying to climb into her bed with her, that it was the one last person that she'd ever invite to sleep with her or have any type of sexual encounter with. Here, Big Girl was trying to force herself onto Izzi. Izzi tried her best to fight Big Girl off, but after the third punch to her face and the punches she had taken to her ribs, Izzi knew that she wasn't any type of opponent for Big Girl. After trying to return a few punches of her own, she watched Big Girl eat her punches like a subway sandwich, which left her balled up in the corner of the bed and taking blow after blow. Izzi's body couldn't take anymore, so she thought that it would be much easier to just lay there and allow Big Girl to eat her vagina. So, she yelled, "Okay! Okay! Stop! I give up." Big Girl took pleasure in removing her jail uniform and watching Izzi cry after being defeated. Big Girl sucked her vagina so good that after a while, Izzi's womanly hormones began to accept what she was feeling. But Izzi didn't know that after Big Girl pleased her, she would eventually return the favor like she had been doing for the last two hours. Izzi knew that she would have been tapped out even with a man giving her oral sex, but Big Girl was going like the energizer bunny.

When the lights came on and the guard announced good morning, ladies. Get ready; y'all have five minutes for breakfast. That gave them a warning that the doors would be popped soon. Big Girl still has her arms wrapped around Izzi when they both awaken to the guard's announcement. Big Girl kissed Izzi on the forehead and removed herself from the bed. She made one final threat to put fear into Izzi, not to tell. Izzi promised that she wouldn't say anything and that she'd say that she just bumped her face. Izzi hadn't seen her face yet, but waking up, she had her waking to a black eye. Big Girl saw the black eye, and that made her want to have sex all over again, but the doors popped on the cells, and Big Girl made her way to the breakfast line. All the other female inmates watched Izzi as she exited her cell. Caroline had tears rolling down her face because she felt like she had betrayed her cellmate. But Caroline knew that she wasn't a match for Big Girl either, so she just did as she was told. The guard watching the inmate serve breakfast didn't notice anything out of line because Izzi didn't say anything, and she pulled her hair over her face. After breakfast, all the inmates, including Big Girl, returned to their regular cells. Caroline hugged Izzi and told her that she was sorry, but she couldn't get involved. Izzi forgave her and told her that she understood. Caroline told Izzi that Big Girl won't stop hurting her. Now she feels that Izzi belongs to her. Izzi already knew that, and she sat on the bed crying. Caroline sat next to her and hugged her.

$ $ $ $ $

Tyler sat on the living room couch, redialing Kahi'Lee's cell phone number. He was so upset that he couldn't contact her that instead of pressing send on his phone, he just kept dialing her number. After calling and speaking to Kahi'Lee's younger sister, Ariel, he was told that Kahi'Lee hadn't been over there in over two weeks. Out of frustration from his guilt, he and Kahi'Lee had gotten into a serious argument after she came back from Fuzzi's house.

Tyler felt that being in the condition that Kahi'Lee saw him in, he would never have left her side. But all Kahi'Lee did was express her love for her best friend, Izzi. But what caused Kahi'Lee to leave, storming out of the house and still not returning, were the words that Tyler heard come out of the mouth of Mr. Pakulski. He told Tyler that maybe the reason why Kahi'Lee was getting good modeling jobs was because she was sleeping with different modeling agents. Tyler started accusing Kahi'Lee of sleeping with her modeling agents. Kahi'Lee couldn't believe Tyler's degrading words towards her, not after just defending him from her friends. Here, she believed in him and his career, and he thought the lowest of her. When it came to her career and the hard work that she put in to make a name for herself, before Kahi'Lee walked out, she said fuck you, Tyler Bronson. You may stoop that low to get somewhere, but not meeeee!

Tyler didn't know that Kahi'Lee knew what he had just done, but her words cut through him like a sharp knife. Pow! Slap! Tyler's countenance showed the anger and rage on his face, it put a fear in Kahi'Lee that she nor Tyler had ever seen on her face before. Tyler had always been her protector and comfort zone. His every word meant the world to her and now her fear was being in her own home. Kahi'Lee grabbed a few clothes and ran to her car. Tyler tried to stop her, but her yelling, "don't touch me," made Tyler come to his senses and back away from her car. Kahi'Lee, at first, had truly no intentions of following through with Fuzzi's little plan to help Izzi, but after Tyler slapped her, the only people in the whole world that Kahi'Lee felt she still loved were Izzi, Fuzzi, Emma, and Ashley, because Tyler could no longer be trusted.

After leaving home and checking into a Motel, Kahi'Lee stood in the shower crying her eyes out. This was a time that she wished and missed having older brothers because she'd enjoy them kicking Tyler's ass right about now, but it's just her and her baby sister. The next day, when Kahi'Lee met up with Fuzzi and Emma to go shopping, she never even mentioned the argument and fight that she and Tyler had before she met back up with them. After crying all night in the Motel, that's when Kahi'Lee made up her mind that Izzi was worth doing anything for. She knew that Izzi wouldn't even have thought twice if it was her, Fuzzi, Emma, or Ashley in trouble. Tyler's mind was all over the place. One minute, he was leaving sweet 'I love you' and 'miss you' messages and the next minute, he was leaving angry and intimidating messages. But as of yet, Kahi'Lee hasn't returned any of his calls. Tyler's next move was to get in his car and go by all Kahi'Lee's friends' houses. He didn't want to hurt her. He was just missing her and knew that he had fucked up and made a big mistake.

Chapter Six
SLY AND CRAFTY

uzzie, Emma, and Kahi'Lee were all looking beautiful and attractive. They all have brand-new outfits. They have gone to give Mr. Shelton $50,000 in cash to take Izzi's case. But Fuzzi was concerned about the large amount of cash that they were taking to Mr. Shelton. But he told the ladies not to worry. He promised to handle the whole transaction between them. But to even Fuzzi's surprise, he was even, after taking care of business, he was asking Fuzzi to see her again, and Fuzzi told Mr. Shelton only this time on my terms and he still agreed to see her.

They left his office feeling good about themselves now, knowing that Izzi had someone representable in her corner. The only problem that melted their hearts was to learn about the time Izzi was facing. She was charged with First Degree Murder, and the prosecutor was offering life without, or hopefully, she'll receive the death penalty. Mr. Shelton told them that they had got a lot of work and more money ahead of them to raise. Fuzzi didn't tell Mr.

Shelton, but just in case they ran into this problem, they, after all, received $100,000 apiece. They still had $80,000 left over for Izzi's case. So, they still got another $30,000 for Izzi's attorney fee. They tried to have Ashley meet up with them to take her out to lunch, but Ashley couldn't meet them; she was in the middle of removing some children from another unsafe home. They all promised to meet up later in the week. So, they all decided to visit Izzi to give her the great news.

Fuzzi, Emma, and Kahi'Lee were laughing and joking about all the women who were walking out of the jail crying and would be going home to cheat or enjoying a wonderful night with a vibrator. Fuzzi told them, "Look at that Bitch right there? She probably got her vibrator in her purse. She looks like her shit could be for pleasure and a weapon." All that hot fish between her legs. Look! Lookkk! Sancho is trying to jump out of that vagina right now. A fat Mexican lady was shaking and squeezing her legs together, looking like she was trying to stop something from coming out from between her legs. But Emma figured she was either nervous or had to use the bathroom. But Fuzzi was the type of person that found a way to make a joke out of everything. The guard finally called them for their visit. They were all excited to see Izzi when she came walking into the visiting room. They thought that they were going to hug her. But because she was charged with murder, they had put her in a higher level of jail. Her custody level made them have to visit her behind the glass. At this point, they were just happy to see Izzi.

Everybody was all smiles until Fuzzi, Emma, and Kahi'Lee saw the black eye on her face. Aye! What the fuckkk! Why does your face look like that, Izzi? Fuzzi grabbed the phone and was going crazy and getting wild. Tears started running down Izzi's face. She was so embarrassed for them to see her like that. Just being in jail was terrible enough, but to be all beaten up was another thing. Who in the fuck has done that to your face? Fuzzi yelled at Izzi like she was her mother, seeing her face bruised from leaving grade school. Izzi tried to change the subject by saying, "hello, I love y'all. I miss you guys." Naw, fuck that, Izzi, tell me who done that. Izzi looked at Emma and then Kahi'Lee. Seeing them made her cry even more. I'm okay, Fuzzi, don't worry about me, let's just enjoy our visit. But Izzi knew Fuzzi well and knew that she wasn't about to stop asking until she got a straight answer. Okay! Okay! Okayyy! Some man looking dike bitch did it, okay. Why Izzi? Because I wouldn't sleep with her, but I should have. Tears started rolling down Fuzzi's face. She already knew what Izzi was going through. It happens to every person who comes off weak in jail or prison. Fuzzi remembers her early days of getting locked up as a homosexual boy in jail. Fuzzi told Izzi, "you listen to me, and I mean you listen good." Fuzzi told Izzi that if she didn't defend herself, not only would Big Girl treat her that way, but every female that came in that door would treat her that way. But she has to make an example out of Big Girl to let the rest of them know to never fuck with Izzi never again, or they can get the same treatment.

Izzi's grandmother raised her not to fight in school. Besides, Izzi always had friends just like Fuzzi, Emma, and Kahi'Lee who wouldn't allow anybody to hurt her in school or around their neighborhood. It wasn't that Izzi couldn't fight; she just never really had to but once. The first time Izzi got into a fight was in the ninth grade. A girl took her boyfriend, that cheered for the football team, and she was rubbing it into Izzi's face. So, a girl that Izzi always spends time with convinced Izzi to fight her after school. If La'Bella had known Izzi back then, she would have known that when it came to a man that Izzi cared about, you don't mess with them because Izzi beat her so bad that it took the whole school security team to get Izzi off her.

After Fuzzi was okay with telling Izzi how to defend herself, they all took turns switching and taking turns talking to each other. Izzi was so grateful to have friends like them. She learned that she already has a lawyer who seems to have a crush on Fuzzi. After Fuzzi told Izzi what she had done to him, Izzi told them that it would be pretty hard not to laugh in his face knowing that she gave him a blow job over dinner. Fuzzi stood up and shook her ass at Izzi. Bitch, you always talking about this ass. I see it got you the best lawyer that money could buy. Izzi put her lips up on the glass. Girl, right about now, what y'all did for me, I'll kiss all y'all asses. Emma said, "we got to hurry up and get you out of there." You sound like that woman then already turned you out. They all, for the first time, busted up laughing together. Izzi asked why Ashley didn't come, and they all told her, "You know how busy her job keeps her." You know she is coming to see you. She going crazy knowing you in this hell hole. That made Izzi start crying again. But this time, the guard was ending their visit. They all blew kisses and promised to come back soon. Izzi left excited to see them, but she couldn't help but wonder what her friends had done to raise $50,000 for a lawyer so fast. It wasn't that she wasn't grateful, but she didn't want to put them in the type of situation to wind up in a place like she was in.

Izzi's mind went back to what Fuzzi said about her defending herself from Big Girl. Izzi didn't know what the outcome would be. But she knew that it had to be done for the abuse to stop and the unwanted sexual encounters. Fuzzi walked out of the jail explaining to Emma and Kahi'Lee what Izzi was experiencing in jail with Big Girl. But she told them after Izzi put that ivory on her ass, Izzi would be just fine. Bitch! Don't that dyke bitch know she is fucking with a different type of dog?

Bitchhh! These some pretty Bitches! You can't be fucking up our faces. We Foxes, girl! Some beautiful, sexy, attractive, and phenomenal women. But just like a fox, we are sly and crafty. Emma and Kahi'Lee loved the sound of that. And Fuzzi had just created a devil in all types of color dresses. Fuzzi told Emma and Kahi'Lee that it was time for them to look like foxy-ass women all the time. Whenever somebody sees them coming, they should leave a spectacular impression on them foxes. We got over $300,000 between the three of us, let's hit the malls and make the world eat out of our asses. It's time to get rid of them buckets that y'all driving. Let's shop till we drop. They all slapped hands and headed to replace the old everything for the new. Three hours later, Emma and Kahi'Lee were driving off the lot in a Royal Blue Lexus 430 and a BMW 325i Convertible. Emma bought the BMW, and Kahi'Lee bought the Lexus. That was a car she noticed that caught Tyler's eye every time that one passed by. She even got his favorite color. As much as she was hurting from him hitting her, Kahi'Lee still loved her man and was missing him dearly.

Fuzzi didn't buy another car because she was still getting used to her Corvette. But she did come up with a great idea that Emma and Kahi'Lee didn't mind agreeing to. They all put up $10,000 apiece and bought Ashley a new Jaguar, black with a tan interior. It was the car that Ashley and La'Bella always dreamed of having one day. But the way La'Bella got her Jaquar seems to cost her, her life after getting it from DuVall. Fuzzi had the Jaguar sent to her job with a Christmas card that said, "from the Foxes, Bitch! We love you, Merry Christmas, and this is our New Year." They all left the car lot trailing each other, headed for the mall to do as Fuzzi said earlier at the jail. Let's go shopping till we drop.

Chapter Seven
THIS OUR NEW YEAR

Hey! Watch it, asshole! Keep your dirty hands off, my baby. Mr. Shelton was meeting another lawyer, Philip Preacher, for a cup of coffee and to discuss a case that he was giving Philip advice on. Mr. Shelton was parking his Maybach Mercedez Benz, and Philip walked up and pulled his Mercedez Benz symbol on the hood of his car, and Mr. Shelton was cursing him out about it as they entered the Star Bucks'. Hey, it looks like you finally spent some of your money and not your wife's. Do I detect you're wearing a new suit, Philip? Philip ran his fingers through his new haircut. Oh wow! Somebody is definitely about to get found not guilty. They both busted up laughing while they stood in line, waiting to be helped. After getting their expensive cups of coffee, they went to sit at a table. Mr. Shelton pulled out his chair then Philips. Here, honey, have a seat. Oh, my goodness! Dave, you must've gotten some pussy. All of a sudden you got some manners. Nope, but I definitely got the best blow job in the whole world. What? My goodness, Philip, trust me, I've never experienced anything like this before. I've had my pricks up before by many women and prostitutes, but nothing like what I got from this colored chick the other day. Awe come on, Dave, a blow job is a blow job. It doesn't matter, Dave, who's giving it; just as long as she knows how to suck and swallow, then that's my type of girl. Both Attorney's started laughing.

So, does she have another friend, or is there a number on hot cheeks? Oh, Nooo! You'll never get that tired old cock of yours in my little black berry. Awe, stop it, Dave! That slut will take my money just like she took yours. Excuse me! I never gave her a dime of my money for that nice, sweet mouth of hers. In fact, after she blew my cock, she came and gave me $50,000. Philip was laughing so hard that he spit out the coffee they were drinking. What the hell did she give you $50,000 for? To take shots at your lying ass. Hell, you're lucky to even have Dolly as your wife. If you didn't pay for that home and new Mercedez Benz she's driving and pay for those extravagant trips, I'm sure she would have been left your old ass for a much younger man, Dave. My wife loves me, thank you. I guess, we all can't get lucky and marry a stripper. Remember those tits bounced around in my face before they did yours. If it weren't for me, you wouldn't even know Marlena. Hey! Hey! Heyyyy! Leave Marlena out of this. She didn't suck your old dead balls. Ok! Don't get all choked up behind this. Let's be real, Philip. We both are paying to have a good piece of pussy laying around the house. We both are better off just paying a prostitute. Trust me, it's so much cheaper. So, what's the $50,000 for? The Dawson case. When Philip heard Mr. Shelton say that he was taking the Dawson case, he turned completely red in the face. "Oh, by the way, your wife did suck my old cock." Philip starts going off on Mr. Shelton. Are you fucking serious, Dave? You can't take that case; do you know what it would do to your career and reputation? Absolutely nothing! People die every fucking day. Who in the hell is he to stop putting food on my plate? He's a lawyer, just like you and me. Besides that, Dave, he was a real good friend of mine and many other lawyers around here. You can't take that goddamn case! Do you hear me, Dave Shelton?

Yeah, I hear you. But neither you nor your friends pay any of my bills, but in this case and any other case I take, do. So, get over it, Phil. I'm already on the case, and I'm not getting off of it. So, get over it already; it's just a case. Philip got so mad that he stood up and slammed his cup of coffee on the table. Dave, trust me on this one; you take that case, I'll personally myself handle your ass first before anybody lays into you. So, are you threatening me, Philip? I'm telling you, and you can take it however the fuck you want to. Philip turned and walked away from the table. Everyone in the Star bucks seems to be looking at Mr. Shelton. But he didn't care because one thing he didn't tolerate was someone threatening him. Mr. Shelton downed his cup of coffee, and now not only was he taking Izzi's case, he wanted to win it to prove to all the other lawyers that when he set out to do something, he not only wanted to do it, but he would come out on the winning end.

$ $ $ $ $

Hello Ashley, did you get that paperwork I placed on your desk? No, I'm sorry. I haven't made it into my office yet. I just came back from the courts. I had to testify in the Mullins case. There was no way that I was going to allow those kids to ever experience that type of abuse. As a matter of fact, Shelly, do you have a moment? We can go over that paperwork now. Plus, I got something else that I need to run past you on the Peterson case. Ok! Give me a second, and I'll be down to your office. Hello Mark, are you buying us lunch today? No, actually, I got a date for lunch. Which girl is this one? He placed his finger on his lips as if to tell Ashley to be quiet. Ok boy! That thing go fall off; you better find you a woman. I did find me a woman, but she won't have me. They both laughed, knowing that he was talking about Ashley. Naw, man, you a bit too much for me. You not go have me fighting females. That's ok, Mark, I'll buy my own food.

Ashley flicked her hand to her co-worker and headed to her office. After placing her purse on the desk, she sat down and started looking through the files that Shelly had sat on her desk. Her answering machine showed that she had 22 unheard messages. Ashley pushed the button on her phone and started checking her messages when Mark came rushing into her office. Damn baller, "maybe you need to be taking me out to lunch." What you do, get a raise? Ashley looked at Mark like he was crazy while she listened to her messages. Aye, baller, there's somebody here to see you, just let me get the keys. Now Shelly came rushing into her office, almost repeating the same words, asking Ashley what other job she got besides that one. Ashley finally hung up the phone, "man, what's wrong with y'all?" I couldn't even hear my messages. Girl, come on here. Somebody is waiting to see you with some keys. What! Ashley looked at Shelly and Mark; she followed Mark while Shelly guided her by the hand. Hello, Ma'am, are you Ashley Washington? Hmmmmn! Yes, I am, may I help you. Would you show me some identification and sign these papers please? Show you my ID for what and sign what papers? Shelly had already left to go grab Ashley's purse. Here girl! Sign them papers so we can bounce.

The man told her that he was from a car lot in Scottsdale and someone bought her a car. Ashley couldn't believe what she was hearing and kept thinking that maybe the man made a mistake, or it was some type of prank because Mark and Shelly joked a lot at her job. But the man showed her the paperwork and handed her the keys. After showing her ID and signing the papers, Ashley, Mark, and Shelly, all headed out into the parking lot. When Ashley saw the black Jaguar, she grabbed her heart. But it wasn't until she opened the door that there was a card sitting on the armrest, and Ashley picked it up. When she read it, it said, "Enjoy Sis from the Foxes bitch!" We love you. Merry Christmas, and this is our New Year.

Ashley couldn't believe what Fuzzi, Kahi'Lee, and Emma had done for her. Tears started running down her face, and her body started shaking. Mark and Shelly didn't know what was going on, but they knew it had something to do with what she read. What they thought was going to be a happy moment had turned into a very emotional one. Shelly and Ashley were good friends but not like Fuzzi, Emma, Kahi'Lee, Izzi, and La'Bella. But Shelly hugged Ashley and told her, "Girl, it's okay, somebody loves you to buy you that car." Mark and Shelly were ready to go for a ride, but now Ashley was sitting there wondering why and how they bought her a new car when Emma and Kahi'Lee didn't have good cars themselves. She knew Fuzzi drove a new Corvette, but how could they all afford to buy her a new Jaguar. Ashley kept trying to call Fuzzi, Emma, and Kahi'Lee, but neither one of them answered her phone calls. They were too busy shopping and laughing at what they knew was Ashley's suspicion. To Shelly's surprise, Ashley told her that she could have her Ford Taurus, and that started her to cry. Now, she really knew how Ashley felt because Shelly didn't have a car. She had been catching rides and taking the bus. Mark said, "Hey, who go give me a car?" He stood there with his arms in the air while Shelly and Ashley stood there hugging and crying.

Ashley was the type of person that she believed in helping people. She couldn't think of a much better person to bless with her old car than to bless Shelly. She was your typical white girl, 5'8, 135 pounds, 36-26-30, with blonde hair and blue eyes. Mark always told her that she looked like Gwyneth Paltrow. Shelly would say, "No sir, I look just like my mom." After completing their work, they all later wind up taking that car ride, and Ashley falls in love with her new Jaguar. But she would rather be riding with her real girlfriends instead of Mark and Shelly. Her mind couldn't help but wonder how they could afford to buy her a car.

Chapter Eight
BLACK BERRY

Izzi's name and booking number were being called over the intercom. Dawson 58224, you got a legal visit. Izzi was talking to another inmate who was getting her hair braided. When she heard her name being called. That made her smile to know that the lawyer was finally coming to visit her. She ran and brushed her hair and tried to look her best. Her cellmate Caroline wished Izzi good luck. I hope he can get you out. You don't deserve to be in here. Izzi kissed her cheek and said, "Thanks, Caroline, you either." Izzi started looking around for whom she really had no idea. All she knew was Mr. Shelton's name and that he had been retained to represent her. The guard directed Izzi to where the old gentleman sat in a room. Hello, "You must be Mrs. Dawson?" Izzi smiled and said, "Yes." Well, I don't know if you know already but I've been retained by your closest friends to represent you on this case. Yeah! I knew you were coming. Well, Mrs. Dawson, I won't bullshit you or play any games. We got a real serious fight on our hands. And the only way that you're going to come out of here is that we put our heads together on this thing. I'm not your enemy, and I'm here to help you. But the only way that I can help you is that you help me, help you. You have got to tell me everything from the beginning to the end. But it's got to be the truth and nothing but the truth. Leave it all up to me to do all the thinking for you. The only way I can help make up a story, if need be, is I know the whole true story.

Do you know what type of time you're facing? Mr. Shelton looked Izzi right in the eyes. Izzi put her head down and said, "Life or either maybe the death penalty." Then she busted up crying. Mr. Shelton allowed her to get it all out before he started asking questions. The first question he wanted to ask for himself was, Mrs. Dawson, did you love your husband? And did you intentionally kill Mr. Dawson? Izzi looked at him and said, "I loved my husband, and no, I didn't intentionally kill him." I had no choice. I didn't want to wind up like my best friend, La'Bella. There were two things that Izzi had just said that Mr. Shelton didn't overlook. The first was that Izzi said that she loved her husband, not that she loved him, and the other thing was she called the female that they found dead next to Mr. Dawson, her best friend.

Now, Mr. Shelton couldn't help but want to hear the whole story. Ok! "Start from the beginning, and don't leave out nothing." Mr. Shelton took out a pen and notepad from his briefcase. Turned out that Izzi was a lot smarter than everyone expected her to be, including her own husband, DuVall. After Izzi went home and found La'Bella at home in their bed, she had committed the perfect crime, knowing that she would spend the rest of her natural life in prison. At that point, she didn't feel that DuVall nor La'Bella was worth her dying in prison. The reason Izzi made DuVall kill La'Bella would be her defense for killing DuVall. After Izzi shot DuVall, she removed her panties and straddled La'Bella's face, leaving her DNA on La'Bella's face like she ate her vagina. Then she ate La'Bella's vagina again, leaving her DNA. After that, she gave DuVall head again, leaving her DNA.

She told Mr. Shelton that she came home and found them in the bed together. She said that she started yelling at La'Bella to get out of her house, but DuVall angrily insisted that Izzi joined them in sex. She declined his offer and ran into the kitchen, and that's when she retrieved DuVall's hunting knife and went back to threaten La'Bella to leave their home. When she returned to the room, DuVall saw the knife in her hand, he grabbed his 9mm automatic and forced her to drop the knife. Izzi said, "That's when he slapped her and ordered her and La'Bella to engage in sex." Izzi told Mr. Shelton that after he watched them have sex, he forced them both to give him oral sex. Izzi said that while she was giving him oral, La'Bella grabbed the knife, and that's when he started fighting with her. Izzi said DuVall got the knife from her after La'Bella cut him across the arm. Then he started stabbing her repeatedly over and over. Izzi told Mr. Shelton I thought that he was going to kill me next, so I grabbed the gun. He rushed at me, and that's when I pulled the trigger. Izzi busted up crying uncontrollably like she was reliving the whole incident over again. Mr. Shelton sat there, blown away by her story. Izzi said that he wouldn't stop coming toward her, so she shot him again in the same leg. Mr. Shelton felt that if everything checked out, he could easily find Izzi innocent and found not guilty. Any female on her jury that heard Izzi's story would quickly find her not guilty and think DuVall was a piece of shit. Mr. Shelton knew that he had to see the police report and autopsy. Mr. Shelton asked Izzi if there was anything that she had left out or forgotten. Yes, sir, at one point, I remember picking up the knife and cutting him across the arm with it. Izzi said that "he would drink heavily after losing a case and would fight her because of all the weapons that DuVall owned. Mr. Shelton asked just about how many guns your husband owns. Over 30 different types of guns, I really don't care for guns. So, I don't know what all that he has. Mr. Shelton was so happy to hear that he almost smiled in Izzi's face. Ok, Mrs. Dawson, let me go check on a few things, and either I or my private investigator will be back to see you to get any more information from you if I feel we need to know anything else.

By the way, Mrs. Dawson! You can call me Izzi. Ok, Izzi! My guy's name is Sydney Fletcher. If he comes to see you, it's okay to tell him anything that you would tell me, and other than that, don't discuss your case with anybody, whether in jail or on the phone. We got a good case so don't blow it. I already know not to talk to anybody. Fuzzi made sure I kept my mouth shut. Hearing Fuzzi's name made Mr. Shelton smile. Yeah, she's pretty smart and beautiful. Izzi and Mr. Shelton smiled at his comment. I'm glad that you didn't talk when you got arrested. That really will help our defense. You really have some great, loving, and loyal friends. That Fuzzi is really special. Yeah, I know she is. I trust her with my life. Mr. Shelton was about to wrap things up with Izzi, but he couldn't help but notice her black eye. Did you get that shiner from your husband? No, that happened since I been here. Are you okay? Do I need to have you moved or something? Izzi smiled. No! No! Noooo! Trust me, I'll be just fine. Just get me out of this place, pleaseeeeeee!

Oh! One more thing before I go. How long have you and DuVall been married? We have been married for six years. Do you know that he was arrested in 2012 for assault on his ex-wife? She said, "Yes, I do." It was at his law firm. I was there when it happened. I was his secretary at the time of the incident. I'm the one who stopped him from killing her. What? You're kidding me, right? No serious. I was there. Mr. Shelton opened his briefcase and looked through some paperwork. After reading something, he said, "Schumer!" He said that name and pointed at Izzi. Ummmm yeah! That's my maiden name. This time, Mr. Shelton couldn't hold back his excitement. He jumped up and grabbed his briefcase, now rushing to leave. Ok! Ok! Okayyyyy! You'll hear from me real soon and stay out of trouble. Izzi stood there looking at him, but she knew that he was already on her case. When he mentioned that she was innocent, Izzi had even forgotten about DuVall's old behavior with women just might come back to haunt him before he could even make it down in his grave. Mr. Shelton was dialing his private investigator, Sydney, before he could even leave the jail. Hey Syd, meet me at my office. I'm on my way there now. Click!

He wasted no time calling Fuzzi, and she answered on the second ring. Hello! Ms. Armstrong, this is Mr. Shelton. Did I catch you at a bad time? No! No! Actually, you didn't. I just got out of the shower. Oh, "I'm sorry. Should I call you back?" Mr. Shelton was now trying to envision Fuzzi standing there naked. He grew very fond of Fuzzi and wanted to spend more time with her. Man, didn't I just tell you I'm not busy? Mr. Shelton started laughing. Well, if I'm going to be attacked, can I at least come and get attacked in person? Fuzzi started laughing. Wouldn't you love to be here right about now? This chocolate vagina is sitting here hot and looking real pretty right now. But too bad there's nobody that feels like I should take her on a shopping spree. Fuzzi started making sexual sounds to drive Mr. Shelton crazy. Ooooooh! Yes! Ummmmmm Daddyyyy! Daddy, don't you want to taste mama's chocolateeee! Mr. Shelton was sitting in his car, getting aroused by the sound of Fuzzi's voice. His penis was about to jump out of his pants. Ok! Ok! Okayyyy! You win, but I'll have to handle some business first. Plus, I'll have to stop by the bank, that chocolate is very expensive. Well, I'm sure if you're looking for a prostitute, there are some out there waiting for someone like you. Imma Queen and have bills and desirable wants just like you.

I've never been with a white man before, so I'll be stepping out of my comfort zone just to please you, daddy. So, don't you think that's worth me going out and buying me something nice, after giving you my blackberry and juices? Hey, let's not even look at it that way because, don't get me wrong, you're a very beautiful African American woman. You deserve more than a few thousand dollars, but I am a married man. If I wasn't spoiling her, trust me Fuzzi, you will definitely be the woman I would love to spoil. That made Fuzzi smile to hear him being honest about his wife. But to also hear that he would want to spoil her. Fuzzi said, "Well, I'm not mad at her. It takes a lot to take care of a man." I'm sure she deserves the type of lifestyle that you offer her, but I'm a woman just like her and I also know my worth, too. So, I hope you don't blame me for wanting to climb out of the mud. No! No! No! Trust me. I'm a real man, and I know anything worth having is definitely worth paying for, but I know that I have to be careful with you. Why do you say that Mr. Shelton? Because, to be honest with you, Fuzzi, since I last saw you, I can't seem to get you off my mind. I think about you all day long. Aweeeeee, that's so sweet. See, you already made me forget why I even called you in the first place. Oh, yeah! I just came from seeing Mrs. Dawson, and before I forget, she told me to tell you and the other ladies that she loves and misses y'all. I noticed that she ran into a little problem in there. I offered to have her moved to another unit, but she declined my offer and said that you told her how to handle her situation. Fuzzi started laughing, I'm sorry, but I did tell her to Ivory her big ass. He said, "What?" Nothing. That's something you will never have to deal with. So, Mr. Shelton, how's her case looking? That's what I called you for until you and your vagina stopped my train of thought. Hey! Don't blame me, that was you and her. They both laughed. Yeah, I really believe that we have a great case. I'm on my way now to meet up with my private investigator. A few good things came up that would help Mrs. Dawson a lot. So, if you don't mind, do you think I can take a rain check for a few hours and meet up with blackberry a little later? Oh, that's what you naming my pussy now? Yes! I like blackberries. Did you hear what you said about blackberries? Yeah, I said I liked them. Well, Daddy, this is a different type of blackberry. If you taste this blackberry, your ass go be loving berries. Mr. Shelton busted up laughing. Yeah, I know that's what scares me. Is eight o'clock good for you? Well, I guess that bank envelope will decide that. Okay, then, that tells me that eight o'clock will be just fine. Click!

Chapter Nine
BAD BREAK

Kahi'Lee sat on the floor in her and Tyler's condominium. She was wrapping gifts that she had bought Tyler and herself. Kahi'Lee was happy that she and Tyler would actually have a good Christmas together. Kahi'Lee was shocked by the new woman she was starting to become. Even thou Xerxes had forced himself on top of Kahi'Lee in a strange way inside of her own mind, she found herself really liking it. At first, she told herself that Xerxes had raped her, but now she was questioning herself. Because she had enjoyed every minute of their interaction. Tyler always made her feel good when they had sex, but it was like Xerxes was owning her vagina. He took her control and made her love it. Tyler had never made her body feel like Xerxes did. Of course, Tyler was the only man that Kahi'Lee had ever given her love box to, and she thought he was the greatest lover. But after Xerxes, Donkey Kong the shit out of her vagina. Now, Kahi'Lee knew that Tyler had to step it up if he ever wanted to take Xerxes, Donkey Kong off her mind. Kahi'Lee was sitting there horny and couldn't wait until Tyler came home, make-up sex with them was always great, but deep down, inside, if she was listening to her vagina's wants, Kahi'Lee knew that she would be boarding another airplane and heading back to Atlanta to say I'm sorry for what I've done to Xerxes and get the type of lovin her body crave right now. Kahi'Lee jumped when she heard her cell phone ringing. She was so deep in thought, thinking about Xerxes, that Kahi'Lee didn't even hear her cell phone ringing the first time that it had been ringing before now.

Hello! Kahi'Lee stood there listening to the person on the other end. Moments later, she started jumping up and down but also screaming at the top of her voice. Yes! Yes! Yessss! Ok! Okayy! I will, when do you want me to come? Kahi'Lee has just received a phone call from IMG, one of the biggest modeling agencies in the world. Some of the biggest models in the world modeled for this company, and if they call you, then that means that you definitely made it in the modeling world. They were asking to do a photoshoot with Kahi'Lee. Kahi'Lee knew that this was the break that she and Tyler dreamed about together. Kahi'Lee knew that their life was about to change for the good. The lifestyle that Fuzzi had introduced her to was almost about to take over her life. After buying the car and pitching in on Ashley's one, the shopping spree and gift shopping that she had done for her and Tyler, Kahi'Lee and Emma's money was starting to get real low. The thing about getting your hands on any type of real money is that it begins to disappear, and you want more and more and more money. Kahi'Lee knew that there was a part of her that wouldn't allow her to ever be broke again. Fuzzi's last words to her and Emma stuck in her mind like gum to a shoe heel. Foxes, let me know when y'all are ready to go get paidddd! Kahi'Lee ended her call and rushed to take a shower. While she was taking a shower, her female hormones overcame her. There wasn't the type of penis that she wanted around. So, she took her vibrator into the shower with her and began to relieve her tension. Ummmm! Ummmm! Yeah! Ummmm! Yes, slow down! Take it, baby. Don't hurt me, pleaseeeee!

Tyler pulled up to the condominium and saw the brand-new Lexus 430 in the driveway. This was a car that he dreamed of for many nights of him taking a ride down the highway with him behind the wheel and his Queen Kahi'Lee in the passenger seat rubbing on his earlobe and telling him how handsome he looked behind the wheel of his Lexus. Tyler wondered who brought Kahi'Lee home as he took in the fine automobile. He couldn't help but stop and admire the vehicle. Tyler took a deep breath like yeah, someday, one day. He walked into the house and didn't see Kahi'Lee or anyone else. He quickly noticed all the gifts under the Christmas tree. He put a look of amazement on his face, but really, all he wanted was to see Kahi'Lee. Tyler didn't make himself noticeable at home. He just slowly walked, headed towards their bedroom. Tyler saw the three new dresses Kahi'Lee had laid across the bed. Now, Tyler's facial expression and attitude begin to change because he could hear the same sexual sounds that Kahi'Lee made whenever they made love or had any sexual encounter. Rage and anger overcame Tyler. How could Kahi'Lee leave him worrying to death about her, then come back home and bring another man home to sleep within their bed? All Tyler heard was the shower water running and Kahi'Lee yelling and screaming out another man's name. Tyler didn't have a gun, and at this point, he was glad because he knew that he would kill Kahi'Lee and her boyfriend. Xerxes, Xerxes! Yes! Yes! Daddy don't stop! Don't stop, baby! I'm almost; I'm almost about to cum! Ooooooh! Ohhhhh! Yes!

The shower curtain flew open, and Kahi'Lee was lying on her back with her legs wide opened and raised up in the air with a footlong, big, round, beige-colored dildo. Wham! Wham! Wham! Wham! Kahi'Lee was slamming it in and out of her vagina. She had her whole hand over the top of the dildo and was pounding away. When Tyler pulled the curtain back, her eyes opened wider than they did the day she heard Fuzzi shoot that gun at Tremendous. Baby! What are you doing? Before she could get out another word, Tyler lost it and started punching Kahi'Lee like a boxer. Bam! Bam! Bam! Bam! Bam! She tried to fight back. She even hit him a few times with her dildo, but he kept on punching her in the face and body. Kahi'Lee finally got out of the tub and was fighting back, but there was blood everywhere. Kahi'Lee finally got the break that she was looking for. While they were fighting, Tyler slipped and fell, and that's when Kahi'Lee ran and grabbed one of her dresses on the bed and ran naked out of the house. She was yelling and screaming. Help! Help! Help! Somebody, help me, pleaseeee!

The next thing Tyle knew, the whole condo was surrounded by police officers drawing their guns. Mr. Bronson! Mr. Bronson! This is the Mesa Police Department. Come out with your hands up. Tyler made a few phone calls and finally surrendered to the cops. After they took Tyler into custody, Kahi'Lee stood looking in the mirror at herself and knew that fast as her break came fast as it went out the door, thanks to Tyler and his temper. Kahi'Lee was supposed to have a photoshoot in two hours, but her face and body looked like she had been hit by a car. And both of her eyes were black. Kahi'Lee stood there crying uncontrollably. IMG would never hire her under those conditions and with those types of problems. Kahi'Lee heard a loud knock at the door, and as much as she needed them right now, she didn't want Ashley, Fuzzi, or Emma to see her face looking like that. Kahi'Lee took a deep breath and opened the door. Girllll! Bitch! Where the fuck is he at?" Oooooh! Kahi'Lee, baby, Noooooooo!

Chapter Ten
TURNED OUT

Detective's Galvin and Kunis were trembling and shaking from the cold weather in New York. This was part of the job that they both hated going to and giving a parent or relative the bad news of losing a family member. They were the lead detectives in the Dawson murder case. Galvin, who was a heavy-set white man, 5'8 over 265 pounds, with a big nose and half of a bald head. Almost couldn't stomach DuVall's mom passing out after they gave her the news. Galvin's partner Kunis and DuVall's dad helped her recover from passing out. Kunis was also like 5'10, slender built with black curly hair and thick glasses, who didn't care too much for DuVall's grandmother, Selma. She kept telling Galvin and Kunis that she told DuVall you honkeys don't care about him. Selma said that she knew that white girl would do something to hurt DuVall. The detectives asked her why she say that. Mrs. Selma said 'cause she is white, just like you all.

Hell, if she didn't kill him, maybe one of y'all would have. DuVall's dad asked the detectives to please forgive his mom. DuVall and his dad could pass for twins. Even Detective Galvin and Kunis had to do a double take after he answered the door and welcomed them into their home. Now Galvin and Kunis were trying to make it back to the Airport, not knowing if they'd even get a flight back out to Arizona because it was now snowing much harder than it was when the two detectives arrived in New York. This was a time when the two detectives enjoyed working in the sunny climate. They appreciated the hospitality of their fellow police officers in New York, but they would rather be back home. Galvin and Kunis took this time to have a warm cup of coffee and look over the Dawson's case. They had already learned that DuVall had killed La'Bella with that hunting knife. Also, from the admission that she shot DuVall, her DNA was on the weapons and DuVall's DNA only on the knife. They, in their own minds, tried to wonder what happened in that bedroom. There were two bodies that needed someone to talk with them. Galvin and Kunis couldn't wait to interview Izzi with her lawyer. All they could get out of Izzi at the crime scene was that she shot DuVall. But when they got her downtown, she lawyered up and wouldn't talk. Galvin heard the females that were there telling her not to talk. He knew that if he got to get a one-on-one with her, he would have all the information that he needed to solve the case. Now, he must do his job. Right now, at this point, Galvin felt that Izzi had come home and found her husband in bed with La'Bella and killed them both, but every time he wanted to wrap his mind around that, he couldn't come up with no explanation for DuVall's killing La'Bella. Damn! That is what he always was left saying.

$ $ $ $ $

Ashley was glad to finally hook up with her girlfriends, but not under the circumstances they were all meeting under. They wind up taking Kahi'Lee to the hospital, and Fuzzi comes up with a miraculous story for IMG. She saved her friend from losing that spot with that modeling agency by telling them that her best friend got into a bad car accident. The agency said that they understood and told Kahi'Lee to take as much time as she needed and that they're still looking forward to working with her. Ladies Ok, y'all can see her now. A doctor came and gave Ashley, Fuzzi, and Emma the ok to visit Kahi'Lee. The doctor told them that she was a little swollen and in pain, but luckily, everything came back ok with her test. Ashley, Fuzzi, and Emma were all happy for Kahi'Lee. They all knew how much she loved modeling. It was her childhood dream, and here she finally made it. To come really close to blowing it was a wake-up call for Kahi'Lee and them. "Hey, Foxy lady!" Fuzzi said as they all walked through the door. For the first time Kahi'Lee had finally smiled hearing Fuzzi say that. They all went and gave her hugs and kisses. Girl! What happened? Kahi'Lee began to tell them everything that happened, but she left out one thing, and that was her calling out Xerxes name while masturbating. She knew that Fuzzi and Emma wouldn't understand that and would clown on her

99

even though her story did sound a little suspicious to all three of them. Kahi'Lee was their baby sister, and fuck Tyler. Fuzzi told them that Tyler go make me shoot his ass. Kahi'Lee and Emma looked at each other because they knew Fuzzi meant what she said. Well, girl, I'm glad you're ok. Oh, by the way, I spoke with the IMG agency, and they said that you can take all the time you need to heal up, and they'll still be looking forward to working with you. Kahi'Lee sat up real fast in the bed. You're lying, Fuzzi, don't play with me like that. Bitch! Do I look like I'm playing with you? It sounds like you did a good job by yourself. Everybody started laughing except Kahi'Lee. She started crying and telling her friends how much she loved them all. Girl, we all love you too.

Ashley started kissing Fuzzi, Kahi'Lee and Emma. Girl, watch out. I don't know who weenies you've been sucking on. Ashley punched Fuzzi in the arm. Bitch, if you still had yours, I probably would have sucked yours after that Christmas present that y'all bought me. I love my sisters, that was the best gift in the world. Now a Bitch goes to work feeling like I'm somebody. They all said thank you except Fuzzi. She didn't like Ashley smart ass comment about her penis. Well, Bitch! I ain't got that penis no more, but I got a lot of vagina you could taste. Emma and Kahi'Lee started laughing. Ashley stuck her finger in her own vagina and stuck her finger in her mouth. Mmmnm! Sorry, bitch! I got enough real pussy to taste. Fuzzi playfully rushed at Ashley, fighting her. Bitch that's why I can't stand your stankin ass. I know, 'cause you love my stankin ass.

Ashley slapped her butt with her hand, making a loud sound. Kahi'Lee was about to talk about how she hates Tyler and men now, but Ashley cut her short. Girl fuck all of that, your stupid ass will be riding his penis as soon as he gets out of jail, and we all know it, so stop it. Kahi'Lee looked at Ashley crazy, but she really meant what she said. She knew that they would have to just see for themselves. Ok! Now somebody tell me how y'all bought all those new cars that are out there in that parking lot? Everybody looked at each other, but nobody answered Ashley's question.

Fuzzi changed the conversation by talking about Izzi. Fuzzi knew that once she spoke about Izzi having a black eye, Ashley wouldn't think anymore about the question she just asked. Girl, do you know when we went to visit Izzi, somebody gave her a black eye? What! You are lying, Fuzzi. They all started talking about Izzi's case until Kahi'Lee was released from the hospital. Emma even told them about some dude she met coming home from work yesterday, how he cut her off in a brand-new Phantom Rolls Royce wearing a few hundred thousand dollars in jewelry. Ashley told Emma that he was probably one of the professional ball players.

A lot of them and celebrities are starting to move to Arizona. Girl, I saw Ice T and Coco in the grocery store yesterday. Naw, Girl, this dude was a baller, but nobody else's team but his own, trust me. He asked me to ride with him and some dude to Las Vegas for two days. But I told him that I had to work. That's when he said if I was his woman that I wouldn't have to work." Girl, where he at, hell, I'll be his girlfriend if a bitch doesn't have to work no more. Because I want to kill some of these parents the way they are treating these kids. What's his name? 2 Much. What? He had on a diamond necklace that was blinding the hell out of me. It had the number 2 and the word Much next to it. 2 Much, girl. I don't know for sure what he does, but I got the feeling that he was a drug dealer or something like that. Fuzzi said, "Why is that?" Because while we were talking, he sent the dude he was riding with into the store for some orange juice and water. He pulled out a wad of 100-dollar bills, knowing the store couldn't break one. Girl, you know he wanted me to see all that money to change my mind. But since a bitch stepped her game up, I went in my bra and pulled out a roll of 100-dollar bills on his ass. Then I grabbed a 20-dollar bill from my pocket and told him I'll buy it. Girl, you should have seen that nigga eyes light up. He tried to clap back by saying, "shit, you need to be taking me to Las Vegas; you're too much yourself." I told him naw, "You're too much, I'm not enough. That's why I got to be at work in the morning." All of them busted up laughing. Fuzzi asked, did they exchange numbers? Emma winked her eye. I'm a Fox. I got his ass on speed dial. Fuzzi and Emma slapped their hands. That's when Ashley said, "What's all this Fox shit?" Emma and Fuzzi walked out of the room. Okay, y'all bitches go stop ignoring me. I know that. She walked out behind them, cursing at them for not telling her what they were all up to. Y'all on that bullshit. Now I hate all you bitches again.

$ $ $ $ $

Fuzzi was in the kitchen cooking, listening to Lyfe Jennings, "Stick up, kid." She sang along to the words. Nobody knows the trouble I see. Nobody knows but me. The last time she and Mr. Shelton were together, he told Fuzzi that he loved Sea Food. So, she was making Lobster, Crab, Prawns, and stuffed swordfish with a Shrimp salad and a bottle of Merlot, which is what they first drank together. Fuzzi was wearing a dark pink rose bra and panty set with a pair of 3-inch-high-thigh pink shiny, glossy boots. Her hair was up in a little girl's pigtails with heart-shaped diamond earrings and necklace. She heard the doorbell ring and smiled when she looked at her clock. It was 7:59 on her way to the door. She switched the music to Jazz, Michael Franks, A Lady Want to Know. Fuzzi took a deep breath and opened the door. Mr. Shelton almost had a heart attack when he saw the beautiful chocolate woman that he called his blackberry. Well, Hello, Mr. I see you a man of your word. Mr. Shelton smiled and reached into his coat pocket. He handed Fuzzi a bank envelope. She laughed and took it, then she invited him in. After he removed his coat, Fuzzi kissed him, to his surprise, on the lips. Mmmmm! Something sure smells good. Yeah, come on, let me show you what I prepared for you. She grabbed him by the hand and led him to her kitchen. Mr. Shelton couldn't help but take in her perfect butt cheeks that shook and bounced like a basketball. Wow! I didn't know you cooked. I'm the best. She smiled and looked back at him and noticed how he was watching her ass.

When they were looking over the food, Mr. Shelton's eyes couldn't believe how well-prepared everything was. You sure you are not a professional chef? Fuzzi just smiled while she let him taste her cooking. Damn! This tastes better than the restaurant food that I have been going to. Thank you! Fuzzi turned off the food and asked Mr. Shelton to join her with a glass of wine. They went back to Fuzzi's dinner table and, shared a bottle of Merlot and talked. Mr. Shelton told Fuzzi that he should have played professional football, but an accident happened while he was playing college football. What position did you play? I was the No 1 wide receiver in the State of California until a bad accident changed my life. Mr. Shelton put his hand down, and Fuzzi saw that whatever happened still bothered him. Do you want to talk about it, baby? He looked up. No! But it all worked itself out because I made my dad a promise that I didn't keep; that's why I'm a lawyer today. I promised my dad that if his friend, who was a lawyer himself, got me out of trouble, I would study and take the bar and go to law school.

Fuzzi smiled at him, and then you're right. Whatever happened, it definitely worked itself out. Look at you now; you're definitely a big-time lawyer. While Fuzzi was talking, Mr. Shelton felt that he would pay her back for their last time eating dinner. Mr. Shelton got down on his knees and went under the table. Before Fuzzi could ask him what he was doing, Fuzzi's legs departed, and Mr. Shelton's tongue was invading her vagina. Fuzzi put both of her legs on the table and allowed Mr. Shelton to eat her vagina like a bowl of blackberry ice cream covered in chocolate. Ohhhhh! Ohhhhhh! Yes! Mmmmmm! Get to that berry! Get to it, baby! Oh, my god, you good pussy eating mother fucker, you. Mr. Shelton had Fuzzi talking in English, Spanish, Arabic and Ghetto Slang. After eating Fuzzi's vagina, they sat and enjoyed the seafood dinner, and the night ended with Fuzzi allowing Mr. Shelton to enter every hole in her body. What Fuzzi didn't know was the same way that Do' Dirty turned her out at the age of 12, Fuzzi didn't know it, but she had just turned out Mr. Shelton. He had never experienced that type of sex before in his entire life. If Fuzzi had just taken one minute to look into his eyes before he left, she would have seen that Mr. Shelton had left her home in love with her sweet blackberry vagina.

Chapter Eleven
CHASING THE FOX

I got both Jokers and the Ace, y'all set. Damn! Damn! Diana, why did you go seven, and you didn't even have a joker? Shit! You be messing up; we could have won the game. Izzi and her cellmate Caroline were playing spades when Big Girl came and whispered something in her ear. Whatever she said completely changed Izzi's happy mood, that she was just in while playing cards with Caroline. Big Girl kissed Izzi on the neck, then walked away, but not before grabbing half of the cards off the table and tossing them on the floor. Diana wasn't afraid of Big Girl, so she started cursing her out. You stupid man looking ass bitch, I hate your punk ass. Girl, you go make me fuck you up. Big Girl turned around to fight with Diana, but a few other females stopped them. Man, come on, y'all about to get us locked down early. So what, fuck, getting locked down. I'm sick of this bull-looking ass bitch. Everybody laughed at Diana's comment. Yeah, I'm a run-over you like a bull too soon as they move out the way. The female still kept them separated and wouldn't let them fight.

Izzi got up and headed to her bedroom. She didn't want any part of what Big Girl was doing. Plus, when Big Girl whispered in her ear, she told Izzi that she was coming to sleep in Izzi's bed with her tonight. Izzi didn't want to be with Big Girl, and she knew that she had to put a stop to her bullying sexual behavior. After Diana and Big Girl got through arguing, Izzi saw Big Girl go up to Caroline and she already knew what they were talking about. So Izzi knew that she had to prepare for the night that was ahead of her. The guard gave everybody their normal warning. Okay, ladies, get it together, y'all got five minutes before lockdown. Everybody in the pod started scattering like roaches coming in contact with the light, trying to get, give, or receive whatever they needed before the doors locked. Before Big Girl walked into the cell with Izzi, she had wet her hair and put it up in a bonnet. Izzi has a towel damping it at the back of her neck. When Big Girl walked into the cell, they both stared at each other. Well, hello, Strawberry Sherbert. Did you miss me? Izzi didn't say anything. She just put a halfway smile on her face. Big Girl turned around to locate where the guard was that was working that pod, but like normally, the guards weren't taking their final walks yet. So Big Girl knew that she should get covered up before the guard came in and noticed her. Because anyone that got caught out of place in the way that Big Girl was at the moment would be an automatic escape charge for any inmate. Before Big

Girl jumped up on the bunk, she walked up to Izzi, ready to have fun tonight, Strawberry Sherbert? Unexpectedly, Izzi smiled and said, "Yes, I am." Big Girl gave Izzi a weird look and then she jumped up on the bunk. It's about time you came around Strawberry Sherbert. You know that belongs to me. Izzi removed that fake smile the moment that Big Girl looked away.

Izzi sat down on the bed, and she thought about Fuzzi. Go put an end to that shit, you a Fox. You're too pretty to be getting your face fucked up. Izzi closed her eyes, and all she could see was DuVall and La'Bella having sex in her bed. She could hear the moans and sounds that La'Bella made as she came down the hallway. The more she thought about it; the more anger and rage came over her. The guards were taking their walk and were counting the inmates, really trying their best to get the hell out of there. The guards stopped at Izzi's door and surprised Izzi and Big Girl. Big Girl's heart was pounding and almost ready to jump out of her chest. Damn! She thought to herself, "Did one of these bitches snitch me off." Big Girl could already hear herself beating the shit out of Caroline and Vick, her cellmate. Good night, Mrs. Dawson. Good night! The guard looked at Big Girl and was about to pound on the door, but Big Girl turned and shifted her body to the other side, allowing the guard to see movement so that he knew Caroline was alive while he was counting on his shift. The guard got just what he wanted, and that was to see a live body. He nodded his head at Izzi and kept it moving to the next cell. Big Girl could hear him telling another inmate good night. That's when she took a deep breath and removed the covers. Damn! Strawberry Sherbert, I thought your little cellmate tried to save your ass. I thought I was going to have to put her ass in check too. Izzi said, "who in check?" Hearing that, Big Girl jumped up and was on her way down from the bunk to show Izzi just who she meant was in check. As Big Girl was coming down off the bunk by the toilet and sink, just as Big Girl took one step down off the toilet, Izzi swung just as hard as she could catching Big Girl right in the throat. Wham! The pressure that Izzi applied to her punch caused Big Girl to choke and try to catch her breath. Izzi didn't stop. Izzi swung with her left hand and caught a clean punch to the face. Wham! Big Girl already couldn't breathe and was off balance coming off the toilet. Big Girl went crashing into the wall and then she hit the floor. While Big Girl tried to catch her breath, she wasn't ready for what was coming next. Wham! Wham! Wham! Wham! Wham! Blood started shooting in every direction. Wham! Wham! Wham! Wham! Wham! The sock that Izzi held in her hand was full of bars of State soap, connecting every time to a different part of Big Girl's body. Wham! Wham! Wham! Izzi had completely blacked out and was beating Big Girl, who really looked like La'Bella at that moment.

What snapped Izzi back to the norm was hearing Diana, and a few other inmates yell out. "Kill that man-looking bitch!" "Beat her ass, Izzi!" Hearing her name made her notice the bloody body in front of her. Izzi stopped swinging and her hands were shaking uncontrollably. Fear overcame Izzi because Big Girl wasn't moving. She thought that she had just beaten her to death. Out of fear but still angry, Izzi kicked Big Girl in the stomach. And when she started choking and coughing, that's when she knew that Big Girl was still alive. Izzi grabbed the towel that was lying on her bed and threw it to Big Girl. Big Girl looked up at Izzi through swollen eyes and tears. Izzi stepped over her, drew the sock back, and was ready to finish the job. But, to Izzi's surprise, Big Girl begged Izzi to stop. Izzi looked at her and was tired of people fucking over her. Today was the day for it to stop. You like sucking pussy? You want Strawberry Sherbert? Wham! Wham! Wham! All three blows landed on Big Girl's head. Izzi removed her black and white jail pants. Izzi walked over to Big Girl and grabbed a handful of her hair. She dragged her on her knees over to the bed, sat down, and spread her legs open wide. Bitch! Since you think my pussy is ice cream, then come get you a triple scoop, and I better enjoy it, or I'm beating your ass again. Big Girl pulled her panties to the side and licked and sucked until Izzi got tired. Izzi didn't even give her the satisfaction of letting her know that she was enjoying it. Izzi lay there with her eyes focused on her every move. Izzi was destined to walk out of that cell letting every female in that pod know that the cat got trapped chasing the quiet fox.

Chapter Twelve
VIOLATED

One by one, extravagant and expensive vehicles were pulling up to Mr. and Mrs. Lehmann's Mansion in North Scottsdale. Thompson, their driver, was out front directing all the Lehmann's guests into the Mansion and showing them where to park. This was a big party that the Billionaires throw every year. Everybody that was anybody was always invited to their parties. The Lehmann's were friends to all types of Celebrities, Basketball, Football players, Actors and high-paid lawyers. Mr. William Lehmann and his wife Amirah own Abusan Real Estate Company. Most of all, the homes that the celebrities, basketball players, football players and lawyers live in, more than likely, came from Abusan Real Estate. This was a party that the Lehmann's threw to say thank you to all their top-notch clients who purchased homes with them. John Legend was hired to perform a few of his soul-felt songs on the piano. Every type of food was laid out between their guests. Just about everyone that showed up always brought Christmas gifts for the Lehmann's seeming that it was so close to Christmas. Mr. Lehmann was 5'10, slender built, with blonde hair and blue eyes that put you in the mind of Prince Harry. His wife Amirah was 10 years younger than him and was drop-dead gorgeous. Her 5'9 model built frame accommodated her 40DD breast, 24-inch waist, and 36 inches butter melting backside. The 10-carat diamond ring that she wears on her finger doesn't go unnoticed either. Hello! William, Amirah, what a beautiful dress. Their guests one by one kissed and complimented them as they arrived. Hello Judge! William, Amirah, you guys sure know how to throw a party. Yeah, we hope you and your lovely wife enjoy yourself. We don't get out like this much, I'm sure we will. Thanks for the invite. Yeah! Sure. We'll talk later, Josh. Even though Josh Hemsworth was one of the biggest Judges in the State of Arizona, William was on a first-name basis with all his guests. Besides being a Billionaire, he was well respected by all his peers.

Mr. and Mrs. Lehmann, Hello! "Here, Merry Christmas." Amirah, what's wrong with this shit head have he been drinking already? I thought I forgot things love, but it damn sure isn't Christmas yet. What's this Mr. and Mrs. bullshit, Dave? They all started laughing at William's sense of humor. How about this attractive lady right here instead of this? He held up the gift that Mr. Shelton and his wife gave to them. Love, can we have her instead of this? William pointed at Dave's young, attractive wife, Dolly. Yeah, sure, why not. If I can unwrap that treasured gift you got. Dolly punched Dave in the arm and gave him an evil look. Well, maybe we can trade gifts after the party. No, thank you. Only I have the say, as to who can unwrap this gift. Come on, Dave. Dolly looked William in the eyes to let him know to keep dreaming. William and Dave winked at each other as they walked away and headed into the Lehmann's home. William and Amirah kissed, knowing that no matter how tough and in control people thought they were, there was always a price that everyone gave into. Amirah told her husband, "We'll be tasting that vagina before the sun come up." They continued to welcome their guests as they arrived.

The party was in full swing when Philip and his wife Marlena came walking through the door. Everyone held a drink and was singing along to "Love Me Now." John was serenading them on the piano. All the lovers were looking into each other's eyes and enjoying the music. Mr. Shelton was conversing with three other lawyers and a couple while Amirah was having a deep conversation with his wife, Dolly, about joining her and William in a three-some after the party. After John left the party, a DJ started playing music and livened up the party. Everyone was dancing and having a good time. Mr. Shelton saw Philip talking to a few other attorneys, and he went over to speak to them.

Hey Philip, Chris, Winston, and Evan, long time no see Joseph. Great party, isn't it? Mr. Shelton reached out to shake the other lawyers' hands, but they all dissed him and walked away. Joseph stayed and shook Mr. Shelton's hand. Hey Dave, what's that all about? Oh, nothing much, Phil just a little uptight over a case I took. Oh Yeah! Ok! How have you been, Dave? How's the wife? For the first time Mr. Shelton hadn't even realized that Dolly wasn't even by his side. While talking to Joseph, he kept looking around the party, trying to see if he could locate his wife, but she wasn't nowhere in sight. The mansion was so big, and it had so many rooms that it was hard to spot Dolly through all the people that were there. The host walked up to Mr. Shelton and offered him another drink. He grabbed one off her tray and proceeded through the house, looking for his wife. But every time he tried to find her; he was interrupted by someone else. Two Black Tahoe's pulled up in front of the mansion and stopped, the two vehicles pulled side-by-side, and the two drivers were conversing with each other. Someone else pulled up, trying to attend the party. They had to blow their horns to get their attention to allow them to pass by them. The two Tahoe's pulled out of the way to allow the Lamborghini to go passed them.

$ $ $ $ $

William Lehmann stood there in his gold boxers with a drink in his hand, and he watched as his wife Amirah slowly undressed Dolly. Just as soon as Amirah unzipped her black Tommy Ford dress, her 44DD breasts stood up like they were saluting Mr. Lehmann. Dolly stood there in her red Victoria's Secret silk panties and Black Alexander McQueen high heels. After her dress hit the floor, Dolly stepped out of it. Amirah and Dolly started kissing each other, flicking their tongues in and out of each other's mouths. Amirah took one of Dolly's nipples into her mouth while her other hand massaged her other breast. That's when Mr. Lehmann let his Gold Boxers hit the floor. He walked up behind Dolly and kissed her on the neck while Amirah let each breast dance from one side to the other, taking each nipple into her mouth. Mmmmm! Dolly moaned at the attention that her body was receiving. William removed her red panties and watched as they slid down to the floor. He placed his hands on each shoulder and allowed his hands to move freely down her back. He rubbed and massaged her back until his hands reached her butt cheeks.

William explored each cheek, getting to know them personally. He spread her cheeks, making a draft of air penetrating her asshole and Lovebox. William encouraged Dolly to spread her legs more, and she gladly accepted. To her surprise, while she and Amirah were sucking each other's nipples, William came from under in between her legs and let his tongue flicker her clitoris. Dolly's legs staggered, but William held each butt cheek so she couldn't fall because his hands and legs controlled her balance. Ooooooh! Oooooh! Mmmmm! William started to suck and bite on her clitoris and gradually allowed his tongue to maneuver her Lovebox. That started to drive Dolly crazy. Mmmm! Mmmm! Ooooh! Smack! Smack! William started slapping her ass while eating her vagina like a bowl of applesauce. Amirah started tongue kissing her and took her finger and played with her clitoris while William let his tongue dance around in her vagina. Dolly let out a loud roar. Ooooh! No! No! No! Wait! Wait! Wait! I can't take this. Stop! Wait! No! Ooooooh! Yes! Yes! Yes! Owwwww! Owwwww! Mmmmm! Agggh! What are y'all doing to meeee? Woah! Ooooh! Oooohhh! Wait! Wait! I'm cuming. I'm Cuming! I'm fucking cuminggg! Dolly exploded like the 4th of July fireworks. Amirah and William both had to catch her because her whole body completely gave out, but William and Amirah have such chemistry together. Before she could even recover from her climax, William cuffed both ass cheeks and picked Dolly up in the air. To keep her balance, she had to grab him from behind his head. William walked Dolly over to their king-size bed and laid her down. Amirah was already removing her blue and pink Chanel panties. She crawled slowly across the bed but straddled Dolly's face putting her ass cheeks in Dolly's face. She leaned across Dolly's body and grabbed both legs giving William a clear landing into her vagina like her vagina was a runway for an airplane. William strapped up with a magnum and welcomed his penis into Dolly's hot soaking vagina. Mmmmm! Aaaaa! She felt him slide his way into her vagina hole. Dolly spread Amirah's ass cheeks and started teasing her newfound friend. Oh Yes! Mmmm! While William pounded away into Dolly's vagina, he and Amirah came together and kissed each other.

Mr. Shelton had searched the whole mansion, looking for Dolly. It wasn't until he realized William and Amirah weren't also nowhere to be found. That is when he ran up the stairs and started opening bedroom doors. Dolly, are you in here? Dolly, are you in here? Every door he opened, there wasn't anyone in either bedroom. Mr. Shelton was about to turn around and go back downstairs. He was starting to feel stupid searching in another man's house, searching for his wife, but the two double doors aroused his suspicion. He opened the door. Dolly, you in here? His heart almost jumped out of his chest when he saw the ass cheeks that he knew so well. Dolly's ass was up in the air because she was in between William's legs giving him a blow job, while Amirah sat across William's face. Dolly, what the fuck are you doing? Everybody jumped up when they heard Mr. Shelton at the door roaring like a lion. You nasty trifling bitchhh! Tears started falling while Dolly explained that she was doing what she thought he had wanted her to do. I thought we were going to have a three-some with you too, baby. William had retrieved his boxers and pants while Mr. Shelton and Dolly went back and forth. I was just joking with this prick. I had no idea that you would go along with this stupid shit. Come on, baby, let's go home, and we'll talk about it then. Go home! Go home! Are you fucking crazy? Do you think that I would go home with you after seeing another man's prick in your dirty ass mouth? Dolly dropped down to her knees in front of Mr. Shelton and pleaded for his forgiveness. Mr. Shelton rushed Mr. Lehmann, and they started fighting. Then Amirah jumped on Mr. Shelton's back, and Dolly jumped on Amirah's back. Wham! Wham! Wham! Smack! Smack! Wham! Smack! Smack! Wham! Fist and opened palms were flying in every direction. By the time they were all tired out, it looked like they had a caged orgy fight. Fighting until the last woman or man was standing. There was blood and scratches on all four of them.

The music was too loud for anyone else to know what was even going on upstairs in the bedroom. When they all stopped fighting, Dolly was crying and told Amirah that she tricked her. You promised me a million dollars to sleep with you with our husbands. So, where's my money? Come on slut let's please my husband. Slobber and spit were coming out of Dolly's mouth. She was crying and was so upset. William told Dolly that her vagina wasn't worth $100, and it's three things that I'll never share. That's my money, food and pussy. Both of y'all can get the fuck out of my house before I have y'all thrown out on y'all fucking heads. He was wiping his mouth with his Kenneth Cole silk shirt because Mr. Shelton had busted it wide open during their fight. Mr. Shelton looked at all of them with rage and disgust, y'all are perfect for each other, and he turned and walked out the door. Dolly grabbed her dress and put it on then ran after her husband. Dave! Dave! Wait, honey, I'm sorry. Amirah quickly got dressed, and she and William went and followed them both. But William didn't have on a shirt because the one he had in his hand was too bloody to put on, and it would have freaked out his guest. Still, nobody didn't know what was going on until they saw 6 men come barging into the mansion, pointing semiautomatic weapons with black masks covering their faces.

BBBRRRRRRRRRTTTTTTTT! Everybody, get the fuck down on the floor, now! The men started moving through the mansion so fast and swiftly like it was their own home. They knew just what doors to hit and where to bring everybody. One of the robbers ordered the music to be turned off. Two of the guys ran upstairs to clear all the rooms, but nobody was upstairs in Mr. Lehmann's bedrooms. Okay, Ladies and Gentlemen, I'm sure we all know what the fuck is going on here. It's time for you rich motherfuckers to pay y'all taxes. Please forgive me for not sending out any tax forms, but I figured I'd personally come and rob the rich in the same way that y'all rob the poor. One dude stood up and started flexing his muscles, and he was half drunk. Fuck you low-life motherfuckers. Do y'all know who the fuck I am? Pow! Pow! Pow! No, I don't, tough guy, and I guess I'll never know you now. A few females started screaming, seeing the bodybuilder lying dead on the floor. Pow! Shut the fuck up! Okay, are there any more tough guys in the fucking party that wants me to know them? The whole mansion went quiet. Okay! Now that I got everybody's attention, my man is going to come around, and all y'all wallets, purses, and jewelry will be going in both these two black bags. If there is anyone here who refuses to pay their taxes today, he walked over by the dead guy. You will be joining this piece of shit right here. He kicked the dude to make sure that everybody heard him loud and clear. Now can someone tell me who owns this beautiful fucking house. Nobody said anything. The robber pointed his 357 Magnum to some female head. Pretty lady, can you please tell me who and before he could even get the words out, she pointed at Mr. Lehmann. William gave her a mean look like you, bitchhh! He tapped William on the top of his head with the tip of his 357 Magnum. Come on, buddy, stand up. Man, what the fuck happened to you.

Mr. Lehmann told the man that he could let all of his guests go. Don't take their things, anything that you want, I'll give to you. The guy looked around the room now this is a good man right here. I can see why all of you came to this party now. He looked back at Mr. Lehmann; don't you know that I would love to tap into all those Millions you got. Oh, excuse me for assaulting you, Billions you got. I know who you are, Mr. William Lehmann, trust me. I've contemplated breaking your rich ass, but I'm not trying to deal with Federal agents in banks where you keep all of your money. There are codes and special names that you have to know when you're dealing with that type of money, right? Mr. Lehmann shook his head and was praying that the man didn't kill him. He hugged William, Mr. Lehmann, do you know what the worst feeling in the world is? Mr. Lehmann said, "I don't know." The worst feeling in the world is what everyone in this room feels. Violated! Taking y'all money isn't shit, you can make more money. But it's how you're losing your money that makes y'all feel violated, right? For the first time, Mr. Lehmann gave him a mean look as if to say I'll get even. Now you see that look right there, that's that real shit right there. That look is what's going to make you follow my partner back upstairs and get me what I came for. Your wife knows all the codes and where that shit at I want.

If your wife doesn't get up right now and get what I came for, Mr. Lehmann, guess what? I already know. Good! We understand each other, my friend. I wish your driver was as smart as you are. Mr. Lehmann put his head down, and tears came to his eyes because he knew that Malik was dead. To everyone's surprise, he turned and pointed the gun at Amirah. Mrs. Lehmann, you want to get up and go handle that business for me and your husband? Amirah looked at William, and he just nodded his head. She got up and followed the two men back upstairs. The other two men had removed every wallet, purse, chain, Rolex watches and anything else of value. When Amirah walked into the room, she wanted to make sure that they weren't going to kill her after she gave them everything that they wanted. But the two men were less talkative than their boss. Pointing their weapons made Amirah empty that safe real fast. They removed jewelry and cash from a black bag, but they didn't reveal what was inside it. Amirah stood there crying because she was counting the minutes until she died. But to her surprise, the men marched her back down the stairs. All cell phones were also collected, and the house phones were smashed up. Everyone was ordered to line up in two rows, men and women. They laid them all in between each other's legs, face down, and then they left. They could hear the black Tahoe's burning rubber away from the mansion. The lead driver removed his mask, and he looked at the

passenger who had just removed his mask. Man, you are 2 Much.
He smiled and laid his 357 Magnum in his lap.

Chapter Thirteen
YA HEARD ME

Good! Good! Nice! Okay! Give me more of that. Give it to me! Look! Click! Click! Click! Click! Nice Kahi'Lee! Nice! Nice! Now come towards me and give me a few turns. Click! Click! Click! Click! Click! Let's go! Try that again. Make your body talk to the camera. I like! I like! Noooo! I love it. Come on! That's it, Kahi'Lee! Beautiful! I got it. I got you. Everyone clapped and applauded Kahi'Lee at work behind the camera. The agents were glad that they were now working with Kahi'Lee. A few months had passed, and she was feeling greater than before. The rest and time off were much needed. She had returned all of Tyler's Christmas gifts and spent Christmas with her girlfriends. Even though she had put a restraining order out against him, Tyler was still calling and showing up at their home. Every time that Kahi'Lee or a neighbor called the police, Tyler would disappear before they showed up. But the police would always tell her to call them back if he harassed her or showed up again. Kahi'Lee's bills were starting to come in, and it was much easier splitting the bills with Tyler, but now all the bills were on her. She refused to take Tyler back because now, deep down inside of her, Kahi'Lee kind of feared being with him or around him. Even though she was now fulfilling her childhood goals, there were still a few more hoops that Kahi'Lee saw that she had to overcome. It seemed that no matter how hard you work for something, somehow her vagina always seemed to be wanted in some type of way. She was starting to feel like women were only born to spread their legs. Even though her photoshoot went well, her mind kept going back and forth, pussy, bills; pussy, bills; pussy, bills; pussy paid for bills; and bills make men want pussy. Damn! "What? Did you say something?" Oh no, please forgive me, Stanley. I was just thinking about something. So, what do you think about the pictures? Kahi'Lee halfway looked at them and said, "They look good, thank you, you're a superstar with that camera." No darling! The superstar is taking the photos, and you make my job easy. They both smiled and gave a half hug and kiss on the cheeks. So, is that it? Yep, for today. We'll be shooting you again bright and early in the morning, so make sure that you get plenty of sleep. Ok, Stanley, I'll be ready. Smooches!

Kahi'Lee headed to her dressing room to change back into her own clothes. She grabbed her cell phone and took a deep breath. The one person that she hated to call right now, she had to call her. Fuzzi picked up on the third ring. Hello, mind reader. What? You must have got burning ears. Why you say that? Because me and Emma were just sitting here at Cracker Barrels eating and talking about you. Then my cell phone started ringing, and your hot ass picture popped up on my screen. Kahi'Lee told Fuzzi to screw herself because they didn't call her out to eat with them. Fuzzi told her that Emma had invited her and that she didn't bring any money, and she looked a hot mess. She doesn't know why she let her talk her into coming out looking like I'm about to beg all these people for their food. Kahi'Lee started laughing and told her about her photoshoot. After Fuzzi listened to Kahi'Lee explore her modeling career, Fuzzi caught her off guard and said, "Bitch I know your ass is broke. That's what you're calling me for." Kahi'Lee said, "then maybe it isn't me that's doing the mind reading. Maybe that's your Cleopatra ass." They both got a good laugh. We are thinking about shaking up that New Orleans. Maybe a bitch a get lucky and spend some of that rapper's money, Ya Heard Me! Kahi'Lee busted up laughing because Fuzzi sounded just like Birdman. You broke, Whoadi? "Then a motherfucker!" Well, start packing bitch so somebody can pay our bills. Fuzzi told Kahi'Lee that they'll come by after they get through eating, so that they all could talk about their next payday. Kahi'Lee didn't want to say anything, but she was more ready than Fuzzi and Emma. Her mind started wondering again. Pussy, bills; pussy, bills; pussy, bills; pussy, bills. Pussy about to pay the bills. Kahi'Lee laughed at her own little mind games that she was now playing with herself. Okay, girl! "Tell Emma I said Hi." I'll see y'all later. Click!

While Fuzzi was telling Emma that Kahi'Lee was ready to shake, Emma's cell phone started ringing. She started hitting Fuzzi. Hey! This old boy I was telling you about that I met a while back. Fuzzi had no idea who Emma was talking about. But it didn't take long for her to catch on to who was calling. Hello! Emma acted like she didn't know who was calling. Being that it took him so long to finally call her. Wait, man, you can't get mad at a lady for not knowing who you are. Damn! Wasn't that over two months ago that I met you and now you are just calling? What you and your woman arguing with each other? Is that why you are calling me now? 2 Much asked Emma, "How did you know that I was about to make you my woman?" Emma said, "Wouldn't I have to be the one to determine that with you?" Well, you asked me if I was arguing with my woman. It wasn't until you answered the phone that we started arguing. OK! OK! I see you are one of them smooth talkers. 2 Much said, "Oh, and I see you missed your man and just isn't woman enough to tell me." That must mean that you ain't my man. Because if you were, then I wouldn't mind telling you that I missed you. Click! Hello! Hello! Hello! Girl, I know this man ain't just hung up on me. Emma was looking at her cell phone when it started ringing in her hand. Hello! She answered angrily, showing that 2 Much had her frustrated. Hello, baby, what you doing? I miss you; do you miss me? Emma couldn't help but start laughing. Man, you ain't about to get on my last nerve. As much as Emma hated to admit it, it was something about 2 Much that made her hardened vagina want to give in to the man that was on the other end of the line. 2 Much asked

Emma if he could spend time with her later, and that's when she got him back. See, I told you that you weren't my man. Why is that? Because my man wouldn't ask to see me, he would already know that I'd want to see him. 2 Much asked for her address and told Emma that I'd be home at 8 o'clock, and they both laughed and ended their call. Click!

Fuzzi was giving Emma the blues after she and 2 Much finished talking. Well bitch, I know that you're about to go and give that dick gobbler away. Emma's cheeks were turning red. Fuzzi was making her feel so embarrassed about her phone call. Bitch when the phone first started ringing, your nasty ass legs were closed, then while y'all were talking, your legs were like this. Fuzzi was slowly opening her legs. Then when he hung up on your stankin ass them legs went dripppp, and your ass closed them right up. But by the time you ended that call, your legs opened up this wide. Fuzzi put both of her legs up on the table and Emma fell on the floor laughing. I hate you, Fuzzi, you make me sick. Naw bitch, 2 Much, 2 Big, 2 Long, its what's go have your ass sick not me. At first, you wanted to rob the nigga, now you want to give yourself away. Fuzzi started singing like she was in church. Emma got up and sat back in the chair. Girl, I'm glad I'm on your side because you are too smart for your own good.

After Fuzzi, Kahi'Lee, and Emma had put their plan together to go to New Orleans to catch their next baller, Fuzzi winded up cussing Tyler out because he kept calling. While they were there, he kept interrupting them from putting their plan into effect. Fuzzi got a phone call from Mr. Shelton, Izzi's lawyer, and had to leave. So, Emma went home to find something sexy and attractive to go out with 2 Much and get to learn what he was about. Even though Emma was acting overly excited to meet 2 Much, she promised her girls that if he had what they're looking for that, it was Foxes over penis and relationships. Fuzzi and Kahi'Lee kissed Emma. Okay, now you're acting like a hungry Fox, bitch. Foxes pick and choose the penises that we want, but we don't want a penis that piss where we sleep and mark their territory. Those were the Foxes' words that they swore by unto each other.

Emma was a real girly type of female, so she laid back in her bathtub with strawberry candles burning around her tub. The music was on a low tone and put her in a relaxed state of mind. K'Michelle, "Can't Raise a Man" played while Emma thought about her job, life and a man, which for some reason, she couldn't get off her mind. Emma smiled at the way that he asked her out, even though it had been a while since she had given herself to a man. Sex wasn't really on her mind with 2 Much. She just wanted to go out and dance and enjoy a good conversation. But without even knowing 2 Much, it was something about him that Emma wanted to allow him to invade her space. It had been a long time since she felt that love bug in her stomach. But 2 Much had her lying back in the tub, holding onto her stomach. Emma knew that it would be a matter of time before her heart would be following right behind. She even a couple of times grabbed her cell phone to call and make an excuse to cancel their outing tonight. But the black, white, and gold Versace mini dress with the back out said that she would be enjoying 2 Much company tonight. She pulled out a pair of gold Versace heels that would show off her French tip pedicure. Emma has a bra and panty set Fuzi bought her for Christmas that she has been dying to put on for a special occasion. Emma thought, what better time to wear them than now, out with 2 Much. Emma was looking at herself in the mirror when she heard the doorbell ring. She looked at her watch and it said 8:10, and it surprised her that it was not 9:10 because most men never did show up on time when they asked you out.

Emma opened the door, and 2 Much had on a black Gucci suit, white silk shirt and hanky, with a black, white and gold tie. He held roses in one hand and a black box in the other one. His Tom Ford cologne hit Emma in her nose the moment she opened the door. Well, Hello, beautiful lady! 2 Much extended his arm and gave Emma the roses. Awwwe, how sweet. Look at you all, handsome. He complimented how well she was wearing her dress. Emma invited him into her home. 2 Much felt comfortable and was grateful to see how well she kept everything in order and so neatly. After Emma put her roses into a vase, she asked, 2 Much was he ready? He said, "Not yet beautiful, I have one more thing to give you." 2 Much walked behind Emma, and her whole body froze. She had no idea what he was about to do to her, but strangely, it made Emma feel uncomfortable because he walked up behind her. To Emma's surprise, he placed an all-diamond necklace around her neck. Emma figured that it was a nice gold chain. 2 Much turned her around to him, ok! Now I'm ready. Emma walked over to the mirror and couldn't believe her eyes. The necklace had to be worth $50,000. Her mouth opened wide. Is this real? 2 Much laughed, "I don't know, maybe you have to ask your jeweler." Emma knew that she didn't have a jeweler, knowing that she hadn't worn a piece of jewelry so expensive. Beautiful, are you going to look at that chain all night, or are we going to have fun? Emma didn't want 2 Much to see the tears in her eyes, but she couldn't compose herself. 2 Much walked up to her and grabbed her face. My lady! I want to see those types of tears in your eyes every day. Emma asked him, "Why do you want to see me cry?" He kissed her lips softly and said, "Because those are happy tears." Emma looked up at 2 Much and said, "See, man, I knew you were too much for me." They both laughed because Emma realized that she had just said his name.

Emma felt like she was a big-time movie star riding in the front seat of 2 Much Rolls Royce Phantom. Twice, she had removed his sun visor to look at the diamond necklace. 2 Much smiled. He had on so many diamonds it looked like the sun was still out. 2 Much pulled up in front of a club in Scottsdale, and it was packed with sexy, attractive women. Emma thought, damn! How am I going to keep his attention around all these Dimes? The valet opened 2 Much doors, and he put a $100 bill in his palm. Another guy helped Emma out on her side. All eyes were cutting their ways, and Emma could see it. Club Top Notch was in full swing. Lil Wayne "What about Me" had everybody on the dance floor. 2 Much and Emma were taken to the VIP Room, when 2 Much whispered to the waitress and grabbed Emma by the hand. He took her straight to the dance floor. 2 Much put on a show. Emma couldn't believe that he would be so much fun. She expected him to lay back and look cool, but 2 Much was the life of the party. Five songs had gone by before they even made it back to VIP. Emma couldn't believe it; all the women had rudely tried to step in while they were dancing, but 2 Much never took his eyes off of Emma all night. He was melting her heart every second that she was in his company. The phone numbers and drinks that were sent to him, he had them all returned. He was lacing Emma at the same time. He told her that any man that was in her company and didn't know that he had a Queen by his side then you don't need him no way, because he will never become a King in life himself. You're like the woman that had me, and I'd never disrespect her or any woman of her quality. Right now, Emma didn't care who saw her crying. Like 2 Much told her back at the house, those are happy tears. She toasted to them, downed their Don Perignon, and returned to the dance floor. Emma walked out of the club feeling really tipsy but on top of the world. So, what now, are you ready to take me home now? 2 Much looked at her, you know that's the best thing I heard all week. Emma gave him a strange look like you're happy to take me home. She was having so much fun and didn't want the night to ever end. She sat back and got real quiet.

A few minutes later, they were driving through the mountains. Emma kept looking at the scenery, and she felt that maybe he had to make a stop before taking her home, maybe he had to take care of some business. Every dealer that tried to have fun, somehow, business would always come up. They got to get that fast money before someone else pockets that cash. 2 Much turned off, and before Emma knew it, he was pulling up to what appeared to her was a resort. Wow! This is a nice place to vacation. What's the name of this resort? I didn't even know that this place was even here. 2 Much looked at Emma and smiled. It's called 2 Much. What! Yeah right! Ain't no resort called 2 Much. Emma started laughing and he quickly busted her bubble. No, ain't no resort named that, but my home is. 2 Much pressed the button in his vehicle, and a big, large gate opened. Emma was more than sure that she had just had an orgasm right there in his seat. What! This is your house. Yeah, you asked me if I were going to take you home now. This is our home now unless you break up with me again. Emma looked at 2 Much, but no words would come out of her mouth. He stopped in front of a bunch of garage doors. It was seven because Emma started counting them. He hit another button, and one of the doors opened. 2 Much pulled inside, and Emma thought that she was in a high-priced car auction. 2 Much has parked in each stall a Porche 911, GT2 RS White Convertible; a Lamborghini Aventador S.V.J Red; a black Mercedes Benz Maybach; a Bentley Continental GTL, Blue; a McLaren 720S Spider; and a custom Becker Mercedes Benz

Metris Van with a 60-inch drop screen with surround sound sitting on custom 24-inch rims.

2 Much closed the garage, welcome to my home until you decide to make it yours. He let those words linger in the air until he came around and opened her door. Emma walked into the house, and nothing else needed to be said. The mansion was so plush that Emma felt out of place being there. All the things that she dreamed of having or accomplished were, right before her eyes, the dreams that Fuzzi gave her. It was all real but only here it all belonged to someone else. If you don't mind, make yourself comfortable. I like to get out of these clothes before I have everything that the club has. Pour us a nightcap if you don't mind. Yeah, sure. Emma started looking around in amazement. 2 Much came walking off his elevator. I'm sorry, baby, but I feel much better. He has on a Gucci robe with mink Gucci house slippers. Emma had removed her shoes, and she handed 2 Much a drink. He said, "Let's make a toast." This is to our new future together. Can you envision that? Emma's mind went to the Foxes sworn words that it was Foxes over penis and relationships. We don't won't know penis that pisses where we sleep. Yeah, I can, to our future.

Emma was about to drink her Don Perignon after they toasted but 2 Much stopped her. He said, "You give me yours, and I'll give you mine." Emma put her glass up to his lips, and while he was drinking it, her mind went to something Fuzzi said, A real boss won't ever drink what's been poured for him; only fools and suckers do that. It wasn't all the materialistic things that made 2 Much stand out from other men, but it was what he had just done, is what made her know that she was in the presence of a Boss and wasn't slipping for a pretty face. 2 Much let her drink from his glass, and that's when they engaged in their first passionate kiss. Emma found herself completely naked, lying next to 2 Much in his extravagant bedroom. Her vagina wanted to explore every inch of his 9-and-a-half-inch penis that she kept staring at, but to Emma's surprise, 2 Much didn't make any advance towards her sexually at all. Her body anticipated exploring his long muscular black penis, but what 2 Much did to Emma no man had ever done before in her life. He made love to her mind, and that was an orgasm that her mind and heart will never in life will ever forget. He allowed Emma to lie on his chest and her tears rolled down it until she cried herself to sleep.

Chapter Fourteen
FOXES OVER PENISES

Kahi'Lee had taken Stanley's advice and got plenty of rest for her photoshoot, but while she was dressing to go to her photoshoot, Kahi'Lee received a phone call from her agent telling her that someone had seen the photos that she had last taken with Stanley, and they wanted to hire her to be in a New Water commercial coming out. They had picked Kahi'Lee to be one of the models in their commercial. Kahi'Lee learned that her role in the commercial would be a female track runner training for the Olympic games. After she crosses the finish line her coach runs up to her and hands her a bottle of Aqua Thirst Cranberry Water. Ms. Neidhart, "Do you think that you'll be interested in anything like that?" Kahi'Lee was jumping up and down. I'm so sorry that this is short notice, but yes! Yes! Yes! I love to do a commercial, and it's going to be shown on television. Yeah, don't worry about acting because you won't be talking. It's your facial expressions, and of course, your look is what landed you the part in the commercial. I guess you can kindly thank Stanley for showing off your pictures to the company's owner. After you shoot the commercial, you can have that photo session with Stanley. That's if you feel up to it. You can easily reconsider changing the date and time. Plus, they'll discuss your pay when you get there. Yeah, sure, no problem. I'll do them both. Okay, Kahi'Lee, I'll see you there. Here's the address and be on time. This is very important for you, Kahi'Lee. Good luck, I know you'll nail it. Click!

Kahi'Lee was so excited that she started calling her girlfriends. She called Ashley first, and she was so happy for her, but Ashley was rushing through traffic trying to get to work. So, she told Kahi'Lee that they'll all celebrate later. Her treat, but she has to get off the phone before she gets into an accident. They told each other that they loved each other and ended the call.

Kahi'Lee called Fuzzi next but got no answer. But she knew that Fuzzi would return her call later. Kahi'Lee thought that maybe she was still sleeping because it was still early in the morning. She dialed Emma's cell phone number, and Emma answered. Wow, you're up early to not have to be going to work. Kahi'Lee was so excited that Emma had gone on a date. Girl, my agent just called me and offered me a part in a commercial. What! Are you serious? Yeah, Girl, I'm about to go shoot it in a little while. Okay, don't be turning all big time on us. They both laughed. Never that, y'all, my sisters for life. But girl, can you believe that? Yes, I can, Kahi'Lee, you so much deserve it. Thank you. Well, you kind of caught us at a bad time. I'm having breakfast with 2 Much right now. Oh Girl! I forgot that y'all went out on a date last night. It must have gone well; he picked you back up this early in the morning. Yo, nasty ass gave it up, didn't you? No! No! Noooo! Girl, I'll call you later, bye Kahi'Lee. Before Kahi'Lee could say something else, Click!

Emma didn't want Kahi'Lee to know, but what Kahi'Lee didn't know was Emma was still on the same date and was sitting at 2 Much breakfast table being served breakfast by 2 Much personal chef. When Emma woke up, she and 2 Much were being called to breakfast. Upon going to the kitchen, Emma noticed that not only was a chef there, but there were three maids cleaning 2 Much's Mansion. Emma wondered where in the hell did all these people come from. After they showered and bathed each other, Emma had a Valentino dress and Vera Wang high heels laying across the bed with a bra and panty set from Chanel all in her size and that blew her mind. On their way to the kitchen, Emma kept asking 2 Much how and where her clothes came from. 2 Much just laughed and said, "Any man should know his woman's size and taste in clothes." Emma seemed overwhelmed by everything that 2 Much had done because she knew that he hadn't left his bed all night. Because he had held her all night and morning until the knock at his bedroom door awoke them both. Emma didn't know what to think because he didn't seem to be shocked by it. She just hoped that it wasn't his wife to shoot them both. When Emma saw the table set for the both of them, she thought that the chef and maids would be joining them, because every type of breakfast food was laid out across the table. Emma thought that if he was still trying to impress her, he had already surpassed that stage. Even though the dinner table was so long, the main thing that Emma loved about 2 Much was everything that he did with her was up close and personal. Just like now, 2 Much sat right next to Emma, engaging in a mature conversation, looking Emma right in the eyes, taking in every word he or she spoke. Emma didn't see any signs of any drug dealer. She just felt that maybe he had made it so big that he didn't even have to touch the drugs anymore.

Emma was so happy that she wasn't the one to bring up the topic of their lifestyle. Because 2 Much asked Emma what she does for a living, Emma said that she works for the Electric company. I'm the one to oversee people's collective payments and turning off your power or restoring it after you pay your bill if it gets shut off. 2 Much shook his head and asked Emma if she enjoyed her job. Yeah, I do. I just wished that it had paid me more money. Well, what about you, Mr. Rich man? Oh no! Please don't let this little stuff fool you. I'm far from rich. Man, I think you mean the opposite, that you're far from being broke. That's what makes me wonder why you want to be with somebody that's broke like I am. 2 Much grabbed Emma's hand and placed it over her heart, beautiful woman when you got a heart like yours, then you're never broke. You just ain't listening to what your heart is asking you for. Me, I did. My heart told me is all I'm missing is you in my life. Before Emma could allow her emotions to set in and start tearing up, 2 Much reached over and kissed her on the lips.

Emma told 2 Much a little more about herself, and then she said, "Okay, enough about me. What is it that you do for a living because it seems to be treating you well." 2 Much laughed. I'm a neighborhood tax collector. What! What is that? After the rich rob the poor, I go and collect what the rich owe the poor: taxes, baby. Taxes! To Emma's surprise, whatever 2 Much had just told her, it made him laugh nonstop uncontrollably. That made Emma laugh at something that she didn't even know why she was laughing. 2 Much asked Emma if she'd go with him to Atlanta, Georgia. Her eyes got big from just even hearing Atlanta. Baby I would love to, but I already made plans with my sisters. 2 Much told her that he understood. Maybe we can take a trip together when I come home. Emma smiled; that sounds great. Why don't we do that? Okay! I'll see what I can put together for us. You know that I'm going to miss you. That made 2 Much smile to even hear Emma say that. That told him that she was feeling him. I'll miss you too, sexy, but I won't be gone too long. Maybe I'll bring you something from ATL back. Emma kissed him and smiled. 2 Much removed an envelope from his shirt pocket and gave Emma $5,000 before he dropped her off. He told her to go shopping and buy herself something nice to wear for their trip when he got back. Emma kissed 2 Much at her doorstep passionately, making sure that she stayed on his mind. Emma watched as he drove away in his Lamborghini Aventador S.V.J.

Emma counted the money for the second time and wondered what she had gotten herself into dealing with 2 Much. She knew that Fuzzi, Ashley, and Kahi'Lee go think that she is going a bit overboard when she tells them about her date. Emma didn't want to lose her trust with her girlfriends even though she could hear Ashley say, girl, forget them. You better not lose no man. Hell, give him to me, I'll date his ass. Emma laughed because she knew how Ashley thought. But on the other hand, Fuzzi and Kahi'Lee would say, bitch fucked that we are robbing that motherfucker. Emma's emotions were all over the place because deep down inside, she knew that she already was developing feelings for 2 Much. He treated her better in one day than any man had before in her entire life, and her mind, body, and heart wanted to experience more of what he had to offer. Emma turned on the television, something that she never got a chance to watch. She was flicking through the channels and a story on the news caught her attention. Six African American men did a home invasion a few months back on a billionaire who was throwing a party at his home, and two men were killed while the home invasion was taking place. Mr. William Lehmann of Abusan Real Estate lost his driver and dear close friend, along with a guest who attended his party that night. The robbers got away with a non-disclosed amount of jewelry, cash and diamonds. Emma put her hand over her mouth, damn! I wish that were us. Somebody came up. Mr. William Lehmann is offering Five Million Dollars to help find and get these men convicted. We'll keep updating you on this story as it comes in. I'm Mark Kenzinger with Fox10 News.

Emma thought about 2 Much home and the way he was living. She knew that if she and the Foxes could catch a break like she had just seen on the news, they could be living just like that, too. Emma knew that she wouldn't need 2 Much or any other man. That put her back in the frame of mind Foxes over penises and relationships. No man would piss and mark his territory in Emma's domain.

Chapter Fifteen
HOLD ON TO IT

Tyler had finally gotten the break, and he received a call from Mr. Pakulski for a modeling job. Tyler was excited because the job would pay good money. He knew this was the way to win Kahi'Lee back. The GQ magazine had seen photos of Tyler and agreed to allow him to do a photoshoot. Mr. Pakulski had called in a favor from an old friend. Tyler needed to go by the condominium and retrieve some clothes. He kept trying to call Kahi'Lee, but she kept rejecting his phone calls. The messages that Tyler left for her, Kahi'Lee, didn't even bother to listen to them. When they got into a fight, and Tyler went to jail, upon being released from jail, the Judge ordered Tyler to stay away from Kahi'Lee. He also told Tyler that if he needed to go back to their home to make sure he called the police officer to accompany him back into their home. Tyler pulled up in front of their condominium, and he saw Kahi'Lee putting a bag of clothes into her vehicle. He still wondered who Lexus 430 she was driving. Seeing her made him smile, and she looked so beautiful.

But seeing her driving another man's car put anger back inside him. Tyler didn't want to go back to jail again, so he kept his composure and got control of his temper. He had a photo shoot that he needed to get to. He figured that after Kahi'Lee left, he could just grab some clothes and leave. Tyler figured that he would call Kahi'Lee later and give her the good news. Tyler watched as Kahi'Lee drove away and waited until she left. He pulled into their driveway and exited his vehicle. He looked around to make sure that Kahi'Lee hadn't forgotten something and was coming back, if she did, he knew that he would get busted. So, he started moving faster, already getting his key ready to unlock the door.

Hello Tyler! One of their neighbors spoke to him as she headed to her vehicle. "Hi Brittany! Good morning. How you doing?" Oh, I've been fine and am on my way to work. I'll talk to you later. He waved at her and walked to the door. Tyler stuck his key into the door and couldn't believe that it still worked. He smiled and walked into the house. He started gathering a few clothes after learning the locks hadn't changed. That gave Tyler some hope that he hadn't completely lost Kahi'Lee. He felt so comfortable that he showered and changed clothes. Tyler grabbed his bag and opened the door, getting ready to leave, when he heard Tyler Bronson get down, get down, you're under arrest for trespassing. Wait! Wait! This is my home. Man, I live here! Three police officers who had their weapons drawn placed Tyler in handcuffs and hauled him off to jail. Fuck you bitch! Tyler said to their neighbor Brittany as she watched them take him to jail.

$ $ $ $ $

Room service! Mr. Shelton went and opened the door. Hello! Good morning, Sir. Will we be setting you up this morning, Mr. Shelton, or should I leave it here by the door? No, here is fine. I'll take it from here. He tried to give the man a tip but being that they were at a five-star hotel, the service tip came out of his bill. No, thank you, Sir; please enjoy your breakfast. Mr. Shelton nodded his head and wheeled the tray into his room. Who's that, baby, room service? Yeah! Everything looks and smells good. He was removing the trays and checking out the food until Fuzzi came walking out of the bathroom completely naked with a towel wrapped around her head, making Mr. Shelton's penis come to life. Fuzzi walked up to him and noticed his erection, and she grabbed his penis. Oh, I see you still have a sweet tooth. I thought you were ordering out. He kissed her on the neck. Yeah, I did, but you do something to me every time I look at you. Fuzzi smiled and grabbed a piece of bacon. So, tell me, baby, "How long do you plan on hiding in this hotel?" She put the rest of her bacon in Mr. Shelton's mouth. Until I get that slut out of my house, or my divorce is final. Hell, you can buy your own hotel by the time all that happens. Come on now, do you really think that she's going to walk away that easily? Fuzzi's words played around in Mr. Shelton's head a little because Dolly promised him that she wasn't leaving him, and he wasn't leaving her.

For the last few months, Mr. Shelton had been meeting Fuzzi at the hotel for sex. Every time that she showed up, her gifts seemed to get more expensive each time. That's not counting the large amount of cash that he kept putting in her bra. Fuzzi told him that she doesn't allow men to sleep over in her bed, so if he wanted to wake up next to her, he had to buy them a home or keep paying that hotel bill. Mr. Shelton promised Fuzzi that his divorce was going to happen much faster than Dolly or Fuzzi could expect it to happen. Mr. Shelton told Fuzzi that his wife had signed a prenuptial agreement, so she wouldn't be leaving with anything that he didn't give or offer her. They sat down and finally enjoyed their breakfast together. Fuzzi wasn't expecting Mr. Shelton to do what he was about to do. He walked up to her and kneeled down on one knee. Fuzzi, I know everything has been happening really fast between us, but like I said before, there's something about you that completes me. I feel like there's nothing that I can't do with you by my side. I think about you all day until I see you again. The real truth is, what I'm trying to say is, I believe, no, I know that I love you. Fuzzi's eyes got real big; she stood up and said, "Dave, I know that your wife just hurt you, and right now, I know that you're a little confused right now. Maybe after your divorce is finalized and you still feel that way, then maybe I can believe that you really do love me." But I can't allow you to hurt me and play with my mind because yours is a little cloudy right now.

Mr. Shelton walked over to his suit coat and removed something. Fuzzi was trying to tell him that she wasn't trying to hurt his feelings. But he dropped down on one knee and showed Fuzzi the biggest diamond that she had ever seen up close. Ok then, uncloud my mind, Fuzzi. "Will you marry me? I love you?" Fuzzi didn't expect everything to go this far between her and Mr. Shelton. In fact, she hadn't even realized that she had any type of feelings for or towards him. But his proposal caught Fuzzi off guard and unexpectedly. Tears started rolling down her face. Man, you're serious, aren't you? I am serious as the first day that I asked you out. Fuzzi grabbed the ring out of the box, and she stared at it for a long time. Mr. Shelton was the second man in her whole life to ever ask Fuzzi to marry them. The first was Micheal Minghella, a millionaire. The man who paid for Fuzzi's sex change operation. Fuzzi thought about him right now while she stared at Mr. Shelton's ring. She snapped out of the last moment she had spent with Michael. She told Mr. Shelton the same thing that she told Mr. Michael Minghella. She handed Mr. Shelton his ring back, here! I'm not saying no but you're still married right now. When you get a divorce, I'll wait for you to ask me that same question again. Until that happens, you hold onto this for us and I'll be waiting. Mr. Shelton smiled. He was happy that Fuzzi didn't say no. He stood up and kissed Fuzzi on the lips for the first time, and to his surprise, Fuzzi allowed him to, and she kissed him back in the mouth. Fuzzi always told him that she didn't kiss men in that way. But this kiss meant a lot to them both right at that moment. Fuzzi knew that the last time she spoke those words to Michael, he died right after he left her because his wife shot him four times because she found out that Michael was sleeping with another man and had paid for him to have a sex change. Michael had bought Fuzzi flowers and a card. After Fuzzi had her operation, and they met up like they always do, Fuzzi accidentally left the card in his convertible Bentley after she gave him a blow job.

The next day, his wife drove the car and found the card. James, I just want to say thank you for making me the happiest man in the world. I want you to know that the first night that I picked you up, I knew that you were born a male, but that didn't stop me from getting to know you. In fact, that night I spent with you was the greatest sex that I ever had in my entire life. That money that I gave you to have your operation was worth every penny. Tomorrow, after my wife gets served with the divorce papers, after they're finalized, then you can accept that ring that you told me to hold on to. I can't wait until we walk down that aisle together. Then you won't be James Armstrong anymore. You will be Sabrina Renee Minghella. No, please excuse me. You'll be Mrs. Sabrina Renee Minghella. Fuzzi called and called but never got any answer. Michael never called her again after she left him that day. It wasn't until she was in a motel dating a trick is when the news showed his home and wife in a standoff. It was his convertible Bentley in front of the mansion is what caught Fuzzi's attention. She was watching on live television when Micheal's wife shot him and then turned the gun on herself. Pow! Pow! Pow! Pow! Pow!

Chapter Sixteen
TELL MAMA I SAID BYE

Fuzzi, Emma, and Kahi'Lee were on American Airlines headed to Louisiana. They were sharing their experiences with the male figures in their lives. Kahi'Lee had them laughing at how stupid Tyler was by getting himself arrested after the Judge ordered him to stay away from her. He had thought that he was being nice to one of their neighbors, but she turned out to be the one to call the police on him. They all had got a big laugh out of that story. Then Kahi'Lee talked about how she couldn't wait for the commercial she shot to come out. Girl, I'm going to be on television. Can y'all believe that? Everyone was excited that Kahi'Lee had gotten the break she wanted, but when Emma started talking about 2 Much, that's when she got everybody's attention, even the female that sat on the plane in front of them. Eaves had dropped in on Emma's conversation. The way that Emma had explained her date, it was like she was explaining every woman's knight in shining armor. Fuzzi had even taken Emma to have her necklace appraised by a jeweler that Fuzzi knew. He told Emma that the necklace was worth $35,000 but she could get up to $50,000 with the right buyer. Emma told them about his home, private chef and maids. Fuzzi asked Emma were there any signs of a woman living there. Emma told her that she got a chance to walk in his closet while he got dressed but all she saw was male clothes and shoes. He was too comfortable and relaxed with her being there for a woman to live there. Fuzzi told Emma trust me Bitch, most men don't give a damn where their woman is when their eyes are focused on a new vagina that they ain't eating, sniffed, or fucked yet.

The female sitting in front of them couldn't help but join in their conversation. She turned around and said, "Girl, ain't that the truth." Fuzzi said, "No! The real truth is Bitchhhh! You know he is fucked! Get you some business and earphones your way out of our conversation." Emma and Kahi'Lee put their hands over their mouth and face, embarrassed at Fuzzi's comment. The woman gave Fuzzi a nasty look and turned back around. She put her headphones back on, and Emma, Fuzzi, and Kahi'Lee all laughed. Thirsty ass bitch! By the time Emma shared 2 Much intimacy with her when Emma had finished talking and repeated the things that he said to her, plus told them how he just held her all night without even trying to even sex her nude body that laid on top of him. Fuzzi and Kahi'Lee were ready to go to the bathroom because both of their vagina's were nice and wet. What made them both hate to hear Emma's story about her date was that she told them that 2 Much didn't want her to ever leave him. That lifestyle she had shared with them, he also offered it to her. She made all of their hearts beat when she said, girl, he asked me to go to Atlanta, Ga, with him. But Fuzzi stole the whole conversation when she told them that. Mr. Shelton asked her to marry him with the ring and all. Emma and Kahi'Lee both grabbed their chest. What! Are you serious? I thought that he was already married. Emma hit Fuzzi, Bitch! You gave that old white man some pussy, didn't you? Fuzzi said, "Bitch, is you crazy!" Hell, naw, I ain't gave him no pussy, but I did sale him some, though. Kahi'Lee asked Fuzzi, "what did you say?" Fuzzi lied and said I told him hell to the naw, bitch. They all sat back and enjoyed the plane ride, but their minds were on 2 Much, Tyler, and Mr. Shelton because they were missing them. As much as they all pretended not to care much for any of them, they all cared about them more than they wanted each other to know how they truly felt.

$ $ $ $ $

CSI and homicide investigators were coming in and out of the house. When Ashley pulled up in her Jaguar, she exited her vehicle after she grabbed her badge off of her rearview mirror. A police officer was about to tell her that she couldn't come over to the house, but when she held up her badge, he quickly realized that Ashley was there to pick up the two little kids. A man had come home from work and shot his wife and killed her in front of their two kids, which were

5 and 7-year-old girls. A female officer was trying to comfort the two kids until Ashley showed up. Ashley introduced herself to the female officer, then she kneeled and introduced herself to the two kids. Hi! Wow, you guys are sure some pretty little girls, what's y'all name? The 5-year-old Spanish girl stepped back and hid behind her sister. She held onto her arm. I'm Ashley, what's your name? The 7-year-old said, "don't worry about Heather; she shy, but I'm not." My name is Bonetha, and that's Heather. Ashley and the police lady smiled at each other. My daddy killed my mommy, and she was fighting and biting him. That made Ashley stop smiling because she knew that Bonetha had stood there and watched her father kill her mother. Ashley knew that the two girls would wind up going through years of therapy behind what they saw. Then the little girl asked Ashley, ma'am, "Is our mommy going to be ok?" That's when Ashley realized that the little girl really didn't know what the word killed meant. Ashley thought that maybe she was repeating what one of the police officers said. Ashley looked at the girl, not really knowing how to answer the question. Maybe we'll just have to let the police officer do their job, and then we'll see what happens. I'm going to take you and your sister to call someone to get y'all, okay? The little girl grabbed her sister's hand, okay, come on, Heather. Is that your car, it's nice? Yeah, that's my car; you and your sister are going to get to ride in it. You want to ride in it? Yeah, could I drive? No, not yet; you better let me do that so we can make it there safe. Ashley and the police officer shook hands, and she helped Ashley put the girls in her car. Ashley reached into her purse and pulled out

two blow pop suckers. Here Bonetha, she grabbed the sucker and said, "thank you." Well, I know that you're not talking to me, but do you want a sucker? She shook her head yeah and took it out of Ashley's hands like the matrix. Ashley busted up laughing and strapped them to her vehicle.

$ $ $ $ $

Fuzzi stood at the rental car desk fighting with a half-breed, man you better look out for us with your handsome self. Maybe the next time I come to Louisiana, it might just be to come visit your fine ass. The guy smiled and took in Fuzzi's figure. Damn! No disrespect, Ms. Armstrong, but you are beautiful. I'd love for you to come and visit me. Well, let me see how you treat a girl. Maybe that might just happen, and thanks for the compliment. They smiled at each other and his fingers got busy on his computer. Emma said, "Aye, where all the good spots at to party and eat around here? The spot where all the ballers and players at making it rain. Babydolls be off the hook and the Pink Devil. Y'all got to check out the hub shack, and they got that mouthwatering food. But we have so many spots to eat out here. This is Louisiana shawty. Hit up the French quarters, all the spots down there. Ya heard me! I heard you. They all started laughing at Emma, trying to sound like him. Ms. Armstrong, here you go; I got your reservations right here. I see that you reserved two Corvettes and a Cadillac SUV. Let me see what I can do to get you a much better price. He tapped in a few more keys, okay, there we go. What I did was charge you the price of a small compact vehicle. Now, that would take the price to almost half of what you paid. Fuzzi smiled and looked at Emma and Kahi'Lee. Wow! I see you are trying to get a visit from a girl. Write your number on one of the invoices, and who knows, you just might get a phone call while I'm here now. He pulled out one of his business cards and slid it to Fuzzi. She read the card. Okay, Mr. Marcus Epps, you might can be my personal guide if I get lost. He told Fuzzi that he'd be her personal anything.

Fuzzi, Emma and Kahi'Lee all grabbed their luggage and headed to their rental cars. This time, Fuzzi drove the Cadillac Escalade and let Emma and Kahi'Lee drive the Corvettes. They went and checked into their hotel and discussed putting their plan together. Emma ordered pizza and wings because neither of them didn't feel like going out to eat. After eating pizza and drinking Monet, Fuzzi, Emma, and Kahi'Lee, all fell asleep and didn't get a chance to explore New Orleans. Fuzzi was the first one to wake up the next morning. She looked at Emma lying across the bed in her blue panties and no bra. Fuzzi laughed because she already knew how they all felt about bras. She walked into the next adjoined room that they also had and saw Kahi'Lee wrapped up like a mummy under the covers. They had got so full of food and liquor that they didn't even take their luggage out of the rental cars. Fuzzi wanted to take a shower, so she put her dress back on and headed to get her luggage. Fuzzi grabbed the key to the Cadillac Escalade and went towards the parking lot. On her way walking across the parking lot, she heard loud music and turned around, only to find the front end of a Lamborghini inches from her back leg. Urrrrrrr! The Lamborghini came to a complete stop, but it still made Fuzzi jump out the way, trying to prevent from being hit by the Lamborghini. Man, what you trying to do? Kill me? Are you crazy? The driver turned down his music and said, "Sexy, I'm sorry you have to forgive my car; it's got a mind of its own." When it sees someone as attractive and beautiful as you are, I don't know if it does something to my motor or me. He smiled, showing off a mouthful of diamond teeth.

Well, I think it's you because you're the one driving the car. What you do, ride around all day trying to run down, pretty woman? Naw Shawty! I ride around all day stacking this. He held up a wad of cash wrapped around a rubber band that made Fuzzi's vagina tingle. Shawty, excuse me, let me make my introduction more appropriate. The Lambo door went up, and the man exited his vehicle. Hello, beautiful lady, my name is Popa Dolla, and yours, sexy? Hi, I'm Fuzzi. You are not from around here, huh? Why you say that? Shawty, I know everybody in the pit, and we ain't never met before. No. I'm not from here. I'm just here on vacation, and if you don't run over me, I'll make it home safe. Where is home? I'm from Seattle. Oh, now I see why you are so sexy. I'm blowing some of that humble county right now. Fuzzi didn't have any idea as to where Humble County was in Seattle, so she played it off. I smoke a little bit every now and then. Yeah, my boy, be sending me some from out of that Portland area. Now Fuzzi knew that Humble County was in Portland. Oh yeah! So, how long you go be out here? Maybe we can get to know each other much better. You not out here with your man, are you? Nope, I don't have one of them yet. I'm out here with a few of my girlfriends. Damn! You brung some more females that look like you out here? Yeah, they all beautiful ladies, just like me. Mmmmmm! So, what's up? Can we hook up or what? I got a few soldiers that I can hook them up with. Baby, we don't do soldiers. My sisters don't deal with anything but bosses. Well, that means that I will be taking all y'all out then because I'm the only boss in this town that I know. I ain't mad at you. If you don't feel that way about yourself, then why should anyone else? Naw shawty! For real. If you knew who Popa Dolla was, then you'd be saying the same thing.

Well, I'll let my vacation here determine that. Aye, I got a room up in here so why don't you come holla at me? Let's blow something and get to know each other. What suite you in? Didn't I tell you that I was a boss? Yeah, what does that mean? Popa Dolla headed back to his vehicle and sat back in the car. He put the Lamborghini in reverse. Shawty, I don't know what type of bosses you been around, but everything is Presidential with me. I'll see you after you get your act together. He turned his music back up then, backed up then drove away. Fuzzi put a smile on her face. Her mind went back to when Do Dirty first turned her out. He said real bitches don't look for tricks to get their money; tricks will find a bitch that he wants to spend his money on. Fuzzi almost skip all the way to her rental car. By the time she came walking back into the room, Emma and Kahi'Lee were already up. Girl, we were wondering where you went to. Why didn't you grab our stuff? It's because I ain't a mule. Get y'all asses to them cars. Ya heard. They all laughed. Fuzzi started telling them about the dude who exposed a wad of cash to her. Fuzzi said that he claimed to be a boss. When I get through with his punk ass, he go be looking for a job. They all slapped hands and started getting dressed. Before Fuzzi headed to Popa Dolla's hotel room, she had Emma and Kahi'Lee go take pictures of his Lambo. She knew that she had to go and season the turkey before she put it in the oven. If her ass is what got his attention, then Fuzzi made sure that he would stay mesmerized by it. Fuzzi put on a body Gucci catsuit and some Gucci diamond heels that matched her earrings and purse. She knew that she was about to be his little eye candy for the day. Anybody that was somebody under his feet, he was about to introduce her to them. The thing about Fuzzi was that it gave her the upper hand over men, and they didn't know that she was born a man and knew just how they think and talk. Fuzzi lightly tapped on Popa Dolla's door. Turned out that he was in the Presidential suite which Fuzzi wasn't impressed with at all. He opened the door, turned, and walked away. Fuzzi didn't know it but he was on his cell phone talking business. Fuzzi walked in as he summoned her to come in and close the door. He was going back and forth with somebody over prices that they were going to pay him for his product. He kept saying I can do 10,5 a piece all depends on how many. His last words to the dude were then you talking about 50. I'll see you tomorrow at the same place as the last time. Click! Sorry Shawty, you know I got to stay at this spinach. Damn! Look at you, shawty, turn around. Look like you then melt yourself in that outfit. Fuzzi turned around slowly so he could lust his little heart out.

Hey, shawty, have you had breakfast yet? Nope. I had just woke up when you tried to kill me. Awe, he rolled back in his chair, laughing. You ain't go let me get away with that, is you shawty? Baby, I'm not trying to hurt you. I'm about to spoil you, Ms. Seattle, you just don't know it yet. Is that right? Yeah, Popa Dolla, lovin your style, Shawty. Fuzzi smiled, but she wanted to slap the shit out of him if he called her Shawty one more time. Yeah, breakfast sounds good. I ain't got to be out here fighting your woman or wife, do I? Shawty, somebody hurt a hair on your head, and I'll be trying to send them to meet their maker, shawty. Okay, then, I'm all yours then. Don't tell me that because I take a man and woman at their word. I'm all yours then. Fuzzi gave him a seductive look. He stood up, placed his hand on her back, and allowed his hand to find her butt. Fuzzi didn't say anything; that's when she knew that the bait on the hook had made the fisherman feel like he had the fish that he had been sitting and waiting for. Come on, shawty, we out of here. Popa Dolla was feeling himself, sitting next to what he felt was going to be his queen to make him shine on his thrown like a King. Popa Dolla did just as Fuzzi thought he would do. Everywhere he took Fuzzi his chest was puffed up like a mad toddler. Fuzzi didn't disappoint Popa Dolla's ego at all. She allowed the touching and popping on the ass and helped him shine. The part that bothered Fuzzi was when he introduced her to his mother. Turned out that Fuzzi and his mom hit it off better than they did. He kept telling his mother that Fuzzi was going to be her daughter-in-law. To Fuzzi's surprise, Popa Dolla, whom she learned his real name was Kenneth Trotter, didn't have a bunch of kids and baby mamas. He spoiled and treated his mother, Mary, like a queen, and Fuzzi loved that. But Fuzzi thought to herself, sorry Mary, but I'm the next queen that he's about to spoil. Before they left his mother's house, she told Fuzzi, "girl, he must really like you because he ain't never brung no female over here." Y'all look good together. Don't be no stranger, and take care of Kenneth, you hear me? Fuzzi kissed her on the cheek and promised she'd come back. But when it came to Kenneth Fuzzi didn't make any promises before she left. Popa Dolla was happy that Mary approved of Fuzzi, and when they left, he and Fuzzi got into a deep conversation about his lifestyle and business. Fuzzi couldn't believe that a woman he had just met a few hours ago was sitting there telling her all his business.

Popa Dolla took Fuzzi all over New Orleans, shopping and spending close to five thousand dollars on clothes and shoes. He wanted to take her to one of their clubs, and she was dressed looking like a black barbie doll. Fuzzi knew that she had to play it out until Popa Dolla completely exposed himself. Fuzzi quickly recognized where she was the moment that he pulled up to the club. The sign said the Pink Bubble, it was a strip club that was packed. Upon walking into the club, Fuzzi quickly learns the love and respect that Popa Dolla has. Everyone treated him like a hood star and made it known to Fuzzi. Females hollered at him but kept it majorly respectful. Dudes surrounded them and kept him protected. Fuzzi excused herself and went to the ladies' room, where she texted Emma and Kahi'Lee, letting them know where to come. She had already put her plan into effect. Less than an hour later, Kahi'Lee and Emma came walking into the strip club. Fuzzi had them working the club and getting at the rest of the other players. It didn't take long to see Popa Dolla's nose open wide when he acknowledged the two other females drawing attention. They were popping major bottles and making it rain on the strippers. Another dude entered the club, and Fuzzi noticed Popa Dolla's facial expression change. A lot of dudes approached him and showed respect in the same way they did Popa Dolla. Baby, everything okay? Popa Dolla didn't know that Fuzzi had sensed a change in his behavior. Oh Yeah, shawty, I'm good. Here, take some more of these ones. He handed her a handful of ones in a stack. Fuzzi kept making it rain but still kept one eye on Popa Dolla. He noticed the dude that had just come into the club was pressing up against the two females that also had just come into the club. It looked like they knew each other, but Fuzzi knew that whoever the guy was, he had to have just met Kahi'Lee and Emma in the parking lot. Fuzzi kissed Popa Dolla on the cheek, and that made him focus back on her. Popa Dolla was 6 feet tall with long, thick dread locks, a very muscular build with a full beard and a dark complexion. He favored Taye Diggs a lot but had Rick Ross style. Really when it came to stunted up in the club, Fuzzi had enough of their boring strippers, and she figured that it was time for her to take a little of their attention. Fuzzi has on a fishnet bodysuit with the mink hoodie and mink down the leg of the bodysuit. She wasn't wearing any panties or bra, just a pair of high-back gator boots past her knees. Lil Boosie & Webbie 'Bout dat' came on, and Fuzzi stood up and started dancing on Popa Dolla. Before he knew it, almost the whole club had them surrounded, and they were making it rain on Fuzzi in the club. She popped and wiggled her ass, making it buck and jump like a wild horse.

Kahi'Lee, Emma and the Dude, who have given them stacks of cash, were all making it rain on Fuzzi along with the strippers. Everybody clapped and cheered Fuzzi on after she got through dancing. Females and dudes were coming up to her, trying to pay for a table dance. The D.J. gave her a shout-out and told Fuzzi that the owner wanted to see her. Fuzzi stayed focused on her mark. She hugged Popa Dolla and turned everybody down who requested her to dance. Popa Dolla was all smiles and stood there with his chest poked out. To really show her class, Fuzzi took all the money and gave it to all the strippers. That told Popa Dolla that Fuzzi was a woman in her own class. He and Fuzzi kept enjoying themselves. Baby, who's that man you keep watching, is he a threat to us? That turned Popa Dolla on the way that she said to us. That's that nigga that owes me money, but I'm out with you, and I ain't gonna go there, shawty. Fuzzi got up in his face and went in for the kill shot, and she kissed compassionately for the first time. Well, if he owes you, I see you been eyeballing his two little bitches. Do you want me to bring them home with us? Popa Dolla's heart almost stops beating to hear Fuzzi offer him the two attractive females. Seeing them two shawty's walk away from his enemy will make him feel like a real boss playa. You not tripping off me fucking with them? Not as long as you know who your queen is. I'm down with pleasing my king. Didn't I tell you that I'm going to spoil you? Okay then, I want to spoil you too. Fuzzi kissed his lips and walked away, headed toward Emma and Kahi'Lee. She whispered something into Emma's ear, then Kahi'Lee's ear. Fuzzi went towards the bathroom, and Emma and Kahi'Lee followed her.

Popa Dolla started smiling, thinking that he had met the greatest woman in the whole world. He watched as Fuzzi came walking out of the bathroom with the two females following right behind her. Fuzzi had told Emma and Kahi'Lee what was going on and to play along. Let him think that y'all into me and with whatever I'm with. Fuzzi told them that he knew her by Fuzzi because he had caught her off guard, and she couldn't think of anything at the time. The other dude held up two drinks as they all exited the bathroom, but they walked right past him as if he wasn't standing there. Popa Dolla started laughing. Baby, this is Jasmine and Veronica. They are coming with us. She kissed Popa Dolla to pour it on think, and then she turned to Emma and Kahi'Lee. Y'all coming with me and my man? Yeah, why not you so sexy? Emma walked up to Fuzzi and kissed her. Popa Dolla tossed all the stacks of ones on the stage, and they left. He turned and smiled at the dude on the way out. Emma and Kahi'Lee drove right behind them in one of the Corvettes. Fuzzi's wheels were turning because she knew that Kahi'Lee and Emma wouldn't want to sleep with Popa Dolla. Time was running out, and she had to come up with something fast. They were getting close to the hotel, and Popa Dolla was bobbing his head to the music. Fuzzi tapped his leg, and he turned down the music, yeah, shawty.

Baby, I got to ask you an important question and be honest, okay? I won't get mad at your answer. What's that, shawty? Where do you see our relationship going? Are you trying to be my man, or do you want to just have fun tonight? Popa Dolla looked at Fuzzi seriously, baby, I told you, shawty, that it's me and you. Okay, if it's me and you then, as me being your woman how do you think I'll feel about you if I sleep with you and these females? Before me and you even get to enjoy each other's company. That question hit Popa Dolla like a ton of bricks. Damn! Shawty, you right; I didn't even think about that. I don't mind sharing you with nobody if that makes you happy, but we have to be happy first together. But if you want to be with me and them because they want to be with me, then I can't tell you that I'll want to be with you afterward. Because if you are a real man like I know you is, then I won't respect you to respect me afterwards. Popa Dolla said, "Shawty, see that's why I have to have you in my life and can't lose you." Even my mother told me I'd be a fool if I let you get away. Fuzzi looked at him and smiled. So, you not mad, are you? You do understand that I'm a real woman. Naw shawty! I ain't mad, and you are a real Queen. I'm about my money, shawty, not pussy. Them females don't mean nothing to me, but you do. Fuzzi kissed him on the cheek, pull over, baby. I'll get their numbers, and I'll make it up to you later. Popa Dolla pulled over and Fuzzi went and talked to Emma and Kahi'Lee.

The next day, after they had breakfast together, Popa Dolla took Fuzzi to his trap house and made the deal for 40 kilos. He got $525,000. Fuzzi saw where he got the kilos from and saw that it was more of them there. She figured that if he made that much money off of them, then she needed to get her hands on the rest of his drugs, also. But she knew that she couldn't take them on the airplane. Damn! Her mind raced, and that's when Fuzzi thought best. Okay, shawty, we got to come back later. I got somebody coming for 20 at 1 o'clock. Fuzzi did the math in her head. He was about to collect another $210,000. That would be $735,000, plus whatever was left over in kilos. Popa Dolla put the money in a black gym bag and put a few clothes over the money. He looked at his Rolex, shawty, we got three hours to kill. What do you want to do? Fuzzi looked at the AK47 that lay on the kitchen table. She knew what she wanted to do but she figured that she better play it cool and not allow him to take that money anywhere. If I'm going to move out here, shouldn't we find me a place to live? Popa Dolla started laughing, shawty, wherever I lay my head, that's where you're going to lay yours.

Fuzzi already knew that he didn't live with no woman. Mrs. Mary had already slipped and given up that information. After we handle this last business, we'll go back to the hotel and grab our stuff, and then we can go home, okay? Fuzzi said, "You mean my home is with you?" Shawty, your life is with me. They kissed, and Fuzzi said okay. Shawty, I think that I like that. Popa Dolla started laughing, oh, I'm, shawty, now. Baby, that's what you call me. He slapped her on the butt, come on, let's go buy you some more clothes. I'm sure that would take up a lot of time. He locked up his trap house, and they headed back to the mall, but this time really went on a shopping spree. The first chance Fuzzi got, she went into the bathroom and called Emma and Kahi'Lee. Fuzzi told them about everything that she had planned. She told Emma that she'd text her when they got to the hotel and what to do. She told Emma to move the rental cars before he recognized them driving that Corvette. Before they hung up, Emma said, girl, how do you think up this type of crazy stuff? I told you, bitch, all foxes are sly and crafty. Be ready. Click! After shopping, Popa Dolla headed back to his trap house and handled his business. Fuzzi knew that he was real smooth with handling his business. Most dealers have a gang of dudes around them, plus they always kept some dude up under them like a puppy, a yes man, a right-hand man, but not Popa Dolla, he moves solo-bolo. On their way to the hotel, Fuzzi asked him, "Why don't you got dudes all around you watching your back?" Shawty, that shit overrated. The homeboy shit, Naw! Every man out here is trying to come up just like me. I've served time before, shawty. The same nigga that was under me all day, that I ate with and would die for, was the same motherfucker that turned State's evidence on me. If I can't trust you, then I don't fuck with you. That's why I wasn't living with no woman either. I seem them turn a nigga in, too, and go sleep with the next man that's Ballin'.

That's crazy, baby! I'd never betray you or turn you into no police. I'd leave you first if you didn't want me. Popa Dolla said, "I knew you were a different type of woman when you left that money on the floor at the strip club." Let's grab our stuff and go home. After you beat this pussy up first. Popa Dolla smiled. Look at you now. You already reading my mind. They jumped out of his Lambo and went to go have sex. Fuzzi went to the bathroom and texted Emma. Fuzzi came out of the bathroom and started kissing Popa Dolla and massaging his penis. He felt his manhood come to life in her hands. Mmmmmm! Yeah, baby! You go fuck me and teach me a lesson, baby? Fuzzi removed his penis and slowly jacked him off. She started removing his clothes, and he pulled his shirt over his head. He kicked off his Jordans and allowed Fuzzi to remove his pants. She dropped down to the floor and removed one leg at a time. Fuzzi reached up, grabbed his penis, and guided it into her mouth. She licked at his head and then slowly allowed him to enter her mouth. By the time Fuzzi started taking him whole, Popa Dolla was grabbing her hair and forcing his penis down her throat. Mmmmm! Mmmmm! Yes, shawty! Suck Daddy dick! Suck it! Fuzzi took it out of her mouth and looked at him, Daddyyyyyy! I've been a bad girl, Daddy! Dog me out, Daddy, make your bitch mind you. Popa Dolla was starting to get more turned on by the way Fuzzi was talking to him than the head that Fuzzi was just giving him. She put his penis back into her mouth and allowed him to fuck her mouth like it was a vagina. Fuzzi stayed with him all the way. After she felt him about to climax, she stopped. No, daddy! Noooo! Don't bust yet, yo bitch been bad; teach me, daddy! Choke the shit out of me and dog yo pussy out. Fuzzi stood up and whipped her silk Prada shirt off. She threw it on the floor and unzipped her mini-skirt. It fell down on the floor. Fuzzi ripped her panties off. Everything she was doing was turning Popa Dolla on. Fuzzi laid on the bed holding her panties in her hand. Come punish me, daddy! Punish your bitch! Popa Dolla slid her and started slamming his penis up in her like he wanted to see it pop out of her chest. Mmmmm! Yeah! Yeah! Yeah! Daddy! Teach me, Daddy! Oooh, Yeah Ahhhhhhah! Yes, Baby! Mmmmm! Choke me, daddy!

Popa Dolla looked at Fuzzi like she was crazy. Choke me, daddy, make me cum. Fuzzi grabbed his hands and put it around her neck. Choke me, daddy, Pleaseee! Punish me! Popa Dolla started choking her and thrusting his penis in and out of Fuzzi. Ooooooo! Oooo! Why! Why daddy! Why you treating me like this? No daddy! Nooo! Noooo! Please! Please! Please! Stop! Stop! Stop! You're hurting me. Ahhhhhhhh! Fuzzi started screaming. Bammm! Bammm! Bammm! New Orleans Police open up. Bammm! Bammm! Bammm! Ahhhhhh! Ahhhh! No, stopppp! Boom! The hotel door flew open, and Popa Dolla was choking Fuzzi when the police busted up in the room. Popa Dolla jumped up. Get down! Get Down! New Orleans Police. Get down! A few police officers had their weapons drawn on Popa Dolla. Fuzzi jumped up, crying. See, I told you nooooo. Why you do this to me? I hate you! I hate you! She screamed it loudly in his face. Fuzzi grabbed her shirt and put it on. She got her shirt and tried to cover up, but it was all ripped up. Bitch what the fuck are you talking about? You better stop playing and tell them the truth. Popa Dolla went to grab his pants, but the police grabbed him and cuffed him. Popa Dolla started trying to fight with them. Man, y'all got this all wrong. Ma'am, are you okay? Yeah, I am now.

My boyfriend kidnapped and forced me to come here to have sex with him. Popa Dolla tried to rush Fuzzi, bitch, you are lying. That bitch is lying, man. Fuzzi squatted down and started crying harder. Man, I just met her yesterday, that bitch lying, mannn. Popa Dolla was screaming! The police searched his pants, and they held them. Put them on. They started walking him out the door. Ma'am, look at my wallet, my I.D. in there. She is lying. I'm not her boyfriend; she doesn't even know me. The police stopped at the door and pulled out his ID. He removed it and showed it to another police officer. Ma'am, you said this is your boyfriend. Can you tell us his name? Popa Dolla just knew that they would have to uncuff him. Yes, Sir, It's Keith Trotter. Popa Dolla heard his name and almost had a heart attack. They looked at each other and took him toward their police car. They took Fuzzi's statement, and she refused to take a rape kit or go to the hospital. The police told her that he'll get charged with rape and kidnapping, but it could easily get dropped if she didn't cooperate. Emma and Kahi'Lee came to the door. Is my sister okay? Is she okay? A police officer took them to her. They all hugged, and Emma said, "See, what I told you, girl, you need to leave Keith alone, mama going crazy." When the police asked Fuzzi for her information, she gave them a fake name and Keith's mother's address and phone number. She grabbed her stuff and his car keys. After the police left, they went and got his black gym bag, went back to his trap house, and took the other 46 kilos. Fuzzi took her lipstick and wrote on the mirror of his trap house, tell mama that I said bye, and I'll come visit her soon, okay, shawty? Fuzzi returned the two Corvettes, and they drove the Cadillac Escalade back to Arizona and $735,000 in cash and 46 kilos of cocaine.

Chapter Seventeen
NEVER AGAIN IN LIFE

Y'all need to stop cheating. I saw you Vicki, pass her that card. What! We not cheating, Izzi. Okay! Stand up. For what, girl, we don't have to cheat y'all to win. That's you and Caroline who be cheating. Stand up then, Vicki. She tried to knock the Joker on her lap, but it fell on the floor when she stood up. Dirty ass bitch! Look, I knew y'all was cheating. I'm not paying y'all shit. Y'all been cheating the whole time. Vicki started laughing. Damn! Carla, Yo, punk ass didn't even try to distract them, while I bitch, hide the card. That ain't my fault that yo slow old ass got busted cheating. They all busted up laughing. Ok! Okkkk! Izzi, that game is y'all's since you playing inspector gadget on a bitch. Izzi and Caroline won the $10.00 pot. Dawson 58224, you got a visit. Ahhhhh Man! Shit! We were about to get our money back. Now you got a damn visit. That's okay. We will finish kicking that ass when I get back. Just grab another partner, Caroline. No! No! No! Noooo! Caroline, you wait until I get back. Cellie, you know I'm not about to play with anybody else but you. Izzi and Caroline slapped hands, and she went and got ready for her visit.

Izzi had gotten her hair braided and was looking like a white Aleshia Keys. Ever since Izzi had taught Big Girl a lesson about bothering her, Izzi had become a whole new person, but Big Girl wind up being taken out of their pod. Three other girls had gotten sick of her bullying them, and they all jumped her in the dayroom. They came and got her on a stretcher and took the three females to the hole.

$ $ $ $ $

Hi Mrs. Dawson! I'm sorry that I didn't get back up here to see you; I want to have a sit down with the prosecutor first before I even come to see you. Hello Mr. Shelton, good to see you. I knew that whenever you were ready or had something that you'd be down to see me. Well, I got some good news, but I don't want you to get excited until the Judge accepts my motion on your behalf. Izzi sat up in her seat, waiting to hear what he was about to say next. Well, Mrs. Dawson, I filed a motion the other day to have all charges dismissed against you. Izzi put her hands over her face and started crying. Thank you! Thank you! Thank you, Mr. Shelton. Well, we got to wait for five business days to see how the Judge ruled on the dismissal. But what I presented to the Judge at this point, the prosecutor doesn't seem to be fighting it too much, but he is asking if it's possible at all to be dismissed without prejudice. Meaning that it can be refiled at a later date. Izzi just stared at Mr. Shelton, so you mean they're going to arrest me again and charge me with murder? He shook his head yes that it could happen if they refile. If they do that, are you still going to be my lawyer? Well, let's not get ahead of ourselves. One thing at a time.

Let's just get you out of here first, and they might not even refile. Mrs. Dawson, do you believe in God? Yes! I go to church, me and my husband. Well, at least we used to. Well, Mrs. Dawson, you had better start doing a lot of praying. Izzi shook her head okay. Have you told my friends? Not yet, I'm still your lawyer and have to confide in you first. Besides, I do believe that Ms. Armstrong is out of town on vacation or business. Izzi sensed him missing Fuzzi in the way that he said it. Maybe you can call and contact her because I didn't get any answer when I called. He almost wanted to tell Izzi to have Fuzzi call him whenever she contacted Fuzzi, but he thought twice about it and didn't. Well, if I hear anything any time soon, I'll come back and talk to you about it. But Mrs. Dawson, if they release you, make sure that you call or come see me. Fuzzi maybe can bring you into my office. Izzi was just glad to hear the words getting released that she didn't know what to think or how to act. Well, good luck, Mrs. Dawson. Go back and get some girls and pray. Thank you again so much for everything, Mr. Shelton. Well, if anything goes against us right now, don't be disappointed. Something similar came up about your husband when he was much younger. Besides that, I'm still with you, and we got a good case. Mr. Shelton grabbed his briefcase and walked out of the room. Izzi burst into tears, but she started praying right there in the visiting room.

$ $ $ $ $

Fuzzi and Kahi'Lee had drifted off to sleep and left Emma behind the wheel, driving them back to Arizona, but she was getting sleepy herself. They all had been taking turns driving from Louisiana, and it was Emma's turn. But she had gotten a little heavy foot from getting tired and was speeding. Trying to drive the speed limit with the vehicle on cruise control was making Emma's body get a little too relaxed, so she took it off and drove the truck regularly by pushing the gas pedal. Whoop!! Whoop! Whoop! Fuzzi, Kahi'Lee, y'all wake up; we're being pulled over by the highway patrol. Fuzzi jumped up and all of their hearts were beating fast. Bitch! Why are they pulling you over, were you swerving or speeding? No, I don't think I was. What if they are looking for money and drugs? Fuzzi and Kahi'Lee were already thinking the same thing. Damn, bitch! I can't be sucking on no vaginas for 25 years. I'm too pretty, they go be passing me around all night. Emma was pulling over to the side of the highway. They were in New Mexico. Bitch don't be acting nervous. Just be your normal self. They can't be searching this truck girl, or we all going to prison. Rip your panties, rip your panties, Bitch! What, Fuzzi, are you crazy?

Bitch, they put them cuffs on your ass, you go be looking crazy. Okay! Oka! Okayyy! I'm ripping them, I'm ripping them, Fuzzi damn. I can't even do it; Emma started panicking because the two officers were exiting their patrol car. How many of them are coming? It's two! It's two! Kahi'Lee, rip your panties too and spread y'all legs open. Make sure that they can see some pussy bitch. Fuzzi had already ripped her panties. They were all wearing dresses.

Hi, Hello officer, did I do something wrong? Yes, Ma'am, you were speeding back there. What! Oh! I'm so sorry, please forgive me. The officer was flashing his flashlight throughout the vehicle. May I see your driver's license and insurance, ma'am? Mmmm! Yeah, let me see. She asked Kahi'Lee to pass her purse. Now, Emma can see that the police were taking Fuzzi's bait because he was shining his flashlight right between her legs and trying to catch a better look. His partner started tapping on Kahi'Lee's window and asking to see her ID. Emma gave him her driver's license and the rental agreement. Ma'am, you must not have rented the vehicle; the name says Murchison. Oh, that's my girlfriend, she is right behind me. Excuse me, sir, can I roll down my window? Fuzzi said that in her most sexiest voice. Yes, ma'am, you can. He stepped back, placing his hand on his gun until Fuzzi rolled down the window. Fuzzi held up her driver's license, and as he reached for it, she gave him a nice clear view of a clean Brazilian shaved vagina.

The officer smiled at Fuzzi, letting her know I see that fat chocolate vagina. It made the officer ask them, excuse me, are you ladies' dancers? Emma was about to say no, but Fuzzi said yes; how did you know? How are the strip clubs out here? Can a girl make a lot of money? Yeah, I bet y'all coming to dance at the Foxy Tail. Yeah, are the men nice gentlemen there? Hey, Bruce, they are in town to dance at the Foxy Tail. Fuzzi didn't know if she had just made a big mistake by saying that name. The way that the officer got excited and told his partner. Had the officer just tricked them into telling a lie? Hey, maybe we'll see y'all there Saturday night. One of our buddies is having a big birthday party there. Oh, maybe I can give you a private show. The big white officer's cheeks turned red. Well, I can't discuss that while I'm in uniform, but who knows what might happen Saturday. Fuzzi opened her legs wider and winked at the officer, and he just smiled. Well, let me just run you, and if everything comes back okay, we'll get you ladies on your way. The patrolman went to his patrol car, and in a few minutes, he came and returned Emma her license.

Ok! You ladies drive safe and slow it down. Here, sign right here. Oh, you gave me a ticket? No, ma'am. I let you off with a warning. Awwwww! Look like we all owe y'all a couple of free dances. Okay, my partner and I will remember that you ladies drive safe. Emma pulled off. Damn. Girl! That was close, Fuzzi, yo ass be coming up with some shit. Hell, Bitch I didn't come up with a good idea this time. My pussy feels like it's then caught the flu. I'm go have to get her some Nyquil. Emma and Kahi'Lee busted up laughing. Bitch, pull over as soon as you can so I can get us home safe. You got all of our nerves up in our vaginas too. We got 46 kilos of cocaine in this truck, and yo ass speeding. Kahi'Lee said, "Telling me to rip my panties only almost got y'all pissed on because I was scared as fuck." Y'all ain't never talking me into driving around with no drugs never again in life. Well, Bitch! You weren't about to piss on nobody but yourself. That leather in that seat was go make it roll right back on yo ass. When I find somebody to buy them kilos, make sure you don't want any of the money then with yo scary ass. Awwwe, Fuzzi, Bitch, you was scared too. Fuzzi said hell yeah, I was, you heard me! They all busted up laughing.

Chapter Eighteen
BITCH YOU SHOULD HAVE DIED

A close friend of the Billionaire, Mr. Lehmann, who was at his party the night of the home invasion, staged a meeting with a lot of the street bosses that were from different neighborhoods. Bring that the price was so high out for the men that entered Mr. Lehmann's home, the crips and bloods and different types of gang members were all sitting at the same park waiting to have a meeting with Mr. Lehmann and Trigger, who all the gang members respected ad trusted to bring Mr. Lehmann in their presence. They all watched as the Hummer limousine pulled into Estaban Park. Trigger called a meeting there at the park to make sure that nobody was comfortable on their own turf. All seven bosses that showed up were given $10,000 just for their time but mainly to hear Mr. Lehmann out. He exited the back of the Limousine after his new driver opened his door. All the gang members took in the white man that has the type of money they all dreamed of having someday. Mr. Lehmann and two bodyguards approached the group of men. Hey, Mr. Lehmann, Trigger extended his arm to shake hands with the Billionaire. Here is a group of fellows that have a lot of power in these streets. He pointed to each Boss, and they told him where they were from and their names. I'm Solo from 19th Avenue. I'm D-Nice, D-Nice from the Eastside. I'm Danger from the Westside. I'm Menace from Maryvale. I'm Rocky from the Vistas. I'm Low Down from Park South. And I'm Hard Time from up North. Low Down said, "aye, man, let's get this clear. We not here on no snitch shit." You say that you are trying to retrieve something back from these dudes that they took from your crib, right? Mr. Lehmann told them, "I didn't call the police and get them involved." One of my guests did, but if they got arrested, I have to deal with that because they took somebody close and dear to me. There was no reason to harm anyone because nobody at the party refused their request. If somebody killed one of your homeboys and you couldn't get to them, I'm sure that you would want to see them rot in prison, too. But what bothered me about these dudes were two things. Solo said, "And what's that?" What they took out of my safe, I want it returned because it has sentimental value. I'm even willing to buy it back with no trouble. So, what's the second thing? He looked each one of them in the eyes. I got a million dollars for anyone who takes their leader's life. He seems to find pleasure in letting me know that he came to violate me and my guest. Solo said, "A million dollars." Yes, that's what I said, a million dollars. All the gang members looked at each other and thought about what they could do with a million dollars. They all shook Mr. Lehmann's hand and prayed that they would be the ones collecting the reward. Rocky said, "Hey, one question." Yeah, what's that? Man, how would you know if we got the right person? Mr. Lehmann said, "Because I'll forget my mother's face before I ever forget his." He turned and walked away.

$ $ $ $ $

Dolly was trying to do almost everything that she could think of to save their marriage. But nothing she had done or said would change Mr. Shelton's mind. His mind and heart were far away from being married to Dolly any longer. There were police officers and paramedics in Mr. Shelton's beautiful Scottsdale home. Dolly had taken a bunch of unknown pills, and they were trying to stop her from going under. The police were asking Mr. Shelton a bunch of questions that he really didn't know the answer to, but he assisted them the best way he could. It was Dolly's best friend who found her passed out in the living room. Dolly, luckily, had told her on the phone that she had taken the pills. Not being too sure, Aries went to their home to find Dolly passed out next to an empty bottle of pills and a bottle of Seagram's Gin. She dialed 911 and then got Dolly's cellphone and called Mr. Shelton. He was leaving from court on the Dawson's case when he received the call and had to rush home to police officers and paramedics in his home. Even seeing his wife surrounded, his feelings weren't making him feel any more passionate towards Dolly. Truth be told, Mr. Shelton really didn't care if she pulled through or not. He only followed Dolly in the back of the ambulance because her best friend, Aries, rode in the ambulance with her, plus he didn't want to make himself look like a terrible husband or person. He listened to Aries tell the police that Dolly was upset about losing her husband and getting a divorce. Something that Mr. Shelton already knew because they had been arguing continually every day. That was how he left the house this morning telling her to just sign the divorce papers. Mr. Shelton felt like the whole taking of the pills and overdosing was just to make him feel sorry for her and accept her back into his life. But walking into Mr. Lehmann's bedroom and seeing Dolly's mouth wrapped around his penis, that ended their marriage the moment he saw that. Mr. Shelton left her at the party and stayed away from her and their home as much as he could. After they pumped her stomach and he saw that she was still alive, Mr. Shelton walked out of the room and headed to his car and left. His last words before leaving the parking lot were, "Bitch, you should have died."

Mr. Shelton grabbed his cell phone and called Fuzzi to give her the good news. On the third ring, to his surprise, Fuzzi answered. Hello! Hello, hi baby! Hi, I missed you, are you standing in the rain? Oh no, I'm in the shower. Can I call you right back? Yeah, sure, but I thought that you just might want to know that Mrs. Dawson will be coming home tomorrow. What? What, baby, don't play with me. Are you serious? Yep, I just got the news early this morning. Fuzzi started screaming, Ahhhhhhhhhh! My little sister is coming home.

Mr. Shelton started laughing, hearing how excited Fuzzi was. So, when are you coming back home? Baby, I'm at home in my shower. Thank God! What's wrong? Did you have a bad vacation? Oh no, my trip was wonderful. Thank you, baby, so much for everything. I don't know why I believe in you so much, but I do. Mr. Shelton said that makes two of us because I believe in you, too. Baby, does Izzi know that she coming home? No, she doesn't know yet; I just found out. But she knows that I filed a motion for her release. I told her that it would take five working days, but I found out much sooner. Oh my God, baby, I can't believe she coming home. I got to call Ashley, Emma, and Kahi'Lee. Maybe I shouldn't say anything and just surprise them. What do you think? I don't know. You know your friends better than I do. I don't want you to put the blame on me. They both laughed. They all seem like a tough group of ladies; I don't want any trouble with them. Fuzzi told him that the only one that he was going to have trouble with was her if he didn't get over there to see her. Hearing that made Mr. Shelton feel like a Billionaire. Baby, I don't want any trouble with you either, so when do you want to see me? Right now! Then I'm on my way, and you just stay right there in the shower. Just leave the front door open for me. I'm unlocking it now. Click!

Chapter Nineteen
SHE DEFINITELY THE ONE

Tremendous and his boss Xerxes was riding in Tremendous truck with his boss's brother. He had come into town to check on Xerxes after he learned he had gotten robbed. Xerxes was telling his brother how they had been robbed. His brother told him that they were lucky that the females didn't kill them. Xerxes knew that his brother was telling them the truth. His brother said, "Whoever they were must have been amateurs if they left all that dope behind." Yeah, big bro, you right, even I thought about that myself. Tremendous said, "I know I'm going to kill them bitches whenever I see they asses." Man, can you believe them stupid bitches shot me? Naw, boy, what I can't believe they didn't find both of y'all ass dead. Hey bro, why don't you take a little time away from this shit and go back with me? Come on, bro, you know how this game goes. You lay off too long, and new players and drugs hit the streets.

That's what you got Tremendous for. He can hold it down for a few weeks. Right, Tremendous? Yeah, 2 Much, Xerxes knows that I got his back. Xerxes said, "that nigga had my back when he got shot in his ass too." Xerxes and 2 Much started laughing. Man, I didn't get shot in the ass; I got shot in the leg. That's only because she couldn't shoot that good. I know she tried to shoot you in the ass that bitch just missed. Man, fuck you. They all busted up laughing. 2 Much started telling them about the attractive female that he met back in Arizona. Bro, you got to meet her; she the most loving, attractive and innocent woman that I've ever met before in my life. I'm taking her to Miami, Florida, when I go back home. Why don't you and Karmela come and join us, bro? Yeah, that really sounds good. I love Miami, and they have some freaks out there. But, bro, I got a lot of shit going on right now around here. Man, I don't know where that gold-digging ass bitch at. She prolly somewhere right now stealing from some nigga. Right now, as we speak about her punk ass. Xerxes started laughing. Yeah, a lot of females fucked up in the head like that. A nigga a do anything for them already as it is, and they still find a way to pitch a nigga pocket. Hey, let me check with Karmela and see what her work schedule looks like, and I'll get back at'cha. Yeah, you do that, Sam, in the meantime take me to see my real Queen. Yeah, mama, go start crying just as soon as she sees you. Me too, Xerxes, me too!

$ $ $ $ $

Emma was at work and hated that she had to be there. Being that her, Fuzzi, and Kahi'Lee had just split up $735,000, giving them $245,000 apiece. She figured that she could be taking shopping bags to her car instead of listening to people lie about paying their Electric Bills. But Fuzzi told them that it was important that they went on about their normal lives and not change anything up. They all agreed to give Ashley $20,000 a piece, but to make sure they didn't get loose lips and tell her anything about their hustle. Fuzzi said that she'll find some type of way to find somebody to sell the kilos for them then they will split up the money. Until then, she told them she would put the drugs in storage because she had a few things that she wanted to put in storage so that she could make room for the new furniture that she bought herself. Yes, ma'am, I could look that up for you if you just give me one minute here. Emma typed something on the computer, and she was waiting for it to come back up. When she spotted the same dude walking into her job that always flashed all the stacks of cash in front of her to capture her attention. But, this time, he wasn't with his girlfriend or baby mama, whoever the female that usually is with him. She wasn't there to roll her eyes at every female that her man looked at. Ok, Ms. White, I do believe that we have it right here. You can pay the whole $263 today, which will catch you up on your bill, or you can pay the $140 that will keep your lights on, but for your next bill, we'll be sending out another notice. Emma kept her eyes on the guy while she helped her other customers. Okay, ma'am, thank you. Have a good day.

Hello, sir. What can we do to help you? Hello, sexy woman. You can do a lot of things to help me. I bet if your wife was with you, you wouldn't be telling me that. What you do, sneak out the house to come pay your bill? Naw, sexy, that headache gone baby girl. That's why I'm down here paying my own bill. In fact, I need your help switching everything into my name. Emma started laughing. Oh, I see here that she had your lights disconnected at that address. She requested that we take her name off this account and leave it disconnected. That's cold-blooded. You must have really pissed her off. Naw! I just can't deal with a woman that doesn't appreciate what you do for her while she sits her ass. Yeah, I have to agree with you then on that. If she ain't doing nothing to make sure that y'all bills are paid, nothing shit, just spending my money and looking pretty but sitting on her ass, though. That's why I need a real woman in my life, like you. Is that right? Yep! But I see you never hit me up. What's up with that? I'm headache-free, baby. I don't need to be fighting any female over no man. That's too high school for me, plus I don't need any man to take care of me. I do just a wonderful job at that myself. Ok, you do know that you're going to have to pay a new deposit, right? Yeah, sexy, I'll pay anything just get her off my shit. Emma started laughing.

So, when are you going to let me take you out? Never! Damn! That's cold. No, don't take that in the wrong way. I'm not looking for no boss. I already got one of them, but only for 8 hours then, when I walk out that door and into my door, baby, I'm the boss. He started laughing. I'm not trying to be your boss, sexy lady. I just got out of that bullshit. Somebody telling me where I should be and accusing me of everything. I don't want any boss either. But hey, we all need a friend. Somebody to talk to and spend time with. You can have all the money in the world, but we all get lonely sometimes, right? Don't you get lonely sometimes, sexy? For the first time, Emma got serious about what he had said and finally hit a soft spot in her heart. Emma knew that he wasn't the type of man that would please her. The only man that could do that, she had already found. What he had said made Emma realize just how much she needed to accept what 2 Much was offering her. But she also loved the man's confidence that stood in front of her. Emma knew the type of lifestyle that he lived and thought about the 46 kilos. Maybe this dude can lace her pockets while, at the same time, she laces his. A major red light came on inside Emma. She told the guy, okay, Mr. Jackson, we got everything set here. I put the order in, and you should be playing your video games before 5 p.m. today. He looked at Emma, sorry, sexy, you mistaken me for somebody else. I don't play video games, nor do I play with women. Maybe you need glasses. They say looking at computers all day can really fuck up your eyes; that's why I don't play video games. Emma was about to let him go, but he struck a nerve with what he had just said to her, but a good nerve. Because his words had just changed his life, Emma gave him his paperwork and said, "I get off at 5 o'clock, if you here, then you win and if you're not here, then you'll spend the rest of your life wondering what life would have been like without me in it." He told Emma, "Don't say it like that because I'll go sit my ass right there in that chair and won't move." He turned around and pointed to a seat in the lobby. Emma started laughing. Man, you crazy, just meet me in the parking lot after work. Man, what's wrong with y'all woman? See, there you go, ordering me around already. Emma threw her pen at him and started laughing.

$ $ $ $ $

Fuzzi was expecting Mr. Shelton to come by as she stood there in the shower. Thinking back over her life and how far she had come from being born a male and changing over to a female. She kept playing Mr. Shelton's words back in her mind over and over again. Will you marry me? Will you marry me? Fuzzi knew that she was getting older, and she didn't know if she would ever get an opportunity to marry a lawyer. In all the years that had passed, she always kept herself happy. The lifestyle that she learned since the age of 12 had always paid her bills and kept her up to date on all the latest gear. But there have been many nights that Fuzzi wished that she had someone keeping her bed and vagina warm. Fuzzi knew that men always come and go because they're always looking for everything that's got sex appeal to lock it and knock it down. Fuzzi knew the games that men played because he was born one. He just never wanted a pussy unless it was in between his legs and the dicks was being served to him. Fuzzi wasn't about to play the street life game and be nobody side chick or eye candy. If a man was going to lock her down, his lifestyle had to secure hers. That's what made her miss and think about Mr. Shelton. His lifestyle can secure hers in so many ways. Fuzzi knew that she could still be herself and still play wifey until she had stacked up enough money to say goodbye when the time came. Fuzzi knew that it would be a matter of time before she accepted Mr. Shelton's offer and walked down that aisle. But until that time comes, she has to make it do what it do.

Fuzzi was a little nervous, knowing that she really didn't have to be. Fuzzi wondered how drug dealers kept drugs in their houses and trap spots. She ain't have the kilos, but a few hours and every noise that she heard made her think that the police were coming to kick her door in. Having all them drugs in her house was about to drive her insane. Fuzzi knew that she needed to get a storage ASAP before she went I.I.H.O.H. Insane in her own home. A mischievous smile came over Fuzzi's face, and she knew that she had the perfect plan to tuck away those 46 kilos. Fuzzi knew that she had better hurry up and get dressed before Mr. Shelton came and wanted his Blackberry. Fuzzi said, "It's about to be some fucking, but not up in here, at least not now." Fuzzi jumped out of the shower, and her cell phone started ringing. Damn! He couldn't have gotten here that fast. She grabbed her phone and turned the shower water back on because her plan would have to be done after spending time with Dave. Hello! You here already? Nope, I'm on my lunch break, and who yo hot ass waiting on. Awwwe, Bitch! I thought you were somebody else. Well, I figured that out by my damn self already. Girl, I ain't got but a few more minutes left on my break, but I got to run something by you real quick. Emma started telling Fuzzi why she called, and Fuzzi told her that bitch I'm glad that you called me before I left because you almost were ass'd out. But I'm waiting to see Mr. Shelton; he has something to tell me about Izzi's case. So, I'll see if he'll take me up there. When I come, girl, just act like I'm bringing you your lunch. I'll call you when I'm almost there. But let me go, child, before he comes, and I don't have time. Okay, bye! Click!

Fuzzi felt bad because she didn't tell Emma about Izzi. She turned the shower off for the third time and started putting her plan into action. Fuzzi got a few things together that she was going to put in storage. She placed as many kilos as she could in each box and stacked them at the door. Fuzzi was completely dressed and ready to walk out the door; just as soon as Mr. Shelton showed up, she was rushing him back out the door. She didn't even give his mind or penis time to even think about the vagina. Before Mr. Shelton could even realize what was happening, he was putting his credit card upon the storage counter and paying for a storage spot. Fuzzi also had him put the storage in his name. Now, he helped her unload kilos out of his Maybach into her storage. After they finished unloading 45 kilos, they stopped at Taco Bell so that Fuzzi could act like she was buying Emma lunch. But really, she was putting a kilo in a bag with a few tacos. Fuzzi called Emma when they pulled into the parking lot. Emma came out and got her lunch bag, which contained four tacos and a kilo of cocaine. Thanks, Sis! I love you but I got to get back to work. They hugged and kissed each other on the cheek. Hello, Mr. Shelton, when you going to get my sister out of that nasty jail? Hi Emma, trust me, it will be soon. Maybe even sooner than you think. I hope so. Bye, I got to get back in here before I don't have a job. Okay, good to see you again. Fuzzi and Mr. Shelton pulled off, and Emma put the bag in her trunk. On her way back to work, she tossed the tacos into a trash can. Fuzzi knew that she had just done the most, and she figured that Mr. Shelton had just earned him some pussy, and it was time for Fuzzi to put out. So, she took him back to their favorite hotel and allowed him to taste her Blackberry. After they had sex and talked about Izzi coming home, Mr. Shelton tried to give Fuzzi $2,000, but to his surprise, she refused and handed him a black box. What's this? Open it, baby, and see. Mr. Shelton opened the box, and when he saw the Rolex watch, tears started rolling down his face. All the years of dating women or even marrying one, no woman had ever bought him a gift as nice as the one he held. Thank you, gorgeous. He kissed Fuzzi and told himself she was definitely the one.

Chapter Twenty
YOU SICK FUCK!

Kahi'Lee was looking through her dresser drawer, trying to decide what panties and bra set she wanted to put on. She had brought so many sets being that it was all new to her. Having so many outfits and lingerie now deciding what to wear, it was starting to get complicated, but this was a complication that she was going to love. Kahi'Lee's cell phone started to ring as she was putting on a set of pink and white panties. Hello! Yes, this is Kahi'Lee. She sat down on the bed, and tears started rolling down her face. Kahi'Lee had been waiting for this call all of her life. An agency had called her to model on the stage with all the top models. A new clothing line was coming out and Kahi'Lee was picked out of 100 other girls to model the clothing in the show. Kahi'Lee thought that at a moment like this, she would be screaming her head off, but here she sat on her bed crying. The call that Kahi'Lee had just received had just told her that all of her hard work had just paid off. She doesn't know why she felt the way she was feeling right now. But the one person that she wanted to share this moment with wasn't anywhere around. That's what made Kahi'Lee feel sad to know that Tyler wasn't anywhere around. Right now, she was missing him more than she had ever missed him before.

Sir, can you hold on a minute while I go grab a pen? Kahi'Lee wiped her face and ran into her kitchen to retrieve a pen from her kitchen drawer. Okay, sir, I'm ready. His name is Mr. Pakulski, and his address is 5260 Hatcher Rd Suite B. He'll be expecting you today at 10 a.m. What! Kahi'Lee looked up at the clock, and it was 8:15. What's the matter, Ms. HeidHart? Will that be a problem for you? No! No! Noooo! I'll be there! I'll be there! I promise that I will be there. No, thank you very much. Click!

Kahi'Lee wondered why modeling agencies never gave you time to prepare. She thought that they made sudden calls to clients to see if and who they could depend on. Kahi'Lee ran back to her room and started rambling through her closet trying to find the perfect outfit to impress the agency that she was about to go see. Kahi'Lee grabbed a Royal Blue Mini Dress and a pair of Louis Vuitton Black High Heel Shoes. Before she got dressed, Kahi'Lee knew that it was just one more thing that she had to do. She picked up her cell phone and strolled through her Rolo desk until she found the number she was looking for, then she pressed the send button. After the second ring, the voice that her heart and body craved to hear answered. Hello! Baby, is this you? Kahi'Lee didn't say anything, a part of her said that she was making a big mistake, and she was about to hang up when she heard, baby, I'm sorry that I hurt you; I'll never do that again. Please! Please, Kahi'Lee, forgive me. Tears rolled down her face. I forgive you, and I love you too, Tyler.

Kahi'Lee talked to him for about 20 minutes, and then she promised to see him later for dinner. Kahi'Lee told him that she had great news. She told Tyler that she'll tell him everything later when they see each other. Before they hung up, Kahi'Lee told Tyler that she had a super big surprise for him later. At this point, Tyler really didn't care what her surprise was; he was just happy that she was even agreeing to see him later. Tyler looked at himself in the mirror and knew that he needed a shave and haircut. Life without Kahi'Lee was weighing on him tough. They blew kisses to each other and promised to see each other at 8 o'clock. Kahi'Lee had planned to even cook Tyler his favorite meal. A T-bone Steak, macaroni n cheese, and a baked potato. Kahi'Lee got dressed and thought about all the things that Fuzzi, Emma, Izzi and Ashley would have to say to her about taking Tyler back, but Kahi'Lee didn't care. It wasn't their heart that was broken. It was hers. Kahi'Lee kissed a picture of her and Tyler before she left the house. I love you, baby, wish me luck.

$ $ $ $ $

9:45 Kahi'Lee went walking into Suite B, and she saw the attractive white secretary that sat behind her desk and was having a conversation with someone on the phone. Kahi'Lee took in the nice office and grabbed a seat until the secretary finished her phone call. Kahi'Lee grabbed a magazine and started looking through the magazine. Hi! Hello Ma'am! "Can I help you?" Kahi'Lee looked up at the secretary, Oh yeah! I'm sorry, ma'am, I didn't want to interrupt your phone call. Thank you, because most people are normally rude and interrupt anyway. That's mighty kind of you. I'm here to see, and Kahi'Lee looked at the paper that she held in her hand. Oh Yeah, a Mr. Pakulski, I'm Kahi'Lee HeidHart. Yes, ma'am, I see you have a 10 o'clock appointment. Let me give Mr. Pakulski a call and let him know that you're here. The secretary placed a call to her boss, and she told Kahi'Lee that Mr. Pakulski would see her now. Hi! Hello, Ms. HeidHart! Wow! You're even more attractive in person. Kahi'Lee smiled and extended her hand while saying thank you. Come in and have a seat. I'm so grateful for this opportunity. I've waited all my life for something like this. Oh, trust me, you have done great work, and you deserve this shot more than anyone else does, Ms. HeidHart. I've seen the commercial you have just done; you've done a wonderful job. Now, the whole world is going to get a glimpse of your beautiful face. Kahi'Lee smiled, thank you. But I'll also tell you this, Ms. HeidHart, after this show that's coming up, the whole world is going to know your name. Kahi'Lee put her hand up to her mouth, excited about what Mr. Pakulski had just said. That's something Kahi'Lee has been dying to do: make herself known to the world.

Mr. Pakulski stood up and walked over to Kahi'Lee's chair. Ms. HeidHart, do you feel like you're ready? He placed a hand gently on Kahi'Lee's shoulder. Kahi'Lee looked up at him. Yeah, I'm more than ready. I'll do anything to land a job like this. Mr. Pakulski smiled. Kahi'Lee had just said the magic words. Yeah, I hear a lot of people say that, but when it comes time to put out, they clam up like a turtle in its shell. No, sir. You don't have to worry about that, not with me. I always give 110%. Mr. Pakulski walked over to his door and turned the lock on it. Click! So, I'll tell you what, how about we celebrate you and your new modeling job. He walked over to retrieve two glasses and a bottle of clear liquor. He set the glasses down on his desk in front of Kahi'Lee. He looked at her real seductively while he poured them a drink. Kahi'Lee closed her legs, now sensing his attraction to her. Kahi'Lee stood up and tried to change the mood. So, how long have you been doing this type of work, Mr. Pakulski? Oh, for over four years now. I've given a lot of beautiful women like you a remarkable lifestyle behind me, giving the okay for them to take the high-paying jobs. I've even helped a lot of men also. He handed Kahi'Lee one of the glasses, but she declined his offer. No, thank you, I'll pass, but I'll toast with you if you like me too. Mr. Pakulski put an evil expression on his face. Well, I don't enjoy drinking too much alone. I'm sure that you can have at least one drink with me, right? Kahi'Lee felt a strange feeling in her stomach. She didn't want to blow her opportunity to lose this modeling job, but still, she didn't want to have a drink with Mr. Pakulski.

Hmmmm! I see now why you and Mr. Bronson are dating. When he said that, Kahi'Lee's heart almost jumped out of her chest. How do you know who I'm dating? Because I thought you were smart like him and knew when not to blow an opportunity. He walked up on Kahi'Lee, closing off her space to move. He put his hand on her back and let it slide down her back until it reached Kahi'Lee's butt, and she quickly removed his hand. Excuse me, sir, Kahi'Lee stepped to the side of him. Mr. Pakulski said, "I'm the one who tried to help Mr. Bronson, but he couldn't even show up for the job." Kahi'Lee played his name back in her head. I'll meet you at the house after I leave Mr. Pakulski's office. Mr. Pakulski picked up a remote control off of his desk. You do know that Tyler's career was over, but I gave him a second chance, and he blew it like you're about to do. He turned and looked Kahi'Lee straight in the face, making her question not to have a drink with him. Mr. Pakulski turned on his television, so you still don't want to have that drink? Kahi'Lee looked at Mr. Pakulski and walked back over to his desk. He put a smile on his face but quickly changed it when he saw Kahi'Lee grab her purse and started walking toward the door. Mr. Pakulski stopped her right in her tracks when he said, "That's okay. I'm sure his lips are much better than yours anyway." What? What did you just say? Kahi'Lee turned around and walked up to him. What the fuck did you just say? You heard me right. He went and grabbed one of the drinks off of his desk and downed it. He pressed play on the remote control; at least your boyfriend didn't deny me. Kahi'Lee watched as Tyler removed his own penis from his pants and laid-back enjoying Mr. Pakulski giving him oral sex. Kahi'Lee grabbed her mouth and stomach. She felt herself about to throw up watching the man that she loves allow another man to please him in the same way that he enjoys when they had sex. Kahi'Lee looked at Mr. Pakulski, you sick fuck! She ran and opened the door, but it wouldn't open because Mr. Pakulski had locked the door. That's when Kahi'Lee knew that he had plans of sexually assaulting her. Because she sure wasn't about to willingly agree to any sexual act with him.

Kahi'Lee felt her head spinning around in circles, and the room seemed to close in on her. Kahi'Lee started beating on the door. Let me out of here! Let me out of here! Before Mr. Pakulski could even get to the door, Kahi'Lee had unlocked the door and ran out of his office. Kahi'Lee didn't stop running until she reached her Lexus. She jumped into her car and burned rubber, leaving the parking lot. Kahi'Lee's mind was racing a mile a minute. Tears begin to cover her face. She couldn't imagine never seeing Tyler engage in a homosexual act. Kahi'Lee raced through traffic and around cars. Honk! Honk! Honk! Honk! People were blowing their horns, but Kahi'Lee didn't care about nothing or nobody. Her heart was hurting. Her whole world had just been turned upside down. Just as Kahi'Lee maneuvered her way through traffic, her cell phone started ringing. It was sitting next to her gear shift, and she saw Tyler's face come across the screen. Her heart started racing, making her foot more heavier on the gas pedal. Kahi'Lee reached for her phone, snatching it to give Tyler a piece of her mind. But the cell phone fell out of her hand, tumbling onto the passenger floor. Without thinking, Kahi'Lee reached over, trying to retrieve her phone, but as she reached for her phone, her leg caught the steering wheel, making her Lexus shift over to the next lane. Urrrrrrr! Urrrrrrrrr! You could hear other vehicles coming to a halt to prevent them from hitting Kahi'Lee. After grabbing her phone and shifting her body back up in her seat, her leg quickly turned the wheel in a different direction, which made Kahi'Lee go spinning like a top into the other traffic that was coming from a different direction. An Impala, a Ford F-150 and an H2 Hummer were coming fast at Kahi'Lee. Just as Kahi'Lee was coming out of her final spin, Urrr! Urrrr! Urrrrrr! Boom! Boom! Urrrrrr! The Impala tried to prevent from hitting Kahi'Lee and ran into a Ford Expedition. The Ford F-150 stopped in his lane, but the H2 Hummer came inches from completely trampling over Kahi'Lee's Lexus. Urrrrrrrrrr! Kahi'Lee's eyes got wider than a smoker taking a fresh hit of crack cocaine. She looked at the Hummer driver, who was almost about to roll over her. Kahi'Lee held her chest, breathing rapidly fast. She couldn't believe that her car didn't have a scratch on it but mainly couldn't believe that she was still alive. People started jumping out of their vehicles to make sure that Kahi'Lee, and the man in the Impala was okay.

Ma'am, are you okay? At this point, Kahi'Lee really didn't care about herself. She wanted to make sure that the man in the Impala was okay. Yeah! Yeah! I'm fine, but what about them? Kahi'Lee was looking at a 6'1, tall, muscular, dark-skinned, handsome man that she was looking at like a child seeing their superhero. He opened up Kahi'Lee's door, and now she could see that her mind wasn't playing tricks on her because his Ralph Lauren Safari Cologne invaded her nostrils, and her female private parts came to life. He told Kahi'Lee to put her car in park, and he reached over her, unlatching her seatbelt and turning off the engine. He reached for Kahi'Lee's hand to help her out of the car. Ma'am, are you alright? Kahi'Lee thought that just in case she ever got a role in the movies or a commercial that she needed to practice her acting, right now would be a perfect time to see how she acted. Kahi'Lee started crying and reached up to her leading man. He pulled Kahi'Lee closer to comfort her, and Kahi'Lee melted right in his arms. Damn! She told herself after really getting a chance to rest on his chest and smell his cologne up close. He rubbed and patted Kahi'Lee's back, making her want to remove her panties right on the hood of her car in front of all those people. Kahi'Lee told herself that if he rubbed my back one more time, I'm going to climax right now, and she didn't want to change it.

So, she stepped back to give them a little breathing space, well, at least her anyway. Kahi'Lee turned to the Impala driver, is he-he-he, okay? He went and grabbed Kahi'Lee by her waist and led her towards the accident. Come on, let's go check on them. While walking side-by-side, Kahi'Lee grabbed his arm like he was her man and walked next to him. Kahi'Lee told herself, "Tyler, you can go suck all the dicks you like." This was a man Kahi'Lee told herself that she had to see him again after all this clear up. She looked at his finger ring, yes! No ring appeared on his finger. What snapped Kahi'Lee back to reality was when she heard the police siren and ambulance. Damn! I hope they don't take me to jail. Now, Kahi'Lee was being checked out by the ambulance because she told the police officer that she caught a pain in her chest. That's what made her lose control of her vehicle. They have moved all of the cars out of the road. The Impala driver wasn't hurt but they did have to tow his vehicle. After the police realized that Kahi'Lee didn't have any alcohol in her system, she received a few tickets and was released.

Kahi'Lee couldn't believe that after all the time that had passed, her black superhero was still waiting by her side. She had told him twice that he could leave but he declined both times and was now escorting Kahi'Lee to her car. I'm so sorry to have ruined your day. I'm Kahi'Lee, by the way. I'm Tyler. What! Kahi'Lee jumped back and started laughing. I'm sorry. Did I say the wrong name? Kahi'Lee was still laughing. No! No! No! I love your name. I was just laughing because God got a sense of humor. Your name is fine, but not as fine as you are. That made Tyler smile to hear that she was feeling him. Well, everybody calls me B.S. What the B.S stand for, Bull shitter? Tayler smiled and rubbed his penis. Naw, baby girl, that stands for Black Stallion. Kahi'Lee's vagina started beating like a heart monitor. Okay B.S., Kahi'Lee told him that she was a model, and he told her that he owns his own car lot right down the street, from where they were standing from his H2 Hummer. Oh, I was wondering why you have dealer plates on your truck. Yeah, I own it, but I hope somebody buys it soon. They consume a lot of gas, but they're great safe vehicles. Well, do you mind if I give you a call sometime? Yeah, sure, thought you would never ask. Of course, I'd ask, or I'll never get you out of my mind; you're so beautiful. Kahi'Lee started blushing and thanked him for his compliment. They could tell that neither one wanted to leave the other. Hey, how about I take you to dinner tonight? How about I cook dinner and I'll be your dessert? Shit! That sounds even better. 8 o'clock? 8 o'clock works for me. He kissed Kahi'Lee on the forehead and walked up to her car. He stood and watched as she drove away. His cell phone rang; he answered and said I'm on my way; I'm down the street. Click!

Chapter Twenty-One
YOU ABOUT YOUR PAPER

Emma came walking out of her job, and everyone was saying their goodbyes. It didn't take her long to see the handsome young man resting against his Tahoe, listening to Gucci Man. Emma put on her sexiest female walk over to her Mercedez Benz. Well, hello, Mr. He smiled, happier to see Emma than she was him. Hey, Sexy Lady. I told you that I'll be here. I never didn't expect you not to be. They both reached out for a hug. Mmmm! I like that you smell good. Ain't nothing like a good-smelling man. So, man, where you taking me so that we can talk? Wherever you want to go. Anywhere I want to go? Yeah! To his surprise, Emma said, "Then take me to meet your mama." What? Are you serious? Yeah! I feel like if you really want to know the real man, you should see how he is around his mother. If you ain't loving her right, then I'm in trouble. Not unless you and another woman already share that warm welcome. Naw, sexy! I'd love for you to meet my mama and my whole family.

You following me, or are we riding together? Emma knew that she had a kilo of cocaine in her trunk, but she knew her vehicle was safe. There would still be a few hours before everybody would leave her job. I'll ride with you if you don't mind bringing me back. He didn't even respond and just headed to open his passenger door. Okay, Mr. Jackson. He reached for Emma's hand to help her in his truck. Oh, and a gentleman, too, huh! Yeah, I'm a lot of things that you go be shocked to learn about, and Rozay will be just fine. That ain't what your account says, it says, Tony Jackson. Tony. They both busted up laughing. But I could get used to Rozay, and I know you a street boss. Rozay shook his head and went to the driver's side.

Less than 30 minutes later, they were pulling into a nice neighborhood. These homes are nice. They shared a blunt of some HighDro, while both bobbing their head to the music. Turned out that Emma and Rozay were enjoying each other's company. They laughed and joked with each other the whole time. After Emma met his mother, Silvia, and her boyfriend, Michael, she also met his two youngest sisters, who they called Porsha and Tasty and were faster than a racing car. Emma even met his best friend who they call Flakes because he stopped by. She felt comfortable being around all of them. Emma stayed for about an hour and a half, then she told Rozay, "Baby, you know that I been working all day and have to go back early in the morning." After Rozay's mom learned that Emma worked at the Electric company, she said, "Tony, it's about time you found somebody with a job." Rozay looked at Emma, "See what I told you." They all busted up laughing. That last heffa was lazy and trifling. I can't even stand being around her, and you are so much prettier. Emma smiled. She knew that her and Rozay wouldn't be a couple only business partners, but she didn't want to bust his bubble not in front of his family. Well, I won't promise that we'll be family I got to see how he treat me first. Emma playfully hit Rozay on the arm. She ain't going nowhere, mama. I hope so. Well, nice meeting you anyway, and you're welcome to come back anytime. They hugged, and Emma said goodbye.

On the ride back, Emma asked Rozay to cut the music off. Her whole demeanor quickly changed. Look, Rozay, I really think that you're an attractive man, but I'm already in a relationship. Rozay's whole facial expression changed. Then why did you lead me to like you? Why did you even want to meet my mother? Why did we go to her house? He found a place to pull over and look Emma in her face. Okay, here's the deal. Emma tricked him into believing she spoke to her man about Rozay and wanted to help him. Emma told Rozay that he would never have to spend his money ever again and that she would supply him with all the drugs that he needed, and they would split the money. Emma told him, Rozay, I didn't know if you would take my offer or not, but I had to know something about you if I'm going to be able to trust you with the type of weight that I'm giving you. Emma had no idea about the drug game, but she knew that dealing with Rozay, she would learn the game from him and how to charge him from what she gave him. So, you want me to work for y'all? Baby girl, I get my own money. I don't need your man's help. He started getting upset that Emma thought less of him. Rozay, how much work are you doing right now? I brought a quarter-brick, but with my own money. Baby, I'm not asking you to work for no nigga. I like you, Rozay, but I'm not like your girlfriend, I could've fuck with my man and you, and nobody wouldn't even know shit. Me and you live here; my dude live in another State. But I'm a real woman. If I were with you, man, I wouldn't cheat on you either. That made him chill a little, knowing that Emma could have played them both. So, what do you want from me? Nothing, I just thought that we could help each other. If I'm fronting you work and you ain't paying shit for it, you're making the same amount as me, then what are you complaining about? Emma watched as he ran her offer through his mind. Before he could even answer, Emma said, "Plus things ain't all that solid between me and him." I know, he probably sees other bitches, but he good to me, so how can I complain about something I don't know about? But if his ass is cheating on me, then I guess that means that I already found somebody that I do know would treat me right and won't hurt me, right? Rozay smiled, naw, sexy, I'll never hurt you.

Emma kissed him on the cheek. Maybe I shouldn't, but for some reason, I believe you, Rozay. 50/50 every dollar. But what if I take a loss, then we take a loss together. Okay, then you got a deal. Let's just see how it works out. But if we not happy then we split it even and go our separate ways, cool. Cool! I'm with that. You don't have to report to me, Rozay, or no shit like that. You do your own thing. Just let me know ahead of time before you run out. You bring me my cut, and I got you. Alright, sis. Alright, lil bro. They both busted up laughing. Yeah, maybe we'll be better off that way anyway. Whatever you want, lil daddy. So, when do we start this thing? Today! Now take me to my car so I can get back to my hustle. After they got back to Emma's car, she told him to hold up. She didn't know what type of money to expect, so she ran it to him like this. If I give you half a kilo, what type of money can I expect? Man, my spot be popping. I'm getting like 13.5 off of nine or better all depends on the deals. Emma stopped him, hold up I'll be right back. Emma returned and said, "I got something better than that for you." What's that? Here, just give me $21,000, and if you make $54,000 of better that's all you. He looked in the bag and saw the brick. Sis, you aint bullshitting about your paper, ain't you? She looked at Rozay to send a message to him. Yeah, I am clean or with blood, Holla! They exchanged numbers, and Emma jumped out of his truck, closed the door, and didn't look back at him. She jumped in her Mercedez Benz and smashed off, leaving him watching her and saying to himself, I got to keep it 100 and make this hook up work for us.

Chapter Twenty-Two
LET'S DO THE DAMN THING

Everyone was cheering and clapping when they heard the guard say inmate 58224 Dawson, roll up. You're being kicked out. Izzi started crying, and she never thought that she would ever hear those words again. Out of all the females there, Izzi really cared about her cellmate, Caroline. They stood in their room, hugging and crying. Izzi wanted so badly to take Caroline with her. Izzi gave Caroline her address and phone number. She told Caroline to call anytime and that she'll keep money on her books for the commissary. Izzi even promised to have Mr. Shelton look into her case, but Caroline knew there wasn't any hope for her. She and her boyfriend got caught transporting 500 lbs of Marijuana from Mexico into the United States and were facing a lot of time. Izzi kissed Caroline on the cheek and said bye. It wasn't until almost midnight that Izzi got released from jail. The $240 that she got released with, she put every dollar on Caroline's books and waited for Fuzzi to pick her up. When Fuzzi showed up, they held each other and cried like a mother losing her child. Izzi didn't want to go to her home, so she chose to stay at Fuzzi's. Izzi wanted to call Emma, Ashley and Kahi'Lee so bad, but Fuzzi had a better idea if they could wait until morning. They sat up talking all night, plus Izzi was curious to know how they raised so much money to get a lawyer like Mr. Shelton.

Fuzzi started beating around the bush until Izzi told Fuzzi that she didn't have Duvall around anymore to support her, so whatever it was, she wanted in. Fuzzi promised that they would help Izzi get by until she found a job. Izzi said, "Bitch, this is me, your best friend." Fuzzi, you don't got a job, and you look better than anybody I know. Stop trying to baby me and let me be my own woman. If you, Emma, and Kahi'Lee risk y'all lives for me, then I'm woman enough to risk my life for y'all to be happy, too. Tears started rolling down Izzi's face. Who do you know got friends like y'all? Fuzzi, I know you know the woman who went to jail, but you don't have any idea about the woman who came out of there. I see how real life is now and how important it is to stand up on your own two feet and be the woman that you want to be. I know that I used to be the main person judging you, Fuzzi. But now I can look you in the eyes woman to Queen and say, "Now I truly understand you." Tears started rolling down Fuzzi face to hear Izzi call her a Queen. Fuzzi said, "You are a Queen to Izzi. That's why I came for you." Izzi said, "thank you." But I'm not where you are yet. But if you'll give me a chance then maybe one day I'll accept you calling me a Queen.

But right now, I'm just a student, a prospect to a Queen. Bitch! Now teach me what it is that you know that I don't know. Fuzzi said, "So that means that you're ready to be a Fox then." Izzi smiled, yeah bitch! I'm ready to be a Fox. Fuzzi told Izzi that she thinks that she better sit down to hear what it is that she's about to tell her.

After they finished talking, Fuzzi explained the whole get down to her. To Fuzzi's surprise, Izzi didn't seem to flinch or blink at what Fuzzi had to say. Emma and Kahi'Lee went against Fuzzi right away but Fuzzi told Izzi that something inside that jail changed her. Izzi told Fuzzi jail didn't change me, bitch. You and life changed me. You taught me how to be a woman in jail. And now you're about to teach me how to become a woman, Queen, and a Fox out of jail. So, you tell me who really changed me? They hugged each other. Child, come on, we got to get some type of sleep before morning. We have a big day ahead of us. I can't wait to see the looks on Emma, Kahi'Lee, and Ashley's faces when they see that you got out of jail. Yeah, I know, they go be so happy and shocked. So, what about Ashley, she don't go on jobs with y'all? Bitch! Hell naw, that girl got a good job and I don't want to ruin that for her. Izzi looked at Fuzzi, let me tell you something, girl. You don't know Ashley like you think you do. Her ass is more of a Fox then any one of us. We done had some conversations that I didn't believe was coming out of her mouth. Fuzzi, she the one that always defended you when we thought that you was a little on the deep end. Ashley always said that she rather play them men in the streets then be waking up at

5:30 in the morning to be arguing with people over their children being taken away from them. Yeah, I couldn't do her job; I'll be cussing them people out. I'd be like bitch, get off them drugs you ain't fit enough to be a parent to a kid. Izzi busted up laughing, girl yo ass is crazy. But I'm telling you if you explain it to her, I'm willing to bet that she'll be down with it. All five of us together, the world will be in trouble. Really with Ashley's aggressive ass, she just like you, and you know it, Fuzzi. Fuzzi started laughing. Yeah, that bitch is aggressive and say whatever the fuck is on her mind. I guess if she can deal with kids all day, then dealing with men wouldn't be too much of a problem. They all act just alike, right! Izzi and Fuzzi slapped hands, bitch, I'm going to bed; we'll holla at Ashley tomorrow.

Fuzzi started walking to her bedroom, and Izzi went walking behind her. Fuzzi turned around, Bitch where the hell you going? I'm getting ready to go to sleep, too. No, you ain't, not in my bed. This the only vagina that's laying in that King size bed in there, bitch, plus, you know, I sleep naked. Izzi said, "Trust me, Fuzzi, I don't want you." Besides, the last bitch that offered me her vagina, I tried to kill her. Izzi looked at Fuzzi crazy. Well, I aint offer you no vagina, so you can stop looking at me like Jason. Haaaaaaaa! Izzi made that sound, and they started laughing. Bitch, if you start snoring, you getting yo ass out of my bed. While Izzi was sleeping, Fuzzi got up and called Ashley, Emma, and Kahi'Lee. She told them all to come to her house for breakfast.

$ $ $ $ $

It was Saturday morning, and Fuzzi told them that they all going shopping. She knew how long it would take them all to get dressed. So Fuzzi said, "ponytails and no make-up, bitch." Get y'all asses up and get to my house now. Click! One by one, they all showed up to Fuzzi's house. Emma was the last one to show up. Fuzzi had all of them at the table while she fixed their plates. After putting the plates on the table, Kahi'Lee asked Fuzzi, "Girl, I know you losing your mind but why you make five plates and it ain't but four of us?" Because I ain't losing my mind, I got a friend coming to say a prayer for us. Well, bitch, they better hurry up and get here because I ain't about to let my food get cold waiting on your guest.

Fuzzi walked over to the table, okay, bitch, bow y'all heads. I'll say a prayer because you need one. Everyone bowed their heads and closed their eyes. Heavenly Father, I want to thank you for this meal, but I really want to thank you for my beautiful sisters and for giving me a wonderful family that loves me. At the same time, everybody started thinking that Fuzzi sure sounded a lot like Izzi, but nobody opened their eyes, and Izzi kept praying. Lord, thank you for giving me back my freedom even though I didn't deserve it. Will you please forgive me for my sins? Kahi'Lee looked up first and started screaming after she saw Izzi. What! What! Iz-Iz-Izziii! Oh my God girl, you're home! Emma and Ashley opened their eyes, and they all rushed to Izzi. Izzi! Izzi! Izzi! Izzi! They were giving her hugs and kisses. Everybody in the kitchen eyes were filled with tears from being so happy to see that Izzi was home. When did you come home? They released me after midnight. Why y'all didn't call nobody, Fuzzi? Emma said, "I hate both of y'all." No, I don't. Yall know that I love y'all dirty asses. But that was so mean though. Fuzzi hunched her shoulders at Kahi'Lee, I know it was, bitch! I'm sorry, okay!

Fuck it! Y'all gone and crucify me, damn. I just tried to surprise you, sorry, bitches. They all busted up laughing. Emma patted Izzi's butt, damn! I see somebody gain some weight in there. Fuzzi said, "Child, don't be touching that heffa's ass." You already threaten to kill me about her vagina last night. Y'all already know she got her twinkie took in jail already. Fuzzi started laughing, and Izzi started chasing Fuzzi around her kitchen table. Stop! Stop! Stoppp! Bitch, you can't have none of this pussy; I then told you already. I'm not that type of lady. Stop, Izzi! Come on, y'all let's eat before our food get cold. They all sat down and started telling each other about their experiences. Izzi started the conversation off by talking about her jail experiences. Then, Fuzzi told Izzi that Mr. Shelton asked her to marry him, but she said no. What, girl, are you serious? That's when Izzi told them that they could still refile the charges against her. Fuzzi said that she'll talk to Mr. Shelton about them refiling. Emma said, yeah, girl talk to your husband because they can't be doing that shit. Everybody laughed at Emma, saying that Mr. Shelton was Fuzzi's husband. Emma started telling Izzi about 2 Much and how he treats her. But she was acting like Fuzzi, like she really didn't care. Ashley started telling them about some sad custody case she had been dealing with. And how she hates taking kids from their mothers. Kahi'Lee wanted to tell them about Tyler and Mr. Pakulski, but she was too embarrassed to let them know that she saw her man getting his penis sucked by another man. So, she told Izzi about the commercial that she shot. What, are you serious, Kahi'Lee, you shot a commercial? Yeah, girl, I sure did, plus I met somebody that I'm kind of feeling. Girl, you know your ass ain't about to leave Tyler for nobody else. Hearing Tyler's name made her sick to her stomach. Well, I already did Ashley, and his name is Tyler, too. We had dinner together, and he told my ex-boyfriend to get lost and don't come back around me. What, girl? You lying? Kahi'Lee had that I'm in love look on her face.

So Fuzzi, Ashley, Emma, and Izzi started to believe her. When did you meet him? That's when Kahi'Lee knew that she had to tell them the truth. She started with the phone call for the modeling job then she told them about Tyler and Mr. Pakulski's homosexual encounter. What? Bitch! You lying, Kahi'Lee? Fuzzi's mouth was wide open. But the conversation turned serious when Kahi'Lee told them that she almost died in a car accident. Girl, you wrecked your car. No! No! No! It's fine. She finished telling the story clear up to her and the new Tyler having dinner and the gay Tyler showing up and almost got beat up by the new Tyler that Kahi'Lee rolled out of bed with this morning when Fuzzi called for her to make this important breakfast. Oooooooww, bitch! I wouldn't have showed up. I'd be still riding that Black Stallion. Kahi'Lee started laughing, girl, I thought that y'all would be making fun of the way that I'm walking. That's his nick name and he is hanging like a horse. For real, bitch? My vagina is so sore I want to go soak in your tub, Fuzzi. They all started laughing. Girl, don't God got a sense of humor. The man's name Tyler, girl. They all raised their orange juice glasses. Well, here's to the straight Tyler. Black Stallion! Black Stallion! Bitch!

Izzi stood up after everything calmed down a little. She said to Ashley, "Fuzzi has something important that we all need to talk about." I already accepted her offer, but I feel that we all shouldn't keep anything from each other because we are all sisters, and we all definitely love each other. Emma and Kahi'Lee were looking at Fuzzi. "Yeah, bitch, she knows everything," Ashley said, "Well, how she knows everything, and I don't. I been asking you bitches what y'all been up to, and y'all just blow me off." Izzi come home and 10 minutes, and she know everything, fuck y'all, bitches. Y'all think I'm dumb and don't know what y'all talking about. I don't know what y'all been doing, but I know one damn thing, y'all better include me in on it. too. I don't want no handouts; I want my cut, too, bitch. Fuzzi, Emma, and Kahi'Lee started laughing. Oh, you want to be a Fox too, bitch. I am a Fox. Look at me. Y'all got me fucked up. She started spinning around in circles with her hands on her hips. Okay! Once I open my mouth, ain't no turning back. Does everybody agree with that? Everybody agreed, including Ashley. Fuzzi started running everything down, and Emma and Kahi'Lee backed her up. They shared their last few hustles and the amount of money that they made on them. Ashley's nose was wide open like a bull, and she wanted in, which they all were glad to hear. That led Emma to put them up on Rozay and their little deal with the cocaine. Fuzzi said, "That's great, girl." Now, we can take all their shit. We just need to figure out how to find somebody else to transport the drugs back here. Izzi thought about Caroline and how she told her all the exciting stories about drug trafficking from Mexico. Caroline seemed to enjoy doing it, and her boyfriend got all the money. What if Caroline was hustling for herself? Aye, Fuzzi, I got just the perfect person, but we got one problem. What's that? She already locked up for trafficking marijuana. Damn, Izzi, then what good is that going to do us. Fuzzi, you got the lawyer wrapped around your finger. Maybe he can spring her. Damn, bitch, you have turned into the perfect criminal. Naw, Fuzzi, I'm just saying. If we go do this, then let's go all the way but be smart about it.

Do you want to know something else? Fuzzi said. Now having Cookie and Lucious in you, bitch, I'm afraid to ask. Emma, Kahi'Lee, and Ashley started laughing. Naw! Naw! Serious. Maybe you do need to marry Mr. Shelton. He could be a major ace in the whole for us. Bitch! I know you didn't just come home and marry me off. After killing your husband, you want me to be stuck and you free? Deep down inside, Fuzzi, Emma, Kahi'Lee, and Ashley all knew that Izzi made perfect sense. But what they didn't know was that Fuzzi had already planned to marry Mr. Shelton but for her own personal reasons. Plus, she had grew feelings for him and wanted him to be her husband. To cut the suspicion in half, Fuzzi said, "Bitch, I'll have to sleep on that one because I ain't the wifey type." But what you said made a lot of sense. I see jail did do you some good. I'll talk to him about your criminal cellmate, and I'll get back to you on that. Izzi told them that she left $240 on her books and gave her, her phone number. Emma said, "That's good, Izzi, at least she'll know that we won't leave her behind if something went wrong." If Mr. Shelton gets her out of jail, then she'll be loyal to us.

Fuzzi told them well, y'all Foxes need to get y'all bathing suits up because we all our headed to Miami, Fl. I know they got a deposit for five beautiful Foxes. What y'all think, Foxes? Hell yeah, let's do the damn thing. Izzi, Ashley, this is what we do when we get there. Fuzzi started giving them the rundown on how they hook the bait, but she has a new plan since they had five hungry Foxes on the prowl. Instead of three, they could kill two animals with five Foxes. After breakfast, they all went shopping and then helped Izzi clean up her house and settle back in. It was time to introduce the Foxes to the whole world and the dope game. They all vowed to Foxes over money, men, and anything that comes in between them for life until death do them part.

Chapter Twenty-Three
2 DAMN MUCH

Solo, D-Nice, Danger, Menace, Rocky, Hard Time, and Low Down, all decided to work together and claim that 1-million-dollar jackpot. They had heard that one of the other players in the street had been spending big money lately and bragging about how up he was in the game. They decided to go and pay him a little visit at his home, just to see he was that 1-million-dollar man. Top Notched pulled into his 2-story double garage home. He and one of his baby mamas had just come from the Super Walmart grocery store shopping. He had just bought a Mercedes Benz G Wagon white sitting on 26-inch Sprewell rims. He turned down the loud music that he was listening to because the type of music that he had in his truck always rattled their neighbors' windows, and he didn't want them complaining to the neighborhood association and getting him evicted. Danger said, "Man, it looks like the nigga doing pretty good for himself." I've already counted a few $100,000 in vehicles. He a little too young to be buying that house. Maybe that little redbone riding with him on section 8. "They are not giving out them types of houses not like this one on section 8," Menace said. All my chicken heads on section 8, and I'm not pulling up into nothing that looks like this. Maybe, they just renting. I don't give a fuck if they are renting, buying or on section 9, if that nigga got what we are looking for then his ass is mine. Solo cocked back his 9mm and said fuck all this real estate talk. Lets bag this nigga and his bitch. Low Down said, "Naw, fam, we need to search this house before we take this boy with us." Yeah, Low Down, right. Maybe what we're looking for is in that crib, and that's some extra bread on top of that Million.

Low Down and Rocky gave each other a dap. The black van that they were in had dark-tinted windows, so nobody could see inside it. No other neighbors were out so everything was looking good. Top Notched parked in the driveway waiting for one of the garage doors to open. Soon, as it opened, it revealed a 66 Convertible Blue Impala. Yeah, this boy doing his thang. Top Notched was tall, about 6'2', slim with long dreadlocks, and a close-shaved beard. Soon, as he pulled into the driveway, he and his girl could be heard laughing. She grabbed a few bags and headed into the home from a side door that connected to the garage. Top Notched was about to close the garage door by a button on the wall, but before he could, Solo, D-Nice, Danger, Rocky and Low Down rushed into the garage, drawing their weapons. Top Notched tried to reach for his gun, but he held a few grocery bags in one hand, and the other one had hit the button to close the garage door. Don't make me blow your brains out, party man. The information that Low Down got from a few strippers who Top Notched had been partying with said that he loved partying. Top Notched threw his hands up, letting the groceries hit the garage floor. The door had completely closed behind Solo, D-Nice, Danger, Rocky, and Low Down just as they entered.

Baby, who you talking to? Aghhhhhhhhh! His girl screamed after she saw all the men pointing guns. Bitch, shut up! You scream again, and that would be the last sound you hear. She put her hand over her mouth. I'm sorry! I'm sorry, sir! Okay, now that's much better. Low Down pointed his gun at Top Notched. Hey, party man, let your girl remove that gun, and you hand that to my man right there. He pointed to Danger. She did just as she was told. Then, they were led back into the house. Low Down asked his girl what's your name, redbone? Tiffany. Okay, Tiffany, if you do like I tell you, I promise you that when we leave here, you won't be hurt. This is nothing personal between your man and me; this all business. I got a woman, and this could happen to me, and I wouldn't want anyone to hurt her or my kids, feel me. She shook her head as tears rolled down her face. I know, it's rough fucking with men like him, but this shit comes with the shine, Tiffany, and you shinning. Low Down nodded his head, Danger and D-Nice started cuffing Top Notched up. They laid him face down on the floor because they didn't know where else he had kept weapons in his house. Top Notched was trying his best to look at their faces, but the black mask, gloves, and long sleeve shirts they had on were making it pretty hard to say if there was anybody he knew or seen before. Tiffany, you come with me. You go be a good girl, right? Yeah! Yeah! I mean, yes, sir. Okay. Danger was letting Rocky and Menace into the house. Tiffany looked at the other men coming in and got even more frightened. Tiffany, that robbery that your man pulled, where he keeping all his stuff at? What robbery? What stuff? Okay, see, I thought we were going to be cool, Tiffany. Low Down put his hand on his hip like Bitch don't try to play games with me. I'm telling the truth; he aint rob nobody. My man sales drugs. So, where all this money coming from? He wasn't balling like this a few months ago. That's because he got a new connection from Mexico. The Mexicans been fronting him kilos. Low Down looked at Danger, Solo, Tone, Rocky and Hard Time. Hard Time said where all the drugs at? He don't keep that stuff here; our kids live in this house, too. Turn this fag over. Low Down was mad because he believed Tiffany. After they turned Top Notched, Low Down took a couple of photos of him and then sent them with the message attached to them. He told Solo, D-Nice, and Menace to search the house. Tiffany said yall don't have to tear my house up ain't shit in here but money. I'll give it to y'all just don't kill us. Please! Please! Please! My babies need us. Pleaseeee!

Low Down said to Tiffany, "I'm a man of my word, and I pray that you're a woman of yours." If the wrong information comes back on my phone, then you and your man both go to meet y'all maker together. Him because he is who I'm looking for and you for lying to me, but if you're telling me the truth, then we're out of here and sorry for the inconvenience, Tiffany. Top Notched was trying to say something, but the tape on his mouth wouldn't allow him to say anything, and Low Down didn't care to hear it anyway. Tiffany's heart was beating like an alarm clock on a nightstand. She didn't know if they were about to die or not. 20 Minutes later, Low Down's cell phone beeped, letting him know that he had a message. He looked at the message and was really disappointed. The text said that Top Notched wasn't the man who robbed Mr. Lehmann, the Billionaire. Low Down watched as Solo, D-Nice, and Menace came down carrying the safe. Tiffany was anxious to know what that text said. So, sir, did I lie? Open that safe then I'll tell you. No, you tell me. Nowwww! Low Down pointed his gun at Top Notched head, and the safe got opened in 2.2 seconds. It was close to $200,000, and some male and female jewelry. They took the money and left the custom jewelry. Low Down said, "I'll let you keep your big bling, Tiffany, because you told the truth." But since your man tricks his coins off with strippers, then I'm sure he won't mind making it rain on our bitches. Tie Ms. Tiffany up, then we out of here. Before they left, Low Down walked up to Top Notched, party man, Tiffany sexy than a mother fucker; don't blow that fam, or I'll be on her bumper. Besides, since you up now and got a new plug, maybe we can do some business together one day. They left with them both cuffed together.

$ $ $ $ $

Emma was waiting on a customer when she saw Rozay walk into her job holding a Church's Chicken bag. She smiled at him letting him know that she saw him. She put her car keys up on the counter, "Aye, Lil Bro, I'll get a break after I help my customers. Here's my keys you can grab mama's gift out of the trunk." Here you go, sis, I bought you lunch. Awwwwe, thank you, bro. He handed Emma the bag that contained $21,000 in cash and 3 pieces of chicken. Emma couldn't help but watch Rozay walk out. He looked good to her in his all-Nike gear and his cologne still lingered in her nose. Even the lady that Emma was helping said, "Damn! Your brother sure smells good with his handsome self." Girl, is he married? Naw, just a few baby mamas. Emma was hoping that what she said would turn the attractive white girl off from trying to holla at Rozay when he came back, but to just be sure, Emma hurried the woman up and gave her the change and bill. Thank you, ma'am. But she really wanted to say thank you, Bitch now get the hell out of here.

Emma took a break and went and caught up with Rozay. They sat in his truck, and Emma counted the money. Damn! You went through that fast, are you ok with everything? Rozzy has a big smile on his face. Yep! I'm straight. He was bobbing his head to the music. How is Mrs. Silvia doing? Getting on my nerves like always. Emma playfully hit him on the arm. Don't be talking about my buddy. Watch, I'm going tell her what you said. She already knows that she be getting on my nerves, I tell her every day. I see you looking all sexy like always. Thank you. Well, I better get back in here, thanks for the chicken. Rozay grabbed the bag. That ain't your chicken, and that's mine. He opened the box, took out a wing and started eating it. Ooooh boy! You cold-blooded. You go take your food back. Nope! I just gave you $21,000 you can buy your own chicken. Emma snatched the wing out of his hand and put it back in the box. Emma jumped out of his truck. Now your stingy ass can go buy you some more chicken. Rozay rolled down his window you ain't my woman; you my sister, and I ain't got to feed you. Emma put up her middle finger and walked off. She hated to admit that she was falling for Rozay more than he even knew it. Rozay already knew how he felt about her, but now he was playing her game. Rozay pulled off, blowing his horn.

$ $ $ $ $

Fuzzi sat in her bed drinking Monet and listening to Denise Williams, Silly. It was her best friend's favorite song. Fuzzi always heard it and felt terrible on the day Fantasia died. Fantasia was another homosexual that she and Fuzzi always dreamed of living the lifestyle that Fuzzi was living without Fantasia. They both used to prostitute together and watch out for each other. Fuzzi had just come off a date when Fantasia told her to come go with her. It was a bunch of college students in town, and they were picking up prostitutes. Fuzzi and Fantasia got picked up by four guys on the football team. They took them back to their motel, and 2 guys dated Fuzzi, and 2 guys dated Fantasia. Fuzzi kissed Fantasia on the cheek and told her they would meet back up in a few minutes. The two guys with Fantasia were a little more drunk than the two guys that were with Fuzzi. After Fuzzi finished dating her two guys, she walked out of the room to hear Fantasia yelling and screaming in the room that she was in. The two guys learned that Fantasia wasn't a real woman. After they ripped all of Fantasia's clothes off, it revealed that she had a penis. One of the football players took his helmet and repeatedly beat Fantasia. Wham! Wham! Wham! Wham! Wham! But Fuzzi kicked the door open. Fantasia lay on the floor, covered in blood. The football player was still beating Fantasia with the helmet. Wham! Wham! Wham! When Fuzzi busted through the door, she started screaming. Stop! Stop! Stop! You're going to kill her. The other guy said, "don't you mean kill him." That fucking thing got a dick and balls between his legs. Yuck! He kicked Fantasia and walked out of the room, him and his friend. Fuzzi went to help Fantasia. Come on, baby! Get up! Get up, girl! Let's get the hell out of here. Come on, Fantasia. Fuzzi sat on the floor next to Fantasia. She could see Fantasia's eyes rolling around in her head like she was about to black out. Fantasia looked up at Fuzzi, Bitch! You go do it. Do it for me. I love you, brat. That was Fantasia's nickname for her, and she took her last breath in Fuzzi's arms.

Now, every year, Fuzzi relives that day over, every year on Fantasia's birthday like she was doing now. Fuzzi and Fantasia's favorite was Silly by Denise Williams. They both used to sing it to each other when they got dressed for work. Fuzzi looked at Fantasia's picture, and she wanted to be with Fantasia. Every year around this time, Fuzzi wished that she died with Fantasia. She took a swig from the bottle. Why did you leave me, bitch? I hate you, Mark Anthony Williams. Oh, I love Fantasia, I miss you so muchhh! Her emotions were all over the place, and Izzi was concerned about her. They all knew that Fuzzi went through this remorseful experience every year. Fuzzi felt like she never should have left Fantasia alone with the two guys, so she blamed herself for what happened to Fantasia. Bam! Bam! Bam! Fuzzi, open this fucking door now. Fuzzi sat there singing along to the music and ignoring the knocks at the door. Bam! Bam! Bam! Bam! Fuzzi finally staggered out of her bedroom and stood at her door, saying, "Go away, go away, leave me alone." Silly of me to think that I, she was still singing along to Denise Williams's Silly. Izzi, Emma, Ashley, and Kahi'Lee all stood at the door laughing at her trying to sing. Bitch, answer the door, you ain't no Denise Williams. That made Fuzzi start singing even more louder than she already was. Bam! Bam! Bam! Go away! Go away! I'm going to go be with my sister, leave me alone. Now, Fuzzi's cell phone and house phone were ringing right along with the knocks at the door. Bam! Bam! Bam! Bam! Fuck! Fuck! Damn Yall! Okay! Okay! Okayyy! Shit! A bitch can't even die in peace. Fuzzi opens the door. What! What! What do y'all bitches want with me? Do I be beating on y'all fucking doors, go away? Fuzzi dropped the Moet bottle on the floor, and when she tried to pick it up, she fell on the floor. Bam! Look at her drunk ass.

Izzi tried to help her up, but Fuzzi slapped her hand. Leave me alone, what y'all bitches, and she stopped talking. Girl, look at you. Yo ass so drunk you don't even know what you want to say. Emma said, "How you go cuss somebody out, and you can't even talk." I can say bitch get out. Get out, B I- Bitch-es. They all busted up laughing.

Come on, y'all, get her stupid ass off of the floor. Fuzzi, when you go let that woman rest in peace. I'm sure she already knows that you love her, hell, I'm sure she loves you too, Fuzzi. But she is gone, baby. She gone, Fuzzi, and she not coming back. Well, I'm going with her if you bitches stop beating on my door. Ashley and Emma picked her up off the floor. Well, if you're going to go be with Fantasia, what about us? Fuzzi turned and looked at each one of them, fuck it, then y'all can come and go with me. Emma said, "See, bitch, now I know you crazy. Because I ain't about to die for somebody that I don't know." Then Emma, you stay your happy ass here. Fuzzi, stop talking crazy, we ain't going nowhere, and you ain't either, bitch. Come on here so you can go take a shower; you smell like some whino. Kahi'Lee, go turn the shower on, girl, so we can bring her back to earth. Fuck earth! I'm going to heaven with my sister. What about your four sisters that are here on earth? Don't you love us too, Fuzzi? After Izzi said that that's when Fuzzi started crying. Yeah, I love y'all stupid bitches. We Foxes, ain't we, Fuzzi? Right! Fantasia a Fox, too. Fantasia a Fox, but our big sis is gone now, Fuzzi. Fuzzi started crying uncontrollably. Aggh! Aggh! Aggh! Fuzzi started yelling. I'm go kill that motherfucker. I'm go kill him, Izzi, watch. Yeah, girl, let it all out. I'm go kill that white motherfucker. I'm go kill him. I'm go kill you, devil. I'm go kill you. I believe you, Fuzzi. We believe you. Come on, baby, come on. Izzi slowly led her to the bathroom. I love you, Fantasiaaaaa! Fuzzi screamed, walking towards the bathroom. Izzi finally got Fuzzi into the shower, and Kahi'Lee made her some coffee.

Emma changed Denise Williams for Jacquees, "Beauty doesn't cry." Her mind was on 2 Much. He had called, saying that he was back home and wanted to see her. Emma was missing him too but their trip to Miami she knew wouldn't be happening. Emma was imagining how things would be if she took that trip with him, but here she was on her way to Miami to get paid. Emma felt that money would be the only thing to make her miss this trip. After talking to 2 Much, Emma tried to enjoy her favorite sex toy which she named Sharky. But just as she was about to reach an orgasm, Izzi called, saying they needed to go to Fuzzi's before she tried to kill herself. Damn! Sharky was just about to snatch her and take her deep into the ocean. Now, Emma sat waiting for Fuzzi to come out of a drunken state of mind. After seeing Fuzzi, Emma wanted to get drunk herself just to take her sexual frustration away and to get 2 Much off of her mind. They wind up frying fish and French fries, turning it into another lady's day out.

Kahi'Lee treated everybody to a spa day after they all got manicures and pedicures. After leaving from getting Spa treatments,

Emma received a call from 2 Much, and he was waiting in his Rolls Royce Phantom in front of the spa place where she was all smiles to see him. Damn! Oh, boy, riding like that, I told y'all. I'm good, and I'm leaving with him. I'll pick my car up later. 2 Much stepped out of the car, hugging Emma and swinging her around like they just got married and engaged in a romantic kiss. Fuzzi, Izzi, Kahi'Lee, and Ashley all wanted to know who this mystery man was, and they headed to see. Hello. Well, hello, ladies. Baby, this is Fuzzi, Ashley Kahi'Lee, and that's Izzi. 2 Much's diamonds were reflecting off the sun so bright that Fuzzi said, "Damn, you about to blind a bitch." Everybody started laughing. I'm sorry, Ms. Lady, but I enjoy all the finer things in life. That's why I'm here to pick up y'all friend. Emma was showing all 32 of her teeth. Well, I guess she wasn't lying. You sounded a little too good to be true. Naw, ma ain't no liar. But I'm 2 Much; it's my pleasure to have met y'all. But if y'all don't mind, I've been going crazy missing this beautiful lady right here. He held up Emma's hand like he was showing her off. As much as Fuzzi, Izzi, Kahi'Lee, and Ashley hated to admit it, they all, for the first time, felt a little jealous of Emma. They all thought about Emma setting 2 Much up for them to rob him. Well, girl, don't let us hold you up. Shit, I would have been then left with that man, Fuzzi said it in a sexy way. But 2 Much never took his eyes off of Emma, and that pissed Fuzzi off. Even though they were all attractive, 2 Much's heart seems to only beat to Emma's drum. They all stood there watching the white phantom drift off into the sunset.

While the Foxes were plotting to rob 2 Much, Emma was like Cinderella receiving the Gold Slipper from her Prince. Less than an hour later, upon arriving at 2 Much's house, 2 Much and Emma were ripping each other's clothes off of each other like they couldn't wait to taste and share in each other's sexual frustration. They kissed and removed each other's clothes all the way to 2 Much's bedroom. He roughly threw her to the bed and climbed on top of Emma, kissing every inch of her body from head to toe. 2 Much sucked on her toes, and Emma closed her eyes. Mmmmm! Ohhhh! Baby, yes. He gently worked his way up, licking, sucking and biting Emma's legs. 2 Much spread Emma's legs like a football goal as he licked up her right thigh, making her moan. Mmmmm! Ohhhh, baby, that feels so good. 2 Much kissed her vagina lips, making Emma's body jerk. He took both thumbs and spread her love box. 2 Much made his tongue do a little dance around the inner part of her vagina lips. Oooooh, baby! Mmmmm! Baby, right there. He took his two middle fingers and let them slide slowly in and out of her vagina. Mmmmm! Ohhhh! Baby, yes. That feels so damn good. 2 Much let his tongue join the party licking back and forth on her clitoris. Emma's body couldn't take it. Mmmm! Ahhhhh, oh my god, baby, yes. Oooooh! Ohhhhh! Ahhhhh, I'm about to cum, baby. Im cu cu cumminggggg! Ahhhhh, Oooooooh, baby, yes, yes, yesssssss! but 2 Much was just getting started. He grabbed both of Emma's legs and hiked her ass up like she was being towed away. 2 much ran his tongue from the top of her vagina and let it go up and down. He put his tongue in her vagina, and French kissed it, making his tongue dance around inside her. Ooooooh! Oooooh, daddy, what! What! What are you doing to me? 2 much ran his tongue down to the bottom part of her vagina, and he licked between her vagina and anus. He let his tongue flick inside of her anus and around it. Ooooooh! Ooooooh, daddy! Wait! Wait! That's my spot, daddy. That's it, baby! Oooooooh! Ahhh! My, what the fuckkk, Daddy! 2 Much let his fingers work her clitoris while he licked his tongue around her anus. Emma's body started bucking like a wild horse.

She had never had any man explore her body in the way 2 Much was doing. He laid her on her back on the bed and gently kissed her vagina. 2 Much kissed his way back up to Emma's neck, and she rolled him over. She jumped up and grabbed his penis and took it into her mouth. She started slow until she got to know every inch of his penis, then she started to allow 2 Much to slam it down her throat. Mmmmm! Mmmmm! He closed his eyes and let her mouth lick, suck, and bob on his shaft. Emma climbs on top of him and lets her hand guide his penis into her vagina. She started riding 2 Much like she was on a wild bull trying to beat the longest time. Ooooooh, baby! Yeah! Yeah! Yeah, sexy. Ride that dick, ride it. Ooooooh! Daddy! Daddy, it feels like it's in my stomach. 2 Much rolled her over on her back and put her legs on his shoulders. He thrusted his penis into her vagina. Ooooooh! Ooooooh! My fucking god. Ooooooh! Oohhhhh! Oh, daddy! Daddy, wait. You killing my pussy. Daddy! Daddy! Daddy! But 2 Much gave her no mercy. Ouch! Ouch! Ouch! Ahhhhhh! Mmmmm! Mmmmm! Damn, daddy, shit! Ooooooh!

Aaaaahhh! Aahhhhh! Ahhhhhh! Emma started throwing her hips back. Ooooooh, yeah! Oooooh, yeah! Baby, give it to me. I'm about to cu cu cu I'm cumming! 2 Much and Emma's body were shaking like a bad motor. Mmmmmm! Ahhhhhh! Mmmmmmm! Ooooohhh! Ahhhhhhhhhhhh! They both came like thunder and lightning. 2 Much's body flopped down on top of Emma's damn! Damn, baby! Damn, daddy! They both busted up laughing. Emma whispered in 2 Much's ear. I love you 2 Much, please don't hurt me. I'll never do that, baby, and I love you, too. Emma closed her eyes and squeezed his body.

2 Much jumped up, wait right here. I got a little something for you. He left the room, and Emma watched his naked body as he walked away. Moments later, 2 Much came back holding two boxes. Emma sat up, what's this? He opened the first box, and the diamonds hit Emma's eyes. It was a diamond chain that had a diamond pendant that read Mrs. 2 Much. Ahhhhhh baby, it's beautiful. Put it on me. Emma turned around, and it hung longer than the first chain that he gave her. Emma ran her fingers across the chain and pendant. Here! Emma opened the black velvet box, and she started crying. Man, don't play with me. What are you doing. 2 Much got down on one knee. "Emma Myers, will you make me the happiest man in the whole world? I knew the moment that I first laid eyes on you that I can't go through life without you, so Emma, will you marry me?" Tears ran down Emma's face, and she thought about Fuzzi, Ashley, Izzi, and Kahi'Lee. The vows that she had made to the Foxes. Foxes

over money, men and anything that separates us. Emma said, "yes, yes, yesssss, I'll be your wife." I am Mrs. 2 Much. Baby, I love you, Yesssss! 2 Much stood up and kissed his now fiancé. Baby, am I dreaming? No, baby, you're not dreaming, Emma. I can't live without you. I can't live without you either, 2 Much. What's my last name go be? Carter! Emma Carter. Baby, I love it. I love you. Before Emma could even ask him, 2 Much said, "I'm Khalil Carter, AKA 2 Much." But that name is to never be repeated to nobody, understood? Yes, 2 Much, I understand. He smiled because she didn't repeat his real name. One last question: What's that? No! No! 2 questions. Do I keep my job? That would be your choice, baby. Am I moving in with you, or are you going to get us a home together? 2 Much grabbed her hand and walked her through the bedroom. He opened the closet, and Emma's eyes opened up wide. Every name-brand clothes were hanging in the closet. Fendi, Gucci, Prada, Chanel, Versace, Alexander McQueen, and Louis Vuitton. You name it, and it was hanging in her size, plus rows and rows of shoes in her size. Emma stepped into the closet and looked through the clothes and sizes. Baby, how did you know my size and my last name? 2 Much laughed, baby, say my name. 2 Much. Then there's your answer. Emma walked up to him and kissed him. So, you telling me that I'm at home? He turned and walked away. Hey, baby! 2 Much turned around and looked at Emma. I'm about to change your name, baby. And what's that, to 2 Damn Much. 2 much busted up laughing, okay you win, I'll be that.

Chapter Twenty-Four
FEAR ALWAYS COME

Gate 14, flight 187 is now boarding to Miami. Fuzzi, Ashley, Kahi'Lee, Izzi, and Emma all toasted to their next mission, then headed towards the gate to board the plane. Izzi and Ashley looked at each other, not really knowing what to expect. Emma had been hiding a real big secret from them, but she knew how they all seemed to have girl talk time when they all got together and now would be a better time than any. The captain came over the loudspeaker, telling everyone what to do in case of an emergency. To turn off electrical devices and put their seats in an upright position. Ladies and gentlemen, make sure all seat belts are in a locked position. He told them approximately what time the plane should be arriving and what the weather would be and to enjoy their flight. After the plane took off, a few flight attendants walked the aisle, taking orders. Hello, ladies, what can I get y'all today? Fuzzi and Izzi were sitting together with an old white man. Emma,

Kahi'Lee, and Ashley sat together. They all ordered something to drink being that they already had started the party back at the bar in Phoenix. Fuzzi was messing with the man who was sitting next to her. Man, you look like you about ready to switch on your people the way you keep staring at these thick chocolate thighs. The man was turning crayon red in the face. You want this white woman, or you want to taste this chocolate? He looked at both of them but pointed his finger at Fuzzi. You going to Miami on vacation, or do you live there? I'm going on vacation; my younger brother is getting married. Do you have $20,000 that you could get your hands on? Oh, no! I don't have that type of money, ma'am. Fuzzi told him, then you better off looking out that window than roaming your eyes up and down my body if you can't afford it. So, stop looking. You can look at them clouds and dream about all the black pussy you want. Izzi put her hands over her face; Emma trade seats with me because this heffa is crazy. But the man did as he was told and turned to look out the window.

Izzi and Fuzzi started talking about Mr. Shelton. Izzi asked if she had told him about Caroline. Yeah, girl, actually, I did. I forgot to tell you that he promised me he'd look into her case. Hey, what's the story with you and her? Did you sleep with her, too, Izzi? Bitch! Fuck you. I'm still into men. It isn't shit another woman could do for me. We were just close in there and listening to her situation Fuzzi, and the guy was just using her as a mule and not giving her shit. I tried making her see that, but I guess when that love wall goes up, everything else is blocked from you seeing the real person. Look at me with my husband. I was the biggest fool of them all. Tears started rolling down Izzi's face. Fuzzi grabbed her hand, and everybody played the fool at one time or another. But who really was the fool? You are still here enjoying life, they both ten feet deep in the ground. So, it sounds to me like I'm not sitting next to no fool. Fuzzi looked at the White guy and said, "Well, maybe I take that back." Izzi started laughing. She wiped her face; you always know how to make me smile, girl. That's why I'm here, and DuVall ain't, Bitch!

Izzi, let me ask you a serious question. What's that? What's so great about being married? Having somebody in your life that you know loves you unconditionally and put you before everything in the world. Most of the time, even your own self, Fuzzi. That person doesn't really care if you're in a mansion. They'll lay next to you comfortably if you're in a box, just as long as it's you that they're lying next to. What really got to Fuzzi was when Izzi said, do you remember yesterday when you said that you wanted to go lay with Fantasia? Fuzzi shook her head, yes. Well, that's what marriage is like. Nobody in this world has made you feel comfortable and know you like Fantasia did, and your heart misses that type of love. Now tears started rolling down Fuzzi's face. She turned to her and looked her right in the eyes; even though I took DuVall's life, Fuzzi, a part of me wants to go and lay next to him. They looked back at each other, and Izzi knew that she clearly understood. Marriage is also a comfortable and safe place. Fuzzi, you are starting to see that in Mr. Shelton. Sometimes, when you mean for things to be a certain way, that's not how it always turns out. Fuzzi, can I tell you something? Yeah, what's that? Fuzzi, I'll be in debt to you for the rest of my life. Why do you say that, Izzi? I'm not sitting here because of no money y'all gave Mr. Shelton; I'm sitting here because whatever you had done to that man, he didn't want to disappoint you because he loves you, Fuzzi. I saw the look in his eyes every time he came to visit me. The only problem now is when he got bitten by the love bug, Fuzzi, you did, too. I see that same look in your eyes when you mention his name. So, yeah, girl, don't miss out on your own future to make anybody else around you happy. I think they kind of say that to all women. Fuzzi said, "Bitch, when we get back home, I'm taking your ass back to jail and go get my friend Izzi because I don't know who the hell you are, but I love yo ass." Fuzzi reached over and hugged Izzi. Thank you, girl, I love you. What! You didn't call me a bitch. Naw, bitch, I didn't. They both busted up laughing.

Emma reached her hand over the seat; look, I'm getting married too. 2 Much asked me, and I said yes. Fuzzi and Izzi turned around at the same time. What? Izzi grabbed her hand and looked at the 3-carat ring. Girl, I know yo ass ain't about to marry him. Then I know you ain't about to marry Mr. Shelton either. That's different, Emma. And how so? Izzi, what did you just say to Fuzzi? Don't miss out on your future to make anybody else around you happy, right? Emma sat back and looked at all of them crazy. I don't care what y'all say,

I'm marrying 2 Much, and if you don't like it, then don't come. Ashley said, "Both of y'all asses is crazy." Both of them dudes is rich, hell, give them to me I'll marry both of their asses. Kahi'Lee said, "Wait a minute, ain't that going against what we stand for?" Me getting married ain't about to change my life. My man does his thing, and I do mine. If my life changes, then I damn sure wouldn't be on this plane. Him and I had a great talk before I left Phoenix. I'm still keeping my job, and I'm still rocking with the Foxes. Yeah, until he starts telling you what to do and how to do it. Fuzzi, is that what Mr. Shelton go do to you, too? Hell naw. What make you think some white man go tell me what to do? The guy sitting next to her looked at Fuzzi and rolled his eyes. Man, if you roll your eyes at me one more time, they about to see what I'm a do to a white man. I told yo ass to look out that damn window. Look, ma'am, you're not going to sit here and threaten me all the way to Miami. Yes, I am, white boy. But I left a woman just like you at home so that I can enjoy my vacation. Don't let the look fool you. I'm married to an African American woman, and I love my wife. I didn't mean to listen to your conversation, but your friend was telling you right. Don't let the color of that man's skin prevent you from being happy. Then, you better keep watching Denzel's movies but keep sleeping with Brad Pitt. He turned back and looked out the window.

"Yeah, bitch, you did," Izzi said. Fuzzi just got read by a white man. Emma, Kahi'Lee, and Ashley started laughing. Fuzzi nudged Izzi with her elbow. Bitch if he keeps talking to me like that, I'll make him cheat on that bitch. Hell, he got my vagina hot now. Izzi started laughing so loud that everybody on the plane was looking at her. After they exited the plane, Fuzzi had rented a red Ferrari Convertible, a red Convertible Lamborghini, and a white Convertible Corvette. She wanted to make sure that they fit right into the Miami scene. If you were going to catch big fish, Fuzzi told Emma, Izzi, Kahi'Lee, and Ashley, you need to look the part and draw it to you. We're beautiful women looking good and driving nice vehicles. So, any man who's trying to get your attention knows that they have to come with it. Fuzzi had made reservations for the Four Seasons at the Surf Club. Everybody has their own rooms because Fuzzi has a completely different plan for this trip. She knew that it was big money in Miami, and the Foxes came for their share of it.

Emma started screaming, ahhhhhhh! Girl, would you look at this? They had checked out their rooms, and she was looking at the beach from her bedroom window. Wow! This is so pretty. They all were looking down at all the people enjoying themselves. Izzi said, "I don't know about y'all, but I'm about to put my bathing suit on and join them." Fuzzi said, "Bitch, give me 30 minutes, and I'll join you, too." Emma, Ashley, and Kahi'Lee told them y'all not about to leave us, we coming too. They all went to their rooms to get dressed. Fuzzi said, call me when y'all ready. They all went straight to their suitcases and took out their sexiest swimsuit. Izzi put on a white and gold Chanel bodysuit with the stomach and back out. White flat open toes 3-inch heels and put her hair up in a genie ponytail. Kahi'Lee put on a 2-piece Louis Vuitton white with the LV symbol all over the suit. She put on Louis Vuitton laced-up heels to her knee. Ashley wore a pink Fendi swimsuit with an open slit down her backside with matching heels. Fuzzi has on Gucci neon booty shorts with a half top that's neon green and white with some white Gucci open toed flats. Her hair was silky straight, hanging down. Emma put on a Versace swimsuit with the gold Versace belt around her waist and Versace gold 3-inch heels. She was carrying a big Versace beach towel to match her outfit. Her hair was in deep wavy locks. They all started calling each other's rooms. Fuzzi asked everybody to meet in her room so that they could get their new names and know what roles to play.

As they were walking to the elevator, there was a woman sitting in front of a room door crying. Emma walked up to her; baby girl, what's wrong? I'm sick of this motherfucker, he always disrespecting me with any new bitch that gets in his face. Who, baby? My fucking husband. I can't stand his ass; I wish his stupid ass drop dead. Emma looked at Izzi, then she looked at the other girls, like damn. He got 2 bitches in our room fucking them, and won't open the door. Fuzzi threw her hands up in the air like girl, come on, that's not our problem. Okay, you guys go ahead, and I'll meet y'all on the beach. They were on South Beach, and there was every type of beach body walking around and trying to attract the men and money sharks. But Fuzzi, Izzi, Ashley, and Kahi'Lee always made their presence known, no matter what type of woman was in their company. Oh my god, girl, this is living right here. I'm living in the wrong place; this I could get used to. Izzi agreed with Ashley, hell yeah. Men were already making catcalls and giving sexual compliments. Fuzzi and the girls went and found themselves a nice spot on the beach. They started laying down their towels and taking in a good view of the beach.

Izzi was rubbing suntan lotion on when two guys approached them. Ladies, can we give y'all a hand or join y'all? Izzi lied, no, thank you. I don't think that our husbands will appreciate that. They might get really upset to come and find y'all here. Oh! Oh! Please excuse us, but you're so beautiful. Izzi smiled, thank you. Izzi told Fuzzi she thought a shark had come out of the water. Big as the guy's belly was and all the teeth he had when he smiled, all they saw was a shark's mouth. Fuzzi, Ashley, Kahi'Lee, and Izzi started laughing. Damn, maybe we need to go change. Does anybody see Emma? They looked around, and Emma still hadn't exited their hotel yet. I couldn't believe that she let that woman tie her up with that woman and her husband's problems. Maybe Emma came to save their marriage. Girl, can y'all believe that she is going to marry that guy? They all started talking about her and 2 Much. Fuzzi was contemplating robbing him after Emma told them about 2 Much. As for the type of gifts that he was giving Emma, she knew that the big payday would be sweet.

Fuzzi was interrupted by her cell phone ringing. Hello, bitch, you through playing wedding counselor. Fuzzi put a real serious look on her face that made Izzi, Ashley, and Kahi'Lee take notice to her change of expression. Okay, we'll meet you in your room. Fuzzi hung up and started gathering up her things. Come on y'all, let's go. What's wrong? Is Emma okay? Izzi put a concerned look on her face. Come on, I'll explain it on the way up. As they entered Emma's room, they weren't too shocked to see Emma's company. Foxes, this is Genesis, our soon-to-be new friend. They all knew that something was up, but Emma addressed them with Foxes. Hello again, ladies. I'm so sorry about my behavior earlier. No problem. Girl, we definitely understand when your husband is cheating on you. So, did you finally get into the room? Nope! Y'all friend convinced me to pay him back in another way, so I'll just allow him to have his little fun for now. Genesis put a vindictive and malicious smile on her face. So, what's the deal, Genesis? I have a little proposition for y'all, that's if y'all interested. Fuzzi said, "Well, for starters, we need to know what it is that we should or shouldn't be interested in."

My husband is expecting a big shipment of drugs this Sunday, and I want y'all to rob him before the shipment even comes. Fuzzi was about to give Genesis an answer, but Genesis stopped her before she could. Wait! Before you give me an answer, y'all have to kill him and shoot me after the robbery. Ashley stepped back and started shaking her head. Noooo! Fuzzi was glad that Genesis didn't see her because Genesis was facing her and Emma. I'm willing to supply y'all with anything y'all need to complete the job. All y'all have to do is wait until we go to bed and then come in and rob us both. I'll leave the side door open. We have 5 pit bulls on the grounds, but 3 of the dogs usually be in the backyard watching his drugs. They are buried, so you won't have time to dig them up, plus the dogs won't let y'all back there in the yard. The other two dogs stay in the house. How in the hell do you expect us to fight off 2 pit bulls? Don't worry about Rocky and Menace, I got a little something that will put them to sleep. So, what type of money are we talking about? Almost a million dollars, actually, $850,000 in cash, but I'll need $25,000, and y'all can split the rest after his people see that I got shot too. They'll take care of me, but I got to take a bullet.

Fuzzi walked up close to Genesis, almost nose to nose. Genesis, before I even give you an answer, you got to give me the real, baby girl. I'm a woman just like you are, and ain't no woman wakes up and just wants her husband killed unless he done something really fucked up. Men and women cheat every day. I'm not buying that bullshit that you want to kill your husband for cheating. Who in the hell was down there in that room with him? Genesis dropped her head and got quiet. That's what the fuck, I thought. Okay! Okay! Okay! He's in the room fucking my twin sister. Okay! Okay, you happy now, my own fucking blood sister. Tears started rolling down her face. Fuzzi took both hands and wiped her tears away. We'll take the job. Set it up. Fuzzi told her that she was going to need three guns plus to rent them an SUV truck and give them the address so that they could get familiar with their neighborhood. Genesis said, no problem; anything else? I'm going to need $100,000 upfront, just in case you decide to waste our time. Genesis didn't hesitate, no problem. I'll meet you back here at 5 o'clock with everything that you asked for. She looked at Emma. Thank you, baby girl. I'll never forget your kindness. They kissed on the cheek, and Genesis left.

The moment she stepped out of the room, Ashley went crazy. "Bitch, what the fuck is wrong with you, I didn't sign up for this." "If you trying to get paid just like us, then what the fuck you think we're doing here in Miami, Ash? If you are not cut out for the job," then Fuzzi pointed at the door. Ashley threw her hands up and headed out the door. "Ashley wait," Emma went running after her. Izzi asked Fuzzi, "Are you really going to do that?" Hell yeah, bitch, for $850,000, his ass is dead as a dead man walking. Anybody that ain't down with me can catch up with Ashley's tired ass. Now that she's gone, we'll get 212,500 apiece. How in the fuck that we come to get paid, and it's right in our faces. Now everybody acting like their eyes ain't on the prize. Fuzzi said, "Well, I tell y'all what, I'm taking my ass back to the beach and come back to meet this bitch at 5 o'clock if she shows." Fuzzi grabbed her towel and stuff then headed back out the door. See, I told your ass that's why I never wanted to tell her shit. Fuzzi slammed the door. Bam!

Izzi and Kahi'Lee started talking about everything that they heard. Izzi thought that Kahi'Lee would back out too, but Kahi'Lee have a different feeling towards cheating men and really didn't care. She was down with pulling off a job. What about you Izzi, are you in or out? Girl, I got change in my purse, what you think. They both slapped hands and went to check on Ashley. Bam! Bam! Bam! Izzi was beating on Ashley's door, but Ashley had already gotten her suitcase and was in the lobby trying to call a cab to go back to the airport. Emma was trying to talk her out of leaving, but Ashley's mind was already made up. Here, they are right here, Izzi. Ashley, what are you doing? What does it look like I'm doing, Izzi? Take that suitcase back upstairs. Ashley started smiling, because she knew that if she left them then they wouldn't let her live that one down. Fuck, Fuzzi girl, she crazy. Kahi'Lee said, "Then I guess we're crazy too, Ashley, because we're not turning our backs on her." You not either, so come on and bring yo ass on. Ooooooh! I'm not liking y'all bitches right now. They all headed back to the elevators. By the time they made it back to the beach, Fuzzi was being accompanied by two guys that look like football players. Oh, here come my sisters now. Fuzzi and Ashley rolled their eyes at each other. Hello, beautiful ladies! Zack, Curtis. Zack and Fuzzi made up some names introducing them. These guys were telling me where all the hot spots is. They said that one of the clubs is jumping tonight. Hello! Hi! Everybody met each other. Fuzzi, Izzi, Ashley, Kahi'Lee, and Emma stayed awhile and enjoyed the beach. They were covering each other with sand and playing in the water. Fuzzi and Ashley finally broke away and found a comfortable place on the beach to talk.

Hey, I'm sorry that I walked out on y'all earlier. Fuzzi hugged Ashley. No need to apologize you did what your heart told you to do. If you didn't do that, then trust me, Ashley, I would have been a little concerned about you. Fear always comes before any money can bring happiness. If you don't know what you're fearing, then you leave yourself open to never enjoying the happiness because you slip up and let your guards down. Now, I know when we do anything, your guard is going to go up because you'll fear what's at hand and won't slip up. I was turned out by a pimp, and I respected him because one day he told me, Fuzzi, the day that you put your hand on a trick's door handle without fear then I know to never expect to see you again. But as long as fear overcomes you before getting in a car then I'll know that you will be on guard. Expecting for something to go wrong and if it doesn't, then bitch I know you should have my money. Ashley hugged Fuzzi, what a story but I do believe what you're trying to tell me is you're afraid too but going into the situation with fear you'll come out with the money. Ashley, my pimp would have loved you, bitch, you learn fast. Izzi, Kahi'Lee, and Emma walked up. Oh, I see y'all love each other again. Ashley said, "I'm sorry to everyone." But nobody responded they knew that Ashley had never done no street shit. When they met her, all she did was work hard and try to save the world. But after landing a job at children's services, she quickly learned that she couldn't save every child so there wasn't no way that she could save the world. Yeah! Yeah! Yeah! Fuzzi, it's 4:30, did you forget that we got business to handle? No, I didn't forget and until I know that shit is straight up, then I don't want nobody else involved yet.

Let me go by myself, and if everything checks out then I'll give y'all a call. But if y'all don't hear from me by 5:15 then grab y'all shit and head back to Phoenix. Got it. They all looked at each other. Naw, Fuzzi, you go, then we all go. Hey! Hey! Look, I'm the one put y'all in this, Fuzzi. How about I go by myself and if shit checks out, I'll call y'all. Emma gave Fuzzi a serious look. Okay, Emma, me and you will go. Izzi, Kahi'Lee, and Ashley watched as Fuzzi and Emma walked across the beach. Kahi'Lee joked about how big Fuzzi's booty was. They could see Fuzzi's butt shake like a stripper on the stage clear across the beach and so did every man because they were all watching and whistling. It was 5:18, and they started freaking out. Girl, what do we do? Do you think something went wrong? Fuzzi said that she'll call us by 5:15, and it's already 5:18. They all started gathering their things and were about to leave the beach. Izzi's cellphone started ringing. Ring, ring! Hello! Izzi listened for a minute then a smile came across her face. We're on our way up right now. They got the money she was on the up and up.

$ $ $ $ $

Club Rucker was packed and crawling with ballers and street hustlers. Fuzzi pushed the Red Lamborghini up with Izzi and Kahi'Lee in the red Ferrari. Emma and Ashley were pushing that

Convertible Corvette. They all were dressed sexy but provocatively. Every body part was saying come pay your way. Fuzzi wore a pink lace catsuit with no panties and bra. When the Lamborghini doors went up, and she stepped out, every penis rose to her body's arrival. Damn Ma, "Somebody shouted out loud." Izzi and Kahi'Lee stepped out next. Izzi wore a Versace mini skirt with Versace high thigh boots. Kahi'Lee has on a white teddy with fishnet stockings and 3-inch Prada heels. The ooooos and ahhhhhhhs, the damn ma continued. Ashley and Emma exit their vehicle. Ashley made every man do a double take. Her Louis Vuitton nude color booty shorts and top revealing her nipples with diamond high thigh boots shut it down. Dudes were getting up close to make sure she wasn't naked. Emma stepped out in an all-diamond mini skirt with matching heels. The night light made her shine like a million bucks. All the fellows were trying to see who and where the five sexy, beautiful, attractive women come from. The doorman allowed them straight in the club. Ladies, welcome to Club Rucker. Hey, Buck, show them to VIP for me. I'm Yee Billions, baby, whatever y'all want tell them, it's on Yee B. I got y'all everybody knows the name. Fuzzi and the ladies followed the bouncers to VIP. What y'all ladies drinking? Fuzzi said surprise us, it's your town. Hey Kitty, Don P me about six times. You know it's a little something in the diaper bag for your kitty kat. He was telling her that she knows that he tips well. When Kitty returned with their drinks, Yee Billions pulled out about $30,000 in all hundred-dollar bills. They all started poppin bottles. I want to toast to Texas for giving birth to such beautiful women. Everybody cups went up Aaaaaaaa! Aaaaaa! Aaaaaaaaa! The D.J played Rick Ross and Meek Mills, "she on my dick," and the club went up. Yee Billions grabbed Fuzzi and headed to the dance floor. In less than a few minutes, Fuzzi had everybody watching her dance. Ashley was also a great dancer, and they took over Club Rucker. Yee Billions put you in the mind of birdman but was much darker. Fuzzi was throwing ass at him like Beyonce in a music video. Fuzzi was rubbing his penis and his whole-body making Yee Billions hornier than Bill Clinton in the White House.

The next song came on, and a female who knew Yee Billions stepped in. She was getting jealous of the attention that he was giving Fuzzi. Fuzzi whispered something into Ashley's ear while she was dancing, and they exited the dance floor. They went and got Emma, Kahi'Lee, and Izzi. They all left the club. While they were driving away, they heard Yee Billions hollering. Hey, bitch, say bitch. Imma kill your ass, bitch, when I catch you. After he finished dancing, they returned to the table. He noticed that Fuzzi, Emma, Kahi'Lee, Izzi, and Ashley were all gone. He put his hands in his pocket, and all his money was gone. Turned out to be $37,000 because Fuzzi was back at their hotel counting his money. Emma said, "Girl, that dude had money. Why we didn't take him for all of it?" He had to have on over $100,000 in just jewelry. Fuzzi threw them all $6,000 a piece on the bed. Bitch, that jewelry wasn't worth shit. How you know that? Fuzzi walked up to Emma and started dancing then they all heard beet, beet, beet! Ashley said what's that noise. That's Emma's diamonds. Bitch, they're real. His shit didn't even light up. Fuzzi tossed her diamond tester to Ashley. Bitch, I'm a Fox for real, sly and crafty. They all busted up laughing.

$ $ $ $ $

It was 3 in the morning, and Fuzzi had already turned the Lambo, Ferrari, and Corvette back in. They were now in a Cadillac SUV, pulling into a nice neighborhood in Miami. They all loved every home that they passed. The GPS let them know they were back at the house they had been scoping for the last two nights. Fuzzi told Emma to kill the lights as they pulled up in front of Genesis's home. Foxes, are y'all ready to get this money? Hell yeah, Emma said, "Okay, everybody knows what to do, right?" All heads nodded yep. Fuzzi, Emma, and Kahi'Lee checked their weapons. Fuzzi has 40 semi-automatic Glock, and Emma and Kahi'Lee both have 9 mm. They checked their weapons one last time before exiting the truck. They all have on black with black gloves and black cat masks. Fuzzi walked up to the door and turned the knob. They waited a second to see if they got any response from the dogs, but nothing happened. Fuzzi nodded her head to say let's go. They opened the door and entered the house. Their weapons were pointed and aimed, ready to shoot at anything that jumped out at them. Fuzzi put her finger to her lips and told them to follow her up the stairs. They slowly maneuvered through the large, luxurious home. Fuzzi could hear a television blaring loudly at the end of the hall. She pointed towards the bedroom to say to them that this had to be their room with the two big double doors. They could see the reflection of their fireplace glistening off the bedroom wall.

When they entered the bedroom, to their surprise, Genesis was lying next to her husband. Her legs were wide open, and she was sliding the vibrator in and out of her vagina. She was watching a porno film while her husband slept. When they entered the room, Genesis didn't even respond or act surprised. But they have caught her releasing herself to a porno flick. Mmmmm! Mmmmmmmmm! Ooooooh! Ahhhhhhh! Genesis was just keeping up with the two porno stars. Fuzzi looked at the heavy-set fat man that lay peacefully sleeping on his back. Fuzzi kicked his leg, and when he quickly turned over to see what was happening. Pow! Pow! Pow! Fuzzi put three bullets into Genesis's husband, and his body jerked to every bullet. His head fell over to the side, and that's when Genesis showed any reaction to what was even taking place. She looked at her husband and smiled. Then she removed the vibrator and sucked on it. Mmmmmmmmm! She grabbed the remote and lowered the volume. Thank you, ladies. Now his rotten ass won't hurt me no more. Now, he can join his rotten-ass mama. Emma looked at Fuzzi and Kahi'Lee like this bitch is crazy. The money is in that closet; you can leave the Nike bag. I already took out my 25, and the rest is y'all's. Now, here comes the part that I hate. Just shoot me in the leg, and that would look good enough. I'll call the police from downstairs and bleed all through the house to make it look like I crawled to the phone. Fuzzi walked over to shoot Genesis in the leg, but Emma stopped her. Wait! Emma walked over to the bed. Hey, didn't your vows say until death do y'all apart? Genesis said, yeah! Emma said, "Well, death haven't done y'all apart yet. So, you should join him." Pow! Pow! Pow! Pow! Fuzzi and Kahi'Lee both jumped, bitch, why did you do that because I'm not a home wrecker; I don't believe in breaking up a marriage. Fuzzi grabbed her stomach, laughing, and this bitch calls me the crazy one. They grabbed all their bags of money and jewelry and calmly walked out of the house. Soon as they made it back to their hotel, they reheated their lemon pepper wings and split the money. Fuzzi gave everybody $170,000 apiece. The next day, they took the Cadillac SUV and got it washed. They made sure that they wiped down the interior and windows. Then they left the Cadillac SUV in the ghetto with the keys in the ignition, to find its joyriders for the police to pull them over. They boarded their flight back to the dirty desert, leaving no paper trail to them.

Chapter Twenty-Five
YOU MAY KISS THE BRIDE

If life could get any better for someone, then the Foxes were experiencing it. They all experienced life at the highest level in the game. They had hit a few more licks that had put them all over the millionaire status. New York, Texas, and the King Pin who was head over hills for Kahi'Lee whom they met in a night club in California, made life become really comfortable for them. Emma had moved in with 2 Much, and their relationship had become so strong that Mrs. Briggs, 2 Much's mother, was in town helping Emma plan their wedding. They are due to get married in six months, but right now, everyone was walking into the Spirit of God Christian Community Church. There were all types of people from all different lifestyles gathering in the church. Fuzzi and Dave finally decided that it was time for them to spend the rest of their life together. Mr. Shelton was the happiest man in the whole world when his divorce went through. He and Fuzzi were on a plane to the

Bahamas, where he proposed to her with the 3-carat diamond ring, and Fuzzi said, "Yes! Yes! Yes!"

Izzi, somebody needs to go and talk with Fuzzi. That crazy girl in there talking about how she can't do it, and she isn't coming out. What? Are you serious, Ashley? As a heart attack. But they got all these people here. Dave is going to be so heartbroken. Come on, y'all, we got to go do something fast. Fuzzi sat on a stool, looking at herself in the mirror. She looked amazing in an all-white custom Couture laced gown with a matching veil over her face. It appeared to Izzi when they entered the room that Fuzzi was having another Fantasia meltdown. Because Izzi heard Fuzzi saying why aren't you here bitch. You're supposed to be here. Fuzzi, what the hell is wrong with you? You have got all the people in that church waiting on you and you're going out there. No, I'm not bitch! But you're going to go marry that man if I have to drag you out there myself. Fuzzi started crying, and Izzi, Emma, Ashley, and Kahi'Lee all tried to console their friend. Bitch! I can't do it. I can't do it. That man deserves somebody better than me. I'm rotten as hell. Y'all even say so yourselves all the time. Emma said, "Girl, you are rotten." Shut up, Emma. Naw, let her speak her mind. I was going to say before I got interrupted. Emma flicked her hand at Izzi, you're rotten as hell, but that man loves everything rotten about you, Fuzzi. I see how he looks at you and how he lights up whenever you come around him. Fuzzi, give him a chance. Hell, give yourself a chance. We can't live this type of life forever, girl. Fuzzi shook her head no and put it down. I can't marry him, Emma. They all were interrupted by a knock at the door. The preacher's wife, Mrs. Arnold, stuck her head in the door. Ladies, it's almost time. Is the bride ready? Ma'am, it almost looks like it ain't about to be a no wedding. Why? What's the matter? She came walking into the room and saw Fuzzi crying. Baby, what's the matter? Are you okay? Fuzzi looked up at Mrs. Arnold, who reminded her of her aunt. I can't go through with this. Baby, do you love him? Yes, I do. Do you know that beyond a shadow of a doubt that he loves you? Yes, Ma'am, I do. Mrs. Arnold asked if she and Fuzzi be left alone. Izzi, Kahi'Lee, Ashley, and Emma all kissed Fuzzi on the cheek and walked out. Thank you, Ma'am. Mrs. Arnold winked her eye at them and closed the door behind them.

Okay, girl, now what's really going on with you? Mrs. Arnold, no, you can call me Mary. Why are you in this room and your future is out there? You already know how you feel; you don't really know if you could love him, right? Fuzzi raised her head and looked at her. Yeah, you're right. Baby, the type of man that you're expecting to wake up to might not be the man that God sent to love you. I've been married three times, and the fly handsome guy that every woman would expect on their arm, child, turned out to be the worst man and caused me the worst pain. The next one that I really loved and cared about turned out he wanted to be more of a woman than I am. I didn't think that I'd ever find happiness. So, I prayed and told God that if he wanted me to be with a man and have a husband, he sent me one. When he came into my life, I felt the same way you're sitting there feeling. He wasn't the most handsome man, nor did he look like the type of man I wanted. But God had sent him, so it turned out that he was perfect in his own way because he loved me, so I had to turn him into the type of man that I wanted and needed in my life. So, Mrs. Mary, what happened to him? Nothing, Baby, he out there waiting to marry you and your husband. We were in the streets together, and we turned to God together. But that wasn't me or him who done that. What he asked for was a woman and wife, and what I asked for was a man and husband. God gave us each other, and I've been happy with his decision, and trust me, baby, you'll be happy too. That man go protect you and love you. The next man just go be offering you pleasure the same thing he go be offering the next woman. But that man out there is offering you a lifetime. Now, you fix that beautiful face of yours, and you go get your blessing. Fuzzi stood up and hugged Mrs. Arnold. Thank you, ma'am. Now, when I can't figure it out, I got somebody that I can talk to. Baby, you can call me anytime; I'll be right here for you. Fuzzi turned around and fixed her make-up. Before Mrs. Arnold walked out, she said, "Baby, if he loves you, then he'll be who he knows whom he should be to keep you." Fuzzi smiled, and Mrs. Arnold walked out.

Izzi, Emma, Kahi'Lee, and Ashley came rushing into the room. So, is there going to be a wedding or not? Fuzzi stood up. You can go tell them that I'm ready. God sent me a husband and a mother also, bitch. Izzi looked at Emma, Kahi'Lee, and Ashley, not knowing what Fuzzi meant by that. They went and told Mr. Shelton that the wedding was about to start. He was talking to his best friend and Billionaire, Mr. William Lehmann, when they told him that the wedding was about to start. Come on, Dave, let's go get you married, buddy. They all came walking down the aisle, and Mr. Shelton waved at a few friends. He and his best friend from high school, Garrett Bryson, walked up front and stood with Pastor Arnold. The pastor shook Mr. Shelton's hand. The music started playing, and Fuzzi walked down the aisle. Mr. Shelton put the biggest smile on his face. 2 Much walked her down the aisle and gave her to Mr. Shelton. Mr. Shelton told Fuzzi, "You're beautiful, baby," and she smiled at him. Pastor Arnold went on with the wedding. He asked who was here to give Fuzzi away. 2 much raised his hand that he was. After Mr. Shelton and Fuzzi said their vows, Pastor Arnold said, "I now pronounce y'all man and wife. You may kiss your bride." Mr. Shelton raised Fuzzi's veil and kissed his wife. Everybody congratulated them by hugging and shaking hands. 2 Much turned around, and just for a moment, he and the Billionaire, Mr. Lehmann, looked right at each other. But 2 Much quickly turned his head and walked out of the church. 2 Much knew who Mr. Lehmann was, but Mr. Lehmann hadn't seen him long enough to recognize who 2 Much was. He was too busy with the wedding.

While everybody was congratulating Fuzzi, Mr. Lehmann's wife, Amirah, walked up to congratulate Fuzzi. Izzi, Kahi'Lee,

Ashley, and Emma were also standing next to Fuzzi. Congratulations, you're a very pretty wife. Amirah and Fuzzi were hugging when she saw the diamond necklace on Emma's neck. She walked up to Emma. Hello, your dress is beautiful. Oh, thank you. Then Mrs. Lehmann touched her necklace. Oh my, that is beautiful. Where did you buy that? I didn't; my fiancé gave it to me as a gift. Ahhhh! Who's your fiancé? He right over there, and when they turned around, 2 Much was nowhere around. He was just standing right there. Oh well, he's around here somewhere. Emma went to hug Fuzzi, and Mrs. Lehmann went towards her husband.

When everyone was leaving to attend their reception, Emma didn't know it, but she was having pictures taken of her. Click! Click! Click! Click! Click! Emma noticed that 2 Much Phantom wasn't in the parking lot. She called him because they came together, and it wasn't like him to take off and leave her nowhere really without giving her notice. 2 Much answered on the second ring. Hello! He told Emma to ride to the reception with Kahi'Lee, and he'll meet her there. But even after the reception was over 2 Much still never showed up. But Emma was so drunk that it really didn't phase her. Because they lived in the same home, and one thing they didn't do in their relationship was to question each other's movements. The Billionaire, Mr. Lehmann, had pulled Mr. Shelton to the side to inquire about Emma, which he thought that Mr. Lehmann was inquiring with his penis. So, he said, yeah, she beautiful, ain't she? That's one of my wife's girlfriends. Do you want me to give her your number? Naw, that's fine; I'm here for you, buddy. Today is all about you. They hugged, and no more was said about Emma. Emma had given Fuzzi and Mr. Shelton matching Rolex watches from her and 2 Much as their wedding gift. They were all so happy for Fuzzi, and Mr. Shelton was on cloud 9. Glad that they were finally Mr. and Mrs. Shelton.

Mr. Shelton didn't know it, but his ex-wife was also there. She sat in the parking lot drinking a bottle of Seagram's gin and holding a 9 mm in her other hand. Luckily, she got so drunk that she fell asleep in the car. When the reception was over, they said their goodbyes to everyone. Now, the newlywed couple, Mr. and Mrs. Shelton, left to go on their honeymoon in Rome for two weeks.

Chapter Twenty-Six

BE A WOMAN AND TELL THE TRUTH

Even though six months had passed, things were going great for the Foxes. Izzi was still a nervous wreck because Mr. Shelton told her that the prosecutor got up to a year to refile on her after dismissing her case. So, every day, Izzi was waking up expecting some of these same police officers to be back at her door, but this time to rearrest her for the same murder charges as before. Also, maybe even add a few more charges of robbery and murder. The one thing she promised to stay away from is the main thing she has been doing ever since she was released from jail. If Izzi didn't have dreams of killing DuVall, then she was having dreams of being rearrested. Izzi laid in her bed that she had just been delivered. She couldn't sleep in the same bed as her best friend and husband shared their little escapade in. Just as soon as they returned from Miami, Izzi bought a whole brand-new bedroom set and all new furniture. She didn't want any old memories of DuVall and her together. Izzi

259

was happy, at first, being free and out of jail, but this was the first time in her life that she was all alone. Seeing all her girlfriends with good men was starting to make her feel more alone. Fuzzi's wedding made her think about when she and DuVall first met and when he asked her to marry him. Just thinking about how he allowed La'Bella to destroy their marriage made tears form in her eyes.

Izzi's cellphone ringing snapped her out of her miserable moment. Hello! Hi, Izzi, it's me, Caroline. Caroline? Hi! Hey girl, how you holding up in there? Hey, wait, how did you just call? It didn't say prepaid when you called. That's because I'm out of jail. Izzi started screaming, Ahhhhh! Ahhhhh! Girl, you are lying. Where you at? I'm standing in front of the lobby where they release us. How did you get out? Some lawyer said that you sent him to take my case. He got me out of jail. Izzi looked up like God had just said her name. Baby girl don't move. I'm on my way to pick you up. Okay, I miss you. I miss you, too. I'm leaving now. Izzi couldn't wait to call Fuzzi and thank her and her husband, but she got no answer, and she knew why. They were still on their honeymoon. Izzi was smiling because she knew things were really about to explode for the Foxes.

They had already clipped one of the dealers for close to 200 kilos but had to leave the drugs in storage back in Dallas, Tx, after Kahi'Lee put them up on a Kingpin. They took his money and kilos but were too scared to bring the kilos back to Arizona. So, Fuzzi suggested that they rent a storage unit and leave it there until they are able to come back and get it from Dallas. Caroline was a splitting image of Charlotte McKinley. Tall, slender 34-24-34, 5'10, with a beautiful smile and green eyes. Her long blonde hair that stopped just above the butt is what always made other women take notice of her. Izzi was smiling from ear to ear as she turned into the Women's Estrella jail. It wasn't hard to spot Caroline.

Some officers patrolling the perimeter of the jail seemed to be giving her a hard time. When Izzi pulled up, she blew the horn, but Caroline didn't know who was blowing the Mercedez Benz horn. Izzi rolled down the window, Caroline, Caroline. Whatever the officer was saying wasn't important because Caroline took off running towards Izzi. She jumped out of the car, and they hugged and kissed each other. Look at you. No, look at you. Is this your car, Izzi? Yeah, I have something for you to drive too. What? I've never owned my own car before. Well, don't worry about that, you'll have your own everything now. Let's get the fuck away from here, girl, I hate this place. On their way to Izzi's home, they reminisce on their time in jail. Izzi told Caroline about everything that had happened since she got released. She even told Caroline about her new lifestyle. Caroline already knew about Fuzzi, Emma, Kahi'Lee, and Ashley, but now she was learning that they all called themselves Foxes.

Izzi told Caroline that her past lifestyle is why the Foxes all agreed to get her a lawyer to get her released from jail. Caroline cried to even hear that someone even cared anything about her. She reached over and kissed Izzi on the cheek. Thank y'all so much, girl. I miss you so much. You know I love you, right? I love you too, Caroline. I told you that I have your back. Now, we have each other's back, let's do the damn thing. Izzi, count me in. Izzi smiled, girl, fuck a man. All we need is each other. Caroline thought about Justin, and she was hoping to work on freeing him now that she was out. But Izzi started telling Caroline, after all those trips that you told me you took, what do you have to show for it? Girl, and how many times have you told me that he cheated on you right after you sacrificed your life for him? Tears started rolling down Caroline's face, and Izzi knew that she was listening. Caroline knew that she didn't even have a pair of panties to wear. All of her things by now are for sure long gone because any motel only keeps your things for 30 days, and then you lose them.

Caroline had been locked up for over a year. Her lifestyle treated her very well before she got locked up. When Izzi pulled up to the house, there was another H2 Hummer and Jaguar sitting in the driveway. Turned out that the Jaguar wasn't in La'Bella's name; it was DuVall's, so Izzi got to keep that, too. Come on, baby girl, let's get you situated. When they walked into Izzi's home, that's when it really hit Caroline that Justin really didn't give a fuck about her or himself. Everything that she saw, Caroline knew that they had this a few times. Your home is beautiful, Izzi. Thank you. Well, my home is yours just as long as you want it to be. Caroline started smiling. Do you have a washing machine so that I can wash my clothes? Baby girl, we are throwing that shit away and taking you shopping for a whole new wardrobe. What! Are you fucking serious? Caroline put her hand over her face. Come on, you go take a shower, and I'll fix you something to eat. Izzi and Caroline were different sizes, but Izzi knew that she had to have something to fit her. Izzi was built like a sister, but her butt said that. She then ate a lot of soul food in her lifetime.

While Caroline was taking a shower, Izzi found her a new Prada mini dress and laid her out some new panties. Caroline really didn't need a bra, being the type of dress it was. One thing they did have in common was they both wore size 7 shoes. So, the 3-inch Vera Wang heel will definitely fit her perfectly. Izzi put them both a steak in her new cooker and cut up some potatoes. Izzi heard Caroline calling her name, so she went to see what she wanted. Yeah, baby girl, is everything okay? Yes, thank you, this dress is pretty. I've never owned a real designer dress before. Caroline dropped the towel that she was holding around her breast. She sat on the bed and started applying strawberry lotion to her body. Izzi stood at the door watching. She didn't know if her time spent with Big Girl had changed something in her. But to her own surprise, now she knew why she had missed Caroline so much. Something about Caroline's body was giving Izzi hot flashes. Do you need me to help put lotion on your back? Caroline looked up at her. I was really hoping that you asked me to. Izzi walked over to her, and they started kissing each other passionately. Caroline undressed Izzi and laid her back on the bed. She allowed her tongue to roam Izzi's body until she found her love box. She spread her legs, but Izzi stopped her. Wait! Are you sure that this is what you want? I've only dreamed of this moment ever since I first saw you. Why didn't you tell me this before? Because I've never looked at a woman before, never in life. Your feminism must have brought the lesbian out of me. Izzi started laughing. Izzi, I really wanted to kill Big Girl for taking away your special moment away from you. Izzi kissed her on the lips. That special moment is now; you can take it back. Izzi laid back and spread her legs. Oooooh! Ahhhhh! Yes, Baby! Mark your territory, then. Caroline and Izzi ate each other's vagina so good that they left their steaks in the cooker until the next day.

$ $ $ $ $

Kahi'Lee's career and relationship with B.S., whom she called him most because he had completely made her forget about the name Tyler. The new Tyler was the new beat for Kahi'Lee's heart. And everything else seems to fall into place for her. Her commercial was now being shown on television. She was getting jobs that didn't call for her to remove her clothes first. She and Tyler, AKA B.S. were now talking about moving in together. Neither one of them was trying to rush the other one into marriage; they were happy for Fuzzi and Emma but decided to wait until the time was right. Ashley's heart was still getting the children to a better home, but she was now dating a gentleman who kept pursuing to take her out. Being that he finally persuaded her to go out with him after nine months, Ashley finally accepted, but she still kept her distance because he was a Phoenix Police Officer. They somehow seem to keep crossing each other's paths because their job titles allowed it to happen. Even though the sex was great to Ashley, she managed to shake it off and keep him at a distance.

Fuzzi, Emma, Kahi'Lee, and Izzi didn't even want to meet him. Ashley completely understood, like they all agreed you never know whom your heart might open up to, so out of respect, she kept him away from the Foxes. Of course, Fuzzi was married and now living the same lifestyle. But now she and Mr. Shelton were living in a brand-new home. Fuzzi refused to live in another woman's house. Mr. Lehmann found them a luxurious 7-bedroom home with 4 and a half bathrooms and 3 car garage. They still have been traveling so much that they still haven't unpacked all of their stuff yet. But in the Shelton's home right now, life is good.

Emma was living on top of the world out of the five women. She was having her cake and eating it too. Her and 2 Much relationship were getting stronger every day. They were just preparing for their wedding that was coming up real soon. 2 Much's mother loved Emma and was happy for her son's choice of women.

Emma had checked all the boxes in her eyes. In fact, she and Emma were starting to spend more time together than Emma and 2 Much lately. But 2 Much wasn't complaining at all. Things between Emma and Rozay have been going really swell also. Every now and then, he will shoot his shot, but Emma always seems to find a way to keep his mind focused on them getting paid. He didn't too much like when Emma called him her little brother. Rozay was getting his money up and was actually hoping that things would change between him and Emma. But what he didn't know was Emma was really about to break his heart in a couple more weeks. Her job had given her a raise, and everything was great at work.

Foxes didn't know it, but they were about to add a new member. Caroline was sucking and licking her way into the family. Now, Izzi's life was about to take a major turn. Because she was now starting to feel like the grass was a little more creamer on the other side. She was replacing everything old and exchanging it for something new. Right about now, she didn't care what the other Foxes were going to say about her and Caroline.

$ $ $ $ $

Black Dynamite, talk to me. 2 Much was listening to his right-hand man that his fiancé was sitting in the Cadillac Ext with some young dude at her job. Emma had looked Black Dynamite in the face twice. But she didn't have any idea that Black Dynamite was just waiting for the word. He smiled at her, holding a 357 magnum in his lap, waiting for 2 Much to give him the word to sleep the both of them. Black Dynamite could tell they were being too comfortable with each other. He told 2 Much that the guy was arguing with Emma because he was pointing his finger at Emma and getting loud. But Black Dynamite couldn't hear what they were arguing about. Emma was telling Rozay that she was about to get married. She even invited him to their wedding. 2 Much told Black Dynamite that he didn't know who Rozay was. But Emma wasn't a messy female, so it has to be a good reason why he there. 2 Much trusted Emma so much that he told Black Dynamite to drive off. Bro you serious? I can sleep em' both right now. 2 Much wasn't the type to repeat himself or second guess his thoughts. Click!

Black Dynamite smiled at Emma, and for some reason, Emma's conscience told her that the man watching her wasn't watching her for no reason. Plus, she would have noticed him if he had come in to pay a bill, which he hadn't. Emma ended her and Rozay's conversation and exited his truck. But she caught a glimpse of the 357 magnum that was lying in Black Dynamite's lap. Her heart started racing with every step that she took. It seems like the door got further and further away. Emma started questioning herself: why would this man be here to hurt me? But she kept coming up with nothing. Maybe he is out to rob Rozay. Her heart started racing faster, and she needed to get to a phone and warn him. Normally, she would have her cellphone, damn! She had left it on the counter where she worked. Because Rozay called and said he was out in the parking lot. Shit! I got to get to my phone. Emma turned to take a look just before walking into her job. Rozay was gone, but the black Audi 8 was still there. Black Dynamite wasn't even thinking about Emma anymore. He had got a call from his baby mama and was chopping it up with her. Emma quickly dismissed the idea of the man trying to rob Rozay. So, she didn't want to call him to have him on pens and needles for nothing. Emma finally watched the black Audi 8 leaving the parking lot. Just as she was about to go back to work, a light came on in her head. One day, after having sex with 2 Much, Emma asked him, baby, how do you know so much about me? And I've never told you any of these things about me before. 2 Much didn't say anything; he just looked at her. Emma said I'm going to change your name to 2 Damn Much. Now, Emma knew that a man with 2 Much's standards wouldn't know what type of woman he was about to marry or even have so close to him. Emma smiled again. They say that after a woman is with a man for so long, she begins to act and think just like him. She just was glad she wasn't caught cheating on 2 Much. Because that 357 magnum that was lying in Black Dynamite's lap had just told her that Mr. Khalil Carter, AKA 2 Much, is really playing for keeps. He always mentioned he had business partners, but he never kept any around him. Emma reminded herself that when the time comes, she should always remain a woman and tell the truth.

Chapter Twenty-Seven
WHAT HAPPENS IN VEGAS

702 Las Vegas McCarran International, the Foxes have landed in a town that never sleeps. They say what happens in Vegas stays in Vegas. Fuzzi, Izzi, Kahi'Lee, Emma, Ashley, and Caroline were hoping that the saying was true. Because they all had their game faces on and were coming to the town like it was New York, and they were the ones to take the bite out of the Big Apple. Fuzzi had rented two Ferraris, one red and one white. They didn't have any convertibles available, so she had to settle for hard tops, but she managed to get a red convertible Lamborghini. It was NBA all-star weekend, and Las Vegas was crawling with people from all over the world. Traffic was backed up with cars bumper to bumper. Every club and strip club were throwing parties and offering deals to draw all the partygoers to their functions.

Izzi and Caroline had already come out as a couple, which Fuzzi and the Foxes already knew before they came out. Fuzzi didn't care. She felt that as long as it didn't interfere with their business and relationships, then who were they to come in between the sheets. Fuzzi thought that Caroline was a bit too timid for her, but she knew that after spending time with them, it wouldn't be too much longer before she toughened up. Plus, they had the opportunity to test Caroline already. One day, Emma, Izzi, and Caroline were riding together when Rozay called. He needed 2 kilos ASAP, and Emma had to go meet him. But the police had pulled them over. Before the police officer approached the car, Caroline grabbed the 2 kilos and put them in her purse. She told Emma and Izzi if they find the drugs, then they don't know anything about her or the drugs. They're just giving her a ride because she flagged them down. Emma was sweating bullets, and Izzi was about to cry, but Caroline was acting like they only had a joint of marijuana. She showed no type of fear at all and even talked the officer out of a ticket. When they pulled off, Emma knew right there that Izzi picked the right person. That even brought Fuzzi's guard down about Caroline. Because she had no faith in her at all to bring her into their circle.

After that day, all six of them became inseparable. Fuzzi had only 3 rooms reserved because it was all-star weekend, and all the rooms were booked. They stayed in the MGM Grand suites. They all coupled up, which was already easy for Izzi and Caroline. Fuzzi and Emma shared a suite, and Ashley and Kahi'Lee shared a suite together. They couldn't wait to go to the strip, so they quickly dressed and started gambling in the MGM Grand casino. Fendi, Gucci, Prada, Chanel, Louis Vuitton, and Versace dresses had the body of 6 Foxes and turning heads. And every part of the casino where the Foxes roamed, men one by one slowly approached them, namely all the pimps that were at the casino. They were hoping to knock at least one of the Foxes, if not all of them. Say bitch! Here I am. Let a pimp put the right knowledge on that white rolls. I see you wrecking hearts and eyes around here. Who I got to call this morning about your hoeing.

Another pimp walked up on Izzi and Caroline, yeah bitch, let's get in a dose of that new Oreo. Two fresh bodies on some of this chocolate. Sock it to my pockets, so Nabisco can know about my pimpin'. Binggg! This cashmere pimp trying to take your horn to the next level hit me 305-556-3189. Caroline was laughing and smiling, making the pimps feel like they can have action of moving her. So that made them all surround her. They were stalking her like lions on a laughing hyena. Izzi had talked to other prostitutes when she was in jail and knew they were being pursued to be prostitutes. Girl, come on, them pimps; they trying to turn us out. Caroline quickly caught on because she talked to prostitutes, too before, in jail. Izzi knew just what to do. She went and found Fuzzi, and Fuzzi did just what she expected. Fuzzi started cussing them out and talking slick to the pimps. Yall must be trying to buy some pussy, the way y'all chasing behind a bitch. I thought hoes ran the pimps. If a bitch did want to choose, we wouldn't be looking for no stalkers. The pimps roasted Fuzzi and called her all type of black bitches. But they weren't calling her anything that she wouldn't call herself or either Izzi, Kahi'Lee, Emma, Ashley, or Caroline. Izzi saw that Fuzzi's words must have struck a nerve with the pimps because they stopped chasing Izzi and Caroline, punk bitch! Get off your seat and go bet the concrete with yo man lookin ass. That's why I don't fuck with black bitches. The pimps slapped hands and walked away laughing.

Fuzzi quickly schooled the Foxes on the experiences that they might encounter while they were in Las Vegas working. Las Vegas was like paradise to all pimps. Because almost every day, millions of females come and go year-round and namely with pimps, just to take all the attention off of them from their pimps' encounter. The Foxes took to the strip and blended in with the crowd. They randomly entered different hotels and gambling and meeting different types of men but even ran into a few celebrities they saw in movies. Hey, that's- ooohh, look, girl, ain't that- no wait, there go......they went on for a while before they headed back to the MGM.

On the way up to their rooms, Emma noticed a crowd gathering around two men with turbans on their heads. Hey, somebody must be really winning at that table. The Foxes walked over to the crap table, and two twin brothers were on a roll and catching every point that they got. While the Foxes were standing there, the two men started whistling to each other and were looking at Fuzzi, Emma, Kahi'Lee, Izzi, Ashley, and Caroline. One of the guys called Emma, hey pretty lady, come gamble with me. I need some more good luck. Fuzzi pushed her towards the table. The man held up the dice, blew on them, and let them roll. Give her the dice. How much is that? 50,000, roll the dice. Emma's eyes opened wide, and she was afraid to lose the man's money. 50,000 rolling. He gave Emma the dice. She blew on them and let em' roll. 7, we got a winner. Everybody started clapping. Emma put her hand over her mouth; she had never played dice in her life. And here was her first playing, and she won 50,000. Yes, you're my good luck charm, sweetie. He left the money out, but this time, he rolled the dice. 11, we got a winner.

Now, the man had got up to 600,000. He and his brother had already won 500,000 before they had even walked up. He put all of it back up, making his total come to 220,000, and let it roll. Everybody got quiet at the table, and the two brothers gave each other a high five. He let the dice roll, and the number six came out on the dice. Point is six. Your point is six. He rolled again, and 10 came on the dice. He rolled the dice again, and this time, we got a nine. He looked at Emma and told her to roll the dice. Oh no, no, nooooo. I don't want to lose your money, sir. It's not mine if you lose it. The dice were placed in Emma's hand, and she rolled the dice with her eyes closed. 6, we got a winner. Emma jumped into his arms. We won; we won. Everybody was clapping and whistling, happy that they had won. His brother nodded at his brother to stop playing. That's it, buddy, that's enough. He grabbed their racks of chips and told Emma to come with him. He cashed out and gave Emma 250,000. He invited them to join him and his brother at their home for drinks. He told Emma that they owned a home in North Las Vegas. That they were from Iraq. Emma said, "Oooh, that's what language you and your brother talking in. That's Arabic right." Yeah, so how bout it? What they didn't know they weren't about to allow them to leave with that much money, no way.

Yeah sure. Y'all want to go have a drink with them? Fuzzi gave Emma a look like, bitch is you and him crazy? Hell yeah, we going. They all exited the MGM after the casino tried to offer the men a hotel suite there for free. But they declined to stay there. They all introduced themselves to each other while they waited for his Limousines. I'm Amarri, and that's my brother Amearri. Fuzzi was watching the man who was with them. She figured he had to be their security guard. Emma gave them all false names to the twins. A black Mercedes Benz Ultra Stretched Limousine pulled up, and everybody climbed inside. Turned out the twins have a mansion in North Las Vegas. Fuzzi wanted to follow them, but the twins insisted that they all rode there with them. They all sat around the living room, and the security guard served them drinks as if he had been working in a bar all his life. They all laughed and chatted about Emma rolling the dice and winning. After the third round of drinks, the whole room started spinning, and the girls tried to reach out for each other. But each one of them looked blurry to each other. Em-

em-em-Emmaaaa! Fuzzi was trying to call her name, but her words were sluggish. Bam! Bam! Bam! Bam! Bam! What the F'U? Bam! Fuzzi tried to fight it, but she wasn't any type of competition to fight off the drugs that were placed in their glasses.

Emma, Kahi'Lee, Ashley, and Fuzzi's cell phones were all blowing up. The men in their lives were calling to check on them, but all their cell phones were turned off and tossed into a fireplace. Two days had passed by, and none of them didn't even have any idea that it had. Ashley was the first one to come to. She tried to rub her face but couldn't touch it at all. What the fuck! Oh my God! What the fuck is going on. Ashley started screaming. Ahhhhhh! Ahhhhh! Ahhhhhhhh! No! No! Nooooooooo! Let me out of here. Emma, Kahi'Lee, Caroline, Fuzzi and Izzi started coming around too. Oh my God, what is going on? What the fuck? They all now saw that they were chained up naked on a cement floor to a basement somewhere. They all started yelling and screaming. Ahhhhhh! Ahhhhh! Ahhhhh! Help! Help! Help! Somebody help us, please! Somebody helpppppp! It wasn't nobody responding to their cries for help. They all were using the bathroom on themselves. Plus, they all were starving for not eating for two days. Caroline and Kahi'Lee were starting to panic and hyperventilate. Fuzzi had to calm them down and talk them through their situation. Ladies, listen, listen to me, got damn it. Everyone got quiet. We are not going to die. We're going to get back home, trust me. We done ran into some psycho fucks. We can't show them fear, that's what's gone continue their behavior. Whatever they're expecting from us, we'll just go along with it. When you don't that's when they go try to hurt us. Come on, Kahi'Lee and Caroline, pull it together. Remember, ladies, we're Foxes dealing with regular dogs, and they always return back to their vomit.

It was like Fuzzi was coaching a professional women's team to win a championship game. Izzi, think about what you will do to Caroline after this is over. Emma, I know you whip it on your husband to be. Kahi'Lee, what you call Tyler, B.S? Yeah, black stallion. Mmmmmmm! Bitch, you making my vagina hot. They all started laughing. Ashley, I know your ass has been getting handcuffed. Pull over, pull over bitch. That police go cuff your ass back up, bitch. No, he ain't not after all this. Ummm! Hmmmm! bitch gotcha, Ashley, a freak. Caroline, look at that bitch, Izzi. You got her all in love. You done something right, so keep doing it, Caroline. Caroline looked at Izzi, and she told her I love you, baby. I love you, too. Awwwwwwe! That's so sweet. When Fuzzi was about to say something about herself, the door opened up, and the two twins walked into the room. Glad to see y'all ladies finally decided to join us. It's been 3 days since we all last saw each other. They all were thinking, damn, we been chained up for three days.

So, are you ladies ready to make us some money? Fuzzi didn't want anybody to blow it or upset them. Make y'all some money, how? Y'all will be transporting different things into the United

States for me. Ahhhhhh, daddy, if that's all you wanted, why we have to be treated like animals? We all down with that just as long as we get a cut out of it. My friend helped you out before, and this is how you repay her. He looked at Emma and smiled. I'm giving y'all a cut. Y'all got shelter, and if you ladies are mine, maybe y'all a get fed later. What do you think about that? Not even Fuzzi had any words for what he just said. Tears started rolling down all of their faces. Even though Fuzzi had given a comforting speech, now they all felt like they were about to die. The twins started having their way with the Foxes one by one, starting with Caroline. When the Foxes saw her again, she was high as a kite with her face and body full of cum. Izzi called her name, but she got no response. Tears filled Izzi's eyes until she just let them fall. They looked at Kahi'Lee; after we get back, we'll be ready to see you next. Kahi'Lee just closed her eyes and started praying. They walked out of the room, and their security guards put chicken and a case of sodas down by the door. He pointed a 40-cal at them, I'm going to unleash one of you at a time; whenever one of you gets finished eating, I'll feed the next one. The only problem was Caroline was so high that she didn't even eat. Hours and hours passed, and they didn't hear or see anybody. They all sat there waiting for Caroline to come to.

They couldn't come up with any type of plan because they kept them tied up all the time. Pow! Pow! Pow! Pow! Boom! Boom! Pow! Pow! Boom! All the gunfire made all the girls' eyes open wide. It even brung Caroline back a little. Kahi'Lee started crying. We about to die. We go dieeeeee! As much as Fuzzi wanted to disagree, she couldn't because none of them had no idea what was happening upstairs. Ten minutes later, they could hear footsteps coming their way. Kahi'Lee wanted to throw up. She knew that she wouldn't be able to live with herself after she experienced what Caroline had just experienced. The door opened, and all of their hearts stopped. Amarri came rushing through the door, but he was being pushed to the floor with them. A 357 magnum was being pointed at his head by Black Dynamite. Emma's eyes opened like she saw a ghost. Nobody had any clue as to what was happening until 2 Much and another dude walked into the room. He snapped his finger, and Black Dynamite pulled the trigger. Pow! Pow! Pow! Pow! Pow! Amarri's body went limped. 2 Much snapped his finger again, and the two men left the room. Daddddddy! Emma started crying. Neither she nor anybody in the room would have expected to see 2 Much. Right at that moment, he was all of their knight in shining armor. 2 Much got down and uncuffed Emma, and she hugged him, crying and couldn't let him go. The other Foxes looked at her like, ummmm bitch, can we get out of these cuffs too. One by one, 2 Much uncuffed each one of them, and even though Emma was his woman, they all hugged him, saying thank you, thank you, thank you. 2 Much knew that he had just got a lifetime of royalty and respect. Emma was crying, saying that she was sorry. 2 Much said, "What are you sorry for?" This is a part of the game, too, Ma. Shit don't always go as planned. But it's a win-win when you walk away with what you came for, and y'all did that. Fuzzi and the Foxes looked at each other, what does he mean by that? Y'all come on and get this paper, and let's get the hell out of here.

Even though they were all standing there naked and over a dead man, nobody felt any insecurity or shame at all. 2 Much watched as all that ass and vagina went upstairs in front of him. Even though they weren't in an attractive position right now, 2 Much knew that those asses would clean up just fine, especially, the one that was in front of him. She was about to be his wife in a few days, and 2 Much now knew why he chose this particular woman for a reason. Because Emma has all the right potential. After they went upstairs, 2 Much set himself apart from all the other men in the world. He gave Emma all the money they found and the jewelry they found, plus he returned the jewelry back to her that they had taken. He kissed his fiancé and said, "Be more careful; I'll see y'all when you get home." 2 Much and his 2 partners walked out the door. Fuzzi looked at Emma, bitch, you better marry him. That's another type of breed of man. That bitch, not even the Queen, have seen before. They caught a ride back with 2 Much and Black Dynamite, who was feeling Ashley. They showered, got dressed, and split up 2.5 million dollars, getting $416,000 apiece. They all headed to Treasure Island to watch Emma shoot dice. The $10,000 they watched Emma place on the crap table, now Emma knew why she never tried to gamble because that $10,000 now belongs to Treasure Island. And when she tried to put another $10,000 down on the table, Fuzzi snatched it and said,

"Come on, bitch, your gambling days is over." Caroline had experienced some drastic things back at that house, but when Fuzzi handed her $416,000, which was her cut, all her pain and trouble left her body. They all raised their hands and said, "Foxes over money and men bitch!" Like they say, what happens in Vegas stays in Vegas.

Chapter Twenty-Eight
I TOLD YOU BITCH

On flight 217, the Foxes were on an airplane heading back to Arizona. Emma was looking back over her life and was wondering what she had done to deserve a man like 2 Much in her life. She always wanted her dad to be that man who always was there to protect her. But he walked out of her life when she was three and never looked back. But not 2 Much; he always seems to not want to let anything hurt her. Tears started rolling down her face. Damn! How did he know that I needed him? That one question bothered Emma more than anything. How did he know? Nobody in this world is connected to another person. 2 Much made her happy, but there was a part of him that frightened Emma. He sweated nothing or nobody. Saying that made her think about Rozay. In a strange way, even though he wasn't 2 Much, Emma was turned on by him wanting to fight for her. Emma knew that she couldn't ever act on those feelings. 2 Much would kill them both. He'll kill us both; he'll kill us both! Girl, who go kill you?

Fuzzi snapped her out of her daydream. Emma didn't even realize that she was even thinking out loud. Oh, Oh, nobody. I'm just thinking out loud. Yeah, so I heard. Who got your heart playing tricks with your mind bitch? Girl, I know yo ass ain't gave Rozay no pu'nanny? Naw, is you crazy? That's my money and my friend. Girl, I then fuck some friends before. That's why we ain't friends now. No, Fuzzi. Emma looked at her crazy, but he was trying to holla. Well, if you know the type of man that you'll about to marry, then you better stop the hollering and keep talking, but not softly bitch. She and Emma busted up laughing. Bitch you know my brother-in-law is a beast. Emma knew right then that 2 Much was nobody to play with if he had gained Fuzzi's respect. She called her fiancé's brother-in-law. Yeah! That's my baby. I'd never even want another man but him. Sister to sister, Emma, there's no money that you and Rozay can make together that will even value that man's worth. These types of men would stop talking to their mama if they knew that it would take their happiness away from them. Fuzzi couldn't have described 2 Much any better than she just did. Emma hugged her. Thank you. You helped clear my mind. Emma knew that she wouldn't allow the thought to ever cross her mind again about entertaining any other man. In 5 more days, she will be Mrs. Emma Carter. The plane landed, and they all returned to their normal lives.

Even though they were all back at home, they all were in deep thought. They all came close to God only knows what. But they were happy to know that what didn't happen was that it was 2 Much that prevented it from happening. They were all questioning whether the lifestyle was really worth the money. The funny thing was they all came up with the same answer. They weren't too sure if the lifestyle was worth it or not. But they all were sure 2 Much was definitely worth fighting for. Damn! Those same words left all of their lips in sequence. Fuzzi was so happy to get back home to her husband, Dave. Fuzzi called him, but he was in court and couldn't talk, so she left a text. Your blackberry is at home and missing you. I love you, Mr. Shelton. Thank you for loving me. Your wife, Mrs. Shelton. Fuzzi put her suitcase down and started looking around her home. Ever since they moved in, she has been traveling and ain't had time to make it feel like home for her husband or herself. Fuzzi told herself that she wasn't going anywhere until she had unpacked everything and put their home together. She wanted to go buy Mr. Shelton something nice before he got home. After showering, she changed into something comfortable and went to work in the house. Fuzzi loved oldies, so Anita Baker 'Angel' played in the background while she cleared boxes. Fuzzi poured a glass of Moet and went to work. She started off by taking boxes to each room that it was going into. Mr. Shelton has a nice office in their home so he can work on his cases. Fuzzi was taking all the boxes that read office on it into his office. She told herself that as soon as she finishes the living room and bathrooms then she'll try to fix up his office. She knew that would put a big smile on his face. Plus, a good seafood dinner would top it off.

$ $ $ $ $

Ashley made it home to learn that Melvin, her police officer friend, had been leaving flowers and cards, wanting her to know how much he was missing her. Ashley smiled, but her mind was more on her job. She knew that she missed a lot of important cases. She turned on her cell phone and listened to her messages. She was supposed to be back at work two days ago. They only planned to stay the whole all-star weekend, and here it was Wednesday. Even though Ashley had missed a few days of work, she was just glad to even be alive. Here, she was almost about to die. And here, this big, black, handsome, muscular man came busting through the door to save her life. Then he whispered in her ear that he wanted to change her life. Ashley was trying to block Black Dynamite out of her mind, but right about now, her female hormones wanted to explore his body. Ashley looked at his number several times. He did tell me to call him any time that my heart wanted to feel his beat. Ashley said, "My heart don't want to feel your heartbeat, but my vagina damn sure want to feel you beating it up." Ashley smiled at her own humor until she heard the message that she was listening to now. A family was busted for selling meth and lost 6 little kids. Ashley's boss was telling her to call him ASAP. But, of course, she never received that call because her cell phone was burned up. Fuzzi had bought all of them new cell phones to stay in contact with each other. Ashley was glad that it wasn't her regular cell phone with all of her contact numbers. Fuck that phone, them suckers bought me a lot of phones.

That reminded her of the money that was in her Chanel purse. Another message came up, and it was her boss worrying about her not returning his calls. Ashley stopped the messages; she knew she had to call him.

Hello! Mr. Shepherd, this is Ashley; please don't be mad. When I went out of town, I won some money in Las Vegas. No, I'm not quitting my job. But I left my cell phone by accident, that's why I didn't get your calls. Yes. I heard your messages, so what happened? She talked to her boss and made sure she still had a job. Okay, I'll see you in the morning; I promise I'll be there. Ashley hardly missed any days, plus she was one of their better counselors. Now that everything was good at work, Ashley's mind went back to Black Dynamite. So, she dialed the number and waited until he answered. Hello! This, and he said, my queen, Ashley. By the time her call ended, Black Dynamite was knocking at her door. Wait! Somebody was knocking at my door. Ashley looked through the peephole, and it was him. Well, are you gonna let me in? You better not try anything because I know a man that would take your life behind me. He said that he wanted to change my life. Then Ashley opened the door. I do want to change your life if you'll allow me to. Well, that's just something that we'll have to work on. I guess that we can give it a try and see if we can make each other happy. Black Dynamite pulled his hand from behind his back, and he held a wrapped gift in his hand. What's this? Ashley opened the box; it was a diamond necklace with a gold and diamond treasure chest with a card.

Awwwwe, this is so pretty. She read the card that was in the box. It read, "Ashley, whatever man lost you, I found my treasure, and I'll treasure you for a lifetime if you will allow me to." Ashley looked at Black Dynamite, and she couldn't fight back her tears. Her last boyfriend caused her nothing but pain. So, his words penetrated her heart to the point that Ashley, for some strange reason, knew that she didn't have to protect it from Black Dynamite. She hugged and kissed him, but when she opened her eyes, Melvin, her Police Officer friend, was standing in the doorway, looking like she had just shattered his heart. Excuse me, I'm sorry. It looks like you're more okay than I could even imagine. He gave her a stare that if looks could kill, then Ashley would be getting prayed over and dropped in her grave. He turned and walked away. Melvin, I'm sorry, wait! Ashley rushed past Black Dynamite and went to catch Melvin.

Even though Ashley didn't love him, she still had feelings for him. Baby, Wait! I didn't mean to hurt you. I know how you feel about me, but we're two different types of people, and I don't feel we'll make it together. Melvin said, "I believe I know our problem. It's how I make my living." This uniform, for some reason, puts fear in a lot of people, but I didn't offer you my job, Ashley. I tried to offer you Me and a better life with my job. Everything okay? It looks like your new man is doing well for himself, too. Melvin looked at the Blue Mercedez Benz G 'Wagon on 26-inch rims and headed to his police car. Black Dynamite's heart still was beating like the custom system in his truck. He didn't know if the police were there to arrest him or what. But he made a mental reminder to tell 2 Much about Ashley's boyfriend. He watched Melvin drive away and wondered what type of problem would come from this. Ashley knew what type of man Black Dynamite was and knew that she had to go give him some type of clarity. Baby, please forgive me for that; it's not what you think. Ashley sat down and explained her and Melvin's interactions. Black Dynamite understood her situation and told Ashley, "Beautiful, just make sure he don't cause us any problems and let's just focus on our future." Ashley wanted badly to believe Black Dynamite, but a part of her felt like him seeing Melvin just might change things in him trusting in her.

$ $ $ $ $

Hello! Hello! Where have you been, lady? I thought you ran away to be a movie star. Now, you couldn't have thought that cause you would have been with me, baby. You ain't getting rid of me that easy, Mr. Man. B.S started laughing. How come you just didn't say baby, I miss you? Because you didn't give me a chance to Kahi'Lee, you trying to drive me crazy. Baby, Ooooooh, don't say that. Okay, now I got to tell you, baby, I'm sorry for not calling. I couldn't, and I miss you. You see, I'm calling your ass now; you driving me crazy, boy. Baby, we just got back. It was crazy out there. Well, did you win? Better know it, and I bought my baby something, too. Now, what you got to say? I'm horny and need your sexy, attractive, voluptuous butt in my bed. Sir, if you wish to continue to have a sexy woman pleasure you, please press two and give our operator your credit card number. If you're expecting pleasure, then just hand your credit card over to Ms. Kahi'Lee, and she'll be right over. They both started laughing. Shit, baby, as good as that pussy is, you can have my whole banking account. Is it that good, baby? Hell yeah! Okay, I'm on my way then. I won't charge you this time, but next time, you owe a girl a little something, somethingggg! I'll see you in 30 minutes, and be naked, boyyy!

$ $ $ $ $

Izzi and Caroline were having the time of their life. They have been to two malls already shopping. And they were headed into mall number three. Izzi was happy to see Caroline happy. She knew that Caroline had never been on a shopping spree before, plus they were riding around in La'Bella's new Jaguar, may she rest in peace. Izzi gave the car to Caroline, and they even stopped to get matching tattoos. Izzi's tattoo was a queen crown sitting on Caroline's name, and Caroline had Izzi's name with a crown on it. They both put them on the left cheek of their butt. They bought new sexy lingerie to keep each other sex appeal attracted towards one another. Izzi said, "Come on, baby, I want some pizza." I want some pizza, too, but we have got to go home for me to get a piece. She slapped Izzi across the butt; you better stop before these people see something they don't want to see. You know that shit turns me on, baby. Caroline popped her butt again. Okay, fuck it, we're going back to jail then. Okay! Okay! I'll stop, then. Izzi and Caroline kissed, and everybody was watching them like they were witnessing a robbery in one of their mall stores. Baby, we got to find some dresses for Emma's wedding. I thought that we had our dresses already. No, not them dresses, we got to change into something more comfortable for the reception. I know you don't want to keep on them long hot dresses, do you? Nope! Yeah, you're right. I didn't think about that. Because I've never been a part of a wedding before, baby, all of this stuff is new to me. You got to remember that I was nothing but trailer trash. Izzi stopped, and tears started rolling down her face. She walked up to Caroline. Don't you never again in life let me hear those words come out of your mouth. You ain't nobody's trash. You're smart, beautiful, sexy and attractive. We're all created by God, and he don't make trash. Caroline started crying. I'm sorry, baby, but you don't understand. That's all I have been told all of my life. Nobody has ever treated me the way you do. You make me feel like I'm somebody even if I feel I'm not. Izzi kissed her. Baby, that's because you are somebody. You're my somebody, and I'll always love you. I'll always love you, too. I don't know what I would do without you anymore. Just keep living, baby. Just keep on living. Because that's what I'll have to do if you ever leave me. I'll never leave you, Izzi. Never say never; life doesn't last forever, baby. Neither do love; trust me, I found that out the hard way. They were standing in the pizza place in the food court. Yes, ma'am, can we get four slices of pepperoni, please and two Pepsi's?

$ $ $ $ $

Fuzzi was sitting on the couch watching episodes of RuPaul's Drag Race. She was cracking up at the Drag Queens being overly dramatic with each other. That's right, read that, bitchhh! Oooooo, no, that tramp didn't say that. Work it bitch! Work it! Oh my God, girl, look out. Fuzzi was busting up laughing when her husband, Mr. Shelton came walking into the house. Baby, I'm home; where is my beautiful wife? Baby, I'm right here in the family room. Mr. Shelton could smell the food just as soon as he entered the house. He already knew just how great of a cook his wife was. To him, it was a completely different lifestyle being with Fuzzi compared to his ex-wife. The only way that he could come home and smell a home-cooked meal was when he came home with it in his hand from a restaurant that he had ordered from. As bad as he wanted to go into the kitchen and sneak a piece of meat, it's been almost a week since he saw his wife, and she filled him up just by seeing her beautiful face. It didn't take Mr. Shelton long to see that Fuzzi had been fixing up their house. That made him smile, seeing their house start to look and feel like a home. Mr. Shelton rushed into the room to see his wife. Hey, honey! Hey, hubby. Hi, sexy woman, I missed you. Fuzzi stood up to hug him, still trying to watch the television. Mr. Shelton went in for a kiss. Mmmmm! I missed you, too, Mr. Oh. I see they came and put the tv's up. Yeah, baby, I love this one a lot; it was an 80-inch TV screen.

Oh my God, why are you watching this? What? RuPaul's Drag Race, baby, I love this show. Awwwe these fagots are so disgusted and degrading to men. When he said that, Fuzzis' whole demeanor changed. What the fuck is that supposed to mean? There not men; those are woman that's trapped in a man's body, and they are not fagots. They're homosexuals, not nobody's fagots, baby. Fuzzi started snapping her fingers. Snap! Snap! Snap! Snap! Ahhhh, come on, honey, you can't be serious. Any man that's sleeping with another man that's a fucking fag. Mr. Shelton started getting upset now. No, honey, that's a homosexual. They have the same desires of the same sex. You love homosexuals more than you will ever know it, honey, trust me. No, I don't love no homosexual fagot man that thinks he's a woman or anything of the such. I'd die first before I'd sleep with a homosexual, trust me. I've almost lost my whole life and almost blew a wonderful career behind that type of shit. Mr. Shelton watched Fuzzi storm out of the room, throwing the remote control clearly across the room. He could see that Fuzzi was really upset, but why is what he couldn't understand.

Why do homosexual men mean so much to her? Mr. Shelton just figured that maybe she had a family member that maybe lived that type of lifestyle. He wasn't expecting to come home arguing with a woman that he just married weeks ago. They were supposed to be ripping each other's clothes off of each other, having sex in every room in the house, breaking it in. Mr. Shelton felt bad that he had upset his wife behind a subject that personally made her feel disrespected. He wanted to know why she felt so offended by what he had said. But right now, at this moment, he didn't feel like now would be the perfect time to bring it up at this moment. Talking about it right now only seems that it would only upset Fuzzi more. Mr. Shelton went to find his wife, and he just wanted to fix the problem. Seeing Fuzzi upset with him like that bothered him even more than him upsetting Fuzzi. Honey, where are you? He thought that she had gone to their bedroom, but even though Fuzzi was upset, she was trying to be a good wife. Fuzzi was in the kitchen fixing their plates to eat dinner. Oh, honey, here you are. Fuzzi looked at Mr. Shelton and rolled her eyes at him. Fuzzi kind of felt bad herself because she didn't expect any man to understand what a homosexual man felt like in his own skin. That was something that one could only understand by experience. Honey, I'm so sorry. Would you please forgive me? I had no reason to talk like that, no matter what. We are all human beings. He walked up behind Fuzzi and kissed her on the neck. I'm sorry. Would you please forgive me? Fuzzi put a half smile on her face. She turned around smiling, yes baby, I forgive you, and I'm sorry, too. Would you please forgive me for the way I just acted? No need to. Let's just put that behind us. I promise that it won't happen again. Okay then, yes, I forgive you. Now go wash up so I can feed you. I will only if I can have you for dessert. I'll have to see about that; you still made me mad. Fuzzi hit Mr. Shelton playfully. He put his hands up, ok, ok, okkkk! No doghouse, please. Please, pretty please. Fuzzi started laughing ok, ok, no doghouse, wow. Thank you, Jesus.

Mr. Shelton went to go wash his hands to eat dinner, and without even realizing it, Fuzzi went into deep thought of her past growing up, hearing people call her all types of freaks and fagots. Hey freak, hey fagot. Every time Fuzzi thought about growing up, she always thought about Fantasia. Hearing Mr. Shelton's voice coming back towards the kitchen quickly snapped Fuzzi's mind out of the daydream that she had sunk into. She knew that she couldn't allow herself to sink into that hole with Fantasia. At least not now while they were about to have dinner. Fuzzi was placing the food on the table when Mr. Shelton entered the kitchen. Mmmmm! Honey, that smells great. Well, sit down because it tastes better than it smells. They held hands, and Fuzzi thanked God for her husband and then the food. It was little things like that is what made Mr. Shelton happy to be married to Fuzzi. So, how was your trip? Almost breathtaking, and Fuzzi meant that literally. How about you, baby? What you been doing while I been gone, looking for a new wife? Mr. Shelton started laughing. No, I'm afraid of the one that I got now. Naw, I love the one I already got to do a thing like that. Yeah, you better have switched that shit up. Mr. Shelton and Fuzzi were eating and engaging in a more peaceful and relaxed conversation.

Fuzzi said, "Oh baby, wait a minute." I almost forgot. Wait! Wait! I'll be right back. Fuzzi got up and left the kitchen. Five minutes later, she came walking back into the kitchen. Fuzzi didn't have time to wrap it, so she just handed it to Mr. Shelton. Here, baby.

Mr. Shelton grabbed the diamond chain. Awwwe, honey, you didn't have to waste money like this on me. I didn't waste it; you're my husband, baby, I love you. I love you too, honey, and I love it. Here, let me help you. Fuzzi put the necklace on Mr. Shelton, wow. This would get me killed. What did you pay for this? Fuzzi gave him a really crazy look. Yeah, baby, I'm sorry. He knew better to ask that question, or at least he should. Fuzzi went and sat back down. Baby, you got the Rolex watch and the big diamond chain now. My baby looks like one of them rappers. Mr. Shelton stood up and grabbed the saltshaker, acting like a rapper. He swayed from side to side and swung his hand. Fuzzi fell on the floor laughing. Man, no. You don't know nothing about being no rapper. Yes, I do, baby. I'm Mr. smooth white chocolate. Baby, stop it, stop it, you making my side hurt. Mr. Shelton helped Fuzzi up, and they went back to eating their dinner. Mr. Shelton had no idea that he was wearing a dead man's chain. Fuzzi gave him Amarri's chain after 2 Much and Black Dynamite killed him.

Mr. Shelton felt that he should do something romantic for his wife. So, he pulled one of Fuzzi's moves back on her. Mr. Shelton went under the table. Baby, what are you doing? Just as Fuzzi got those words out, she didn't have to wait for an answer. Mr. Shelton spread her legs and slid her panties over to the side. He put both hands behind Fuzzi's back and made her butt slide a little in the chair, giving himself better access to her vagina. He kissed her vagina lips and spread her lips with his tongue. Mmmmm! Ooooooh baby! He placed Fuzzi's legs on her shoulders and licked on her clit. Mmmmm! Mmmmm! Ahhhhh! Yeah! Yeah, baby! Make mama pussy feel good. Fuzzi relaxed and laid back in the chair. She closed her eyes and enjoyed her husband's tongue. Ahhhhh! Yes! Yes! Yessss! Come on, baby, ahhhhh! Yes! Yes! Come on, baby! Wait! Wait! Yeah, baby, right there. That's my spot, baby. Ooooooh! Ooooooh! Ahhhhh! Yes, baby. I'm about to cum, daddy, I'm cummm, im cummmm, im cummmm, Aahhhh! Ooohhhhh! Oohhhh! Yes, daddy! Mmmmmm! Mmmmmm! Aaahhh! Ahhhhh! Yes, daddy. Yes! Fuzzi's body went limp in the seat, and Mr. Shelton couldn't move because Fuzzi had a handful of his hair and was smashing his face deeper into her vagina. Mmmmm! Awwww, baby, that felt so good. Fuzzi finally released Mr. Shelton's hair, and he came back up to the table looking like he did when he wakes up in the morning. Fuzzi started laughing when she saw his hair sticking up. Baby, come here, look at you. My daddy was putting in work on this vagina. She fixed his hair and gave him a romantic kiss. Mmmmmm! My pussy taste good, doesn't it, daddy? Hell yeah, now you see why I'm sucking on it all the time. Fuzzi put her hand over her face like she was embarrassed.

After they ate dinner, Mr. Shelton went into his office to look over an important case, while Fuzzi cleaned up the kitchen and put the food away. Before she headed upstairs, Fuzzi went to their bar and fixed herself a drink. She figured that she'd finish clearing a few more boxes before she called it quits for the day. Plus, she needed to get some rest so she could attend Emma's rehearsal for her wedding. Emma and 2 Much wedding is in two days, and she wanted to make sure everything was on point. Fuzzi headed to one of the bedrooms and started removing boxes and placing them where they go. After unpacking a few boxes, Fuzzi came across a pretty large size box. It has the words important, and office written on the top and side of the box. Since it said important , Fuzzi started pushing it down the hall toward her husband's office. It was too heavy for her to carry to his office. Excuse me, baby, but this is one of your boxes. Baby, it says important on it. Mr. Shelton put up one finger, he was on the phone talking to his secretary. Letting her know that she needed to mail the paperwork that he was working on immediately. Oh, baby, I'm sorry I didn't know you were on the phone. Fuzzi whispered, trying to prevent the person on the line from hearing her. She kept pushing the box into his office. Okay, honey! Sorry baby. No! No! It's okay. That was Holly, she told me to tell you hi anyway. Fuzzi smiled oh and tell her I said hello and her gift was nice. Yeah, I needed her to get this paperwork mailed out first thing in the morning. Baby, do you want me to mail it? No, honey, that's what I pay her for. I'm just glad that I got it finished in time.

Oh, I almost forgot to tell you, Izzi was so grateful for what you had done to get Caroline out of jail. Baby, she really is a sweet girl, I really like her a lot. We'll have to invite them all over for dinner after I get this house in order. No problem, honey. You know I'll do anything in the world for you. They kissed each other, me too, baby.

Here, let me help you with that box. No, baby, it's okay. Go ahead and finish your work. Well, I just so happened to finish it just before you walked in. That's why I called Holly to have it mailed out. Mr. Shelton pulled the box towards him. He opened it, you can help me put this stuff away if you don't mind. Sure, come on. Mr. Shelton started pulling books and different things out of the box. Here, honey, put all this stuff on that shelf right there. It will all fit perfectly; that's where it came from in my other home. Fuzzi looked at him when he said that. But she wasn't tripping because Fuzzi was a lot smarter than his ex-wife. Fuzzi wasn't about to be put out on the streets with nothing. From all the conversations with Mr. Shelton in the past, Fuzzi told him up front if you're going to marry me, we together until death do us apart. Fuzzi refused to sign a prenuptial agreement. Mr. Shelton knew that if Fuzzi was going to be his wife, then he had better not ask her to sign one. Mr. Shelton came out of the box with a football helmet framed in a glass case. Here, baby, put this up there on the top shelf.

Fuzzi said, "Mmmm, baby, what's this?" Fuzzi saw his whole demeanor change when he pulled the helmet out of the box. Awwwwe, baby, I don't even want to talk about that old thing. It almost cost me my life having it. That's why I even kept it in the first place. It's just a reminder to me of how close I came to losing my life. Losing your life, what, baby, are you serious? Yeah, I used to play football in college, and I would have gone to the pros. But I let a couple of players talk me into doing some stupid stuff. We were all kids not thinking and acting stupid. Fuzzi saw a newspaper clipping taped on the inside, and she started reading it. We had a tragedy happen here earlier yesterday in the San Francisco area. Two of the top football players were involved in a senseless crime involving a male victim whom they thought was a female. Fuzzi slammed the glass case on Mr. Shelton's desk and quickly raised the lid so that she could remove the article inside. Tears started rolling down her face while she kept on reading the paper clipping.

Quarterback Bradley Copperfield and wide receiver Dave Shelton of Phoenix, Az, who was being scouted by professional football teams, said that they were out picking up prostitutes and picked up two whom they thought were females. They said when they entered the motel that two men disguised as females drew a gun on them and demanded all of their money. In defense, Dave Shelton used his football helmet to fight off one of the men, killing him with repeated blows to the head. Fuzzi grabbed Mr. Shelton's football helmet, you lying-son-of-a-bitchhhhh! You killed Fantasia. Wham! Wham! Wham! Fuzzi swung the helmet as hard as she could, hitting Mr. Shelton hard across the head. He fell down in front of his desk. We didn't do shit to you, motherfuckers. Wham! Wham! Wham! Wham! Blood was gushing out of his head every time that Fuzzi came down with that helmet. Wham! Wham! Wham! Wham! You killed my sisterrrr! Wham! Wham! Wham! Wham! Wham! Wham! Wham! Wham! Wham! Fuzzi blacked out and kept beating her husband. Wham! Wham! Wham! Wham! By the time Fuzzi realized what she had done, Mr. Shelton looked just like Fantasia did back at that motel room in San Francisco.

Fuzzi started laughing like she was a sadistic, pathetic psychopath not carrying at all. Fuzzi was covered in blood. She went and got Fantasia's picture and held it up over his body. What I tell you, bitch. I love you, girl. Didn't I tell you I was going to get him for doing that to you? Bitch, now you can rest in peace. Fantasia, do you love me now? You were mad at me for getting married. Are you satisfied now, bitch, are you? Fuzzi stood there talking to Fantasia like she was right there in the room. Now, I'm coming to be with you, bitch. I don't got him no more. Fuzzi went to their bedroom and got her 9 mm out of a shoe box. She walked back into Mr. Shelton's office and sat in his chair. She sat down, put the gun in her mouth, and closed her eyes. Fuzzi started yelling shut up, shut up, bitch. Now, you don't want to be with me after what I have done for you. Fuzzi slammed the 9mm down on the desk, got up, and left the room. 10 minutes later, she returned with her cell phone, a glass and a bottle of Moet. Fuzzi sat back down, grabbed the gun again, and put it to her head. She closed her eyes, shut up, shut up, shut up, goddamn it. No, Fantasia, I'm not listening to you. Leave me the fuck alone. She was acting like she could hear Fantasia telling her not to shoot herself. Fuzzi started crying uncontrollably. Why did you leave me? Whyyyy! I hate you, bitch. I hate youuuu! You left me all by myself, bitch. Fuzzi laid the gun down and picked up her cell phone. She scrolled through her numbers and found one particular number. Fuzzi pressed send, and on the third ring, the voice said hello. I need your help. I just killed my husband. What?

Chapter Twenty-Nine
UNTIL DEATH DO US PART

2 Much was one of them real street legends, so when the word got out that he was getting married to some attractive, beautiful woman in Phoenix, AZ, hustlers and players were coming from all around the world to see the woman who found a soft spot in his heart. That nobody even thought that he had inside of him. 2 Much didn't really move too much around Phoenix, Arizona. He just chose to buy a mansion there because the property was cheap, plus the weather was good all year long mainly sunny weather. But he had bumped into his soulmate, and he knew it the moment he saw Emma. Being the type of people that would be attending his wedding, he didn't want to crowd the church with all those sinners. So, 2 Much rented out a ballroom in a nightclub in Scottsdale, AZ. They were really close to each other, and he knew that they were about to turn up. One thing about 2 Much: when he does something, he goes all out, and today, he was doing just that. Emma was in a

room with her own glamour squad and nail techs. A crew was applying her make-up while some did her nails and feet. Her white vera wang wedding dress hung on a rolling hanger waiting for her to be dressed by two fashion designers that were flown into town from New York. 2 Much wanted everything to go perfect for his and his wife's wedding. He didn't want any family or friends assisting him or his wife. Everyone who was there to oversee their wedding were all professionals in their profession. The whole thing was a royal King and Queen setting. Purple, white and gold were displayed throughout the whole ballroom. 2 Much had 12 White Phantom Rolls Royce's and a horse and carriage with white horses ready to take him and Emma through the town. And the Rolls Royce Phantoms were for their family and friends to follow behind.

Emma always wondered what being married would be like, but she had never expected her wedding to be like this. All her sisters were there except Fuzzi, whom they had been trying to call all morning. Izzi, Caroline, Ashley, and Kahi'Lee were looking as beautiful as ever. They wanted badly to be in the room with Emma. But 2 Much gave strict orders to his crew that nobody was to go back and bother Emma. Even though Emma also wanted them back there also. She was too busy being spoiled and respecting her fiancé's wishes. 2 Much's family members were also in town for his wedding. He has an uncle named Bobo who was giving all the women in the ballroom a hard time. Even though he drank a lot, he and 2 Much were really close. Bobo was really more like a father figure to 2 Much and Xerxes, whom 2 Much was expecting to show up to his wedding. Xerxes and his wife Camilla were driving down to Arizona.

Girl, come over here and sit down on my lap. You know that chair can't hold all that ass. B.S had to tell Bobo that Kahi'Lee was his girl and that ass belonged to him. Bobo told B.S. that he should never claim no woman's ass because all asses come attached to two pair of legs, and she'll get up and walk away from you the minute you finish tapping that ass, partna. Kahi'Lee had to grab B.S. because he was getting fed up with all the disrespect. Baby, come on, it's okay he been drinking since he got here. Bobo was about to turn to Ashley, but Black Dynamite and Spicy were already leading him out of the building. There was no way they were about to allow Bobo to disrespect 2 Much's special day of his life. On the way, taking him outside, Bobo started yelling, Nappy, is that you? Nappy was 2 Much's best friend from Atlanta, and 2 Much haven't saw Nappy in 15 years. So, seeing Nappy was going to be one of the biggest wedding gifts to 2 Much, which was next to getting married to Emma. Nappy had to take a 20-year bid for 2 Much and got out early for good behavior. As soon as he heard 2 Much was in Arizona and was about to get married, he jumped on the next Greyhound bus to Arizona to surprise his partner in crime.

Man, when did you get home, he and Bobo were hugging each other. I got out two weeks ago, and your sister told me about the wedding. Where she at, Bobo? Man, she still at the house; wait till you see yo man's crib. Yeah, I been hearing his name ringing while I was down in the pin. Man, look at you, wait until Kahlil see you. For some strange reason, Nappy and Black Dynamite automatically started sizing each other up. It was just that street mentality in both of them that said they both were somebody to pay close attention to. Hey Black, this the cat who used to be where you at now. That really put Black Dynamite and Nappy in an uncomfortable place. But it was Black Dynamite who broke the ice. What's good with you family? They both shook each other's hands. Ahhh, so you, the legendary Nappy. I've heard a lot about you, glad to see you back on the soil family. I'm Black Dynamite. Nappy started smiling. That's smooth. I like that name. You making it known that you'll blow some shit up. Where the fuck is my brother at? He in the back getting himself groomed for his big day. He requested to be alone, but being who you are, I'm sure he won't mind getting interrupted. Come on, fam, right this way. Black Dynamite stopped. Hey, Bobo, can you be cool, my brother, till I come back? Be cool for what nigga. I ain't fucking with nobody. That's them bitches with all that fat ass calling my joint. Fat asses wake him up all the time Black. Shit, it ain't my fault. Nappy and Black Dynamite started laughing at Bobo's comment.

Black Dynamite nodded his head at Spicy as to say watch him till I get back. They made their way through all the other guests and headed back to where 2 Much was at. Black Dynamite knocked at the door, and Nappy stepped off to the side. After about 3 minutes, somebody answered the door. They saw that it was Black Dynamite and let him in. He walked into the room, still not allowing Nappy to follow him. Black Dynamite didn't have any idea as to how 2 Much and Nappy departed, so he wasn't about to let nobody get the ups on his man and catch him off guard. Hey fam, I hate to bother you, but I got something important to run by you. 2 Much was lying on a massage table getting a massage from two white girls.

Black Dynamite whispered something in 2 Much ear, and he jumped up off the table. What? Where that nigga at? Black Dynamite went and opened the door. They ran and hugged each other, but Nappy picked 2 Much up and slammed 2 Much on his back on the massage table. Black Dynamite pulled out his 357 magnum and was about to blow Nappy's brains out. No! No! No! No! Nooooo! 2 Much stopped him just in time before he could pull the trigger. 2 Much pushed him up off of him and caught Nappy with a two-piece, "Bam! Bam!" to the jaw and upside the head. The two females started screaming. Ahhhh! Ahhhhhh! Bitch, shut up! Get them out of here. Nappy hit the floor and jumped back up on his feet. He bobbed, and weaved, and danced on his feet. He swung and caught 2 Much with a good couple of blows. 2 Much flipped over the table, and he stood back up.

Okay, I see prison then taught you a little something. 2 Much walked around the table, and he let off a flurry of punches, and

Nappy blocked a couple. But the six that he didn't sent him flying to the ground, and he was bleeding to the mouth. Nappy took his time getting back up. He sat there and looked at 2 Much and Black Dynamite. Fuck you, nigga, I thought we were family. You left a nigga to rot in that hell hole. What the fuck you talking about, man? I'll never turn my back on you. You my nigga for life, and if I eat, then you eat, motherfucker. 2 Much grabbed Black Dynamite's 357 magnum, and he thought that he was about to kill Nappy.

Man, get this motherfucker off the floor before I blow his god damn brains out, whatever is left in the motherfucker. Punk ass motherfucker. How dare you ever doubt my loyalty to this shit. Yo motherfucker ass didn't wont for shit in that prison. I sent you money every month for 15 years and set yo ass up out here for when you come home. 2 Much was so mad that he went and punched Nappy upside the head again, but Black Dynamite broke his fall. 2 Much walked up on Nappy and handed him a 357 magnum. He looked him in the eyes, man, if you don't see that same real motherfucker right now, then handle yo business, partna. Nappy looked at Black Dynamite man, how you put up with this big head, motherfucker? The reason that you did family, he a real one. Nappy handed Black Dynamite his 357 magnum. Boy! You know the only thing that I can do with that gun is kill me a motherfucker behind you. Now, give me a hug, nigga. They both hugged each other. Nappy looked at Black Dynamite. Don't play that shit, no mind, fam, me and yo big ass go fight one day too. That's what real brothers do sometimes. They all busted up laughing.

Congratulations, man, now where my sister-in-law at? 2 Much looked at Black Dynamite. Didn't I tell you this nappy head motherfucker is crazy. 2 Much went and grabbed his cell phone. After 3 rings, Mrs. Briggs, 2 Much mother answered. We leaving now, baby, is everything okay? Yeah, I'm good, mama, I even got a little surprise for you when you get here. But I need y'all to do me a favor. Can y'all put my man on for me? Yeah, wait a minute, baby, I'll take the phone to him. 2 Much had one of his workers driving Mrs. Briggs around. Yeah, what's good boss. 2 Much told him to switch cars and to drive the Bentley Continental down to the ballroom. He told Razor, who they all call Razz, where the keys were. He told him to come see him just as soon as they got there. Mrs. Briggs is ready, so we leaving right now, fam. Click! Izzi, Ashley, Kahi'Lee, and Caroline were starting to get worried. Fuzzi still wasn't answering her home or cell phone. They all knew that it wasn't like Fuzzi to miss something so important to all of them. She also was one of Emma's bridesmaids. They all have on their Valentino purple laced dresses with gold highlights throughout the dress. All their hairstyles were on point, and they were wearing designer shoes. They knew that the wedding would be starting soon. Even though the ballroom was packed with people, more people were coming. One of Emma's friends that she worked with, her five-year-old daughter, was the flower girl for Emma at the wedding.

They walked through the door, and everybody was complimenting her friend on how beautiful her little girl looked. Awwwwwe, little mamas, look at you, baby. You are so pretty and precious. She was acting shy and standing behind Carla. Girl, if you don't let me go. You don't be acting shy at home. Ashley grabbed her hand and said, leave my little princess alone. Come on, baby! Carla said, "Shit, I wish she was a little princess." At home, she is a little monster. That girl be getting on my nerves, girl. They all laughed.

Izzi told Caroline that maybe we needed to go check on Fuzzi. I can feel that something is wrong. Kahi'Lee told them not to leave because Emma go be upset if we fuck up her wedding. Caroline, let me see your phone, I'll try calling her from a different number, and maybe she'll answer it. Just as Caroline was passing her phone to Kahi'Lee, Fuzzi came walking through the ballroom door. There goes Fuzzi right there. They all rushed over to her, and she was dressed and appeared to them that nothing was wrong with her at all. Girl, where yo ass been, we been worried about you? I lost my cellphone somewhere in the house while I was unpacking. Where is Emma? She back there and they won't let anybody go back there. Oh yeah, her husband did say that he wanted them to be alone. But I'm sure the wedding will start soon. So come on, let's see if she is ready. Ohhhh, look at you, aren't you pretty. Thank you. Precious must have liked Fuzzi because she didn't hide from her. They all went back to go see Emma, but on their way back there, Fuzzi told them I have something very important to tell y'all when the wedding is over. What? What's wrong? Is everything okay, Fuzzi? Izzi asked her with a serious look on her face. Yeah, I'm good. I'll tell y'all later. Fuzzi started knocking on the door, but nobody answered. Here, girl, hold my purse. She handed the purse to Ashley, damn, what you got in here, your purse heavy? Fuzzi was knocking. Bam! Bam! Bam! Bam! But before Ashley could be nosey, she grabbed her purse back. Ashley was about to say something about Fuzzi's purse, but the door opened, and they all rushed inside.

2 Much's mother, his cook, and Razor all came walking into the ballroom. They headed back to where 2 Much was and knocked on the door. Mrs. Briggs saw Nappy and started crying. Come here, boy, and give yo mama a kiss. 2 Much smiled watching them together; it gave him a warm feeling inside. Baby, when did you come home? She popped Nappy and why you haven't been by my house? I did go by there, but you weren't home. I left you flowers at the door with a card that said, "I'll surprise you later." Baby, that was you? I got those flowers, and they were pretty. Thank you, son. Hell, I thought it was one of those crazy men that I then ran off already. Maybe they might have thought that I moved. Nappy hugged her. Mama, you still look young. When are you go ever age? Child don't be rushing me. I still have a whole lot of something to give away. She hunched her shoulders at him. Okay, see, now you trying to send me back to prison for killing somebody. Well, I won't let y'all meet him then because I don't want you back in that nasty place. Me neither, mama.

Here you go, boss. Spicy tossed him the keys. Naw. Hey Black, go take him outside and show Nappy how much I forgot about him. 2 Much gave the keys to Nappy. What's your favorite color, boy? You already know that it's blue. He nodded his head towards the door. Just as they were opening the door, they were coming to tell 2 Much that they were ready for him. Another knock came at the door. Okay, we coming, but the door opened, and it was his baby brother Xerxes. Yeah, yo ass didn't think we was going to show up, did you? 2 Much ran and gave his baby brother a big hug. Now, he knew today would be the happiest day of his life. His best friend Nappy was home, and his mother and brother were there to witness him marry the woman of his life next to his mother. 2 Much was wearing a white pair of Versace pants, a white tuxedo shirt with a purple bow tie and a cummerbund and a purple velvet Versace coat. His dreadlocks were hanging perfectly down his back and his shoulders. His jewelry was sparkling like a club disco ball. 2 Much took one long look at himself before he walked out. His best man was Black Dynamite, and Emma was about to have Kahi'Lee by her side.

They were knocking at the door telling Emma that the wedding was about to begin. Emma was looking at herself in the mirror. Even though she could see herself, she almost couldn't believe that it was really herself that she was seeing. She wanted to cry, but she didn't want to mess up her make-up. This was a time when she wished that her parents were there to see her get married. Even though they weren't there, Emma wasn't about to allow their absence to rob her of the most beautiful day of her life. Nappy was sitting behind the wheel of his Bentley Continental GT. Tears were rolling down his face. All this time, he really did think that 2 Much had forgotten about him. When he pulled the title out of the glove box, it said Anthony Dwayne Hill on the title. He knew that 2 Much wasn't playing any games because that's Nappy birth name. Damn! He hit the steering wheel. He felt stupid. Hey, family, I think we better head back in. I think the wedding is about to start. Man, it ain't too many more real brothers left like 2 Much, is it? Naw, family, it ain't. Everything he told me he go do, 2 Much have always kept his word. Nappy saw a black case sitting in the passenger seat. He picked it up and opened it. It was a camcorder, and he placed it back in the seat. Nappy and Black Dynamite headed back into the ballroom.

Upon entering the door, Mrs. Briggs was walking out of the ballroom. Black, let me see those keys. I forgot to grab my camcorder. Oh, Nappy got the keys. Black Dynamite said let me see the keys, family. I'll run and go get it. When Nappy went to hand Black Dynamite the keys, Mrs. Briggs grabbed them. I'll get it myself. Y'all head on inside. The wedding is about to start, I left my hat on the back seat, too. Nappy kissed Mrs. Briggs on the cheeks. You have done a great job raising your sons. Thank you, baby, now y'all gone get in there. Mrs. Briggs was walking across the parking lot and was meditating on what Nappy had just said. You done a great job raising them boys. Mrs. Briggs put a big smile on her face. She unlocked the Bentley door and retrieved her hat and camcorder.

Mrs. Briggs put the camcorder strap on her arm and headed back toward the ballroom. Urrrrrgh! A black van pulled up alongside Mrs. Briggs, and two men jumped out. They placed a black bag over her head, and Mrs. Briggs dropped her hat and camcorder, trying to fight the men off. But they forced her into the side door and slid the door closed. Urrrrgh! The black van burned rubber, leaving the parking lot. The last few people that were walking into the ballroom turned around to see the van sped through the parking lot but didn't have any idea that Mrs. Briggs had just got kidnapped.

The music started playing in the ballroom. 2 Much, and Black Dynamite stood next to Pastor Blackwell. He came down from Atlanta to personally marry 2 Much and Emma. Mrs. Briggs, 2 Much, and Xerxes have been attending his church ever since they were little kids. Little precious came walking down the aisle with Emma right behind her, looking drop-dead gorgeous. She was looking so beautiful that tears started welling up in 2 Much's eyes to see his lovely wife walking down the aisle. Everybody turned to see the beautiful bride walking down the aisle with Emma's boss, Mr. McKinney. Xerxes looked at Emma and said wow. I see why my bro married her. Emma walked up next to her fiancé, and they held hands facing each other. Fuzzi, Izzi, Kahi'Lee, Ashley, and Caroline were all crying, seeing how beautiful and happy Emma was. Pastor Blackwell begins the ceremony. Mr. Carter, do you accept this woman to be your lawful wedded wife? "I do." He repeated the same thing to Emma, and she said, "I do." I now pronounce you man and wife; you may kiss the bride. 2 Much raised Emma's veil, and when Xerxes saw her face, he put the most evil and hateful look on his face. He stood up and was about to walk out. That's when he noticed Fuzzi and Kahi'Lee sitting next to each other.

Xerxes stormed out of the ballroom in rage. Stupid bitches! Everybody was hugging and congratulating 2 Much and Emma. Izzi, Kahi'Lee, Fuzzi, Caroline and Ashley were all kissing Emma. Congratulations, baby girl, you did it. You a wifey now. They all busted up laughing. Ashley said now we got 2 brothers-in-law. They all went to congratulate 2 Much. Emma was doing the bathroom dance, shuffling her feet from side to side. Baby, I'll be right back; I got to go use the bathroom. Emma kissed 2 Much and headed to the bathroom. She quickly found a stall. Ahhhhhhhhh! Emma has been holding it for a while. After using the bathroom, she stepped out of the stall and to a 40-cal pointing right in her face. Hey stupid bitch, do you remember me? Emma put her hands up. No! No! Please don't. Pow! Pow! Pow! Xerxes' body hit the floor. Bam! Emma's heart stopped. She just knew that she was dead. All she could do was say no, no, please don't when she saw the 40-cal that Xerxes had pointed in her face. The only protection she had was to close her eyes and pray to God, not to call her home on the most specialist day of her life. This was a day she had dreamed about since she was a little girl, and here it was all ending so fast.

Emma has always heard about karma, but how could it pick today to show up in her life? Emma had never been shot before, and she didn't know what to expect or how to feel, but one thing she did know was she just heard three gun shots. But haven't felt anything in her body that said today was her last day on earth. It wasn't until she opened her eyes that she saw Fuzzi standing there holding the gun in her hand, and Xerxes was lying in front of her, lying face down on the floor. Those bullets that was meant for her was rested inside a man she had last seen in Atlanta. Emma knew that her special day was about to turn into one of the worst days of her life. But right now, she knew seeing Fuzzi was worth whatever was about to happen next. Because she was still alive, and right now, life was much more important than marriage. What Xerxes didn't know was that Fuzzi had spotted him much sooner than he had spotted Emma. Before 2 Much removed her veil from her face. Fuzzi watched how he put an angry look on his face and stormed out of the wedding. Fuzzi knew that she had to watch her sisters because he had also spotted her and Kahi'Lee. Fuzzi watched as she saw Emma do that dance that they do when they need to find a toilet and fast. Fuzzi reached and grabbed her purse and made her way through the crowd who was now approaching 2 much and Emma. Fuzzi didn't know where Emma was, but she watched Xerxes walk into the ladies' bathroom. Fuzzi cocked her 9 mm and walked into the bathroom behind Xerxes. He was just asking Emma if she remembered him when Fuzzi fired her weapon.

Fuzzi already knew her life was over before she even left home. Because Mr. Shelton was lying in his office beaten to death with the same helmet that he ended Fantasia's life with. Fuzzi nor Emma had any idea that Xerxes was 2 Much's little brother. Emma opened her eyes to see Fuzzi holding her gun, and Xerxes lying dead on the bathroom floor. Emma rushed over to Fuzzi, and they hugged each other. Emma couldn't even get the words thank you out of her mouth. Fuzzi begins to tell Emma, come on, girl, we got to get out of here. But as they were exiting the bathroom, Black Dynamite came walking towards them with his weapon drawn. What Fuzzi didn't know was while she was watching Xerxes, Black Dynamite was watching Xerxes and sensed that something was disturbing to him the moment 2 much removed Emma's veil. He watched Xerxes storm out of the wedding, but he also saw Emma quickly run to the bathroom, which Fuzzi quickly went behind him. Black Dynamite didn't know what to think of any of it. He was about to bring it to 2 Much's attention later. Because he was about to go check on 2 Much's mother, Mrs. Briggs, because she was about to miss the whole wedding, and he didn't see her anywhere. But his gut instinct told him to check on Emma and Fuzzi. He even planned to talk to Xerxes later to see why he stormed out in the middle of his brother's wedding.

Fuzzi had just put her gun back in her purse as they were exiting the bathroom. Ladies, is everything okay? No, not if you're going to kill us. Fuzzi quickly went into survival mode while easing her hand into her purse. Just in case Black Dynamite was ready to harm her or Emma. No, I'm just making sure that everything is okay. You know how you ladies love getting into trouble. They all started laughing. But Emma still had a look on her face that concerned Black Dynamite. He looked around and didn't see anything to concern him. So, they all headed back to the wedding, but Emma held on to Fuzzi the whole time. Fuzzi and Emma were trying to get to Kahi'Lee, Caroline, Ashley and Izzi, while Black Dynamite was trying to get over to 2 Much, he was still looking through the crowd of people for Mrs. Briggs and Xerxes, but he didn't see any one of them. Just as Black Dynamite made it over to 2 Much, his cell phone started to ring. On a day like today, he would normally have ignored the call. But it was his special ringtone that was going off on his phone. Because the woman that was calling was more special to him than the woman that he had just married. It was his mother, Mrs. Briggs, calling his phone, at least that's what he thought. Until he heard a strange voice say, "So, tell me, how do it feel to get violated, Mr. 2 Much, on your special day?" You have something that has sentimental value to me, and I have something that has sentimental value to you. Before 2 Much could say a word, he heard his mother say Khalil, and the phone went, Click! 2 Much felt like a bullet had just gone right through his chest. But the loud screams quickly snapped him out of his train of thought.

A couple of ladies went to the bathroom and saw Xerxes lying dead on the floor. Ahhhh! Ahhhhh! Ahhhhh! Everyone turned to see the two women holding each other and pointing towards the bathroom doors. The only reason nobody heard the gunshots was the way the ballroom was made; the bathrooms were out of the building and down the hallway. Black Dynamite sensed something was wrong with 2 Much, and he asked Black Dynamite where's my mother? Black Dynamite felt like he had just been shot in the chest. Because he didn't see Mrs. Briggs, nor did he have an answer to 2 Much questions. He just shook his head while he said I don't know. The last time I saw her; she went to grab her camcorder out of the car and her hat. They both rushed out of the ballroom, and it didn't take long to see her black case and hat lying on the ground. 2 Much heart was pounding while he was telling Black Dynamite about the call he had just got. But it was his best friend who changed his whole life. Spicy and Razor were calling 2 Much and Black Dynamite, telling them that Xerxes was dead. 2 Much's mind was so much all over the place that he had completely forgotten that he got married just a few minutes ago. Now, his heart was being snatched out of his chest to see his baby brother lying dead on that bathroom floor. Black Dynamite and Nappy watched as 2 Much cried like a baby holding his baby brother.

When they finally got 2 Much up, Black Dynamite whispered something in 2 Much ear. What? I'll kill those bitches. 2 Much rushed out of the bathroom with Black Dynamite, Nappy, and Bobo trailing behind him. When 2 Much made it to the parking lot, it didn't take them long to know that something went wrong. He noticed the camcorder bag lying down on the ground that he had given to his mother for her birthday last year. One of the hats that she wore with her church clothes was lying a few feet away from the camcorder. 2 Much kneeled down to pick it up, and tears started to form in his eyes, but what changed his frame of mind was he saw his wife, Emma and the Foxes rushing to their vehicles like they were trying to leave. 2 Much stood up and yelled out his wife's name Emma, Emma. As much as her mind knew she should keep going and run for her life, the man that was calling her name held a major place in her heart.

Emma stopped running and turned to see the love of her life standing there and now holding a gun in his hand. Here they were just less than a half hour ago, saying their vows to each other, saying I do, and already here she was running away. Now Emma could hear her name being called from different directions in the parking lot. Not only was 2 Much calling her name, but so was Izzi, Kahi'Lee, Ashley, Caroline, and Fuzzi, who was the closest to Emma because they were running to Fuzzi's Corvette, trying to get away. Fuzzi ran over to Emma, bitch, what are you doing? We got to get out of here. We'll call your husband later and explain. Emma, he'll understand why you left. Tears began to roll down Emma's face, leaving 2 Much was the last thing in life she ever thought of doing. In fact, she wasn't even sure why she was running away. But 2 Much yelling is what snapped her out of wondering why she was running. Fuzzi handed Emma her gun, come on, bitch, let's go. Fuzzi opened up her door to retrieve another weapon and to start the car. All the Foxes were making their way to Emma and Fuzzi with their weapons in their hands. Now, a lot of people were coming out of the ballroom. You could even hear police sirens coming because somebody had called and reported Xerxes body in the bathroom.

2 Much was getting closer to Emma and Fuzzi. Baby, what happened to you is this what we doing? He and Emma have teary eyes locked on each other. You just married me and promised to be the woman of my life. Then you run out on me without saying goodbye. No, baby, wait, you don't understand; I'm not running out on you 2 Much. I love you. Hearing them words pissed 2 Much off even more, and he even started walking faster toward Emma. But Emma also started walking towards 2 Much. Emma, no bitch what are you doing? Fuzzi was yelling at the top of her lungs. They were still a nice distance away, but what stopped 2 Much in his tracks was his cell phone rang. It was his mother's ringtone. Hello! 2 Much listened to the instructions he was being given to get his mother back. He ended the call but this time in a rage. He started walking faster towards Emma and Fuzzi. Ashley, Caroline, Kahi'Lee, and Izzi were all yelling at Emma, telling her to come back. But it was too late. 2 Much and Emma was about 6 feet from each other that's when Emma heard 2 Much say, "Bitch, I give you the world, and you repay me by killing my brother." What? What are you talking about? Pow! Pow! Pow! Pow! Pow! Pow! Pow! Pow! Pow! Pow! Pow! 2 Much and Emma both hit the ground. They both had put

bullet holes in each other. 2 Much found enough strength to look at Emma, and he said, "They said until death do us part," and they both went out. Bam!

THE END

COMING SOON
BY: SHAWN L. BAILEY
THE ROLL'Z ROY$$ OF STORY TELLING

THE ROLL'Z ROY$$
OF $TORY TELLING
GOD HAS THE FINAL SAY;
NOT THE HATERS

www.ingramcontent.com/pod-product-compliance
Lightning Source LLC
Chambersburg PA
CBHW051138300726
48978CB00011B/325